The Cave of
LASCAUX

To the memory of my mother
the Princess Marthe Ruspoli, née de Chambrun,
historian,

and of André Leroi-Gourhan,
my guide in a world of darkness.

M.R.

MARIO RUSPOLI

The Cave of
LASCAUX

THE FINAL PHOTOGRAPHS

Preface by Yves Coppens

Harry N. Abrams, Inc., Publishers, New York

The majority of the photographs in this book are by Mario Ruspoli, taken during the filming of the *Corpus Lascaux* and reproduced by kind permission of the French Ministry of Cultural Affairs. Illustrations from other sources are credited in the individual captions.

The publishers wish to thank Mme Arlette Leroi-Gourhan, who allowed us to make use of various documents published in *Lascaux inconnu*, notably Abbé Glory's tracings.

Translated from the French by Sebastian Wormell
Picture research by Marguerite de Mlodzianowski
Diagrams, plans, and maps by Jean-Pierre Lacroux and Jean Castel

Editor's note
Mario Ruspoli died suddenly in June 1986, while the present volume was in production. It is left to the editor, who was also a friend of long standing, to pay homage to the two years of care and passion which he put into writing and producing this book, down to the minutest detail. All those who cooperated with him on this project were conscious of having lived, in this encounter with the Magdalenians of Lascaux, an exceptional adventure.

Thierry Foulc

Library of Congress Cataloging-in-Publication Data

Ruspoli, Mario, d. 1986
    The cave of Lascaux: the final photographs.

    1. Cave-drawings—France. 2. Art, Prehistoric—France.
3. Lascaux Cave (France)   I. Title.
N5310.5.F7R86   1987   709'.01'1209364   86-22210
ISBN 0-8109-1267-8

Times Mirror Books

Printed and bound in Italy by Amilcare Pizzi, Milan

CONTENTS

PREFACE

When Mario Ruspoli asked me to write the preface to his beautiful book – an honour for me, as well as a great pleasure – I told him how much I was touched by his request and accepted with enthusiasm. But I did not tell him of my curiosity about what he could have new to say about Lascaux. I wondered whether he could do anything other than describe the filming which he had been commissioned to do, and repeat what was already to be found in the various publications of the Abbé Glory, the Abbé Breuil and André Leroi-Gourhan, or the more recent additional researches by Arlette Leroi-Gourhan, Jacques Allain and others in *Lascaux inconnu*, the 1979 publication of the latest discoveries and their interpretations and the extraordinary work being done to safeguard the cave. But I had not reckoned with the vision of a man who deals with images and combines passion with rigour, knowledge with imagination. This enchanting and thorough book does indeed manage to be original.

Mario Ruspoli has read everything about the Upper Palaeolithic and, of all the lovers of that period, he seems to have got closest to its spirit. When he describes the landscapes, the animals, life in the tents of reindeer skin or in makeshift huts built inside the caves, he becomes something of a Magdalenian himself. As he says, 'We were communicating with the mysterious impulses of prehistoric humanity.'

His admirable catalogue of the large mammals (the artists' food and their models), his description, worthy of an ethnologist, of the hunters' and artists' equipment, his summary of the problems of dating at the site or of the interpretation of pollen, to mention only a few, show his ability as a prehistorian. One of the great achievements of the book, dealing as it does with images – always imaginatively – is that it remains a scholarly work. Many observations and comments make one consider a subject afresh, open up a new line of argument and unexplored paths of research. I am thinking of the interpretation of signs in terms of sounds – perhaps the beginnings of writing – or the identification of engravings as the work of painters because of the stylistic conventions of their treatment. The author's eye – perhaps because it is behind a camera – can still reveal to prehistorians what may be an essential trait common to all these works: the paintings and engravings were made to be seen as one moves forward. The Upside-down Horse, curved round a pier and impossible to 'photograph' complete because one cannot step back from it, is probably the best example of an image which only the cinecamera can show in its context.

Mario Ruspoli came to Lascaux on an official mission of the Ministry of Culture. He had been commissioned to create a bank of images of the paintings and engravings in the cave, which for conservation reasons is now closed to the public. In fact the story of the filming began when my colleague Richard Leakey made me a request to film there himself. It seemed that this was an opportunity to put forward my long-considered idea of recording all the works in the cave by means of fixed and mobile cameras, in order to make people everywhere better acquainted with this important, but now inaccessible, part of the world's cultural heritage. At the same time I could propose my plan of forming a team for this made up of members chosen on the grounds of excellence, without reference to nationality. I decided to take the steps necessary to get such a project off the ground. It took me six months. My idea was quickly approved by the then Minister of Culture, Jean-Philippe Lecat, and it also duly obtained the agreement of the Conseil Supérieur de la Recherche Archéologique, of which I was a member, as well as of the Commission des Grottes Ornées which appointed me to report on it. Also, for more circumstantial reasons, agreement was reached with Channel 1 of French television, which was commissioned by the minister, for the sake of convenience, to carry out the project under its own name.

Although the authorities in a ministry which is national in scope are not by habit or inclination very much concerned in 'foreign' relations, the various archaeological services of the Ministry of Culture, once it had dealt with the basic question of safeguarding the cave art, gave their assent fairly quickly – in the time it took to hold several extraordinary committees. André Leroi-Gourhan's support and Denis Vialou's advocacy of the project were influential, but there was general good will.

Television, on the other hand, because of the very nature of its statutes, was in competition with any possible foreign participation and proved much more difficult to convince. I remember that there was much shouting down the telephone. It is not easy to be a citizen of the world in France nowadays! It was then time to choose who would make the film . This was done with exemplary courtesy one Sunday morning in my office at the Musée de l'Homme. Mario Ruspoli and his team were to make the *Corpus* and the four programmes for TF1. Richard Leakey and his producer, Graham Massey, would film the few sequences for their series on the evolution of man. My part in the project was over.

Lastly, after paying due tribute to this fine book, which is at once an essay and a history, I must also pay a particular warm tribute to the extraordinary work of the team that made the *Corpus*. In the face of many technical constraints and the inevitable problems raised by differences in personality, this team completed its pioneering work. All those paintings, engravings, sculptures that have remained in excellent preservation over tens of thousands of years, are still threatened by a number of possible causes of deterioration, some of which are foreseeable, others not: an excess of visitors, vandalism, seepage of water, microclimates etc. The keeping of a photographic and cinematic record of this portion of our heritage will make it possible not only to preserve the information which these works contain, thanks to the fidelity of modern techniques and the quality of those with the skills to use them, but also, by reproducing the images, to teach hundreds of thousands of people, now and in the future, about the magnificent cultures of their ancestors. It represents a great step in the direction of the new universal humanism which is gradually emerging with the increasing knowledge about people of all places and all times. Let us hope that the principles behind this first attempt – as well as the responsible attitude it demonstrates and the quality of the work – will be not only followed but systematically applied in the future.

Yves Coppens
Membre de l'Institut,
Professor of Palaeoanthropology and
Prehistory at the Collège de France

Postscript

Mario Ruspoli will not, alas, have had the pleasure of seeing his book come out; he died on 13 June 1986. May these few lines, added shortly before it went to press, express the writer's sorrow and pay tribute to the memory of a warm, inquiring and passionate man, full of talent and ideas, and a great friend.

INTRODUCTION

'. . . Oh, I should like to think that his first invention,
the first condition for his survival, was a sense of humour.
If he did not have one, it is all too easy to imagine
what a miserable creature he would have been.'

ANDRÉ LEROI-GOURHAN

This book has been devised by a film-maker who is fascinated by prehistory. It originated one day deep in the cave of Lascaux. I had climbed 26 feet down the iron ladder into the Shaft – the most sacred and most inaccessible place, which could be called the 'crypt' of the Palaeolithic sanctuary. There, plunged in total darkness, we were getting ready to film and I was talking in a half whisper to Jacques Marsal, one of the four boys who discovered Lascaux on 12 September 1940. We were using two cameras: beside me my cameramen Michel Bonnat and Noël Véry simultaneously switched on the completely silent mechanism of our Aaton 16 millimetre cameras and the light from our two small quartz lamps was first aimed at the ground, then rose slowly up the rock wall. The administration of the cave had decreed that we could stay in the Shaft no longer than ten minutes. Gradually out of the gloom I saw emerge, like a mythological figure, the enraged bison, its entrails hanging out. It is lashing the air with its tail and has brought down a little spindly puppet of a man, who falls backwards stiffly, with his penis sticking out at a right angle. An image of life and death, a moment fixed in eternity, which has come down to us by chance, this scene is so powerful, so charged with emotion, that I began to think about its creator – the artist who descended that same shaft at the end of a rope, with his lamp and his manganese crayons, 17,000 years ago.

Our scientific mission, spread over three years, was reaching its end: we were filming the last of the 150 reels of the *Corpus Lascaux*, a cinematographic monograph of the famous cave, made at the request of the Ministry of Culture. We had recorded on a long strip of Fujichrome the various stages of our journey in this kingdom of shadows, as well as the mysterious message inscribed on the rock walls by a tribe of reindeer hunters at the dawn of the Magdalenian civilization. In the light of our furtive lamps, fitted with heat shields and hardly any larger than those of prehistoric times, each of the figures, painted or engraved (or both), and the abstract signs that accompany them, had in turn emerged out of the darkness.

The Palaeolithic artists were certainly not consciously making art, and they had no idea of preserving it. They were intent only on fixing momentarily – sometimes using very elaborate techniques – the images of a religious and mythological world in which the elements recur of what could be called a first Genesis, resulting from the relationship between mankind and the deified animals. In the imaginary space, magic and metaphysics are expressed by the interplay of symbols based on tradition, as in primitive religions. The prehistorian uses the findings of research to gather together and reconstruct the scanty and incomplete elements of an impenetrable puzzle which has been left us from a distant prehistoric civilization.

In the course of our underground journey we came close to those first artists, often following in their footsteps. Gradually we solved the problems of filming in the cave by simple but effective means. The new methods are discussed in Chapter 8, 'A Cinematic Approach to Lascaux'. Our cave – a huge receptacle of images – became to us a second, imaginary and secret homeland, another planet, a vanished world, which we became attuned to through the medium of art.

At the bottom of the Shaft I lit the lamp on my forehead. I took a last look at the rhinoceros and slowly climbed back up the vertical ladder. I had resolved to write down what I had learned during those three years and to illustrate it with the working photographs taken with my Leicas.

Two days later we were to leave the Dordogne and Lascaux. The idea of this filled me with melancholy, as it did my five technicians who had christened themselves 'Lascaunauts' because their every descent under ground had been an incursion into space-time.

This book relies on the latest scientific information available to tell the story of what is known about the sanctuary of Lascaux, and, by looking at the tribe that discovered and frequented it, to place it in the context of its times. They were free people living in a wild and magnificent world, with no constraint other than survival in harmony with the laws of nature.

We shall examine in turn their civilization, the variations in climate, pollen and the surrounding vegetation and fauna, their religion, their techniques of hunting and fishing, the development of their art and way of life up to the end of the last glaciation, about 10,000 years ago. We shall look at the invention of the perforated needle, the lamp, the spear, spearthrower, the earliest harpoons, and abstract sign language – the beginnings of a written language – one of the major inventions in human history.

My work is based on the researches of the group of prehistorians and scholars who have studied Lascaux, and on my own personal observations. Where my own knowledge seemed to me incomplete, I asked prehistorians to collaborate directly: Brigitte and Gilles Delluc have put their names to several such valuable contributions to this book.

Marylène Patou, of the Institut de Paléontologie Humaine, worked with me on the fauna.

The classification of Upper Palaeolithic civilizations in the appendix is by Henry de Lumley, professor at the Muséum National d'Histoire Naturelle, who gave me much help and encouragement.

This book certainly could not have been completed without the admirable monograph Lascaux inconnu *(published by the Centre National de la Recherche Scientifique), the work of Arlette Leroi-Gourhan and Dr Jacques Allain, with an excellent team of researchers. To all of them I extend my thanks.*

Yves Coppens and Denis Vialou were responsible for choosing me to make the Corpus Lascaux, *the most fascinating work of my whole film-making career. I am deeply indebted to them, and also to M. Jean-Philippe Lecat, the Minister of Culture at that time, who within a few hours launched this unprecedented scientific project.*

Jacques Marsal, now the guide at Lascaux, our friend and travelling companion, was of invaluable assistance.

Jean Guichard, the curator of the museum of Les Eyzies, and his wife Geneviève became our friends from the moment we met.

Dominating the whole of this book is the incomparable teaching of Professor André Leroi-Gourhan – 'le patron' – whose most humble pupil I am. He showed much attentive and kindly interest during the making of the Corpus Lascaux *and the editing of my television programmes, and it is to him that I owe my conviction that a new profession with many audio-visual possibilities now exists: that of the* cinéaste *of prehistory. When I last saw him and spoke to him of my projected book about Lascaux, his only comment was: 'Well then, you'll have a lot of work to do . . .'*

M.R.

For thousands of years Périgord has been a land of moderate contrasts. Lascaux marks the apogee of the art and civilizations created there in prehistoric times by the Cro-Magnon hunters. (Photo Maurice Bunio.)

THE MAGDALENIAN
CIVILIZATION

W ho were the artists who decorated the sanctuary at Lascaux 17,000 years ago? Where did they come from? How did they live? These are some of the questions that a visitor to Lascaux will ask after being astounded by this most beautiful cave in the world. To find the answers we must take a vertiginous journey back in time.

The artists of Lascaux belonged to the early Magdalenian civilization which gradually evolved about 20,000 years ago during the last phase of the Würm glaciation. The Magdalenian period marks the culmination of prehistoric man's long progress through the Upper Palaeolithic. The people who were living at that time already had more than three million years' slow development behind them, and in the course of these millennia they had instituted many technical innovations and acquired much experience of life.

Predecessors and ancestors

I n the Tertiary era their distant ancestors had begun to walk on two legs and use their hands: a dialogue between the hand (that learns to make a tool) and the brain (that controls it) which lasted thousands of centuries, and in the course of which the process of humanization came about. It is the principal cause of the development of intelligence and the conquest of matter.

The first representatives of the genus *Homo* perfected the strategy of hunting in groups. To subdue a large animal requires several people and they must be able to organize themselves, live in a group and distribute and diversify daily tasks. Two and a half million years ago *Homo habilis*, an early form of the genus, was already making crude implements by knapping flints. He gradually gave way 1,600,000 years ago to *Homo erectus*, who spread all over the earth with the exception of the New World, Australia and Polynesia. This remarkable ancestor crossed straits, taking advantage of the glaciations when the sea-level went down by nearly 330 feet. Travelling on foot, he went to Britain, crossed the Straits of Gibraltar, and also populated the islands of Indonesia. From him are descended the various groups that were to form the enormous human patchwork of the future.

Homo erectus, Acheulean man, evolved greatly during his time on earth during the Lower Palaeolithic which lasted nearly 1,500,000 years, and his cerebral capacity increased by more than a third. In the course of this time he passed through three periods of glaciation: the Gunz, Mindel and Riss. He was responsible for the invention of symmetrical double-sided flint implements, made by the 'Levallois' production process, a new and more sophisticated way of making tools, and it was he who domesticated fire more than 500,000 years ago. He lived in tribes in organized encampments, built huts and occupied rock-shelters from which he would emerge to hunt the great mammals or fish in the nearby rivers. He probably had an articulated language.

Acheulean flint hand-axe. The hand-axe ('biface') was an invention of *Homo erectus* who populated the old continents of the world between 1,500,000 and 200,000 years ago. Its purpose is not known, but it represents man's discovery of symmetry. About 300,000 years old.

Homo erectus gradually disappeared 100,000 years ago, during the interglacial period that preceded the Würm glaciation, and gave way to other human groups, known as *Homo sapiens*, which inherited his long experience and whose subsequent evolution depended on climatic conditions. In Europe, north Africa and the Middle East *Homo sapiens* is represented mainly by Neanderthal man, who was short and stocky and retained many of the anatomical features of *Homo erectus*, in particular the low forehead, the receding chin and the ridge of the eyebrows. He created the Mousterian civilization. A skilful hunter, he lived in huts and tents under the entrances to rock-shelters as well as in encampments in the open air. Neanderthal man was not a homogeneous *Homo sapiens* type: he is found in many more or less localized forms with morphological variations and different industries according to the habitat. Some scholars believe that 'Neanderthal man' lived alongside other contemporary races and base their hypotheses on the enormous variety of industries and the diffusion of Levallois production over great distances.

The earliest ritual burial places were created by the Neanderthals: the dead, sometimes sprinkled with ochre, were buried in specially dug graves, which were supported in some cases with flagstones. The cult of the dead reveals the metaphysical preoccupations of *Homo sapiens* in the Middle Palaeolithic more than 60,000 years ago. Neanderthal man gradually and mysteriously died out during the period known as the 'Châtelperronian' between 35,000 and 30,000 years ago, leaving the way open for the earliest modern man.

The rock-shelter of La Madeleine gave its name to the Magdalenian. It was explored and excavated from 1863 onwards by Lartet and Christy, then between 1910 and 1913 by Denis Peyrony and other archaeologists. The shelter was inhabited only in the final phase of the Magdalenian, between 13,000 and 10,000 years ago. Tursac (Dordogne). (Photo Musée de l'Homme, Paris/Photoeb.)

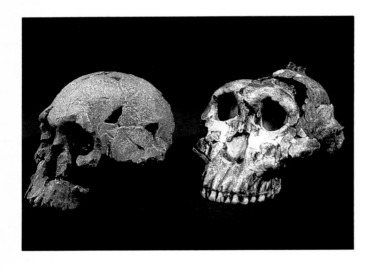

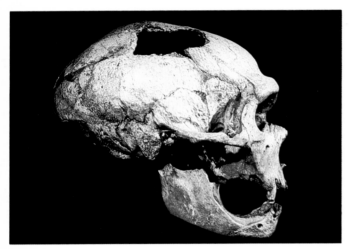

From top to bottom

Homo habilis and *Australopithecus boisei*, 1,800,000 and 2,000,000 years old. (Photo J. Oster – Musée de l'Homme, Paris) *Homo erectus tautavelensis*, 450,000 years old. *Homo sapiens neanderthalensis*, between 35,000 and 100,000 years old. (Photo J. Oster – Musée de l'Homme, Paris) *Homo sapiens fossilis*, this is the Cro-Magnon type. (Photo J. Oster – Musée de l'Homme, Paris)

Above: Mousterian hand-axe made by Neanderthal man. Levallois point. (Photo J. Oster – Musée de l'Homme, Paris)

Below: Aurignacian ornament made by Cro-Magnon man from freshwater and sea shells. (Photo J. Oster – Musée de l'Homme, Paris)

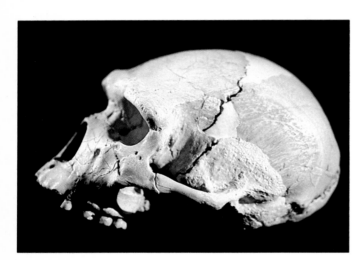

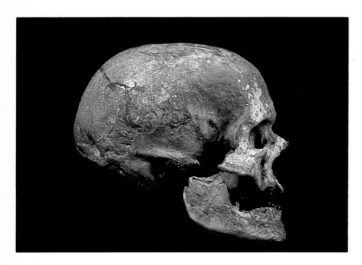

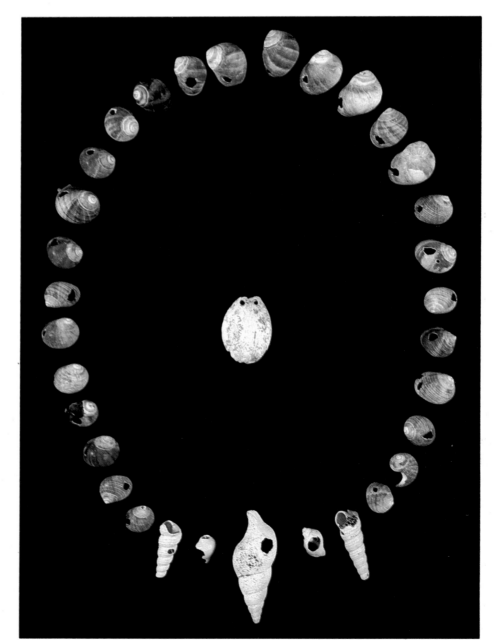

Homo sapiens fossilis

Whole books would be needed to tell the immense history of *Homo sapiens*, who spread over the whole earth creating the countless regional cultures that were to lead to the diversification of races. In western Europe *Homo sapiens* is represented by Cro-Magnon man and Combe-Cappelle man, discovered in 1868 and 1909 respectively, both of whom had archaic features similar to those of Neanderthal man but with different components. Combe-Cappelle is well represented in central Europe but much less common in the Franco-Cantabrian area where most of the fossils are of Cro-Magnon man. The latter was a sturdy hunter, reaching a height of about 5 feet 11 inches; he had a high forehead, a developed chin, and lacked the large eyebrow ridge characteristic of Neanderthal man and *Homo erectus*.

The Reindeer Age

The Reindeer Age', as the Upper Palaeolithic is sometimes known, lasted about 25,000 years and passed through four phases during which there were considerable oscillations in the climate of the glaciation. Periods of greater or lesser cold or humidity were followed by dry and very cold episodes with strong prevailing winds. This had a great influence on the flora and fauna of man's environment. The landscape changed from steppe inhabited by mammoths to varied forestation and grassy prairies where the aurochs and deer roamed. Throughout the Upper Palaeolithic, reindeer provided most of the food for the semi-nomadic tribes, who were continually on the move.

The history of *Homo sapiens fossilis* in western Europe was characterized by an accumulation of experience, with various cultures spreading, overlapping and interpenetrating unevenly. From the very earliest appearance of these cultures 35,000 years ago, there is evidence of a concern for art. In a stratigraphic study of the habitation levels of a rock-shelter one may find one particular culture above another, while at a different site in the same region the layers are in reverse order. The various layers correspond to the remains of each period of human habitation, linked to their industry and the refuse of their consumption. The typology of stone and bone implements characteristic of each layer makes it possible to place in context the periods of successive habitation during the different civilizations. Also, dating by the radiocarbon method or by pollen analysis can give relatively precise dates in some cases and in others an understanding of the vegetation and climate.

Archaeological excavations undertaken since the mid-nineteenth century in hundreds of caves, rock-shelters and, more recently, in open-air encampments have revealed an immense amount of material for study. Millions of objects of stone (particularly flint), bone, ivory or deer antler, weapons, implements, colouring stuffs, items of dress or offerings can thus tell us about how the prehistoric civilizations spread, succeeding one another all through the Upper

Links in the human chain.
Australopithecus boisei was a contemporary of the first human, *Homo habilis*, who made the earliest primitive tools from stone 1,800,000 years ago. Tautavel man, discovered in the rock-shelter of La Caune de l'Arago (Pyrénées orientales) by Henry de Lumley, is the oldest human to be found in France. He did not yet have fire, but he made many tools from flakes of stone. Neanderthal man, discovered in Germany in 1856, populated Europe, north Africa and Asia as far as Iran (the skull on the page opposite comes from La Chapelle-aux-Saints). Cro-Magnon man, discovered in 1868 at Les Eyzies de Teyac (Dordogne), was the first modern man. *Homo erectus* invented the hand-axe more than 700,000 years ago, and it continued to be made by his descendant, Neanderthal man, for more than 60,000 years, though its shape became smaller and flatter, with more refined trimming. The Levallois method was much more complex and sophisticated than the technique for making hand-axes. The earliest known ornaments date from the end of the Neanderthal cycle, 35,000 years ago.

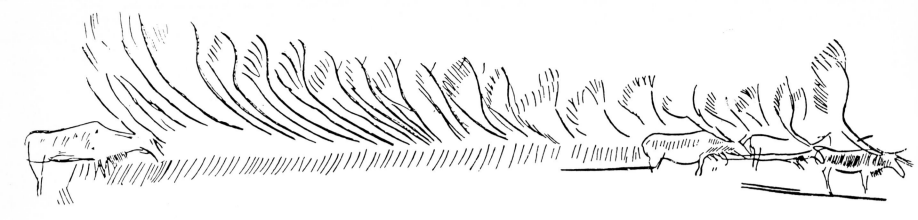

A herd of reindeer. Late Magdalenian engraving. The artist has used a very modern technique to create the illusion of a great number of the animals. Cave of Teyjat (Dordogne), about 10,000 years old. (Copy by the Abbé Breuil)

Palaeolithic. This catalogue is, however, very incomplete since so many objects and ornaments of perishable materials (wood, bark, skin, fur, assembled fibres and basketwork) have vanished and can probably never be included.

Art

Art appeared about 35,000 years ago and bears witness to the religious and symbolic preoccupations of *Homo sapiens fossilis*. It began with geometrical figures, sexual symbols and rudimentary outlines of animals engraved deeply with a pick in a rock wall or on blocks discovered in rock-shelters. Artists then tended towards increasingly elaborate expression. André Leroi-Gourhan has made a detailed study of figurative art in prehistoric times and divides it into four styles (see 'Chronology and the analysis of styles' (pp. 196–7)). Between 29,000 and 21,000 years ago appeared female statuettes made of bone and ivory, the earliest paintings and animal engravings which were still rigid but much more naturalistic. This led 18,000 years ago to a real artistic explosion at the beginning of Magdalenian civilization, and the finest example of this is the sanctuary at Lascaux.

THE LIFE OF THE MAGDALENIAN ARTISTS

The beginning of the Magdalenian opened the way in France and Spain to an unprecedented artistic expansion which increased right up to the last moments of the glaciation and spread over the whole of Europe. The walls of caves and sanctuaries were covered with a network – sometimes impossible to unravel – of fine engravings executed with a flint point. The polychrome compositions codified in the large animal paintings – in the Rotunda at Lascaux, for instance – imply a sophisticated conception of wall space and all sorts of preparations. The artists had perfected their materials: they made good use of a wide variety of pigments, some of which had to be sought many miles away and brought back in skin bags, before being ground down, mixed with water and perhaps urine, to form emulsions. The ochres were 'burned' to obtain cooler or darker shades, black was obtained from manganese or charcoal, and red from haematite. Brushes were made from hair and bristle, and 'sponges' from fur, and the artists even cut out stencils. The techniques inherited from earlier periods developed to a startling degree and were combined with stylistic innovations. The hieratic figures of the previous style were succeeded by well-constructed ensembles: horses and ponies with fat bellies, small heads and hooves, the shape of which evolved. A concern with the representation of movement and perspective characterizes the period of Lascaux and the figures are mostly filled with colour by means of a series of dabbings with a 'sponge'.

About 17,500 years ago the early Magdalenians experienced a great climatic change. The very cold period which they had just passed through suddenly gave

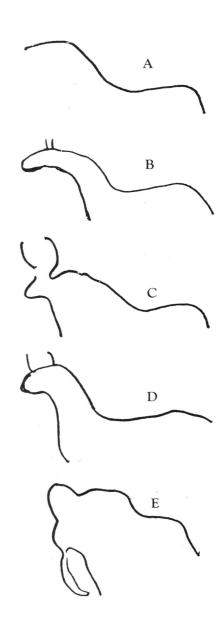

way to one of milder weather. The landscape was completely altered and the fauna increased – as we shall see when we look at dating methods. It was during this interstadial that Lascaux was decorated; the artists of the cave were thus living in a climate similar to that found in the region today.

It is not surprising that during this temperate period the number of hunters increased and new tribes were formed. As they journeyed and encountered each other, exchanges took place resulting in a new demography. Across the whole of Europe new communities were formed with new regional centres, and different cultures grew up parallel with each other, diffusing and interpenetrating. There was a development of languages and dialects and the Magdalenian is punctuated by all sorts of technical inventions and improvements, increasing people's comfort and raising their standard of living. These include the perforated needle invented 20,000 years ago (a legacy of the Solutrean tribes), which revolutionized sewing and the making of clothes, and the fat-burning lamp which considerably improved domestic lighting (see 'Prehistoric lighting' at the end of the chapter). This new means of illumination was convenient and smokeless; no doubt it encouraged the artists to go deeper into the caves and create large polychrome compositions.

Leroi-Gourhan has divided into four chronological stages the strange way the decorated sanctuaries become deeper. For the earliest mural art, 30,000 years ago, the artists did not penetrate underground but inscribed symbols and figures beneath cave entrances. Gradually, about 25,000 years ago, they ventured deeper, but almost always in areas where there was a little daylight. Then, around 20,000 years ago, probably helped by the invention of the lamps, they executed their first works in places further and further from the entrances, decorating gloomy halls and galleries in perpetual darkness, such as those at Le Portel (Ariège), Pech-Merle and Cougnac (Lot) or Lascaux (Dordogne).

In the Middle Magdalenian, 14,000 years ago, nothing seemed to deter the hunter-artists in their subterranean incursions. Armed with their brushes, palettes and colours, and their flint engraving tools, they would set off on expeditions into the depths of the earth and stay there for whole days during their initiation adventures, taking with them provisions of food and fuel for the lamps. The adventurous spirit of the Magdalenian artists does not seem to have been dampened by fear of the dark or the unknown, of their light suddenly going out, or of the subterranean lakes they had to cross, and the stalagmite curtain which they had to break in order to proceed. Their expeditions astound modern speleologists and prehistorians who have discovered images painted or engraved at the ends of almost impenetrable passages nearly a mile and a quarter from the entrances. Finally, towards the end of the Magdalenian, around 11,000 years ago, art moved closer to the cave entrances. Gradually the artists abandoned the deep sanctuaries and great subterranean expeditions.

André Leroi-Gourhan has derived the structure of Palaeolithic drawings from the cervico-dorsal line A, which is used as the basis for drawing the horse B, the aurochs C, the bison D and the mammoth E.

The evolution of the hooves of horses (from A to B) and bison (from C to D) took place during the Magdalenian. (After André Leroi-Gourhan)

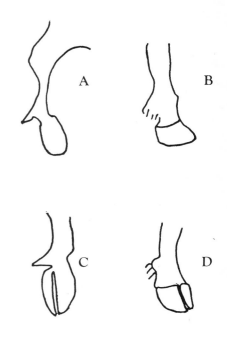

The legs of this engraved bison from the sanctuary of Les Trois Frères are shown in perspective. Its hooves are of the developed type shown in the figure D at the bottom of page 17. Middle Magdalenian, about 13,000 years old. The animal has been pierced by a spear; its tongue is hanging out and it seems to be urinating. (Copy by the Abbé Breuil)

After Lascaux

Around 16,500 years ago the temperate interstadial gave way to a new attack of the Würm glaciation and ice once more moved down to the lower-lying regions. The cold-climate fauna reappeared, including mammoths. However, the artistic impulse remained and decorated sanctuaries proliferated in France and Cantabrian Spain – more than 150 of them are known today. Little by little the art lost its spontaneity and tended towards an academic and realistic perfectionism. The images of animals multiplied everywhere, becoming increasingly detailed and anatomically correct. Horses, bison and mammoths, depicted with their fur, manes and beards, are represented in codified groups conforming to conventional schemas. In the artists' work, studies of movement, details, postures taken from life and perfection in representation vie with a concern to obey canons that had by then become classic. Some of the figures at Font-de-Gaume (Dordogne) and Altamira (Spain) give the impression of belonging to what would later be called schools – or so the Abbé Breuil maintained.

What would it have been like 14,000 years ago during those long winter evenings of the mid-Magdalenian, in the middle of the glacial period?

Outside, the temperature reaches −30°C. (−22°F.). The wind gusts in the enclosed valleys, raising the powdery snow. The rivers are frozen; water must be obtained by melting snow, unless one risks going into the caves to draw it from the pools and basins which collect the drips of the stalactites, or from a subterranean lake or river. Containers are made of grassed and waterproof leather for this purpose.

Crouched under tents pitched in the open air, or beneath rock-shelters, the Magdalenian hunters' families are spending the winter wrapped up in fur clothes.

In the cold season the reindeer wear their thick waterproof winter coat. Once this is modified and sewn together it is ideal as a covering for the tents which are often conical in shape like those of the northern Indians or Arctic peoples. The snowflakes slide off the fur on the outside and do not settle; any hole is carefully patched. Inside, the families are huddled under heaps of furs. There is a good atmosphere here in spite of the acrid smoke from the fires which are kept going by burning the greasy bones of the animals killed in the hunt (the gathering of damp, incombustible and smoky wood is out of the question). Although it is dark in the tents, there is nothing gloomy about life here: laughter frequently erupts. This cheerfulness, the endless discussions and real-life stories told with a sense of humour are characteristic of all hunting peoples.

There are a thousand daily tasks to keep everyone occupied. All around the fire people are scraping, cutting, filing, hammering, smoothing, chipping, piercing, using the flint implements designed for these various activities which have been found in the Magdalenian layers. There are provisions of dried meat and marrowbone preserved in the cold – sometimes frozen in pits dug specially for the purpose, where they are protected from the wolves and foxes. On the hearth a pot made of skin resistant to burning is suspended not too close to the flames. It is filled with broth containing bones with the meat still on them, and brought to the boil by means of red-hot stones. The smoked salmon that has been stored is greedily shared, and the long reindeer bones are cracked open in order to get at their marrow which is eaten raw and is a rich source of proteins.

From time to time, when the wind is not blowing so strongly and a herd of reindeer has been spotted, there is commotion in the tents; the men lace up their thick fur boots, mittens and anoraks, and grasp their long spears which have smooth, sharp points and are their prized possessions, together with their skin haversacks containing the sharp flint blades for cutting up the meat. (It is relatively easy to knap flint – everyone can do it, even children – but the making of a hunting weapon from a material as hard as red deer or reindeer antler involves much more time and work; this is an art that is practised only by men.)

The reindeer are now in sight, passing in single file over the snow. Seven or eight hunters emerge on all fours from the double screens that close the entrances to the tents, armed with their spears and spear-throwers. Their average age is twenty-five, but some are barely fifteen. They pull down their thick fur hoods leaving a narrow slit to see through; dressed as they are, they could be taken at a distance for bears standing on their hind legs. They disappear down to the bottom of the valley, moving between the scattered clumps of trees.

In the evening they return exhausted, carrying quarters of meat, their steps echoing on the slippery ice. The camp celebrates: there is laughter, a festive meal of steaks grilled on the hot stones of the hearths, and mimed reports on how the hunt went, which are eagerly listened to by the children, their eyes shining in the light of the lamps. The women chatter and there is general admiration for the main trophy: the head of a large male with a mighty pair of antlers that will make excellent spears.

The skin of the deer is stretched outside on a circle of stakes where it quickly freezes and becomes as hard as a sheet of metal, making it much easier to work. The next day the women take their flint scrapers to remove the fur and everything stuck to it, producing that inimitable sound: the screeching of the blade against the stiff hide. Good skins, clean and resistant, are cured in the cold weather away from the flies of the warm season. Night falls at four o'clock and there will be no glimmer from the pale northern sun until eight in the morning.

Mobiliary art

Winter is also the time for 'mobiliary' art (the name given to the production of small decorated objects of bone, antler or stone). Every tent contains a workshop, where hands are not idle for a moment. The making of mobiliary art pieces is a more personal, everyday, family activity – a pastime almost – and is not motivated by the same preoccupations as the figures found on the walls of sanctuaries. In excavations such pieces are found mixed with domestic remains in the habitation layers at the entrances to the caves or in rock-shelters.

Few examples are found from the Solutrean, the early Magdalenian and the period of Lascaux, but mobiliary art developed and multiplied enormously in the ensuing periods. From the mid-Magdalenian until the end of the Ice Age, it flourished literally all over Europe, providing evidence of the variety of cultures: engravings, sculptures in bone or antler, perforated staffs, spear-throwers, spear-straighteners, semi-rounded rods, amulets of all sorts, decorated with realistic or abstract designs, marks or ornamental motifs, as well as engravings on pebbles, small stone plaques or limestone slabs. This domestic activity shows the hunters' skill in using very small flint implements in the dark of the night. All these objects – some of which are characteristic of particular regions – give valuable information about the life and thought of the Palaeolithic tribes.

The famous 'carved profiles' made from the hyoid bones of horses or deer are only found in the Pyrenean region, where the climate 14,000 years ago must have reached maximum severity. This unbearable cold even forced some tribes to seek shelter at the back of deep caves (in Ariège, for example) where conditions must have been uncomfortable.

The estate of the Counts Bégouën, whose family has produced three generations of prehistorians, extends over the wooded hills near Saint-Girons, at the foot of the Ariège Pyrenees. Down below is the River Volp, a trout stream which flows partly underground, and three famous caves are hidden among the low, rocky cliffs here: the sanctuary of Les Trois Frères with its many engravings, the cave of Enlène and that of Le Tuc d'Audoubert with its famous statues of bisons modelled in clay. Regular excavations over three-quarters of a

A Late Magdalenian bone awl decorated with engraved horses, about 11,000 years old. (Périgueux Museum)

century have revealed a quantity of decorated artifacts. It is amazing to discover that in the cave of Enlène the Magdalenians travelled underground by the light of their lamps for a distance of 185 yards. They wintered there at various times in two halls right at the back, where they paved the floor with innumerable small schist plaques brought from the outside, in effect converting the cave into a subterranean encampment. Traces of their dwellings still remain.

The scene there can easily be imagined. The Palaeolithic hunters are installed in makeshift huts in the smoke-filled cave, surrounded by hundreds of rodents. All around is scattered kitchen refuse, bones emptied of their marrow, chipped implements – they are literally living in their own rubbish – and there is no privacy at all. Their lighting is provided by the lamps and the pot-shaped hearths hollowed out of the clay, where during the long evenings they burn greasy bones which fill the cave with a sickly smell.

However, these appalling conditions did not discourage remarkable artists, who used their small flint tools to create amazing objects: carved profiles and sculpted staffs – as well as a wonderful salmon that has recently been discovered by Clottes and Robert Bégouën. Excavations have also revealed numerous small engraved plaques, one of which has the only depiction of human copulation so far known in Magdalenian civilization. The series of habitations is about 14,000 years old, as revealed by carbon 14 tests and confirmed by the pollen sequences studied by Arlette Leroi-Gourhan.

Semi-rounded rod, engraved with stylized horses, Late Magdalenian. (Périgueux Museum)

The head of a horse or deer carved on a hyoid bone. Typical of the Middle Magdalenian in the Pyrenees. (Foix Museum)

After the long winter the days gradually lengthen and nature reawakens during the short, late spring. With the melting of the ice, shoals of salmon climb up the swollen rivers. Hundreds of birds wheel in the sky and herds of wild horses and bison graze on the new grass growing between the patches of snow. In preparation for the summer the Magdalenians often leave their base camps and set off in small groups to establish provisional encampments along the reindeer routes, for the purpose of hunting and fishing. The meat and fish will be preserved by smoking or drying and taken back to be eaten during the winter.

The famous seasonal encampment at Pincevent on the banks of the Seine was excavated over several years by André Leroi-Gourhan and his team of researchers. The sophisticated technique of removing the archaeological layers has made it possible to find out a great deal of information about the daily activities of the hunters: it is possible to reconstruct their movements, the places where they knapped flint, the position and orientation of their tents, hearths, left-overs and rubbish heaps, as well as the age of the game (mainly reindeer) that they hunted. Not far away was a ford across the Seine used by reindeer, which always crossed at the same points.

The open-air encampments

This Eskimo summer encampment in Greenland gives a fairly good idea of what such encampments would have been like in Palaeolithic times. (The domestication of the dog occurred much later, in the Mesolithic.) (Photo Dr Gessain – Musée de l'Homme, Paris/Photoeb.)

At Pincevent and at many other sites the hunters would quit the summer camp in the autumn at the first sign of cold, leaving behind their tents – which would be regularly flooded in the spring – and returning the following summer to rebuild the whole camp once the flood waters had gone down. There is almost no mobiliary art among the countless objects left behind or lost there – which is not surprising since the intense activity and the short nights in the summer left little time for aesthetic concerns.

Little is known about camps and settlements by the sea because climatic changes caused the level of the water to vary considerably, thus altering the coastlines. Since the end of the Ice Age the level of the oceans has risen substantially and the remains of Palaeolithic encampments must now be some distance below the sea.

It is very likely that the shaman – guardian of traditions, mediator in rites, bearer of spiritual comfort and medical knowledge – was already in evidence in the life of the group. He was able to drive away and ward off evil, to call up spirits and was even supposed to be able to provide remedies for physical ailments, using powerful psychosomatic methods – recognized as of vital importance by medical science today. If a young hunter succumbed to fatal wounds his family and his companions would be concerned with his passage to the world beyond and the ceremonies that would assure him of an after-life during his long sleep and on his awakening: death had to be exorcized.

Top: a Magdalenian encampment around 11,000 years ago, studied and reconstructed by André Leroi-Gourhan and his team. Tent and hearths, areas for cutting bones etc. and scattered rubbish. A Magdalenian tribe would come every year in the spring and encamp at Pincevent by the banks of the Seine, near to the ford used by reindeer. They would leave again in the autumn.

Bottom: a double hut with three hearths (plus skeleton plan).

Funeral rites

Ancient rites established at the beginning of the Magdalenian evolved throughout almost the whole of the Ice Age. They represent a development of spiritual experience, a religious and cultural legacy which remained in the consciousness of Palaeolithic people over thousands of years.

Ritual burials were already practised by our Neanderthal ancestors and have continued down to the present day. A number of tombs of Magdalenian men, women and children are known in Europe. They have some features in common but there are also notable differences between them due to the diversity of regional cultures.

The Magdalenian dead were usually buried in individual graves, more rarely in groups of two or three persons, laid out in various ways: on their sides with their legs slightly bent, on their backs, or sometimes curled up in a way that suggests that they were tied. They are dressed in their clothes, sprinkled with ochre and wearing their finest ornaments: necklaces, headbands, head-dresses, hairnets, bonnets and hoods decorated with rows of shells and perforated teeth, pendants, rings and bracelets (these last items are rare in France) and no doubt other objects which have not survived because they were made of perishable materials. Antlers, spears made from antler, and flint and bone implements

Magdalenian hearth at Pincevent, surrounded by trimmed flints and broken reindeer bones. (Photo J. Oster – Musée de l'Homme, Paris)

Magdalenian ornament composed of perforated teeth. *Bottom*: two bear's canines (on both sides). *In the middle*: four deer's teeth (on both sides). *Top*: two artificial deer's teeth carved from bone and decorated with striations, about 14,000 years old. (Photo J. Oster – Musée de l'Homme, Paris)

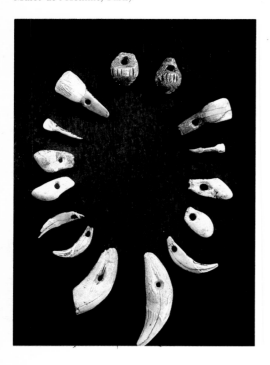

were placed around them; sometimes these are held in their hands or arranged around their heads and on certain parts of the body. Are these offerings, or personal or familiar objects with some symbolic significance? Did the Magdalenians believe in some form of metempsychosis? It is difficult in the present state of knowledge to come up with any verifiable hypotheses. On the other hand, the practice of burying the dead with their weapons, ornaments and familiar objects continued after the Palaeolithic, through the great civilizations, to modern times.

The families of hunters lived in a society which was probably very structured and hierarchical. Tasks would be distributed according to sex. Hunting, protection and the making of weapons would have been done by the men. Gathering, care of the children, making of garments and ornaments, cooking and general maintenance would have been the responsibility of the women and the young. Everyone worked flint from childhood onwards and also enjoyed hunting and trapping small game, fishing and gathering.

The Magdalenian hunters very probably sang and recited epics and genealogies of heroes. They also danced to the sound of instruments made of perishable materials which have now vanished. Flutes and whistles of bone have survived from the beginning of their civilization. In the Soviet Union prehistorians have discovered shoulderblades of mammoths which have traces of being used as percussion instruments together with the bone sticks used to produce the sound: the first 'tam-tams'. The various cultures, languages and dialects would have been diffused and differentiated as much by these audible rhythmical and musical media as by the better known industries.

Scattered over vast tracts of land in little semi-nomadic tribes, the Magdalenians were few in number and survived in a cold climate in the midst of unpolluted nature. Protected from contagion, they probably did not suffer from epidemics, viruses and most modern diseases resulting from the mixing of populations and the denseness of sedentary conglomerations. There is no real evidence of violence among the hunters of the Upper Palaeolithic: they seem not to have experienced tribal struggles, massacres, genocides and slavery. Nor does warfare appear to have been a part of their civilization. One can imagine that, despite the restrictions imposed by the climate, their way of life probably assured them a kind of contentment and freedom which is reflected in their character as creative artists.

Although the Magdalenian cultures did not extend much beyond the frontiers of France and Spain – which are the only areas to have deep sanctuaries decorated with polychrome paintings – other parallel (so-called Epigravettian) cultures were spread over Italy and eastern Europe. However, the slow decline of the Würm glaciation resulted in a sudden upheaval. The glaciers quickly melted in the central regions, causing the sea-level to rise and

because of the heavy rain that resulted from evaporation a rich vegetation sprang up. The new dense and varied forests, lakes and pools led to a transformation of the fauna: red deer multiplied as reindeer disappeared from the southern regions, and rabbits, hares, partridge, roe deer and wild boar proliferated. Soon people could no longer remember having seen a mammoth or a woolly rhinoceros.

This was the beginning of a new age and mankind too had to change. Some Magdalenian tribes must have followed the reindeer as they headed back northwards. Others stayed where they were and experienced a change in their lives and attitudes, while yet others moved up into the mountains now that the glaciers had gone, and hunted the ibex, penetrating into Switzerland, Germany and the Pyrenees as they took over the higher lands that been inaccessible to them until that time. With the departure of these tribes art disappeared from western Europe. The sanctuaries were abandoned 10,000 years ago and their 15,000-year history was hidden until almost a hundred centuries later, when modern explorers made their first incursions.

The Magdalenians must have been brave, resourceful and imaginative to have passed through the coldest period of the Ice Age, despite a high infant mortality rate and the general hardness of life. They were the pioneers of Western civilization; from them we have inherited many ingenious practical and technical inventions, though we are not always aware of their great antiquity, as well as the most beautiful of all human creations – art. The end of Magdalenian civilization saw the turning of the final page in the saga of the reindeer hunters who decorated Lascaux and Altamira and lived in a savage world with no constraints other than survival. The end of a 'dreamtime'.

Methods of dating

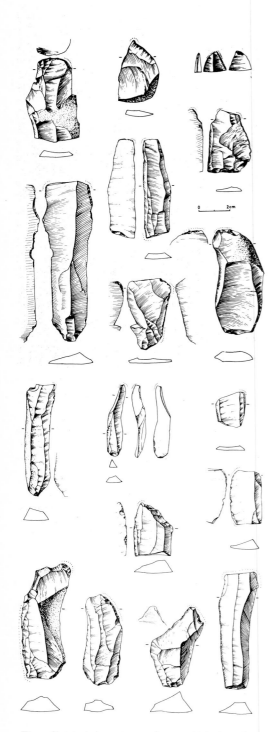

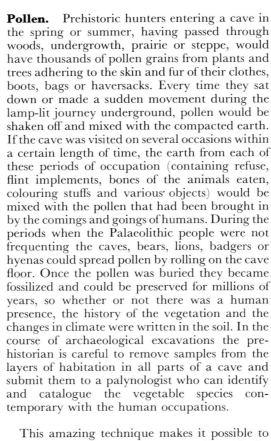

These flint tools have traces of wear which show they were used for engraving. The artists of Lascaux often abandoned them at the bottom of the cave walls. They have been studied by Dr Allain (in *Lascaux inconnu*).

Pollen. Prehistoric hunters entering a cave in the spring or summer, having passed through woods, undergrowth, prairie or steppe, would have thousands of pollen grains from plants and trees adhering to the skin and fur of their clothes, boots, bags or haversacks. Every time they sat down or made a sudden movement during the lamp-lit journey underground, pollen would be shaken off and mixed with the compacted earth. If the cave was visited on several occasions within a certain length of time, the earth from each of these periods of occupation (containing refuse, flint implements, bones of the animals eaten, colouring stuffs and various objects) would be mixed with the pollen that had been brought in by the comings and goings of humans. During the periods when the Palaeolithic people were not frequenting the caves, bears, lions, badgers or hyenas could spread pollen by rolling on the cave floor. Once the pollen was buried they became fossilized and could be preserved for millions of years, so whether or not there was a human presence, the history of the vegetation and the changes in climate were written in the soil. In the course of archaeological excavations the prehistorian is careful to remove samples from the layers of habitation in all parts of a cave and submit them to a palynologist who can identify and catalogue the vegetable species contemporary with the human occupations.

This amazing technique makes it possible to reconstruct precisely the vegetation of the landscape in which the prehistoric hunters evolved. In some cases a single cave may have seen a number of periods of occupation separated by intervals of several thousand years, and the layers related to each of these periods of habitation may contain completely different pollen which provides information about the changes in the climate over a great length of time. Conversely, if the periods are close together, pollen sequences can be established showing the evolution of vegetation within spaces of only a few years – as is the case at Lascaux. Arlette Leroi-Gourhan and Michel Girard's study of pollens collected in the sanctuary (*Lascaux inconnu*) has provided unexpected revelations enabling the coming of the Magdalenians to be pinpointed to a short temperate phase in the middle of glaciation: the so-called Lascaux interstadial. In the period 18,000 years ago, immediately preceding the interstadial, the Solutrean hunters had to struggle against the intense cold of interminable winters. Dry, icy winds swept thin layers of snow across the frozen steppes, over which troops of mammoths and woolly rhinoceros would oc-

casionally pass. The herds of reindeer that followed the rivers and crossed the frozen pools provided the hunters' basic food. The summer temperature rarely exceeded 18°C. (64°F.) and a sparse vegetation consisting of birches and conifers growing in protected valleys gave shelter to bison, while along the edge of the empty expanses of steppe galloped saiga antelope. The marshy areas were inhabited by the huge megaceros deer, with antlers 10 feet wide, an animal depicted in the cave at Cougnac and in the much older cave of Pair-non-Pair (Gironde).

Yet within less than 500 years the landscape had changed completely with the onset of a mild, fairly humid climate comparable to that of the Périgord today – although the winters were colder. In the sheltered bottoms of valleys, trees favouring warmer temperatures multiplied (hornbeam, hazels, junipers, limes, walnuts, oaks and even maritime pines). The grassy prairies were covered with flowers, thousands of salmon and *fario* trout swam up rivers swollen by the melting of the glaciers, and pools were formed where aquatic birds lived. The fauna changed considerably: mammoths seem to have disappeared, together with megaceros deer, as they both headed northwards to the colder regions, and gave way to great herds of herbivores. The reindeer continued to migrate and provided the Magdalenian hunters with an abundance of excellent meat, which was now supplemented by a very varied vegetable diet.

Mankind changed too: the Magdalenians of Lascaux, with an average height of 4 feet 11 inches, were rather smaller than the big Cro-Magnons of the Aurignacian, but no exactly contemporary burial site or human fossil is known. They were probably Cro-Magnoids as represented by the types from La Chancelade and Saint-Germain-la-Rivière. Compared to the severe periods in the past, the 'interstadial' was a short 'golden age' – but the colder weather was to return. The forest cover became extensive, comprising 60 per cent of the vegetation. Pines (which prefer a colder climate) were moderately represented; at first hazels predominated, later giving way to mixed oak woodland. Rarer trees which thrive in a warm climate were present, such as walnuts and maritime pines, and there were also alders, elms and many herbaceous and graminaceous plants still in existence today – even geraniums. Deers and other herbivores thrived in this rich vegetation, as did wild boars, bears, rabbits, hares, carnivores and birds. The prehistoric tribes were able to provide themselves

with excellent supplementary foodstuffs by gathering, and it is certain that the Magdalenians of Lascaux ate large quantities of walnuts and hazelnuts, currents, bilberries, strawberries and blackberries.

'A particular aspect related to the seasons', writes Arlette Leroi-Gourhan, 'is revealed by the fact that most of these plants blossom between July and September. The Magdalenians frequented the cave in the middle of summer and brought plants into the Axial Gallery and the Passageway in this season. The evidence from flowers inside the cave proves that quantities of small herbaceous plants were brought in deliberately, particularly grasses and *artemisia* which indicate that the cave was frequented during the warm season.'

Finally, piles of grass in certain spots (Passageway, the Upside-down Horse in the Axial Gallery) were used as cushions by Palaeolithic people. They may have covered the grass with skins, to make themselves more comfortable when they were resting, talking or working at their art, as in the Passageway or at the end of the Axial Gallery. Gradually the 'warm-climate' pollens become rarer and then disappear from the layers, indicating the return of much colder weather. With the spread of glaciation, people abandoned the sanctuary never to return.

Carbon 14. Since the war the technique of carbon 14 dating has brought about a complete transformation in prehistory, making it possible to date precisely remains of bone and charcoal found in the archaeological layers. It is now possible to establish scientifically-based chronologies for the occupation layers in caves and rock-shelters. Charcoal specimens taken from different parts of Lascaux were sent to four different laboratories to undergo carbon 14 testing; the results showed that they fell into two distinct groups separated by about 9,000 years.

The earlier date – corresponding to the Magdalenian occupation – was recorded for charcoal samples from the Shaft and the Passageway: 17,070 ± 130 years ago (15,120 BC). The later group was dated 8,380 ± 60 years ago (6,430 BC) – i.e., after the Ice Age – and was composed of samples of charcoal taken from *above* the layer of calcite that formed after glaciation. These showed that Mesolithic hunters lighted

fires in the entrance to the cave, but never ventured inside, and the run-off water and the little stream (which began to flow through the cave at the end of the Würm), carried their charcoal debris into the Rotunda and the Meander.

The carbon 14 tests were carried out in 1950 and the results were greeted with great surprise; the Abbé Breuil and the Abbé Glory, together with other prehistorians, had believed the sanctuary to be much older, from before the Magdalenian, and had divided the pictorial compositions into different periods.

Thus the stratigraphic sections, the study of the pollen sequences and carbon 14 dating together have pinpointed exactly the interstadial when the cave was decorated and the period of about two or three centuries when it was frequented by the Magdalenians.

Flints. The typological study of the lithic industry at Lascaux, including all the implements discovered in the layers, dated it stratigraphically to the early Magdalenian, a relatively mediocre period for flint-working compared with the incredible feats of the slightly earlier Solutrean flint workers. Lascaux's is a fairly ordinary collection with no really remarkable piece or type fossil. The flints characteristic of the cave are blades (sometimes converted to scrapers), very many bladelets (with or without a back), burins, flakes (some altered and some not), picks and some nuclei.

A magisterial study by Dr Allain (*Lascaux inconnu*) deals with some 353 pieces. It includes some very interesting discoveries which have made it possible to identify their precise functions by microscopically examining traces of wear. A certain number of implements, all found in the areas with engravings, have been blunted and the signs of wear are clearly the result of the work of the artists who cut the figures on the rock walls. In some instances, it can be seen that the tools were assembled without using ligatures: on nearly sixteen bladelets and one flake there are traces of mastic which show that they were fixed to handles by simply being glued. These raise intriguing questions about the Magdalenians' techniques of assembling tools; they must have made all sorts of glues and mastics, the recipes for which have vanished for ever.

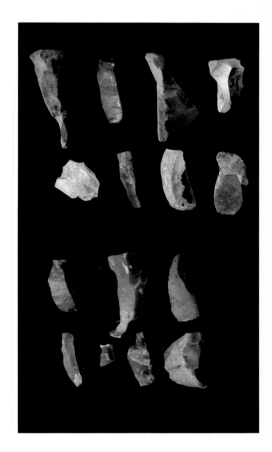

Various flint tools typical of the Early Magdalenian, discovered in the cave.

Top: this flint bladelet found at Lascaux was fixed with mastic to a wooden or bone handle. Traces of the adhesive are still visible, although its composition is unknown. (Photo J. Oster – Musée de l'Homme, Paris)

'Type fossil' is the name given to the very characteristic pieces found in a particular layer, which are used for dating purposes. Examples include the Solutrean 'notched point' and the Late Magdalenian 'parrot-beak'.

Prehistoric lighting

As one moves through the various parts of the prehistoric sanctuary of Lascaux, the great polychrome compositions on the walls emerge out of the darkness as the light from the lamp falls on them, only to sink once again into eternal night as the light moves on. Spellbound visitors naturally try to imagine the Magdalenian artists at work, drawing, painting or engraving the images they now see before them. As they ask themselves how they were able to illuminate their forays underground, they will remember that their grandparents used chandeliers to illuminate their drawing rooms and that millions of candles used to burn slowly in churches, cathedrals, palaces, theatres, and all sorts of human dwellings. In fact, the fat-burning lamp is perhaps one of mankind's oldest inventions. Such lamps were used for illumination throughout the Magdalenian, and they are still burning today in the tents of Eskimos and other increasingly rare ancient peoples who remain cut off from the modern world. At Lascaux more than 130 lamps have been discovered. They were used 17,000 years ago and provide evidence of the movements of the Magdalenian hunters and the activities of the artists, giving answers to some of the questions the visitor will ask. How could they have managed to paint and illuminate the Great Black Cow that raises its majestic silhouette in the Nave, more than 10 feet from the ground, or the rhinoceros 26 feet down at the bottom of the Shaft?

These natural lamps found in large numbers at the foot of the paintings were used for lighting by the Palaeolithic artists. They all have traces of reddening. This sort of lighting, which was convenient and effective, first appeared about 18,000 years ago. (Photo Delluc)

Nowadays much is known about prehistoric lighting and scholars have studied it in detail. There is an inventory and analysis of more than seventy lamps from many Franco-Cantabrian caves and sanctuaries, but not including those from Lascaux. Brigitte and Gilles Delluc have analysed each of the lamps found in the cave at Lascaux and many other sanctuaries, as well as the remains and traces left by the resinous torches, and have made working reconstructions of them. The hunters of the Upper Palaeolithic had two types of lighting: to begin with they used torches, then, in the early Magdalenian, they developed the much more convenient fat-burning lamps. The large quantity of charcoal debris discovered in the archaeological layers – there was some found everywhere in the cave – is evidence of the use of fires which may also have served as illumination.

The lamps found at various points in the cave can be divided into three categories: 'natural' lamps, 'modified' lamps and 'shaped' lamps.

'Natural' lamps. These are by far the most numerous. They have not been shaped and are simply pieces of limestone, 6 to 11 inches long, usually chosen because of their slightly concave shape.

'Modified' lamps. These are derived from the same basic stone but with improvements: cups for holding the fuel may have been hollowed out in more or less rudimentary fashion, the already existing natural cups modified, the base straightened, etc.

Most of these lamps have traces of use, while others are 'new' and had not yet been used. They were discovered piled up in reserve at the foot of the painted walls, mixed with used lamps. Black marks were left by the soot from the burning of the wicks. Reddish marks ('rubefaction') were the result of the heat transforming (desiccating) the iron salts which usually give limestone its ochre colour. Judging by the thickness of the red patina, some lamps seem to have burned for a great many hours. Several have been found in particular situations: at the foot of wall paintings or spattered with paint (proving that they were used by artists), or else – as in the Shaft – they are arranged to form a curious kind of paving.

The 26-foot-deep Shaft is the most inaccessible point in the cave and could be reached only with the aid of a rope. Yet curiously enough, it was much frequented and was apparently the most sacred place in the sanctuary, rather like the crypt of an ancient church. The objects it contained were probably intended as votive offerings. Excavations were conducted there in several stages. Between 2 and 7 September 1949 the Abbé Glory, S. Blanc and M. Bourgon found beneath recent debris 'a thin archaeological layer 0.05 to 0.15 metres [2–6 inches] thick, sloping very steeply and characterized by a sort of paving made up of whole or broken lamps, many of which were inverted. These lamps are pieces of limestone brought from the outside, having either a wide natural cup or a modified cup'. Charcoal, a few fragments of bone or antler, flint blades and spears decorated with signs were associated with these lamps, suggesting to Blanc 'the material remains of ritual ceremonies'. Unfortunately sixty of these lamps (nearly all of them) mysteriously disappeared. In 1951 the charcoal found around them was used in Chicago to establish the first dating of the remains in the cave to 15,566 (± 900) BC. (This was contested at the time because they were thought to be much older.)

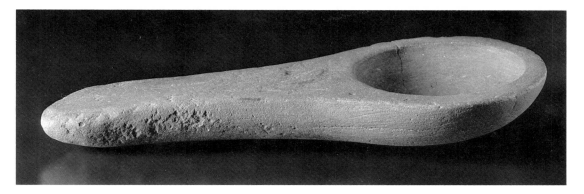

This magnificent lamp of polished sandstone was found at the bottom of the Shaft at Lascaux. One of the most beautiful of prehistoric objects, it may have been used both as a lamp and as an incense-burner. (Photo Musée des Antiquités Nationales, Saint-Germain-en-Laye)

In the course of his explorations in 1957–8 Abbé Glory made nine geological sections in various galleries. The archaeological layer 1 to 2 inches thick provided him with further lithic and bone remains: 'twenty-three palettes made of limestone or schist, four crushers, one pestle, two pots and sixty lamps with charcoal'. Glory draws attention to the fact that the pots, palettes and lamps were arranged with care, 'all were turned over so that the surfaces with soot or paint smears were facing what had been the ground. The lamps were used to give light to the artists, since the minerals (colouring substances) and palettes were always found in the close vicinity'. Finally, the flint blades were often grouped beside the palettes and colours. The Abbé adds: 'There were centres of supply or stockpiles: eleven inverted lamps and palettes, which had certainly never been used, were piled up one against the other and lined up against the wall at the foot of the "blazons" of the Nave, that is to say in the middle of the corridor'. These reserves of lamps and palettes grouped at certain points have been noted in other Magdalenian sanctuaries (for instance, Les Trois Frères in Ariège).

Shaped lamps. Among the most extraordinary objects ever discovered by prehistorians is the famous 'burner' (*brûloir*) – the fragment of another burner found at the same time has been lost. It was found by the Abbé Glory on 8 July 1960 when he was excavating the archaeological layer below the tail of the rhinoceros at the bottom of the Shaft. Shaped like a large spoon made of red sandstone, $8\frac{3}{4}$ inches long by $4\frac{3}{16}$ wide and $1\frac{1}{4}$ thick, the 'burner' is finely polished and symmetrical. Its shallow, oval cup (approximately $3\frac{1}{4}$ inches by 3 inches and $\frac{3}{4}$ inch deep) serves as a receptacle for fuel; it has a capacity of 2 fluid ounces (1.6 American). The perfection and beauty of its shape are startling: it is a true work of art. The upper surface of the handle is decorated with two abstract signs of chevrons fitted into each other, such as are found painted or engraved in various places in the cave. They seem to be characteristic of the period and also perhaps of the ethnic group that decorated Lascaux. These signs were later to appear frequently on spears from the Middle Magdalenian.

When the 'burner' was discovered it still contained sooty substances 'grouped in a circle at the bottom of the cup on a magma of fine dust. This had not adhered or been stalagmitized, clearly indicating that the burner had not been moved since it was last used' (Glory). After several attempts at identification the calcinated particles in the middle of the cup were sent to Dr C. R. Metcalfe of the Royal Botanic Gardens at Kew near London. He indicated the presence of organic matter in such a disorganized state that it was difficult to identify, although part of it at least was wood charcoal which seemed to be associated with an amorphous substance like resin. Such particles could well have been formed by the combustion of resinous conifer wood. The particles of wood charcoal were tested several times, confirming their identification as *juniperus* (juniper).

Modern experiments. Brigitte and Gilles Delluc have experimented with reconstructions of the Lascaux lamps. They used limestone plaques gathered on the hillside just near the cave and identical to the ones used by the Magdalenians. Their only fuel was from the fatty tissues of large mammals, as close as possible to the fuel that could have been used in Palaeolithic times: tallow from oxen or calves, fat from horses and bone marrow are all usable, though they vary in quality. Fats from the renal cavity are the most homogeneous, whereas those from the breast or even from the udder of a heifer are the most heterogeneous. Tallow from the renal cavity of an ox melts at 100°C. (212°F.) and boils at 190°C. (374°F.), while horse fat melts at 85°C. (185°F.) and boils at only 125°C. (257°F.) which makes it difficult to use in open-circuit lamps, whereas it has advantages in closed-circuit lamps, such as the 'burner' in the Shaft. Bone marrow has the same properties but is difficult to obtain in any quantity.

Two sorts of wicks were used. The wicks for kindling were made from lichens taken from the branches of trees or shrubs (*evernia* and *prunellia*) or from the ground. They flare up instantly like paper, causing the tallow to start melting and producing little pieces of charcoal which are transformed into wicks and keep the lamp alight. For illumination, wicks were made of vegetable fragments from various species. The polyporacious amadou fungus, cut in strips and dried, makes excellent wicks which continue to burn after they have ceased to be fed by the fat. Wicks made of dried whitewoods also burn well and are reduced to very fine ash, which is quickly dispersed. On the other hand, juniper, with branches $\frac{1}{4}$ inch in diameter, provides wicks of high quality (whether it is green or dried), and keeps its shape after burning – so that what remains after the fat is consumed is not ash but charcoal.

Kindling is the most difficult stage and requires constant attention. A $1\frac{3}{4}$-ounce piece of tallow is placed preferably at the upper end of the slightly oblique stone. The wicks for illumination are placed flat on the stone connecting the fat with the sloping part, and the whole is covered with dry mosses and lichens which are easily ignited. These are renewed until the illumination wicks have soaked up the melting fat and are alight.

The same lamp shortly after it was discovered; it still contained traces of combustible material, which were subjected to analysis. The charcoal remains were found to be wicks of conifer and juniper, and had been saturated by melted fat. Note the interlocking chevrons on the handle, typical of Lascaux. (Photo Rey Delvert–Spadem)

Top: a natural fat-burning lamp in operation. The wick impregnated with fat will burn without smoke for more than an hour. All it then needs to keep burning without going out is the addition of more tallow.

Bottom: a comparison between the light emitted by a candle and the light from some natural lamps. Using several of these lamps the artist could illuminate the cave wall perfectly. (Experiments by Brigitte and Gilles Delluc)

Only wicks that are soaked and in contact with fat at a high temperature are likely to burn properly without smoke and give enough light. When the person carrying the lamp moves, a draught of air is produced which fans the wicks and speeds up the melting of the tallow and hence the feeding of the wicks. This phenomenon makes clear how the lamp is able to keep itself going, although it is an open circuit, like a candle, and not a closed circuit like an oil or paraffin lamp. As the stone gradually heats up, the process accelerates, and if a stone is heated up beforehand, the lamp can be started more quickly. Gradually the piece of tallow in contact with the wicks is hollowed out and chars a little, so it is advisable to move the wicks closer or alter their positions from time to time to obtain a brighter light. After an hour the lamp must be recharged by adding another piece of tallow.

The intensity of the light. These experimental lamps were tried out in several caves and in the facsimile of Lascaux. Each wick produced about as much light as a candle, and so each lamp was the equivalent of two or three candles. The illumination provided by several lamps placed near the paintings made it easy to examine quite an extensive area of prehistoric rock surface, especially if the rock was light in colour, or white as at Lascaux. The light has the fault of being uneven and having a strong red or orange glow. This method of primitive, but convenient and effective illumination, which is still in use among peoples cut off from the modern world, was used for the decoration of the Magdalenian sanctuary at Lascaux, as well as many others. In the course of our cinematographic approach to prehistory, I often filmed painted or engraved images with no light source other than these lamps, by using corrective filters and films with fast emulsions.

Torches. Torches are another means of illumination for which there is evidence throughout prehistoric times. Although in most instances the wood has disappeared, one still finds the charcoal fragments that were scattered on the ground as people came and went, as well as the 'smears' and black 'marks' on the walls where the torches were 'scraped' to revive them. The Dellucs have made reconstructions of them using resinous, dry hearts of pine, similar to those in existence in the Palaeolithic.

The wood of the torches has to be warmed by the fire and, if possible, covered with animal fat before it can be ignited. They have the disadvantage of being more cumbersome than lamps and more dangerous to manipulate, as well as creating smoke which gradually builds up in the chambers of the caves.

Archaeologists have not so far found many lamps in open-air encampments where the Magdalenians lived, although they were certainly used in tents. It seems unlikely that when the artists of Lascaux returned home in the evening after a visit to the cave, they would not have made use of the same sources of illumination they had used underground. Eskimo, American Indian or Siberian families, holed up in their fur tents or igloos, were until recently still using fat-burning lamps for illumination, heat and cooking in temperatures below $-50°$C. $(-58°$F.) A single lamp burning constantly would maintain the necessary level of heat throughout the winter nights.

As we have seen, the Magdalenians were not afraid of the darkness of the subterranean world and would venture a mile or more from the cave entrances, confronting many dangers. They would of course have prepared in advance the equipment indispensable for these lengthy exploratory journeys sometimes lasting many hours, and sacks and bags would certainly have contained everything needed to reduce the risks. It should be remembered also that they sometimes ventured on incredible journeys alone.

One can guess what these 'survival packs' – the predecessors of the modern speleologist's equipment – contained. The lamp was kept separate, held in the hand to be used throughout the trip, just as the modern prehistorian holds a carbide lamp. A supply of fat was kept in a separate bag. There were spare wicks and strands of moss, as well as what was needed to light the lamp again if it was tipped over and went out: wood for tinder, lichens, amadou and twigs that could be smeared with fat – all these would be well protected from damp. They also took various kinds of trimmed flints, sticks of colours to draw signs or figures and balls of ochre, and they probably had leather thongs or plaited ropes to haul themselves up difficult passages or explore shafts (as at Lascaux). Finally, they would have needed some provisions consisting of dried and/or smoked meat or fish, since hunger and cold come quickly underground and it is essential to eat.

But all this is speculation: the lamps of Lascaux went out 15,000 years before the birth of Christ.

THE FAUNA

In order to obtain a clearer idea of the daily life of the hunters of Lascaux, we shall look one by one at the various animals whose bones have been found among the remains of Magdalenian habitation sites. We shall often be reminded of the great collective hunts in which our prehistoric ancestors exercised their ingenuity, strength and courage. Skilful hunters inspired respect from the tribe as well as keeping it alive, and this basic activity determined their relationship with the wildlife around them.

As we proceed we shall see that only some of the animals hunted and eaten were represented by the artists on the walls of caves or on artifacts. Conversely, there are others that are sometimes depicted but were probably not eaten, or only very occasionally. Moreover, certain basic animals, such as reindeer, were only seldom depicted before the last millennia of the Würm glaciation, yet throughout this period they formed a staple part of man's diet.

Finally we shall see that whereas some prehistoric animals succumbed to the great climatic upheavals at the end of the Ice Age, the descendants of others are now protected, having miraculously survived to our own day. Yet others – alas – have been wiped out, particularly in the last few hundred years, the victims of firearms and poaching.

Animals represented in the cave at Lascaux

The bison and the aurochs were in evidence right through the Ice Age, and from the very beginning of the history of art they are to be found in painted or engraved form on the walls of caves and sanctuaries; in the Magdalenian period they appear on decorated artifacts made of bone or antler. They were already present 28,000 years ago in the Gravettian and continued to inspire artistic expression up to the end of the Palaeolithic. Powerful and magnificent beasts, they were intimately bound up with religious pre-occupations, assuming a central and pre-eminent place beside horses in the decorated sanctuaries, such as Lascaux, Font-de-Gaume or Altamira. These great Ice Age herbivores, living, of course, in their wild state, were much bigger than their present-day counterparts: hardier, stronger, and no doubt more wary and watchful.

They would have been kept constantly on their guard by the presence of many carnivores that could attack the young and sometimes the adults themselves. Lions, panthers, lynxes, bears, wolves and even wolverines lay in wait to fall on a young bison or aurochs calf that had become separated from its mother. Mankind too must have been aware of the danger and the competition on the hunting grounds between packs of hungry wolves, hyenas and lions drawn there by the slaughtered animals. Once the hunters had left, the wild animals and birds of prey would have vied with each other for the viscera and discarded carcasses.

The bison

The European bison is represented seventeen times at Lascaux, notably in the dramatic scene at the bottom of the Shaft. It has been studied and observed by the great naturalist Robert Hainard: 'The most majestic animal of our land fauna and the one most threatened with extinction, it seems to me to be the symbol of our nature in its grandeur and integrity. The bison of prehistoric man, the one we see in those engravings, paintings and sculptures that are one of the peaks of animal art or of any art, was the *Bison priscus*, larger than the *Bison schoetensachi*, the ancestor of the still existing *Bison bonasus*, which is more like the American bison.'

The *Bison priscus* reached a height of 6 feet 6 inches, had a hump at the level of its shoulders, long horns and a powerful jaw with a pronounced forward-jutting beard. In winter it was covered with thick, dark, woolly fur which moulted in the spring, leaving in its place a much lighter coloured coat. It lived in the steppe and became extinct with the spread of the forests, whereas the forest bison continued. Aristotle mentions the latter as living in present-day Bulgaria. Under the Merovingians it became extremely rare in Gaul but it was still living there in the seventh century. There is evidence of its existence in Switzerland in

The Magdalenian artist has shown the bison in the spring during the moulting season. The winter wool is coming off to reveal the lighter coloured summer fleece. Lascaux, Nave, Panel of the Crossed Bison, about 17,000 years old.

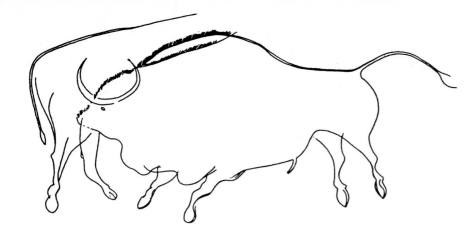

An engraved bison from the Early Magdalenian period. The crescent horns are depicted in 'twisted perspective'. Lascaux, Apse, about 17,000 years old. (Copy by the Abbé Glory)

the eleventh century, and in Transylvania in the eighteenth; the last bison in Germany, a female, was killed by a poacher near Labiau in East Prussia in 1755.

Until the 1914–1918 War there were still two herds of wild bison, under the protection of the Russian tsars: one in the vast forest of Bialowieza (in Poland) and the other in the Caucasus. The animals in Bialowieza were massacred during the First World War, but five herds survive (about forty head), descended from the animals given by the tsars, living on private land and in zoos. In 1929 a bull and two cows were reintroduced into Bialowieza in a 150-acre enclosure. By 1938 there were 96 pure-bred European bison alive: 35 in Germany, 30 in Poland, 9 in Sweden, 8 in Great Britain, 8 in the Netherlands, 6 in various zoos. Later they were interbred with Caucasian and American bison; nevertheless, in 1947, 93 pure-bred animals had survived in the 890-acre 'Saupark of Springe', which is protected by a 10-mile wall; 25 of these were descended from bison given by the tsar to the Prince of Pless at Pszczyna (Silesia) in 1865. Since then the species has been protected from poachers and has held its own, increasing in numbers in both Bialowieza and the Soviet Union. More than half the present population of European bison is crossed with Caucasian bison.

Despite its weight – up to a ton in the case of large males (the females are smaller) – the bison is swift and nimble. It climbs well in rocky terrain and on steep slopes. Galloping with its head down and tail raised, in strides of 11 feet or more, it can leap high obstacles. Bison are lively, frisky and playful, especially the calves. They like to splash about in marshes and swim, but they avoid flooded areas in winter because of ice. They are not afraid of the wind, cold or rain, and enjoy rolling in the sand and basking in the sun, though they can only endure it for a limited time. Wary and difficult to tame, they have a good memory and learn quickly. Their most highly developed senses are smell and hearing. They can spot the presence of a human at 150 to 200 paces in clear, calm weather; but in rain and wind one can get as close to them as 50 to 60 paces.

It seems that the European bison was never a migratory animal, nor was it as gregarious as the American bison, herds of which may number several hundred. It lives in herds of twenty to thirty head, usually consisting of a bull, cows and their calves. The old males live alone and only join the herds for the rut. They graze in the evening, ruminate during the day, and roll in the dust and snow. Their diet consists of branches, bark, lichen, moss, acorns, beechnuts and mushrooms; in winter they eat heather and berry bushes, but grass only in time of dearth. At the end of summer the young bulls tend to wander. In May or June the cows go off on their own to give birth, rejoining the herd one or two weeks later. The calf develops slowly, and is prey to bears, wolves and lynxes, which mainly attack the young and the weak. In the Caucasus there were also leopards, and in Palaeolithic times lions and panthers.

The Magdalenians at the time of Lascaux would doubtless have known all this about the bison's habits. They would also have known that the big herbivore is brave and strong, difficult to surprise and kill, especially with a spear, that it is sometimes violent and aggressive and that a fight between two males can last a whole day. The hunters probably attacked isolated male bison, the young or pregnant females. Four or five hunters would have lain in wait upwind and pounced on the animal, surprising it and attempting to get at its vital organs quickly. Also plausible is the hypothesis that they used snares, pits and disguised traps in the narrow defiles in which the animal could be imprisoned or just held long enough for it to be separated from the protection of the herd.

Every bison killed after a difficult fight represented a considerable windfall for the prehistoric tribe, providing 1000 to 1550 pounds of excellent meat which could be smoked or dried. The fact that no bison bone has been found in the archaeological layers at Lascaux by no means proves that the beast was not consumed generally. The fat was carefully stored to be used as a lubricant in the preparation of skins, or as fuel for the lamps which lighted the interiors of the tents or huts, and which were taken underground when the artists worked in the sanctuaries. The bison's skeleton was particularly useful, providing all sorts of bones which could be engraved and decorated, and innumerable everyday

Charcoal drawing of bison in Style IV, as defined by André Leroi-Gourhan (see appendix, p. 196). The artist's love of realism can be seen in the depiction of the animal's coat and mane. Sanctuary of Niaux (Ariège), Black Salon, about 14,000 years old, Middle Magdalenian.

Two bison, one depicted in detail, the other as a simple sketch. Below, a sketchy ibex has been hit by one spear and seems about to be struck by another. The bison in the middle has also been wounded by two spears. Niaux, Black Salon, about 14,000 years old.

objects including 'trimmers' for knapping flint. The long, strong bones were full of marrow which would happily be eaten raw. Unused bones were used as fuel for keeping the fires going. Stripped of its winter wool or summer coat, the thick yet porous skin – especially that of the young or of foetuses – would have been used for making clothes, bags, moccasins, boots, and mats for covering the floors of the tents. It is quite probable that the horns and hooves of the animals were put to use (though we have no scientific evidence of this, because horn does not last long), as well as the tendons, intestines and membranes. A regal, noble animal, inspiring respect by its size, its beauty and its large eyes with their long protective lashes, the bison was to mankind not only a vital resource, but also a deity; indeed, it was the centre of a cult extending right through the Magdalenian (17,000 to 13,000 years ago).

The European bison has recently been reintroduced and acclimatized in captivity in France. Two examples can be seen at Le Thot – a centre of activity devoted to prehistory – at Montignac near Lascaux.

The aurochs

The Aurochs is the ancestor of most breeds of domestic oxen, notably of the fighting bulls of Spain. It was almost as important as the bison in the life, diet and religion of Upper Palaeolithic hunters. Like the bison it appears in the very earliest representational art, painted, engraved and sculpted in sanctuaries, and is found throughout the Magdalenian period. At Lascaux it is depicted fifty-two times, notably in the majestic figures in the Rotunda (the largest of which measures 18 feet), the cows and bull in the Axial Gallery, the Great Black Cow in the Nave, and the images in the Apse which are – alas – poorly preserved (thirty-five representations).

The first mention of the aurochs is by Julius Caesar, who records it in the hercynian forest by the name *urus*. It was, he writes, the same shape as a bull, in size not much smaller than an elephant, very strong and a fast runner. The early writers of the Christian era speak of the Gauls being passionately fond of hunting the aurochs, and mention its presence in the Pyrenees. Under the Merovingians it was so rare in central France that in the time of Clovis the hunting of the aurochs was reserved exclusively for the king. They were hunted in the Vosges by Charlemagne.

Writing in the sixteenth century, Gessner reported that: 'the aurochses are supposed to be very like our common black bull, but larger and with a longer coat. They have two long thin horns, whitish with black tips pointing forward [see this detail on the Great Cow in the Nave]. The forehead with its tight curly hair has a frightening aspect. The feet are lighter in colour than those of domestic cattle. The cows are smaller and shorter than the bull. At six months it

These magnificent carved aurochses, in Leroi-Gourhan's Style III, belong to the Solutrean civilization which came slightly before the Magdalenian. Le Fourneau du Diable (Dordogne), about 20,000 years old.

An aurochs head drawn in manganese 10 feet above the ground with the help of scaffolding. It may be the work of the artist responsible for the giant aurochses in the Rotunda. Lascaux, Axial Gallery, south wall.

The head of the Great Black Aurochs. The horns are shown in 'half-twisted perspective': the head is in full profile, while the horns are in three-quarter view. Lascaux, Axial Gallery, north wall, 17,000 years old.

is completely black with a lighter stripe on the back. The cows are seldom black. These animals are very strong, very agile and very dangerous. They do not live longer than fifteen years . . . They eat acorns in the autumn and thereby become fatter and sleaker. In winter they browse on leaves and buds, and stay in herds, but in summer they live on their own. They do not come to much harm from wolves, unless they wander off alone after their birth. Man does not frighten the thur [the Polish name for aurochs], and it does not avoid him. If he rouses it, it picks him up on its horns and tosses him in the air. The rut is in September, there are many fights . . .'. The last aurochs, a female, died in 1627, but there are good drawings recording the aurochs, which have made it possible to reconstruct the species (by crossing males and females that resemble these drawings), so creating the neo-aurochses that are found in reserves (Gramat, Chisay).

In earlier times the aurochs was found all over Europe, from Spain and Britain as far as Asia, and from central Sweden as far as north Africa; moreover, there were local breeds. The prehistoric aurochs measured 6 feet 6 inches at the shoulders and weighed up to 2870 pounds, whereas the later animals of recorded history did not exceed 4 feet and 1100 pounds. Heck believes that the aurochs was not a forest-dweller, as has been claimed, but an animal of the clearings and less dense forests, of grasslands and marshes, eating grass rather than bark and foliage. In prehistoric times it seems to have been hunted much less than the bison, no doubt because its habitat was less favourable for hunting than the steppes where the bison lived.

In fact, its readiness to fight and its dangerousness, combined with its strength and speed, must have discouraged the hunters. To understand why, one has only to see its much smaller descendant, the fighting bull, at the corridas of Seville and Cordoba, as it charges blinded with rage – the ease with which it tosses and disembowels the picador's horse or impales the unfortunate torero on its horns and carries him along. In the sixteenth century the Polish voivode Ostrorog made a very interesting observation: he advised against mixing bison and aurochs in game parks, because they would spend their time in terrible fights. This suggests that the two great herbivores avoided each other in nature and that each would chase the other from its territory.

The hunter-artists of Lascaux would certainly have been aware of this, and the antagonism between the bison and the aurochs, two deified animals, is perhaps reflected in the composition of the cave paintings: there is one solitary bison right at the end of the Axial Gallery, far away from the aurochs cows and bull; two bison (incidentally superimposed) on the panel of the Imprint in the nave are surrounded by horses but, significantly, not by aurochses, and finally the famous Crossed Bison have a separate panel to themselves. There are no aurochses in the entourage of the bison in the scene in the Shaft, but there are three engraved bison in the Apse and six in the Chamber of the Felines.

The musk-ox

The musk-ox is an ovibovine, i.e. half-way between an ox and a sheep. It thrives in the cold, avoids damp and suffers in the heat, on account of its long, thick, woolly fleece, which enables it to resist temperatures of −50°C. (−55°F.). Still surviving in the Far North, it inhabits the icy steppes, but particularly the tundra. The musk-ox lives in herds, is an excellent climber and can run very fast. At the beginning of summer it sheds its fleece – which, incidentally, is of a much higher quality than that of the sheep – by rubbing itself against rocks. Considering the way the Magdalenian hunters made use of all possible natural resources, it is hard to believe that they would have ignored the woolly fleece left behind by the ovibovines – but no doubt we shall never have scientific proof of this.

A strong male can pursue a human over many miles and fight so fiercely with his rivals during the rut that he himself may die by having his head split open – in spite of the thickness and strength of his horns which point backwards with their tips curving out sideways. In the Arctic North its enemies are wolves and polar bears. If a herd is attacked it adopts a characteristic tactic: the animals close ranks, pushing forwards, and then charge at the enemy, galloping close together with their heads down. The musk-ox, which is the subject of an excellent study by Dr Gessain, called *Ovibos*, first appeared in the Lower Palaeolithic, is found in the Acheulean layers at Tautavel, and continued through the Würm glaciation. Occasional depictions on blocks of stone occur from the beginning of the Upper Palaeolithic; in the Magdalenian there are engravings on bone or on cave walls, as at Lascaux.

The horse

The horse is the most frequently depicted of all animals from the very beginning of art 30,000 years ago up to the end of the glaciation. No doubt there were numerous wild species and sub-species scattered over the prehistoric landscape, but, as Hainard has observed, the most frequently represented species, to judge from bones and prehistoric drawings, is the Przevalski horse (so named after the traveller who discovered it in 1881), which today is found only in a region of 7,720 square miles in Dzungaria (Mongolia). It lives in the steppes at an altitude of between 3,300 and 4,600 feet, in groups of five to eleven head led by a stallion.

Now that they are a protected species and hunting them is forbidden, they seem to be out of danger, though they came very close to extinction. In 1958 there were only twenty-four males and thirty-four females left in captivity. They are small and broad-backed, with a fat, low belly and short legs. The brush-like mane only rarely falls to one side. The coat is short in the summer, long and thick in the winter, pale yellow to bluish grey ('Isabella'), with a white belly.

A galloping horse. Taken from a painting in red from the Middle Magdalenian. Cave of Altamira (Santander, Spain), about 14,000 years old. (Copy by the Abbé Breuil)

A very old engraving of a horse from the Gravettian period. Leroi-Gourhan groups the figures from this period with Style II. Sanctuary of Pair-non-Pair (Gironde), about 25,000 years old.

Opposite
Horses and outlines of horses facing each other. Some of the figures seem to be preliminary sketches that have been filled in. The winter coat of the bottom horse is visible, drawn with fine brushstrokes. One of the grid signs typical of Lascaux separates this composition from the next. Lascaux, Axial Gallery, south wall, about 17,000 years old.

The coat also has markings; a line on the shoulder (cross of Jerusalem), a stripe like a mule's, and the legs are sometimes striped like a zebra's. The famous Chinese horses of Lascaux certainly seem to belong to this species.

Hainard gives further details: 'Rarer was the tarpan (*Equus caballus*) which also had a brush-like mane but stood taller on its feet. It had a concave profile, a very short muzzle and a dark brown coat which turned a lighter colour in the winter. It was the wild species from which a series of domestic breeds is derived. True wild horses existed until quite recently in Europe and attempts have been made to reconstruct the species. With the spread of the forests, the tarpan withdrew to the steppes of southern Russia where it survived until the end of the nineteenth century; but a forest version remains.'

In 1593 the physician Amédée Roesslin wrote: 'Among the animals which are to be found in the Vosges, we must mention what would be a wonder in many lands – wild horses. They live in the forests and mountains, seeing to their own support, reproducing and multiplying in all seasons. In winter they seek shelter under the rocks and feed, like big game, on broom, heather and branches of trees. They are shier and wilder than the deer are in many regions, and they are as difficult to catch.'

In the Middle Ages wild horses lived in the forests of Silesia, Westphalia and Denmark, while in the fourteenth century they were still to be found in Prussia and Lithuania. In the second half of the eighteenth century, the last woodland tarpans with short manes and tails, mousy grey in colour, were captured in the forest of Bialowieza by Count Zamoyski; they were later distributed among the peasants and are the origin of the breed of little horses (koninks) in the region of Bilgoraj. The ponies of Exmoor and Wales are considered to be wild in origin, but the last truly wild horses are certainly the Przevalski horses; these are very shy and aggressive, and even the strongest male bison avoids them once he has received a few kicks to the head from their hind legs.

It must have been very difficult to hunt horses in prehistoric times because of their strength, speed, stamina and aggressiveness. Their back-kicking and biting must have protected them from most predators, with the exception of lions, panthers and, perhaps, bears. Wolves and wild dogs would no doubt have attacked only the young, weak, foolish or isolated animals, or the old and solitary ones. The Magdalenian hunters' technique would have consisted mainly of beating the countryside to force the animals into narrow blocked defiles where other hunters would be lying in wait armed with their spears, ready to spring from their hiding places at the right moment. It is plausible, but not certain, that they used snares, stretched thongs, and a missile known as the 'bolas'. The flesh of the horse was eaten, as also was its marrow; its skin was sought after for making clothes, boots, moccasins, thongs, and sacks and bags of all sorts. The mane was used to plait cords. The teeth, particularly the incisors,

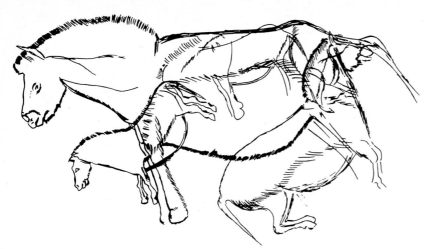

These engraved horses from the Middle Magdalenian look very like the wild Przevalski horse which still lives in Mongolia. Cave of Les Trois Frères (Ariège), about 14,000 years old. (Copy by the Abbé Breuil)

The rarely depicted hemione: a prehistoric donkey with a long neck. Cave of Les Trois Frères, Middle Magdalenian. (Copy by the Abbé Breuil)

were pierced with flint drills and worn as ornaments; the fat was used for, among other things, the 'closed circuit' lamps, because it melts at a low temperature.

The horse is far and away the most frequently depicted animal in all parts of the cave at Lascaux, right down to the bottom of the Shaft. It is first figure on the right, coming before the Unicorn, as one enters the cave. It is also found throughout the decoration of the Rotunda, and there are magnificent groups of horses scattered over both sides of the Axial Gallery. A horse is the final figure at the end of the narrow Meander which terminates the Gallery, and horses are again represented in the remains of paintings and numerous engravings in the Passageway and the Apse (247 in these two areas). The whole eastern wall of the Nave is decorated with them, and one appears on the west wall above the third of the Swimming Stags. A horse also appears at the end of the narrow Chamber of the Felines.

There has been much discussion about the types of the horses represented; they seem to belong to several species. Some are thick-set and massive like the Przevalski horses, others (such as the famous Upside-down Horse) have a narrow muzzle and long legs. Some, especially in the Nave and Apse, have goatee beards. The five woolly, thick-set 'ponies', moving forward one behind the other on the right-hand wall of the Axial Gallery, contrast with the two long-necked horses on the panel with the hemiones, which follow the large black aurochs on the opposite wall.

The hemione which may be depicted at Lascaux was a slender, very swift animal with thin legs, a small, short head, long raised ears and a tail with no hair at its base. It is now extinct. The image of this ancestor of the asses is rarely found in prehistoric times (Le Portel and Les Trois-Frères, in Ariège).

Only one piece of bone from a horse has been discovered in the archaeological layers at Lascaux, which is not enough to prove that it was eaten there.

The deer

The red deer (*Cervus elaphus*, Linnaeus), is represented eighty-five times at Lascaux. It is the direct ancestor of the present-day European deer which already in those far-off times would have been divided into many species and sub-species – just as it is today, especially since the repopulation of the forests, parks and private hunting grounds often depends on animals imported from distant regions. This magnificent cervid varies considerably in height (4 feet to 5 feet 7 inches), colour and antlers; the stags weigh up to 550 pounds in France and as much as 940 pounds in the Carpathians (the antlers themselves can weigh 33 pounds). The colour of the deer varies from almost black grey-brown to light brown, fawn colour and sometimes blond. The young have a fawn-coloured coat spotted with white, which lasts until August.

The male's antlers begin to grow at the end of his first year. They appear first as single spikes which may be various lengths, at which stage the young stag is called a brocket. The antlers are cast every year in March but start growing again soon afterwards – each time with more branches – and are covered with a downy skin called 'velvet'. By June they are completely formed. In July the velvet dries out, giving the animal a strong itching sensation which drives it to get rid of the velvet by rubbing its antlers against trees, thus stripping off the bark. It then goes about with strands of sometimes bloody skin hanging from the antlers. In general there is a new tine (antler point) each year, so that an adult has ten, sometimes twelve or more tines.

The red deer is a noble animal, living in open terrain with scattered trees, as is suggested by its physical make-up and its antlers. Preferring grass to foliage, it grazes in the meadows and fields, though agriculture has forced it into the woods where it can hide. In Scotland it lives on heather-covered, treeless hills. The deer is frequently found in forests of tall, widely spaced oaks, with grasses and ferns as undergrowth. It is equally at home on mountains and plains, even in very rough terrain. Although not venturing into really rocky country, it is agile and not afraid of narrow ledges and steep paths, enjoying climbing above the tree line. Moving generally at a walking pace or an elegant trot, the deer does not run unless it is being pursued or hunted; it likes to swim and can cross rivers and pools. According to Oberthür, it can endure a chase of over 35 miles; he also mentions a deer leaping more than 30 feet and landing 6 feet higher than it started. Leaps have been seen of 45 feet in length and 9 feet in height.

Red deer. Above is a hind, and below are two stags with 'imaginary' antlers, probably painted with a brush on the uneven wall. To the left and right below: 'dabbed' signs reminiscent of the line of a horse's back. Lascaux, Rotunda, north wall, 17,000 years old.

A small engraved stag. Lascaux, Apse, about 17,000 years old. (Copy by the Abbé Glory)

A red deer stag in the classical style. Engraving from Altamira (Santander, Spain). Middle Magdalenian, about 13,000 years old. (Copy by the Abbé Breuil)

The deer's senses are very acute, especially its hearing and smell. The stag is aggressive and fights violently with its rivals, especially in the rutting season; the clash of antlers can be heard at distance of over a mile in the forest. Sometimes both combatants die when their antlers become inextricably locked together. Generally these fights are to the death and when the deer has lost his antlers he fights vigorously with his front legs. The herds move around in areas of 40 to 50 miles, often returning to the same spots. They feed on grass, buds, leaves, acorns, beechnuts, berries and mushrooms; in winter they eat dried grasses, heather and the bark of deciduous and coniferous trees – they need a lot of food.

In rare cases a deer may attack a human being, especially in the rutting season. Their enemies include wolves; they may chase an isolated animal over the snow, but dare not attack a large male with a powerful set of antlers. The hind and the fawn, however, are vulnerable if they become separated from the herd. The other formidable enemy is the lynx, which lies in wait and falls on it from the branches of a tree or from a rock, or straight from the ground – it can jump 16 feet. In the course of the frantic race that ensues, the cat holds on to the deer's shoulders, opens its veins and drinks its blood until the deer is exhausted. Then the lynx feeds on the deer's brains and liver, leaving the rest to the wolves which have been following the chase without daring to approach. The deer is often represented in prehistoric times, especially in the Magdalenian from the period of Lascaux onwards. The warmer climate characteristic of Lascaux was accompanied by a considerable and very rapid spread of a varied vegetation, so that the area covered by forest increased. The winters became milder and not too damp and the steppe became prairie, creating ideal conditions for deer, which had been much rarer in the earlier cold periods of the steppes.

The Magdalenians hunted the deer for its meat, marrow and skin, but no doubt primarily for its antlers, from which they carved their incomparable spearpoints. They probably searched avidly for fallen antlers during the casting season. The canine teeth (or 'craches') were worn as one of the main elements of prehistoric ornament and seem to have had a symbolic significance, judging by the way they are arranged in Magdalenian burials, where thousands of them are found, perforated and sometimes decorated with lines or signs. They were hung as necklaces, pendants, decorative features in head-dresses, headbands and clothes. There are even artificial examples, perfect imitations cut from bone. Bone from deer, particularly the shoulder-blades, was made into engraved artifacts.

It seems that the red deer was much more difficult to hunt than the reindeer, which was the most plentiful source of food in prehistoric times. The hunters must have followed the tracks over the snow, then spotted the deer and lain in wait, attacking them in strategically narrow defiles and fords, as is illustrated in the frieze of the Swimming Stags in the Nave at Lascaux. They may also have immobilized the stags by stretching cords and thongs between the trees and entangling their antlers. The hinds, which have no antlers, may well, like the female reindeer, have been surprised with their fawns or when pregnant, since the skin of the foetus is very fine and was no doubt much sought after for making clothes.

In the cave of Lascaux the deer is depicted only in particular places. The *Rotunda*: four deer, partly superimposed, on the north wall at the end, between the first and second aurochs. A small stag cuts across the breast of the third aurochs on the opposite wall. The *Axial Gallery*: a large, incomplete roaring stag (6 feet 7 inches high) with its head pointing towards the back of the Gallery, where it is represented only by abstract branches, particularly at the very end, in front of the Upside-down Horse; these branches have been interpreted as antlers. The *Apse*: sixty-four more or less complete paintings and engravings. This part of the cave has suffered much from erosion: of the fine sequence of deer halfway up on the south wall only the antlers and hooves are still visible, and of their colouring only the black is preserved. Other paintings of deer, their lines emphasized by engraving, are visible on the ledge on the left (south) wall in the Apse, while on the right (north) wall the famous engraving of the Major Deer, more than 6½ feet long, is difficult to make out among the confusion of superimposed figures, which include other deer and horses. In the *Nave*: on the west wall the famous frieze of five Swimming Stags plunges towards the back of the cavity. It is one of the wonders of the cave. Traces of bone from red deer have been found in the archaeological layer of Lascaux (though they comprise only 1.5 per cent of all the bone remains), proving that the deer was eaten occasionally in the cave. In the *Chamber of the Felines*: many stags and a hind.

A stag engraved on a stalagmite. Cave of Teyjat (Dordogne). Late Magdalenian, about 10,000 years old. (Copy by the Abbé Breuil)

The ibex

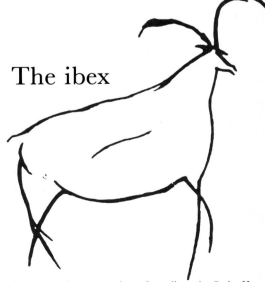

The ibex (*Capra ibex*, Linnaeus) is the fifth 'deified animal' (after the horse, the aurochs, the bison and the deer), and is represented thirty-five times at Lascaux. Like the other four it appears in the very earliest art, the first representations of it dating back to the Aurignacian period more than 30,000 years ago.

There are ibexes in the wall decoration of the very early sanctuary of Pair-non-Pair (Gironde) 26,000 or 27,000 years ago, at Cougnac 20,000 years ago, and throughout the Magdalenian after Lascaux. They are found at Niaux in the Pyrenees 13,000 or 14,000 years ago, and also at Rouffignac in the Dordogne. In most Palaeolithic compositions the ibex is a curious character, occupying a rather marginal place. Absent from some caves and represented in others – though seldom in any numbers or in the central groups – it is an accompanying figure, a kind of witness.

A very ancient engraving of an ibex, in Style II according to Leroi-Gourhan's classification. Pair-non-Pair, Gravettian, about 25,000 years old. (After the copy by Lemozi)

An ibex associated with bison. The charcoal drawing of the legs and hooves in profile is perfectly correct anatomically. Style IV in Leroi-Gourhan's classification. Sanctuary of Niaux, about 14,000 years old.

By a miracle the ibex has survived on the earth. We ought to pay as much attention to it as did the Palaeolithic people, who hunted and ate it, made paintings and engravings of it, and used it as a symbol. The famous Venus of Laussel, carved on a block of stone 25,000 or 26,000 years ago, holds in her hand a large ibex horn, perhaps a drinking horn filled with some mysterious liquid. Unfortunately, horn is a perishable material and it is never found among the familiar objects of prehistoric habitation sites, where it must have been very important and have had many uses.

The male is powerful and stocky, weighing 165 to 220 pounds, with a total length of 55 to 61 inches and a height of $26\frac{1}{2}$ to $33\frac{1}{2}$ inches. Its shape is rounded and full, with the back of its neck rising in a large hump behind its head. It has short, strong legs, a skull wide for its powerful horns, very widely spaced eyes and a short beard. Its nodulous and slightly curving horns can measure up to $35\frac{1}{2}$ inches and weigh 33 pounds. Its wide hooves have elastic, spongy soles and hard, sharp ungulae. The female is very different. She is much smaller, rarely exceeding 110 pounds, and resembles a goat. The colour of the coat is a pale, slightly pinkish fawn, with a white belly and blackish flanks. The males become darker as they grow older and turn almost black. The woolly winter coat becomes frayed and moults in the spring, when the animals get rid of it by rubbing themselves against rocks.

Some writers believe that the ibex was originally not an inhabitant of high mountains, but was relegated there and has not adapted to its new conditions. Lavauden remarks that ibexes appeared suddenly and in great numbers in the deposits of the last glaciation, only to disappear just as quickly. Their sudden spread into low-lying regions would seem to have been the result of the extension of the glaciers. At the end of the Würm glaciation, when the reindeer, the elk and the wolverine returned to the north, the ibex headed towards the mountains with other alpine animals, taking advantage of the melting snows and glaciers which were uncovering new land.

The ibex's decline began in the sixteenth century, even before firearms were widely used. The Emperor Maximilian, a great huntsman, recorded having killed one at 220 yards with a crossbow bolt, after one of his companions had missed it using a 'fire tube'. By the late nineteenth century, poaching, improved firearms and intensive hunting had almost brought about the extinction of the ibex. It was saved by King Victor Emmanuel of Italy, known as 'the hunting king'. Several pairs that had escaped the poachers were captured and taken to populate his game reserves of Valsavaranche. There the animal has prospered, despite being almost exterminated by the Resistance fighters hiding in the mountains during the last war: the 3,865 ibexes in 1913 had been reduced to 419 by 1945, but today the numbers are encouraging: 3,500 in Switzerland, 4,500 in Italy, 2,000 in France, and several hundred in Spain.

The ibex combines the qualities of a climber with those of an incomparable acrobat – excelling even the chamois. The young, when they are at play, will run down almost vertical rocks, touching them only at wide intervals. The large males will throw themselves on all fours against the rock, holding on to it with the points of their front hooves, and swinging their heads forward to pass over the top. It may be that they use the weight of their horns to help them over. Today ibexes seldom descend below 6,600 feet in winter. The snow is less deep on the heights, and can blow or slip away to reveal dry grass.

The rut, which takes place from December to January, involves terrible fights between the males in which they charge at each other and bang their horns together. Two wardens at the 'Gran-Paradiso' reserve told Hainard that they had seen two bucks at ten in the morning running at each other and clashing heads. They would separate, only to charge at each other once again, and as they took off, they sent stones as big as a baby's head flying twenty-five yards. The fight went on all afternoon and the wardens could hear the clash of their horns all night. The animals did not separate until ten the following morning. The naturalist D. Burckhardt recorded hearing 178 such clashes in twenty-five minutes, echoing well over half a mile away!

Hainard continues: 'Unlike the chamois, the ibex is not in part a forest animal. Only rarely does it descend to the sparse upland forests or the trees that

Confronted ibexes (executed in the dabbing technique), with the heads and necks of horses. A grid sign separates the two buck ibexes. Lascaux, Axial Gallery, south wall, about 17,000 years old.

Ibexes associated with a mammoth. Sanctuary of Rouffignac (Dordogne). Later Magdalenian, about 13,000 years old.

cling to the rocks. The males in particular stay very high up. Outside the rutting season they do not live with the females, but neither are they solitary like the chamois. They form little masculine groups often consisting of about thirty individuals, comprising old blackish grey bucks with enormous horns, and others that are younger and browner.' Sometimes when the rutting season comes these groups of bachelors may not pick the right females and instead visit the herds of domesticated goats on the mountains, much to the annoyance of the male goats which are much less strong and have smaller horns. This interbreeding results in a large number of hybrids which often rebel against domestication. The females with their young also live in groups but lower down the mountain.

The males may be aggressive towards humans, especially during the rut, and there is a recorded incident of a beater being killed by a blow from the head hitting him full in the chest. The ibex can provide 65 to 155 pounds of excellent meat, which is the reason why mankind hunted it from the penultimate (Riss) glaciation onwards, notably during the Upper Palaeolithic, 35,000 years ago. In the Alps the species is represented by the *Capra ibex*, which has horns with a rectangular cross-section. In the Pyrenees and the other 'sierras' of Spain as far as the mountains around Gibraltar, the species is the *Capra pyrenica*, and its various sub-species. Its horns have a triangular cross-section. The

Magdalenians of Lascaux hunted the ibex in the rocky hills at a relatively low level, since the species then was not yet acclimatized to the high altitudes (up to 11,500 feet), then under constant snow cover, where it has since taken refuge.

At Lascaux the ibex is represented only in certain places in the cave. There are two ibexes, one black and the other red, incomplete and not very carefully executed, their outlines created by a series of dabs, facing each other on the south wall of the Axial Gallery, near the back, and separated by a 'grid' sign. The famous frieze of the seven ibexes at the entrance to the Nave (east wall) is unfortunately poorly preserved. The horned heads can be clearly distinguished by their deeply engraved outlines, but the polychrome painting has not survived and only vague blotches are visible. There are many engravings of ibexes in the Passageway, the Nave (drawn within the horses) and the Chamber of the Felines.

The reindeer

There is only one depiction of the reindeer (*Rangifer tarandus*) at Lascaux. It is on the north side of the Apse, in the midst of a confusion of engravings, scrapings and graffiti, which resembles a picture puzzle with superimposed and intermingled images. (Indeed the identification has been disputed because the characteristic backward-pointing antlers are not easily recognizable.) Yet the reindeer was the animal most hunted and eaten by the tribes of the Upper Palaeolithic – and of the Magdalenian in particular.

The archaeological layers in the cave contain very many bones, often cracked to extract the marrow: these are the remains of the 'picnics' that the hunter-artists took with them underground when they decorated and frequented the cave. The bones indicate that reindeer constituted 88.7 per cent of the meat eaten underground. This statistic raises many questions about the meaning of prehistoric art. Why were the animals most frequently represented by the artists, such as the bison, the aurochs and the ibex, not eaten? And why does the horse, which is by far the most frequently depicted animal in the paintings and engravings, account for only 0.8 per cent of the food remains, and the red deer for only 1.5 per cent, compared with the reindeer's 88.7 per cent? These statistics are in flagrant contradiction of the old theory proposed in the Abbé Breuil's time, which linked artistic expression to the magic of hunting, the aim of which was to appropriate the animals. According to this theory the animal most hunted should be the one most depicted, and Lascaux should be full of reindeer.

The Upper Palaeolithic has been called the 'Age of the Reindeer' and we must devote as much attention to the animal as the Magdalenians themselves did. The reindeer is restricted to the tundra and cold forests, and is now found only in forest regions of Scandinavia and Siberia. Various species of it inhabit all the Arctic areas: the caribou still lives in the wild in Alaska and Canada, and it is hunted by the Eskimos as well as by the last of the Montagnais and Algonquin

An engraving of reindeer, together with a bison and ibex. This remarkable anatomical study, dating from the later Magdalenian, is in the cave of Les Trois Frères, about 13,000 years old. (Copy by the Abbé Breuil)

Indians. Unlike the European reindeer, which is less migratory, the caribou moves over thousands of kilometres in huge herds, crossing the frozen lakes and sea inlets in the winter, and swimming great rivers in the summer. Most of the description that follows draws on Hainard.

The reindeer belongs to the family of Cervidae. It measures between 3 feet 5 inches and 4 feet high and between 6 feet and 7 feet 3 inches long, weighing 265 to 330 pounds. It stands shorter on its legs and is much smaller than the deer, which can weigh more than 880 pounds. The reindeer is unique among the Cervidae in that both the male and female have characteristic antlers. It has wide hooves with very developed ungulae, which prevent it from sinking into the packed, frozen snow or into the marsh. It has a heavy head, which it holds lower than the deer, a broad muzzle with hair growing on it to the tip, and large eyes. Its antlers are round at the base and then become flatter and wider and are palmate at the end. They vary enormously in shape, but broadly speaking they start by pointing backwards, then curve upwards and forwards, measuring up to 5 feet along the curve; they weigh between $6\frac{1}{2}$ and 24 pounds. One prong, more developed than the others, projects forward from the base extending along the nose and widening into a shovel shape. The male loses his antlers in November to January, the female in June after giving birth. The thick greyish-white winter coat of soft wool and brittle hair is extremely warm and forms a mane. In summer the coat is shorter, darker on the legs and neck and lighter under the neck and breast. The reindeer disappeared from central Europe at the end of the Würm glaciation, at the start of the Azilian (9,000 years ago), and its territory – by then no doubt wooded – was occupied by deer.

The Scandinavian reindeer is a running animal, not a climber like the chamois. It lives on high, rocky, desolate and partly marshy plateaux at an altitude of between 2,600 and 6,600 feet, avoiding forests, and feeding on Alpine plants, buds, branches and particularly lichens. In summer it eats grasses, in autumn mushrooms and occasionally young birds, eggs, small rodents and seaweeds on the shore. In winter it scrapes away the snow to find its food. The herds, composed of females and the young of both sexes, are led by an old female. The adult males live alone or in small groups for most of the time. The herds are often on the move, following particular valleys, with the males in front; in winter they come together to form much larger herds. The principal enemies of reindeer are wolves, which chase them over the fresh snow, lynxes, wolverines and bears. But even more malevolent are the flies and horseflies, whose larvae live under the skin and in the nasal cavities and cause abscesses. The migrations are determined primarily by these flies, and one of the reindeer's most important needs is to stay cool.

In Siberia, reindeer live in herds of thousands, divided into bands of two or three hundred. They migrate from the forest to the tundra, fording or swimming

rivers, where native hunters lie in wait for them, exactly as happened in the Magdalenian at the open-air sites. Pincevent is a famous site in Seine-et-Marne, 60 miles from Paris, excavated over more than twenty years by Leroi-Gourhan and his students. 13,000 years ago some Palaeolithic people established their tent encampment there and hunted the reindeer that crossed the Seine. Reindeer have been domesticated by the Lapps, who catch them with lassoes, and by the peoples of Siberia. The castrated males pull sleighs – 'but the shepherd does not drive the reindeer; the reindeer drive the shepherd'.

To both Neanderthal man and *Homo sapiens fossilis*, the reindeer was not only a living larder, but also the source of many basic materials necessary for daily life. The sheer number of their uses is staggering. We shall attempt to list some of them, though there were probably others. No doubt the prehistoric hunters – whom Leroi-Gourhan must be right in imagining to have had a sense of humour – already knew the saying: 'Everything on the reindeer is good for something'.

From the *antlers* they made pierced needles, spearpoints, harpoons, percussors for knapping flint, anorak buttons and stoppers for waterskins. The *skin* was used for making clothes, hoods and hats, moccasins, boots, blankets, bedding, tent coverings, bags, receptacles, waterskins and flasks, and the particularly fine skin of the foetus was especially prized. The *teeth* were used as implements, scrapers and ornaments. The *offal*, brains and glands provided predigested

The photograph shows a jumble of engravings including the profile of a cervid which may be the only reindeer in Lascaux. If so it would date from the Early Magdalenian (though the depiction of reindeer is rare before the Middle Magdalenian). Below is the same reindeer as shown in a tracing by the Abbé Glory. Lascaux, Apse.

foodstuffs. It is possible that, as they waited, the hungry hunters did as the Eskimos and Indians used to do and ate raw the antlers and contents of the stomachs, which are rich in proteins, vitamins and mineral salts. The *meat*, rich in proteins, was cut up on the spot, carried to the encampment, and roasted on the fire or boiled in pots made of skin by using red-hot stones; it was then cured, dried or smoked and stored. In the archaeological layers of Magdalenian habitation particular parts of reindeer skeletons are often found together, which suggests that the meat was cut up on the hunting-grounds and the best bits brought back. *Tendons and ligaments*: sewing thread made from the long dorsal tendons of the reindeer is still used by the Eskimos, the last of the Indians and the Siberian peoples. The tendons were also used to carry ornaments, to make bindings for weapons, ties for tent frames, and cords of all sorts, notably for making nooses and traps. The thread was also used for fishing lines. The *bones*: the marrow is often still eaten raw by hunting peoples. The Montagnais Indians consider it to be a choice food for pregnant or lactating women. In the Palaeolithic period they were so fond of marrow that it was even extracted from the maxillae (jaw-bones) and tarsals (ankle-bones). In the archaeological layers long bones are found, broken up into regular segments and split to extract the marrow. Bones were also used for implements and objects of all sorts: flint trimmers, bodkins, awls, percussors, body ornaments, beads, discs, cut-out shapes, as well as surfaces for engraving. The remaining bones were used as fuel, the shoulder-blades as plates.

As yet we have no certain proof of the use in Palaeolithic times of reindeer shoulder-blades for 'scapulomancy', a form of divination practised by the shamans of Siberia and Canada. My friend the film-maker Arthur Lamothe watched and filmed a Montagnais shaman one winter in the north-west of Canada at a temperature of −50°C. (−58°F.), as he 'divined', from the small cracks and burns on a shoulder-blade exposed to the fire, the position and numbers of three herds of caribou, how far away they were and what direction they were going in. The *fat* was used as food, as fuel for lamps, as lubricant for skins making them supple and waterproof, and for much else besides.

At Lascaux in the interstadial period – as Jean Bouchud observes in *Lascaux inconnu* – the temperature in summer rose to 22°C. (72°F.). Since reindeer cannot endure a temperature of more than 13°C. (55°F.), they must have left the region at the end of the short spring and climbed up towards the high pastures of the Massif Central, coming back down again in autumn. Certainly the Magdalenians would have done most of their hunting in autumn and winter. Interestingly, archaeology has revealed that the reindeer eaten by the hunter-artists on their 'picnics' in the sanctuary were young.

Reindeer become more common in Palaeolithic wall decorations after Lascaux and are often found on the artifacts of the later Magdalenian millennia.

During the Würm glaciation the steppes of Europe were crossed by herds of rhinoceros (*Rhinoceros tichorhinus* Cuvier = *Coelodonta antiquitatis*), a species which became extinct at the same time as the mammoth at the end of the Ice Age. A great deal is known about the physiology and anatomy of this extraordinary animal, thanks to discoveries made in the Soviet Union. Whole carcases have been found preserved in the ice of Siberia and the salt clay of Galicia, with their skin and even the contents of their stomachs intact, making a very detailed study possible.

This powerful and dangerous mammal was a natural 'tank', measuring 11 feet 6 inches long and 5 feet high. The longer of the two horns, placed one behind the other on its massive head, could be more than a yard long. Its body was protected from the cold by a thick woolly fleece, and its nostrils were partitioned, no doubt also because of the cold. It fed on steppe plants, and remains of conifer branches and willow leaves have been found between its teeth. The rhinoceros was occasionally depicted in prehistoric times, notably at Lascaux at the bottom of the Shaft, as well as perhaps in an engraving which is hard to make out. It does not feature in the classic compositions and almost always occupies a place apart, at the end of dead-end passages. It is possible that the famous unicorn at the entrance to the Rotunda, with its two parallel horns, is a rhinoceros with its head wrongly drawn, a description that might have been passed down by oral tradition. However, the artist responsible for the picture in the Shaft was more successful.

The rhinoceros

The only rhinoceros in Lascaux was drawn 26 feet down at the bottom of the Shaft. The artist went down there by rope 17,000 years ago taking lamps and a supply of manganese, which is used here in a fairly rudimentary, but nonetheless expressive manner. The colour appears to have been spread with the hand and manipulated with the fingers. Note the animal's woolly coat and four of the six black dots, a sign meaning the end, which is also found at the back of the Chamber of the Felines.

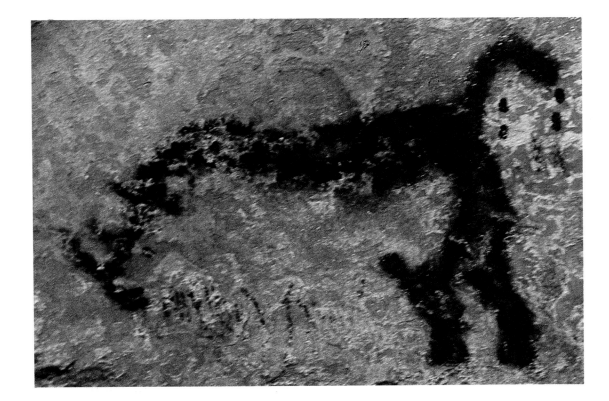

The Frieze of the Three Rhinoceros. The woolly rhinoceros (*Coelodonta antiquitatis*) became extinct about 9,500 years ago. It fed on willow branches. Cave of Rouffignac (Dordogne), Middle Magdalenian, about 14,000 years old.

The fearsome beast would have been invincible: it could fight, and had acute senses of smell and hearing, so it is unlikely that any predators would have threatened it. Similarly it was no doubt eaten only very rarely in the Magdalenian period. It could have been caught in pits – but there was already a wide variety of game available which was both more edible and easier to obtain. The Abbé Breuil thought that the rhinoceros at the bottom of the Shaft at Lascaux had gored the bison which has its entrails hanging out.

The lion

The seven felines of Lascaux (six of which can be identified with certainty) are all grouped in the first small space in the end chamber which bears their name. They are engraved summarily with a flint point, on the walls on either side. To see them you have to crouch down and direct the beam of your lamp obliquely across the surface. They are cave lions and have no manes. The

Ice Age lions, closely related to their present-day counterparts, sought shelter, like the bears, in caves, where they would winter and give birth to their young. They must have been a great danger to humans and have attacked almost all the herbivores.

The figures at Lascaux are interesting in spite of their relatively naïve draughtsmanship – attributed by Leroi-Gourhan simply to the artists' having no opportunity to take a close look at the animals. The attitude of one of the cats is taken from life: the lines coming from its mouth probably signify roaring or growling, and it shoots a jet of urine behind it – the way that cats mark out their territory. The Lascaux engravings are the only known representation of a herd of lions from prehistoric times.

The cave bear and the brown bear

These two species of bear (*Ursus spelaeus* and *Ursus arctus* Linnaeus) were living throughout the Upper Palaeolithic. The first was contemporary with Neanderthal man, but gradually disappeared during the last third of the Ice Age and gave way to the second species. The cave bear was much bigger than the brown bear and seems to have been entirely vegetarian. It spent the winter in relatively dry caves, where it hollowed out nests or 'wallows' in the clay, sometimes more than half a mile from the cave entrance. In some decorated sanctuaries such as Rouffignac, in the Dordogne, there are hundreds of fossilized bear nests. Only one species from the Magdalenian period has survived in Europe in the wild – the brown bear. It measures up to 8 feet long and 4 feet high at the shoulder, and weighs between 550 and 660 pounds – but can reach 880 pounds in the Soviet Union. It still exists in Spain in the Pyrenees and Cantabrian mountains, in the Alps, in Italy in the Abruzzi national park, in Yugoslavia, Albania, Greece, Bulgaria, Rumania, Hungary, Slovakia, Poland, Norway, Finland and Estonia, but the largest unsurveyed population is in the Soviet Union.

Like man, the brown bear is an omnivore: it will feed on anything edible it can find. As a carnivore, it does not hesitate to eat sheep, cows, calves, young wild boar, deer and reindeer – some bears even hunt wild boar. But the animal also likes to feed on snails, insects, larvae, ants, mice, frogs, ceps and other mushrooms of all kinds, roots, nettles, acorns, beechnuts and bulbs. It breaks open beehives and eats the honey. The bear is also an accomplished angler; it will go down into the shallows of rivers and catch salmon and trout, using its paws and teeth with surprising agility. It then throws the fish on to the banks – sometimes from a considerable distance – and climbs up nimbly to eat them.

It is a cunning, intelligent and cautious animal, and seems to have a very clear idea of the danger created by the presence of man on its territory. It can rear up and stand upright, and can also run at up to 30 miles an hour. Robert Hainard writes of a man living in a hut deep in the woods in Slovakia, who is said to have seen a bear throwing stones at dogs that were harassing it on the edge of a torrent. The naturalist continues: 'In Bulgaria my warden maintained that bears fought wolves by backing against a tree and throwing stones and sticks, and I also heard in Croatia that this had happened recently.' The bear's strength is almost incredible: Krementz reports that in 1867 'a bear picked up a cow between its front paws and, walking upright, carried it across a stream in the forest'. Arlette Leroi-Gourhan told me that during her stay among the Ainu on the island of Hokkaido a bear killed three horses.

The bear is remarkably adept at using its front paws; it can undo knots in ropes with its claws like a human. It likes water, bathes frequently in summer, can swim very well and climb like a cat. I myself have seen the peasants in the mountain village of Illica in eastern Anatolia place their hives 50 feet above the ground on platforms in the branches of giant beeches, so that they are out of reach of bears. The bear is reputedly able to build itself shelters sometimes so elaborate that they could be taken as made by humans. It spends the winters there, emerging very rarely during the cold weather.

These accounts of the bear by experienced naturalists make it easy to understand the respect and special feelings that the animal inspires in the hunting peoples of Scandinavia and the Indians of Canada. Its human gait and its affinities with man give it a personality of its own in the minds of primitive peoples. The Ainu of Hokkaido believe that the soul of the ritually sacrificed bear is a link with the world beyond, and some Siberian tribes see the bear as a sort of wild man hidden under a skin from which it can emerge if it wants to. The bear is also the leading character in many legends, stories and traditions, which constitute a very ancient folk memory with its origins lost in the distant past. In a conversation about the depiction of the bear in prehistoric times, André Leroi-Gourhan told me that 'the bear is a creature apart, perhaps a man in disguise'. The one at Lascaux is hidden in the breast of the third aurochs in the Rotunda (on the south side); only its muzzle, ears and clawed back feet are visible. Bear's teeth were very often worn as ornaments and strung on necklaces in prehistoric times. In the sanctuary of Tuc-d'Audoubert (Ariège) the prehistoric hunters discovered some skeletons of long-dead cave bears and salvaged their canine teeth.

The only bear in Lascaux is just visible in the photograph and can be seen more clearly in the reconstruction drawing. It is hidden in the breast of the third aurochs in the Rotunda. 17,000 years old.

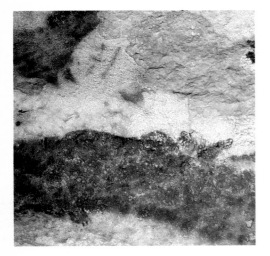

The archaeological excavations at Lascaux were conducted sporadically at various periods. Some were carried out at the same time as the alterations for tourism in the cave and were often salvage excavations which were executed too quickly. Winches and wheelbarrows were used to bring rubble to the surface, destroying irrecoverably the layer of earth trodden by the prehistoric hunters. The earth was not always sifted, and no doubt many bones must have disappeared with it, as did the forty lamps from the Shaft, which the Abbé Breuil had stored in the antichamber to the cave. Jean Bouchud's remarkable study, begun in 1957–8 and published in *Lascaux inconnu*, discusses the fauna found in the cave. The statistics he derived from the 133 bone fragments produced some quite surprising results. Of these bones, 118 came from reindeer (88.7 per cent), two from red deer (1.5 per cent), 6 from roe deer (4.5 per cent), 6 from wild boar (4.5 per cent) and only one (a molar) from a horse (0.8 per cent) – which is not enough to prove that the horse, the animal most frequently depicted, was actually eaten. Oddly enough, the horse's tooth was found in the Chamber of the Felines, at the narrowest point and furthest from the entrance. Similarly, a few sparse bones of hares found at the bottom of the Shaft do not prove that hare was included in the 'picnics' – the scarcity is surprising since the Magdalenians hunted the hare frequently, especially in the temperate period when the climate and vegetation allowed the species to prosper. In the small sanctuary at Gabillou, in the Dordogne, which is contemporary with Lascaux, there is an engraving of a hare.

The remains of wild boar and roe deer are plentiful in prehistoric encampment and habitation sites. They were much hunted and trapped by Palaeolithic peoples, though boar hunting in particular could lead to very dangerous confrontations. A wild boar can weigh up to 440 pounds in France, Spain and Germany, and up to 770 pounds in the Carpathians. Many species and sub-species have been widespread throughout the Palaearctic region for hundreds of thousands of years. The boar is an nocturnal omnivore, and a forest-dweller like the bear. It eats anything: acorns, chestnuts, roots, ferns, bulbs, berries, birds, rabbits, rodents, larvae, caterpillars and bugs, and it will feed off carrion and even eat hedgehogs. Its senses of hearing and smell are very acute, enabling it to detect the presence of a human from a long way off. It has a reputation as a quick, courageous and aggressive animal – this is especially true of the sow when she has her young with her. The boar charges its enemy with formidable force and its long, curved, dagger-like tusks and dangerous bites have often proved fatal to hunters even when they have been armed with guns. The wild boar attacks a person once they are down. A Balkan proverb advises one to 'take a doctor for a bear hunt, but a priest for a boar hunt'.

The roe deer, bounding through the undergrowth and always on the alert, is no doubt much easier to kill with a gunshot than to approach within spear-

ANIMAL BONES
DISCOVERED
IN THE CAVE

throwing range. The almost complete absence of these two animals in the prehistoric cave pictures is somewhat surprising. They were among the game animals eaten but, for reasons unknown to us, not depicted.

There is only one – very doubtful – engraving of a reindeer at Lascaux, yet the animal was eaten in great quantities by the hunters inside the cave. An examination of the bones has led to some interesting conclusions: the fact that the epiphyses of the phalanges are not fused together corresponds with the beginning of the cold season. It follows that the reindeer was hunted in winter, over the snow, because in summer the higher temperature would have forced it to climb up into the Massif Central. The herds, led by an old female, came back down to the Lascaux region at the end of autumn. In conclusion, there were also numerous small animals, the microfauna, which were not eaten but which, like the rodents, provide precise information about the climate.

OTHER ANIMALS DEPICTED IN PREHISTORIC TIMES

The mammoth

This huge and majestic animal lived in the glacial steppe and tundra. Representations of the mammoth are found from the very beginnings of art, in the Gravettian, and continue throughout the Magdalenian. One of the deified animals constituting the engraved compositions in sactuaries, its enormous size and fantastic appearance make it the star among prehistoric beasts. We can imagine the feelings of disquiet, respect and fascination it must have inspired in the Magdalenian hunters if we picture the scene fourteen or fifteen thousand years ago. . . .

It is the beginning of winter and the tribes are living huddled in the tents they have erected under the shelter of a high rocky porch. Suddenly a piercing trumpeting rends the air, as if many alarm sirens in the valley were warning of the arrival of the herd. The hunters wake up with a start, come out of the tents, dressed in their furs, and look intently at the giant pachyderms silhouetted against the morning mist. The hump behind the head of the big male, 10 feet above the ground, is a reserve of the fat which covers its whole body beneath its thick skin and the long woolly fleece extending down to the ground. Two young mammoths are also there looking like balls of fur, and their whimpering mingles with the noise of the herd.

The hunters at their vantage point watch every movement of the enormous beasts. At the moment the mammoths are busy feeding. They clear away the thin layer of fresh snow with their long, curved, ivory tusks. Their elastic trunks, with a prolonged upper lip like a sort of thick flexible finger, coil around the dwarf willows by the water's edge, tear them up and feed them to their giant molars. Even at a distance the scraping sound of their chewing can be heard. A kind of mist rises from the woolly masses, and one of the females shoots out a

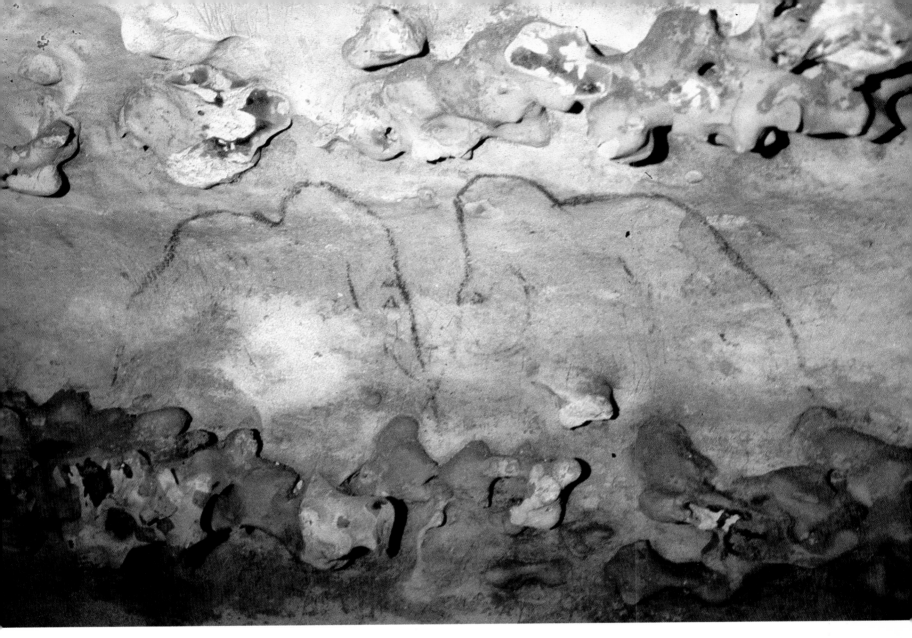

thick jet of steaming urine . . . The herd has now continued on its way and is heading towards the bottom of the valley. The hunters know that down there, by the birch wood, are two deep pits covered with branches and grass, hidden under the snow . . .

The mammoth represented an enormous reserve of meat and fat, and so must have been an important catch. Its tusks provided a large supply of ivory, from which Palaeolithic people made all sorts of implements, weapons, tools and *objets d'art*.

As with the rhinoceros, numerous complete carcases of mammoths have been found, still covered in their skins and wool, preserved in the ice of Siberia or the salt clay of Galicia. Whole cemeteries of mammoths in the Soviet Union have for centuries supplied the trade in ivory; tusks were exported to China, Japan and America. Many statuettes by Chinese and Japanese craftsmen, and other recent works, have been sculpted in fossil ivories dating from the time of the last Palaeolithic people. The end of the Würm glaciation 10,000 years ago led to a great climatic upheaval and Europe became covered with thick forests. The mammoths, needing a cold climate, migrated north in search of the steppes and tundra that had been uncovered by the recession of the ice, but they died in their thousands in the enormous snowstorms that were triggered off by the rise in humidity caused by the post-glacial thaw. In the Ukraine, cabins lived in by prehistoric tribes and built entirely of mammoth bones have been excavated and reconstructed.

Two mammoths. Herds of these huge pachyderms appeared in the Palaeolithic landscape during the colder periods. More than 120 of them are represented in the vast cave of Rouffignac. Here two males confront each other. About 13,000 years old.

Engraved mammoth. Cave of Les Trois Frères, Middle Magdalenian. (Copy by the Abbé Breuil)

59

This powerful figure of a mammoth has recently been discovered. It was carved 13 feet from the ground, no doubt with the help of scaffolding. Representations of the mammoth appear from the Gravettian (25,000 years ago) up to the Middle Magdalenian. They seem to be contemporary with the cold periods of glaciation. Cave of Saint-Front de Domme (Dordogne), Solutrean civilization, 22,000 to 18,000 years old.

The fact that the mammoth is not represented at Lascaux may be due to the mild climate of the interstadial, the disappearance of the steppe, and the consequent migrations. After the warmer weather of the interstadial, the climate again turned very cold. Mammoths returned in large numbers to the region around Lascaux and were once more painted, engraved and sculpted by the Magdalenians.

The megaceros deer

This giant deer (*Megaceros giganteus*) is unquestionably one of the most magnificent antlered animals ever to walk the earth. It evolved all over Europe – from France, Italy and Ireland, as far as the Altai Mountains in the East – during the Pleistocene, and became extinct at the end of the Ice Age. Its antlers, resembling enormous hands with the fingers apart, had a span of up to 10 feet and weighed 160 pounds. The megaceros lived on the great glacial prairies, avoided wooded country where it would only find unpassable obstacles, and fed on grass and broad-leafed bushes.

It was no doubt scarce and seldom hunted by Palaeolithic people, since remains of it are very unusual in the archaeological layers. On the other hand, it does mysteriously appear in the large compositions on the walls of the sanctuaries right from the earliest animal art, perhaps as a substitute for the red deer. The famous cave at Cougnac (Lot), dating from the Solutrean, is one of the few sanctuaries where the horse is not represented, but it does contain a magnificent frieze of megaceroses accompanied by ibexes.

The megaceros ends this list of the deified animals – some present in the cave at Lascaux, and others not – which are part of the depictions as a whole throughout the Upper Palaeolithic. To this catalogue must be added those animals which, like the bear and the felines represented at Lascaux, are rarely or never depicted as part of the classic groups. The saiga (a species of antelope), the fallow deer, the elk and the chamois are among animals whose bones have been found at habitation sites, but which appear to have been ignored by the artists, or only rarely depicted. The image of the wolf is also very rare, that of the hyena is non-existent, or nearly so, as is that of the fox, the badger, the cuon or wild dog, the wolverine, the cave panther, the wildcat, the lynx, the beaver and the marmot.

Depictions of fish are much less common on rock walls or clay floors than they are on small artifacts made of bone, ivory or antler. Pictures of salmon, trout, pike, sole and eel are known. Birds are even rarer than fish on the walls of sanctuaries and not much more frequent on bone objects. Otters, stoats and weasels are exceptional, as also are hares, rabbits, squirrels and various other rodents, and reptiles. And yet all these animals were hunted for their meat, bones, fur, teeth, vertebrae (for ornament), feathers or claws. The marine mammals represented are limited to the seal, engraved on bone or on schist at the end of the Magdalenian – about twenty images of seals have been found in caves, some of them far from the sea. On a perforated staff made of reindeer antler two seals can be seen chasing a salmon, which suggests that the marine mammals followed the salmon up the glacial rivers. Seal bones, belonging to several species, have occasionally been found in the shelters and caves of the Ariège, the Dordogne, the Landes and even at Altamira in Asturias. Did the Magdalenians hunt the seal with harpoons? There is no reason why they should not have done so. A tooth of a sperm whale discovered at Mas d'Asil has two ibexes carved on it.

To conclude this analysis of the Palaeolithic fauna contemporary with Magdalenian civilization, as it related to the life of the hunters and the images created by the artists, we must turn to the human race itself. We must imagine men and women living in a virgin world, very different from ours, ruled entirely by the laws of nature.

In their small tribes of twenty to thirty individuals the Magdalenians depended on and were governed by the animals around them. A territory would be exploited for the necessities of life required by the group. As the people became more numerous they impoverished the stocks of animals and destroyed the ecological equilibrium of the territory. If the region was rich and game was plentiful – which depended to a large extent on the climate and the passing of wild herds – the base camps could remain in one place for quite a long time. In

This gouache by the famous Czech animal painter Zdenck Burian in 1953 shows a reconstruction of *Megaceros giganteus*. Its enormous palm-like antlers reached a width of more than 10 feet. The animal was very occasionally depicted in cave art: at Pair-non-Pair (Gironde) and Cougnac (Lot). (© Artia, Prague)

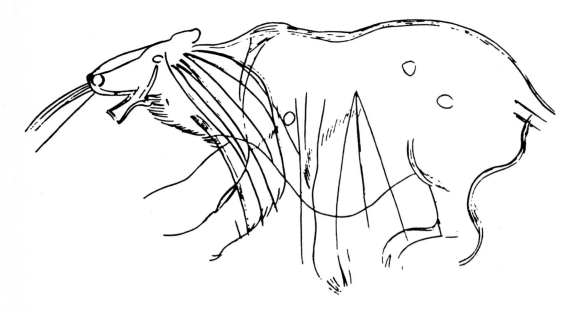

A wounded bear. The animal seems to be bleeding badly. The V and O signs on it represent wounds made by small and large spears. The lines coming from its nostrils indicate its cry or growl. An engraving in the cave of Les Trois Frères, Middle Magdalenian. (Copy by the Abbé Breuil)

THE SPIRIT
OF THE HUNT

the fine season small expeditions would set out, consisting of about eight hunters, including men, women and adolescents, who were not afraid of going away for trips lasting several days. They would set up provisional camps – two or three tents – along the traditional routes followed by the reindeer migrations and come back at the beginning of winter.

But in spite of the wild animals, was there nonetheless a certain sense of security? A group could stay in one place for four or five centuries. We do not know how long the period lasted when Lascaux was frequented during the interstadial: when the cold climate returned the hunters moved on to other parts, leaving the sanctuary for ever. This semi-nomadic existence in the midst of an extremely varied natural world must have been very enriching. It would have developed their powers of observation, hunting techniques and detailed knowledge of the behaviour of the various animal species, all of which we today have lost. For almost all animals living in groups, such as horses, bison, aurochses and ibexes, a complex hierarchy is established in relation to the other animals and the extent and diversity of the territory where it is essential to maintain the ecological equilibrium necessary for life. From the components of this equilibrium there develops a scale of values: the prehistoric hunters' daily experience of life and death inspired in them a religious system – impenetrable to us, but embodying a supreme driving force that emerges in their art.

Is it possible to take that great step into the unknown and understand the prehistoric spirit of the hunt? 10,000 years have passed since the end of the Ice Age; we are separated by more than four hundred generations from the last of the Magdalenian hunters, by more than seven hundred from the hunters of Lascaux. Among these developed peoples, with their cultural, artistic and technical wealth, the spirit of the hunt was necessarily linked to a whole collection of traditions and beliefs in which magic, religion and metaphysics governed the relationship between man and nature. The great ethnologist Evelyne Lot-Falk gives the following definition of them: 'How does man envisage the animals, those mysterious beings with which he lives side by side? Are they simply prey, a means of ensuring his subsistence? Certainly not. Such a materialistic conception would be very far from the mind of the "primitive", who moves in a world impregnated with religiosity, where nothing is inanimate, where everything, right down to the stones, is endowed – if not with an actual soul – at least with life. The primitive man does not classify or group beings according to categories. Nothing is finished or definitive. In accordance with the

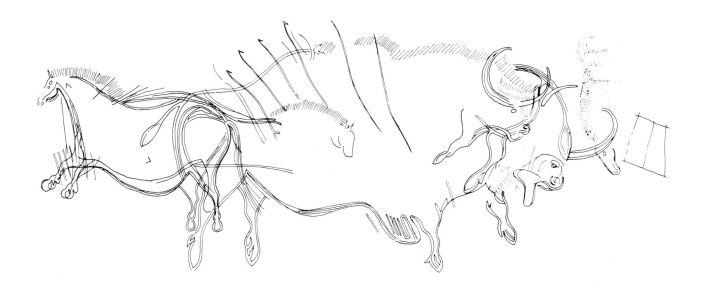

Horses, both painted and engraved, and a bison with
two heads. They have the conventions that are typical of
Style III, as defined by Leroi-Gourhan: small,
expressive heads and swollen bellies. The hooves are
pear-shaped. The bison has seven lines, perhaps
representing spears. This number occurs frequently at
Lascaux and must have had a symbolic significance.
Lascaux, Nave, Panel of the Imprint. (Copy by the
Abbé Glory)

cyclical idea of time, the past is always present, the future is an eternal recommencement. Nature is in perpetual movement, forms are still fluid, undifferentiated, not fixed or stable. In this moving universe no barriers have yet been set up between the animal, vegetable and even mineral kingdoms; there are only different aspects, changing appearances. A single current of life circulates through all creation. Everything that exists is alive, and everything that is alive is united by powerful bonds of solidarity. Man is only a link in the chain. He identifies himself with the world, and communes with what is round about him.'

During the final glaciation, the Magdalenians – as we have seen – were among the direct ancestors of many races and sub-races which populate the old continents of the Northern hemisphere, from America to China, from Europe to Siberia. Until recently, there were still many 'Archaic' or 'primitive' peoples living at various stages of prehistoric development. Although they are now increasingly rare, some, like the Australian Aborigines, have not yet been assimilated or wiped out and have remained the masters of their own culture. They are the inheritors of wisdom handed down over thousands of years, with its origins lost in the distant past. The invaluable contribution made by ethnography, in conjunction with other disciplines of prehistoric research, has made it possible in recent years to get much closer to the daily life of the Ice Age peoples, but an important gap still remains: how are we to imagine the 'spirit of the hunt' as it was experienced by the people of Lascaux and the Magdalenians in general?

Lot-Falk's study of the hunting peoples of Siberia, who live in climates very like those in prehistoric times and who are dependent on similar fauna (with the exception of mammoths), provides an excellent analysis of the 'spirit of the hunt'. Some aspects of this may bring us closer to the Magdalenian world. She writes: 'Hunting is not a luxury activity but a problem of vital importance, requiring an attention, concentration and seriousness which the modern huntsman necessarily lacks. It is not a duel between man and beast in which man succeeds in reassuring himself of his enormous technical superiority. It is not merely a confrontation of adversaries: behind the animal the hunter sees a host of supernatural forces ready to intervene against this irruption into their domain. The roles are reversed: man is puny and seems to be attacking a strong opponent from a position of inferiority. He is faced with a warrior whose resources are no less than his own, who is under the protection of supernatural

A magnificent painted and engraved figure of a bison,
from the Middle Magdalenian. Cave of Les Trois Frères
in the Ariège Pyrenees. (Photo Max Begouën – Musée
de l'Homme, Paris/Photeb.)

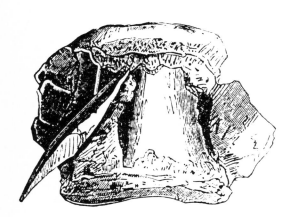

A reindeer vertebra pierced by a flint point, found at Laugerie-Basse and dating from the Magdalenian period. As early as 1872 this engraving was used to illustrate the work of the famous Scottish geologist Sir Charles Lyell, who had been one of Charles Darwin's teachers.

powers and who must consent to his own murder. Left to his own powers alone man would attempt nothing. For himself he does not exist. Of course he does not underestimate the importance of technique. He will not neglect to practise handling his weapons, to develop his strength and skill. He will study the behaviour of animals, the places they frequent and the dates of their migrations. He will recognize the slightest track, will know exactly where to set his traps, lay his snares or position an ambush. Yet for the success of his enterprise he will not rely on his physical abilities alone. On its own, technique can accomplish nothing; it remains a dead letter unless backed by the appropriate rites. Technique and magic are indissolubly linked, but it is the latter that gives the former its efficacy. It is the force that guides the arm of man, that thrusts the weapon in the right direction, that makes it penetrate into the body, that closes the trap on the prey.

'Entering the field of "savagery", man must be in a state of grace, like the priest who is to carry out a sacrifice. This state of grace can only be attained through a number of observances, some of which are positive (offerings, prayers, purification) and some negative (prohibitions). The hunt itself is the final stage after lengthy preparations in which religious and magical concerns predominate (of equal importance are the rites after the murder, which re-establish the order of nature that has been disturbed). There are also various means of involvement which make it possible to affect things at a distance, by means of interposed persons or objects, and which for their part require certain restrictions (for instance between married couples).

'The hunter only commits himself once he has as much luck as possible on his side, and has assured himself of the complicity or neutrality of parties involved, by taking out a kind of insurance with "the other side". This fact gives the undertaking a legal colouring: the right to kill has been paid for, rather like a hunting permit issued by the higher powers. In exchange for sacrifices, the deities will grant game in abundance. Without sacrifice, luck will desert the hunter. Although he is driven by necessity, the hunter is not convinced of the legitimacy of his act; his feelings of guilt clearly emerge in the care he takes to justify himself, to relieve his responsibility, to reconcile himself with his victim. It is in the interests of the group as a whole to watch over the precise observance of the laws, because the error of one person will rebound on all. This fear of the possible consequences of any reprehensible act serves as a great restraint on any infringements. Between the desire and its realization primitive wisdom raises a barrier and maintains a tradition of discipline and moderation.

'Thus it appears that the art of the hunt, among primitive peoples, requires knowledge drawn from the various fields of technique, magic, religion and law. These are the keys needed to open the way to the perilous kingdom.'

HUNTING AND WEAPONS, FISHING AND GATHERING

HUNTING

Although he has been called an 'opportunistic omnivore', man is primarily a hunter. For over two million years one of his principal activities has been to use his cunning and group strategy to capture and kill the animals around him – from the smallest to the largest, the weakest to the most ferocious. The hunting of big game began with *Homo erectus* 1,600,000 years ago and gradually replaced the hunting of smaller game which his predecessors had pursued. To attack and vanquish a beast much larger than himself and equipped with considerable defences (teeth, claws, hooves, horns or antlers) he had to invent strategies or draw inspiration from other predators, such as lions, wolves or wild dogs.

The hunting of big game provided new experiences for *Homo erectus*, bringing about an intensification of the learning process for the young and a considerable increase in the area and distances covered by expeditions. The application of the group tactics and strategies needed to approach and catch big game developed the powers of observation, agility, cunning, memory and knowledge of the habits of each animal species and probably also helped in the development of communication and language. 'The habit of meat-eating led by imperceptible degrees to more complicated hunting techniques and gradually transformed mankind. For the first time culture and tradition became increasingly responsible for changes formerly brought about only by genetic mutation and natural selection.' (J Pfeiller).

As in present-day tribes, the social structure of a group of hunters was restricted to twenty or thirty individuals, although they might regroup on a temporary basis to form associations with other tribes for more important hunts. Was *Homo erectus* already setting traps, digging pits to capture elephants and

A dying bear. The animal is literally covered in V- and O-signs which suggest many spear-thrusts. Blood seems to be spurting from its mouth. Such images provided the basis for the old theory of bewitching magic (see chapter 4, 'Religion and the Sanctuaries'). Cave of Les Trois Frères (Ariège). Middle Magdalenian, about 13,000 years old.

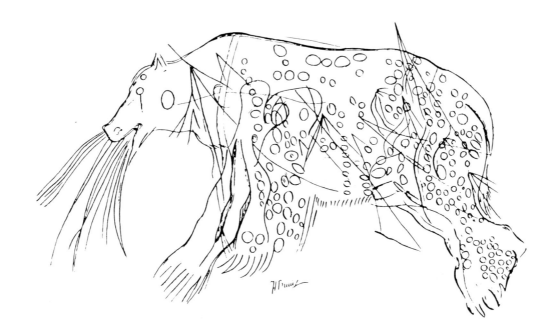

rhinoceros? There are some indications to support this hypothesis, such as the age of the animals killed and the discovery of large spears in the deposits. We also have evidence of ambushes laid by *Homo erectus* at Olduvaï, and at Torralba and Ambrona (Spain).

The forces of natural selection were intense during the last period of glaciation about 100,000 years ago, and evolution favoured the survival of groups or individuals who were endowed with a longer and more extensive memory than average. Thus the development of hunting techniques led to a widening of the gap between 'primitive people', with their considerably enlarged cerebral hemispheres, and the rest of the animal world.

The process of humanization continued from the early *Homo erectus* to the first *Homo sapiens* who inherited his predecessor's skills and knowledge and like him lived by hunting and fishing, but made great advances in his industries and techniques.

R ight from the start, *Homo sapiens fossilis* made use of the special properties of antler – a material which was to be of great and increasing importance throughout the Upper Palaeolithic: 30,000 years ago it was the basis of the principal weapon of all the hunting peoples of the world, the spear. Spears continued to be made throughout the succeeding periods and were particularly numerous in the Magdalenian, when they were often decorated with engravings of schematized animals or with abstract signs which may be an indication of ownership.

The hardness of the material meant that it had to be carved and sharpened using a whole range of flint tools specially made for sawing, trimming, scraping, polishing, rounding, filing and sharpening the sections cut from the best branches of deer or reindeer antler. Since antlers do not have any straight parts, the pieces cut from them are necessarily curved to a greater or lesser extent, and are therefore not very suitable as weapons for throwing. This problem is overcome if the hunter first immerses the antler in water and soaks it before shaping it. Prolonged soaking makes it much softer, more malleable and flexible and easier to carve.

WEAPONS

The hunting spear

A reindeer-antler spear from Lascaux found at the bottom of the Shaft, below the rhinoceros. Length: 17¼ inches. (Photo Delluc)

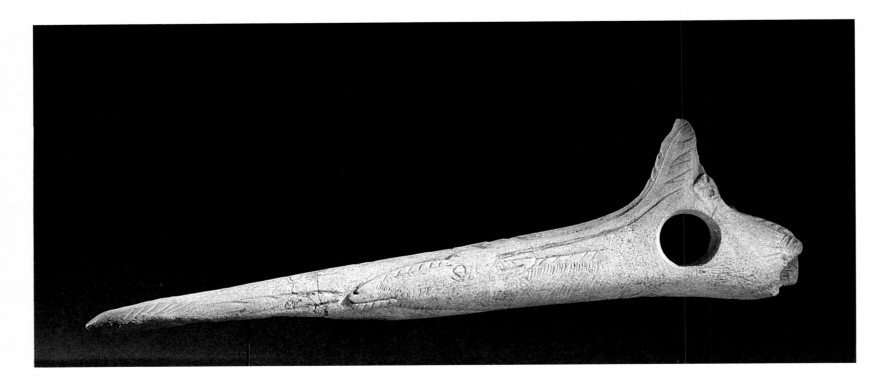

The perforated staff or spear-straightener

The shaped piece is straightened out in the heat of the fire using a special instrument made for the purpose and known as the 'perforated staff' or 'spear-straightener'. This was a *de luxe* tool, a personal object often decorated with signs, engravings and carvings. Hunters were justly proud of them and took them on their expeditions. Once the antler had been softened and made more flexible, it was inserted into the hole in the implement which thus acted as a right-angled lever. The straightener was then moved along the whole length of the spear, correcting the natural curvature until the spear was perfectly straight and had hardened in the heat. Now it was ready to be fixed to a shaft, which could be of hard wood, or sometimes, as at Sungir in the Soviet Union, made from mammoth tusk carved and straightened in the fire. The parts were joined together with ligatures probably coated with glue, mastic or pitch and exposed to the heat in their turn.

It seems very likely that the Magdalenians also used spears with detachable points, perhaps bound to the shaft, like the heads of some harpoons, though there is no direct evidence of this. Harpoons with moveable or detachable heads have existed since prehistoric times among the Arctic peoples, who are the last inheritors of the Magdalenian culture. At the end of the Ice Age, hunting spears underwent many transformations; 12–13,000 years ago they already had grooves for the insertion of rows of small triangular-shaped pieces of razor-sharp flint fixed with glue – which caused a worse wound resulting in greater loss of blood from the animal. This type of weapon continued to be used in the Mesolithic, after the Ice Age, and to spread to peoples all over the world.

When the treated antler forming the spearpoint came into contact with the outside humidity during a hunt, it would gradually curve again and return to its natural shape, necessitating frequent heated straightenings with the 'perforated staff' which the hunter kept constantly to hand. Unlike flint implements, which were easy to shape and could be quickly retouched, the precious antler point, which could be 14 inches long, like those found in the Shaft at Lascaux, must have required a slow and gradual process of manufacture and continual maintenance. Every hunter must have owned several spearpoints and may have changed them in the course of the expeditions, bringing the worn or damaged

Perforated staff or spear-straightener, made from reindeer antler, found at Laugerie-Basse. The engraving of the reindeer's antlers was fitted by the artist to the shape of the object. Note the nested signs in front of the animal's head; they are identical to those at Lascaux. Middle Magdalenian. (Photo J. Oster – Musée de l'Homme, Paris)

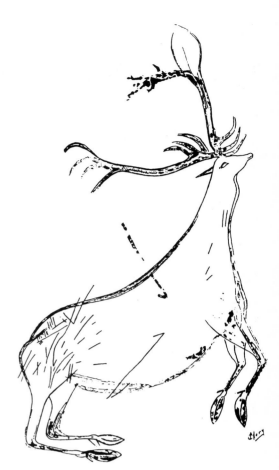

ones back to the camp to repair them. It is therefore very likely that bags or satchels would have been carried, containing thread made of reindeer tendon (for binding), sewing needles, leather thongs, pitch and mastic. There would also have been an assortment of flint tools already prepared for various uses: blades, perforators and scrapers, separated from each other and perhaps rolled up in skins because they were so fragile: in short, a complete repair kit. For expeditions lasting several days, this would also contain means of lighting a fire and some minimal provisions, probably dried and smoked meat or fish.

The spear-thrower

How did Palaeolithic people use the spears that seem to have been their main weapon? Firstly, they could, of course, be held in the hand if the animal could be approached, as in ambushes. They could also be thrown a short distance and would have greater penetrating force if the hunter threw them from a point higher up than the animal he wanted to hit – from the top of a rock, for instance. Later in the Middle Magdalenian, about 14,000 years ago, a new implement appears to have been perfected which considerably altered the effectiveness of the projectile. This was the spear-thrower, a staff cut from deer or reindeer antler and ending in a hook into which the blunt end of the spear was inserted. It could also have been carved in wood like those of the Australian Aborigines, but since such perishable materials have disappeared there is no scientific evidence of this. The thrower acted as an extension of the arm, so that the weapon was accompanied further forward in its trajectory and received a much stronger parting thrust which resulted in a considerably longer trajectory.

I myself have observed and filmed comparable techniques among the last whalers of the Azores, who until recently were still hunting the sperm whale with a hand-held harpoon. This weapon has an iron-weighted tip about 30 inches long and weighing $5\frac{1}{2}$ pounds; the shaft or handle is made of rough-hewn wood weighing about 13 pounds and measuring about 5 feet long and nearly $2\frac{1}{2}$ inches in diameter; the hemp line is wound round the base of the iron head and fixed to the shaft by means of thin cords, which are intended to break as soon as the harpoon has stuck in. Altogether the weapon is fairly heavy, weighing about 22 pounds (not including several loops of line to be released, which the harpoonist holds in his left hand). Firmly wedged in the prow of the dugout canoe with his left leg inserted up to the knee into a crack specially made for the purpose, he throws the harpoon by grasping the end of the shaft in his right hand, while keeping it balanced by holding the middle of it in his left. As soon as he relaxes, his body pivots on itself, making a half turn, and he lurches forward losing his balance, so that his right arm accompanies the heavy shaft on its trajectory until the very last moment. A weapon thrown in this way by the right hand, and unwinding the coils of rope released by the left, may cover a distance

Above: the collapsing stag is pierced by two spear-wound (composite) signs and numerous short strokes which could also be wounds. The hindquarters of the animal seem to be paralysed. Lascaux, engraving in the Apse. 17,000 years old. (Copy by the Abbé Glory)

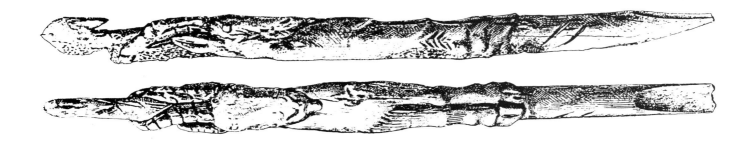

of 30 to 40 feet or more. Although this method of throwing is made more difficult by the movement of the sea, it enables a harpoonist weighing 150 pounds to throw one seventh of his own weight for 30 feet, using his right hand like the hook on a spear-thrower. Thus the projectile used for killing the whale is the direct descendant of the hunting spear and is propelled in the same way.

These observations have no direct bearing on prehistory but they do give us an idea of how a spear weighing $4\frac{1}{2}$ pounds, hurled with the help of a thrower and a strong arm, would have been able to go at least as far as 30 yards. The spear-thrower, like the 'womera' of the Australian Aborigines, was used as a basis for all kinds of embellishments, engravings and carvings and is hence an art object.

What is known about other prehistoric weapons? Did projectile weapons with flint points exist before arrows began being fired from bows at a later period? Flint is so fragile that every 'misfire' or deflected shot would have broken or chipped the point and it would then have to be changed and another one fixed to the shaft. This raises the question of the function of the flint points found in layers earlier than the Magdalenian or, like the Solutrean, from the beginning of the period.

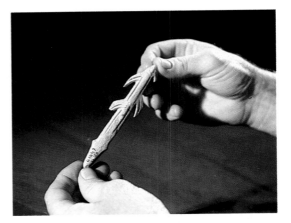

The marvellous 'notched points' and 'laurel or willow leaves', which date from the Solutrean (20,000 years ago), were made by heating the flint before working it – a very lengthy and delicate process. Their great fragility raises problems: if they were really parts of projectile weapons, they would have had to be replaced after every throw. Perhaps they are more likely to have been the cutting and penetrating end of a pointed hand-held weapon, a *bandarilla*, thrust directly into the animal like a sword. If they broke once they had penetrated the flesh of the animal they could cause severe haemorrhages which would weaken it. Mounted on lighter shafts, these points were the forerunners of arrows and could be carried by the hunter together with the heavier weapon made of reindeer antler.

The other weapons are more hypothetical. 'Bolas' attached to thongs, apparently go back millions of years to *Homo habilis*, but apart from the numerous stone balls uncovered at different periods in the archaeological layers, we have no direct evidence of how they were used. On the other hand it is certain that clubs, projectile staffs, bludgeons, cudgels, pikes and daggers of all kinds were in general use. None of the wood from these has survived, nor has the

Laurel leaves

Solutrean 'willow leaf', 20,000 years old, $8\frac{5}{8}$ inch long and $\frac{3}{32}$ inch thick. These remarkable objects represent the zenith of the art of flint-working. They were made from flints that had been heated in the fire, and are too thin and fragile to have been used as weapons. (Périgueux Museum)

Below: harpoon of deer antler with two rows of barbs. Late Magdalenian, 12,000 to 10,000 years old. (Périgueux Museum)

wood used for boomerangs (which seem to have existed only in Australia), but the bow and arrow probably appeared in the late Magdalenian. To conclude this armoury of projectiles, we must not forget that a river pebble thrown accurately by hand is also a formidable weapon.

About 13,500 years ago harpoons begin to appear in the Magdalenian layers. These were new weapons and their exact uses are unknown. The earliest ones have only a single row of barbs and must derive from spears which had triangular flakes of flint embedded in grooves. About 12,000 years ago they were succeeded by a version with two rows of barbs, which it seems clear was used for fishing. As these harpoons gradually evolved they became shorter and, like their predecessors, resembled those used by the ancient Eskimos. Did the harpoon first originate in Magdalenian Europe? We have no certain proof of this, given its appearance at a time when people in all the continents were already concerned with techniques of fishing and hunting.

The hunting of birds

The bones of birds are found in the oldest stratigraphic layers and increase in number in the Upper Palaeolithic layers after the arrival of *Homo sapiens fossilis*.

They come from three sources: first, birds nesting in the entrance of the cave; secondly, the discarded pellets of nocturnal birds of prey; and thirdly, birds hunted or trapped by humans. The number of the latter increased considerably in the Upper Palaeolithic and they have been the subject of several studies. The most frequently found species in prehistoric habitation sites in the Lascaux region are: the willow grouse and the ptarmigan, together with other grouse, partridge, ducks and teal. Large birds, such as swans, bustards, cranes, storks, vultures, lammergeyers and golden eagles, were occasionally caught to be eaten, as well as for their bones.

Bird bones are particularly suitable for the making of perforated needles. Prehistorians – in particular Cécile Mourer Chauviré (1979) – have studied and reconstructed the stages in this manufacturing process which was so important in the daily life of the Magdalenians. The operations required patience and minute detail and the work was probably done by the women and children during the evenings in the tents or huts of the encampment. Using a sharp cutting burin, two parallel grooves were hollowed out of the bone, leaving a narrow strip in between. This strip was gradually cut away, then removed, made thinner, given a point and polished by rubbing in a grooved polisher. The final and most difficult stage was the piercing of the hole with a minute flint piercer probably stuck to a rod and twisted between the palms of the hands – as is still done today by many 'primitive' peoples.

There were also other objects made of bird bones, such as tubes, flasks for 'make-up' (especially for ochre which was used for body painting), needlecases, birdcalls and even flutes. Many other objects, often artistically decorated, must also be added to this list, among them pendants and beads which were skilfully sawn from the long, polished bones. It has been demonstrated by archaeologists that the feathers were carefully removed, no doubt to be used as ornaments in the hair or on the body.

Some ancient methods still practised today may give an indication of how the Magdalenians hunted birds. In the moulting season geese, ducks and swans cannot fly and it is easy to surprise them and beat them to death with a stick. Catching them on their nests is more problematic, especially at night – which all hunting peoples believe is 'peopled with ghosts' and so inspires a salutary fear. We can be sure that the Magdalenians used traps, snares, nooses, nets and birdlime. The presence of hooks, projectile staffs, catapult stones and (at the end of the Palaeolithic) bows and arrows supports the hypothesis that these were used to catch birds. A very curious feature in some late Magdalenian sites is the great abundance of bones of the snowy owl; 1,130 bone fragments of this nocturnal bird of prey, from more than 84 large owls, were associated with tools from this period in the deposit at Pessac-sur-Dordogne.

At the period when the cave at Lascaux was decorated, and throughout the following 4–5,000 years, mankind can be said to have spread across the whole of the earth – except for some remote archipelagos in the middle of the oceans. Maritime navigation, which we can trace back to the Greeks and Egyptians, in fact existed 35,000 years before those great civilizations. Migrations from Asia along the archipelagos of the north Pacific reached Alaska at various periods in the Arctic Palaeolithic and Neolithic. People could have come on foot during the very cold episodes in the glaciation, but, nevertheless, some straits must have been crossed by boat.

American Palaeolithic hunters pursued herds of bison, mammoths, red deer and elk across the prairies, and in the Far North at a later period they followed caribou, musk-ox, seals and perhaps, even at that date, whales. In Australia other Palaeolithic people, the ancestors of the Aborigines, were hunting completely different fauna (with no mammals), hurling their spears at the many species of kangaroos and aiming boomerangs at flocks of birds in flight. Prehistoric Africa was heavily populated and had its own fauna, quite different again from that of Europe, America or Australia. The Magdalenian peoples everywhere hunted the animals which lived in their particular regions and climatic conditions, developing techniques appropriate to the various species of game.

Engravings of snow owls in the cave of Les Trois Frères. (Photo Max Begouën – Musée de l'Homme, Paris/Photoeb.)

PREHISTORIC FISHING

How did prehistoric people fish? This is a matter on which there is very little precise information and on which the imagination has to be exercised. All we can be sure of from the archaeological evidence is that prehistoric hunters ate a great deal of fish: countless fish vertebrae have been discovered in the layers of habitation sites. It follows that they must have fished, but this aspect of research has been seriously studied only fairly recently.

The catching of fish in lakes, rivers and the sea dates back hundreds of thousands of years, but the further back we go, the less material evidence we have. There is after all no reason why the implements used for fishing should have been preserved. 400,000 years ago *Homo erectus* was fishing, and 45,000 years ago Neanderthal man was doing likewise – but what evidence could possibly survive from such distant times to prove the existence of fishing nets, osier hoop nets, hooks (made of wood, thorns or the bones of fish or small animals), lures, lines (made of thread, animal hair or reindeer tendon), all of which are perishable materials?

For the Upper Palaeolithic there is more direct and indirect evidence from rock and mobiliary art, fishing implements and food refuse. Vertebrae have been found even in the depths of the sanctuaries. Radiographic analysis of them has made it possible to identify the species most frequently caught. At the top of the list are the Salmonidae: salmon, trout, grayling and char. However, all we have to help us imagine what Palaeolithic fishing was like are ethnographical comparisons. These provide information about very many fishing techniques still practised by 'primitive' peoples, including those living in climatic conditions similar to prehistoric times: Eskimos, Lapps, American Indians and Siberian hunters. Indeed, some of these techniques must have been handed down over thousands of years and originate from the Magdalenian; but prehistoric fishing techniques still remain open to speculation, owing to the small number of objects – straight and curved hooks, gigs and harpoons carved from bone or antler – that can be connected with them. That is all we have: there is no engraved or painted image depicting fishing, though there is no shortage of images of fish.

At Les Eyzies, in the Dordogne, a magnificent salmon was sculpted in the roof of the 'Shelter of the Fish' about 24,000 years ago, dominating the River Vézère where it was no doubt frequently fished. At Pech-Merle (Lot), a pike is engraved along the back of one of the famous 'dappled horses'; it is 20,000 years old. The sanctuary of Niaux contains the image of a salmon traced in the clay floor. Still more numerous are fish engraved on bone, among them the superb 14,000-year-old salmon recently excavated in the cave of Enlène. Even more extraordinary is the discovery in the sanctuary of Fontanet of a salmon complete with all its vertebrae, which had been left 6 feet under ground on a stalagmite flow and can be dated to 13,810 years ago!

What a delight it would have been to fish at the time of Lascaux in the teeming rivers and glacial torrents! The salmon making their way between the pebbles as they climbed upstream in spring towards the shallow waters of the sources of the rivers would have been a real treat for the young Magdalenian hunters. And we may be sure that they picked up some useful hints from that professional angler, the bear.

The poacher's method of fishing for trout by hand, feeling along the edges of torrents and nimbly slipping his arm under the big projecting rocks, must have made a substantial contribution to Palaeolithic menus. Nets, hoop nets and temporary dams made of stones and branches would have channelled the fish along predetermined routes. In winter the tribes must have obtained a considerable addition to their diet by passing fishing lines through holes cut in the ice. Smoked salmon, so enjoyed by the modern gourmet, must be one of the oldest dishes in the world – though originally it would have been served on a reindeer shoulderblade for a plate.

There are a few certain facts: the earliest harpoons (first with one and then two rows of barbs) and fishgigs appeared in the last millennia of the glaciation. It seems impossible that the Magdalenians, who knew how to fix long shafts to their spears, would not have been able to make rods, attach lines to them, manufacture hooks from various materials and bait them with insects, crustaceans, worms, flies, young fish or lures simulating these. Thread made of reindeer tendon is as resistant as nylon and since it was used for sewing there is scope for speculation about the making of lines, hoop nets and other nets. The Australian Aborigines are evidence that humans have been sailing the sea for 40,000 years and, although there is no proof, we may be certain that the Magdalenians fished in the sea.

A trout drawn with a flint tool in clay. Cave at Niaux. Middle Magdalenian, 14,000 years old.

A salmon engraved on bone. Laugerie-Basse, Middle Magdalenian, about 14,000 years old. (Photo J. Oster – Musée de l'Homme, Paris/Photoeb.)

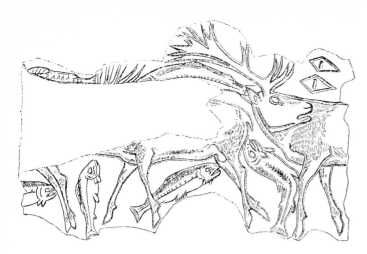

Reindeer and salmon. A balanced protein-rich diet, from a combination of hunting and fishing, would have suited the active life of the Ice Age hunters. This famous bone engraving represents the apogee of Style IV (as defined by Leroi-Gourhan) in mobiliary art. The artist had no hesitation in depicting the backward turn of the reindeer's head. Above are two vulvar signs. Lartet shelter, Les Eyzies (Dordogne). Middle Magdalenian, about 13,000 years old.

GATHERING

The scientific term generally applied to Palaeolithic people is 'hunter-gatherer' and although scientific evidence about the latter activity is even more slender than it is about fishing, hypothesis has become certainty. As 'opportunistic omnivores' using all the resources of nature, humans ate everything edible they could find. There is no doubt that the surrounding vegetation provided all sorts of foodstuffs: berries, bilberries, strawberries, blackberries, walnuts, hazelnuts, chestnuts, leaves, roots, bulbs, broad beans, mushrooms and wild fruit. To these can be added the taking of eggs from nests, and the gathering of crayfish, shellfish and honey – even this is still, no doubt, a very incomplete list of the supplementary food supply. The gathering of it may well have been the responsibility of women and children.

We know very little about the cooking and preparation of the foods. Foot bones of hares, rabbits and birds burned at the ends, found in the remains of habitation sites, prove that these animals were sometimes roasted on spits. Meat and fish could be grilled on red-hot stones from the fires, or eaten raw, or dried and smoked. Palaeolithic hunters could boil food in leather pots heated on the fire by adding hot stones, just as, at a much later period, the Neolithic tribes put stones into the earliest fired clay receptacles.

To end this chapter on a note of comfort: the discovery of some isolated hearths, with no trace of culinary use, outside the tents at the encampment of Pincevent led Leroi-Gourhan to propose the hypothesis that they could have been used for saunas. The hunters may have used low tents for easing away the fatigues of the day through the benefits of a steam bath, as many present-day tribes living in the tunda or steppes of Siberia or Canada have done for thousands of years.

RELIGION
AND
THE SANCTUARIES

The birth of prehistory

As has already been mentioned, the increasingly evident artistic concerns of *Homo sapiens fossilis*, and his principal representative, Cro-Magnon Man, were from the very beginning connected with the expression of an intriguing religious and metaphysical world. There were great controversies in the scientific world at the end of the nineteenth century about what exactly the irresistible impulse was that drove Palaeolithic hunters to express on rock the symbolic components of a system of thought very different from our own, and now lost in the distant past.

We must bear in mind that prehistory is a recent science. For 10,000 years the subterranean world was completely unknown: speleologists and prehistorians began exploring it barely more than a century and a half ago. In the fifty or a hundred years before them there had been a few infrequent expeditions by local curiosity seekers, huntsmen, notables or children equipped with candles or torches, who penetrated sometimes quite far into the caves. They carefully carved their names and occasionally the dates of their exploits – showing little respect for the sites – at the end of dark passages and in chambers where the natural spectacle was made the more impressive by the dimness of their makeshift lights only just enabling them to make out their way.

These furtive visitors would sometimes collect animal bones or natural curiosities from the ground, and return quickly to the outside when their light ran out. They never really recognized the Palaeolithic signs, engravings and paintings on the surfaces, and if they did occasionally notice these images they did not imagine that they could date back to civilizations before the Gauls, the Egyptians – or even the Old Testament. After all, had not mankind been created in a single day? When the first bone objects engraved by the Magdalenians were dug up (around 1836) they were attributed to the Celts.

After excavations such as those of Boucher de Perthes, and later Lartet and Piette, at La Madeleine (1864), the study of prehistory gradually became, in the second half of the nineteenth century, of fundamental interest to the scientific world, and the sequence of discoveries in excavations in Europe continued, provoking passionate polemics from scholars. The publication of these early discoveries came at a time when the great debates about the origin of mankind, the ideas of Darwin and Lamarck and the arguments about antediluvian objects were current issues. The Reindeer Age had become a legitimate subject for scientific inquiry and caves and rock-shelters produced tens of thousands of flint tools and objects made in the Ice Age.

The turning-point came in Spain in 1879, with the chance discovery of cave art at Altamira, the first decorated Palaeolithic sanctuary to be recognized. This was due to a little girl called Maria, whose grandfather Don Marcelino de Sautuola was an archaeologist in the Santander region and had spent three years digging in a cave pointed out to him by local hunters. He took his granddaughter with him to the cave one day, and she was the first person to make out the magnificent 14,000-year-old Magdalenian figures of bison on the ceiling.

Official salon-based art of the last century was restricted by its Western historical preconceptions – tempered though these were by a certain admiration for Pharaonic Egypt or the refinement of China. It could hardly be expected to take to its heart what were believed to be infantile scrawlings. How could those antediluvian ancestors, whom Darwin had said were descended from monkeys and who were imagined as half naked, covered in hair or rolled up in bear-skins with armholes cut in them, have any claim to be considered proper artists? The report published by Don Marcelino passed almost unnoticed. It took another twenty years and some lively polemics before the scholar Emile Carthailac, who had for long refused to recognize the authenticity of the paintings, pronounced his famous *mea culpa*. He visited Altamira and in 1902 gave the young Abbé Breuil the task of making the first records of it. Meanwhile other caves were discovered in France: Font-de-Gaume, Marsoulas, Bernifal and Teyjat (in the Dordogne), and Le Mas d'Azil, Niaux and Gargas (in the Pyrenees). Much later, in 1940, came the discovery of Lascaux.

Two 'negative' hands of children, in the cave of Gargas (Basses-Pyrénées), recall some ancient ceremony. Probably Gravettian, nearly 25,000 years old.

The magic theory

Prehistoric studies in the early part of this century were dominated by the figure of the Abbé Henri Breuil. He was an indefatigable worker who devoted his life to the study of prehistoric art and his huge *oeuvre* constitutes the first detailed approach to the thousands of figurations painted and engraved on the walls of caves and on smaller objects.

Confronted with the problem of explaining all these images which almost always represent animals contemporary with the Ice Age hunters, it was natural that the theory of 'magic' should come to mind. According to Breuil, the images were used to bewitch the animals and put them at the mercy of the hunter. This interpretation, based on ethnographical comparisons, became the official explanation of Palaeolithic art, and it is certainly true that there was no shortage of comparisons to be found in ethnologists' notes about the so-called 'primitive' peoples still left on earth. Customs observed among Arctic, Amazonian or Australian tribes contributed to provide the desired explanation of what happened tens of thousands of years ago. As André Leroi-Gourhan pointed out: 'To have established the religious character of Palaeolithic art and to have brought proofs, even if incomplete, is a glorious achievement for prehistoric studies of the previous generations, but leaves the basic problem unsolved'. These earlier theories have not, therefore, emerged unscathed from more recent analysis, and the great contribution of the Abbé Breuil, who did not yet rely on systematic dating methods, has necessarily been challenged.

A new theory

He was succeeded by two specialists in cave art, Annette Laming-Emperaire (who died prematurely) and Leroi-Gourhan himself. They took on the considerable task of opening up this vast field afresh and have revolutionized the approach to and analysis of Palaeolithic art. Their views coincide to a great extent, but it was Leroi-Gourhan who first undertook statistical study of the evolution of Palaeolithic art, using new research disciplines and analysing the layout of the ensembles of organized cave decoration – thus confirming the existence of 'decorated sanctuaries' distinct from the dwellings of the hunters. His magisterial work gave the study of prehistoric art a new orientation, free of ethnographic parallels and instead seen in the light of metaphysical, religious and symbolic preoccupations. The cave was a sacred place where ceremonies were performed; we have some evidence of what Palaeolithic people did there, but it is still impossible to explain why they did it.

The sanctuaries

Rock-shelters have always attracted people; for more than a million years they have sought refuge beneath them from the weather, the cold and wild animals. The shelters are often in dominant situations above valleys, which made them observation points as well as natural fortresses, ideal for the establishment of encampments. Positioned under these huge rock porches, where rain and snow could not penetrate, the skin tents and huts made of branches could give protection from winds and squalls.

It was in rock-shelters 30,000 years ago, during the first millennia of their expansion into the Franco-Cantabrian region, that the Cro-Magnon branch of *Homo sapiens fossilis* engraved the first images in the history of art. These schematic figures, signs and symbols scratched in the rock or on blocks that had fallen to the ground were a part of the organization of the first exterior sanctuaries. Erosion, frost, winds and run-off water have almost completely obliterated any evidence of these, but we still know of more than twenty-five shelters and cave entrances that are decorated with relief sculptures from various periods – from the early Upper Palaeolithic to the Middle Magdalenian about 14,000 years ago. The fact that no later examples are known suggests that people then left the cave entrances to penetrate further and further into the deeper caves and decorate sanctuaries at the back, or else that painted and engraved compositions replaced sculptures which took too long and were difficult to execute by the light of the lamps.

There are indications that several cave porches have been modified: the prehistorian D. Peyrony wrote that at the site of Fourneau du Diable (at Bourdeilles in the Dordogne), 'the area containing the sculpted blocks had been altered by the construction of a sort of low wall made of blocks of fallen rock and there were several post-holes in front of this artificial partition. Thus the

The oldest painting in the world. It probably shows the belly and hind legs of a horse. The block of rock was detached by erosion and fell naturally face down on to an Aurignacian layer. Blanchard shelter (Dordogne), 30,000 years old.

sanctuary formed a quadrilateral open to the front and probably shielded by a screen which masked the painted and sculpted blocks.' Similar structures have been noticed in the vast and famous shelters of La Madeleine and Laugerie Haute (Dordogne).

The cave which often opens at the back of a porch forms an orifice, at once maternal and mysterious, penetrating into the womb of the earth and charged with great symbolic force. It is an occult place, a gloomy and tranquil refuge, suitable as a retreat for the spirits and deities who rule the primitive imagination, a living temple – for the rock itself is alive, just like the animal and vegetable world, according to a system of values inherent in the cycle of nature.

The forces which contributed to this natural sanctuary's formation and to the unpredictable richness of its internal structure are still at work. It may be a cathedral, a church or sometimes just a simple chapel – depending on its shape, size and arrangement and the richness of its images – and it inspires religious feelings. The images on the walls and the archaeological evidence show that it was used as a sanctuary where people went to inscribe and rediscover ancient memories, symbols and mythologies. To pass from the external world with its bright light to the deep darkness within is to make a journey into the 'beyond', where the spirits of deified animals become embodied in the rocky shapes.

According to Leroi-Gourhan, caves are, symbolically speaking, feminine entities. The underground Palaeolithic sanctuaries were places not for living in but for initiation. If, as at Lascaux, remains of cooking and flint and bone tool-making are discovered in them, these should be attributed to the occasional incursions of those taking part in ceremonies. As we have seen, at the time the art was created the Magdalenian hunters would store or lose such objects, or sometimes deliberately conceal them in cracks in the rock. After these incursions the initiates would leave the sanctuary and return to their encampments, which could be some distance away.

Although there are a few exceptions, Palaeolithic hunters were on the whole reluctant to live in caves. They had serious inconveniences, as they do for us

The message of the human footprints

today: damp, darkness, the unevenness of the internal walls, seepage of water, natural obstacles, a clayey and unstable floor full of pitfalls. As well as these there was also the possible presence of dangerous carnivores such as bears, lions or panthers. In several sanctuaries various cavities were decorated at different periods, sometimes separated by several thousand years. One can imagine the astonishment of Magdalenians 12,000 years ago, when they came to the cave of Le Portel (Ariège), for instance, and discovered images in the chambers at the back that were already 8,000 years old – the interval is almost as long as between the end of the Palaeolithic and the birth of Christ!

Some sanctuaries, like Lascaux, were visited comparatively frequently and the number of initiates must have been quite large, judging by the archaeological remains, the number of lamps and number of figures represented. However, footprints found in other sanctuaries show that they must have been rarely visited. From the Middle Magdalenian (about 14,500 years ago) onwards, the underground expeditions went deeper and deeper and became more and more dangerous, presenting the prehistorian with a series of as yet unresolved enigmas.

The floors of caves have almost never survived intact: sedimentations of calcite have been deposited above the layers that date from the period of human presence, or else modern discoverers and other visitors trampled down the clay or sand on their first visits, destroying irrecoverably precious and fragile traces which could have revealed much. However, there are fairly rare instances where the floor in the sanctuaries has remained unaltered since the last presence of Palaeolithic people, and by studying with the meticulousness of a forensic scientist all the imprints of feet, hands and even other parts of the human body, as well as of animals which entered the galleries and chambers, the prehistorian can gather much information. Around these tracks many other clues are visible: the charcoal that fell from torches, pieces of colouring, objects lost or thrown away, marking out the underground comings and goings of prehistoric people and making it possible to reconstruct their movements and habitual attitudes. They also indicate which areas of the cave were most frequented, the number of persons and sometimes their sex and approximate age.

Some sanctuaries, such as Tuc-d'Audoubert, Fontanet and Niaux (Ariège) and Pech-Merle (Lot), have preserved many imprints of feet which are almost always naked. Fontanet contains the only traces so far discovered of a foot shod probably in a moccasin. It does not follow from this that the Magdalenians usually went about barefoot in the outside world – that would be inconceivable in the cold of the Ice Age – but that they left their fur boots or moccasins at the entrances, perhaps to avoid getting them covered in mud and clay.

'One fact is very striking,' writes Leroi-Gourhan, 'practically all known footprints were made by young people. This of course argues strongly in favour of some sort of initiation ceremony: the long line of prints at Aldène suggests a group of youths running through the cave corridors; at Niaux and Montespan, there are signs of trampling at a point where the ceiling is low; in a puddle at Pech-Merle, we have the footprints of a boy, perhaps accompanied by a woman, and the imprints of small heels in the puddle-shaped depression at Le Tuc d'Audoubert. Thus it is certain that children went inside the caves. Elsewhere the footprints are found at points well away from the normal route through the cave and (except for Aldène) in wet, clayey ground – one must wonder whether this does not simply attest to the fact that children like to step on places where the foot sinks in. Let us say that the children were carefree enough, however solemn the attendant circumstances may have been, to play around in puddles. As for the ritual of initiation, the idea is justified merely by the fact that the young people penetrated the caves as far as the sanctuary. . . . But it is impossible to speak of footprints without mentioning those at Le Tuc d'Audoubert. At the end of the gallery, nearly half a mile from the entrance, there are two bison modelled in clay which are among the very few known examples of sculpture found inside a cave; nearby there are a few piles of clay that may be the remains of other modelled figures, and a few sausage-shaped pieces perhaps representing male symbols. In the clay of a puddle-shaped depression covered by a thin film of stalagmite one can see about fifty heel imprints left by a youth who walked over this soft ground. The Abbé Breuil summed up the evidence with these words: "This track with about fifty human footprints evokes the thought of some initiation ceremony which was performed only once." Moreover, the deeper the sanctuaries are, the less one has the impression that people went there more than a few times; on the contrary, one

Frequency of representations. André Leroi-Gourhan has broken down 2,188 figures (in 66 caves) into their various species:

610 horses	36 bears
510 bison	29 lions
205 mammoths	16 rhinoceros
176 ibexes	8 megaceros
137 aurochses	8 fish
135 hinds (especially in Spanish)	6 birds
112 stags	2 boar
84 reindeer	2 chamois

The central parts of the caves and shelters are occupied by 92 per cent of the aurochses, 91 per cent of the bison, 86 per cent of the horses, and 58 per cent of the mammoths (especially at Rouffignac). But the centres of the sanctuaries contain less than 10 per cent of the rest of the animals.

Deified animals

often has the feeling that there was only one expedition, perhaps even one executant who was to establish once and for ever the sanctuary which was thereafter known to exist in the heart of the earth.'

The images deliberately placed at the rear of caves, always difficult to reach, must have been intended to be private and 'sacralized', and as the Middle Magdalenian progressed these images moved further and further away from the entrances. Perhaps this defiance of the dark and the unknown, which had been shown at a much earlier period by the Neanderthals, had persisted in the collective unconscious and was crystallized around the original idea of an ordeal, a return to origins in the maternal womb of the earth or a consultation with the spirits of the animal-gods on which survival depended. It is certain that in the future more decorated sanctuaries will be discovered containing many imprints and these traces of human activity could bring us closer to the mysterious ceremonies which took place by the light of lamps in the bowels of the earth, during which the walls were decorated by artists – or perhaps shamans – who were the guardians of the powers of revelation.

Very little is known about the real meaning of Palaeolithic religion and its rites and ceremonies. We have only the evidence of archaeology and the study of the representations of animals with associated abstract signs arranged on the walls of sanctuaries where the same basic themes are often repeated, with a few variations. This repetition of similar schemes over several thousand years suggests the existence of an enduring, structured religious system based on central myths that had been handed down from generation to generation.

The earliest underground sanctuaries, not yet very deep, such as Pair-non-Pair (Gironde), dating from 8,000 years before Lascaux, contain ensembles of figures which are still being depicted at the end of the Palaeolithic. These schemes have been the subject of a well-known study by Leroi-Gourhan.

The *first group* consists of four 'noble' animals, all herbivores, occupying central positions in the decorated panels. In accordance with a sort of protocol, a dialogue appears to be taking place between two species, surrounded by witnesses. Statistics reveal the preponderance of the horse throughout the Upper Palaeolithic: it is found in the vast majority of decorated sanctuaries and often takes one of the leading roles, as at Lascaux, although it is sometimes in a peripheral or marginal position. Opposing it is the powerful figure of the aurochs or the bison, which statistically takes second place. Some caves, such as Altamira or Font-de-Gaume, contain many bison and they seem to take the leading role, while at Lascaux and other sanctuaries the aurochs seems to take over the leading role from the bison, which consequently occupies only marginal positions and peripheral panels without being integrated into the central compositions. The fourth of the leading characters in Palaeolithic mythology is the mammoth. The vast and celebrated sanctuary of Rouffignac in the Dordogne is dedicated to this pachyderm, which is represented more than a hundred times, singly, in groups, or associated with horses and bison. It lived in the glacial steppe and is found in the decoration of sanctuaries dating from the cold periods, but is not represented in the temperate interstadial of Lascaux.

The *second group* includes the ibexes and cervids. They occupy positions near the entrance and at the rear of sanctuaries, or on the periphery of the ensembles devoted to the first group. The megaceros and red deer are less often represented than ibexes. The 90 or so representations of red deer at Lascaux (74 of which are in the Apse) are an exception. The megaceros deer is found only eight times in all the caves studied by Leroi-Gourhan, while the reindeer is not found in sanctuaries before Lascaux, but occurs more and more frequently on cave walls and mobiliary art in the last millennia of the glaciation and has an increasingly important role in the compositions of the Late Magdalenian.

The *third group* consists of fearsome and dangerous animals: bears, rhinoceros and felines. There are few representations of these (in all only 36 bears, 29 lions and 16 rhinoceros have been counted) and they are always in secret or marginal situations at the ends of shafts and passages. The rarity of these images and their position in the topography of the caves seem to reflect the fear they inspired in the prehistoric hunters as well as the fact that they were much scarcer than the herbivores. The inventory of animals in cave art includes only 6 birds, 8 fish, 2 wild boar and 2 chamois, although these, like rabbits and hares (also seldom represented) were frequently eaten – as is revealed by the remains found at habitation sites.

What can we learn from this statistical analysis? Firstly that Palaeolithic people depicted only a part of the vast and varied fauna around them and gave a preference – which may seem arbitrary – to certain species. It is somewhat surprising to note the rarity or absence of a number of species: wild boar (which was eaten at the time), fallow deer, roe deer, saiga antelopes, elks, wolverines, foxes, wolves, hyenas, lynxes, badgers, hares and rabbits, as well as most of the birds, notably eagles and other birds of prey. These creatures seem to have been overlooked by the cave artists, or else deliberately but inexplicably omitted.

On the basis of these statistics and a detailed study of the ensembles, Laming-Emperaire and, more exhaustively, Leroi-Gourhan have developed interesting theories from the idea of the complementary natures of the animals represented and their symbolic meaning as male and female principles. 'From the earliest images onwards', observes Leroi-Gourhan, 'one has the impression of being in the presence of a system refined by time, like the ancient religions of the world today, where divine male and female entities can exist without making any overt allusion to sexual reproduction by their actions, even though the male and

In the Rotunda at Lascaux the bovines are represented only by the aurochs; the bison appears at the back of the Axial Gallery and in other parts of the cave. Apparently, as in the wild, one species drives the other from its territory.

An example of the bison-ibex-horse combination. The Black Salon, Niaux (Ariège). Later Magdalenian, about 13,000 years old.

female qualities are necessarily complementary.' The numerous 'couplings' of the horse with the bison or aurochs, and more rarely in other combinations, as well as the frequent presence of the ibex or red deer as accompanying partners in cave compositions, suggest a sort of bipolarized duality 'coupling' the male and female principles which were to be at the centre of mythology throughout the Reindeer Age.

The sexuality of the image

When it comes to sexuality, Palaeolithic animal depictions are extremely discreet and modest. The 'preliminaries to mating' are sometimes represented but the sexual act itself never is. The artist's apparent attitude of reserve with regard to the image of mating seems to indicate some sort of prohibition. Perhaps if the abstract signs accompanying the figures could be interpreted, they would provide explanations. Primary sexual characteristics are seldom depicted, but they occur particularly on aurochses (as in the Rotunda at Lascaux), bison (as in the panel of the Crossed Bison in the Nave) and more rarely on horses, whereas the secondary sexual characteristics (manes, horns, the bovines' large heads, the antlers of the male cervids and courtship displays) are almost never absent. On the other hand, primary sexual characteristics are frequently included in the images of men and women.

In the earliest exterior sanctuaries, about 30,000 years ago, the Aurignacian artists used flint picks to carve deep engravings. This represented a great intellectual step: the representation in two dimensions of what they saw in nature in three dimensions. The images they inscribed on blocks of rock and on the walls of shelters reflected their most vital concerns: the mysteries of reproduction, the sex drive and the first figures of animals.

The authenticity of this beautiful little Gravettian 'Venus', carved in a block of limestone in the Pataud shelter (Dordogne), has been contested. (Photo J. Oster – Musée de l'Homme, Paris)

Women

The earliest known engravings in the Western world come from the rock-shelters of Castelmerle. They represent the vulva, the visible female sexual organ, and, more rarely, the male organ. These vulvas, in various forms – engraved, sculpted, sometimes just suggested by a natural detail in the rock wall smeared with colour – are found throughout the Upper Palaeolithic and raise a number of questions. Were the hunters 30,000 years ago aware of the biological consequences of the sexual act? Or were the mysteries of birth attributed to the intervention of spirits, as some primitive people still believe?

The vulva shown below the distended belly and heavy breasts of a pregnant woman is the theme running through many statuettes in mobiliary art. These symbols of maternity – known as 'Venuses' – are found all over Europe from East to West during the 'Gravettian civilization' 25,000 years ago, and are contemporary with the famous *champlevé* sculpted effigies of Laussel. (Indeed it may be significant that the *Woman with a Horn* from Laussel is symbolically holding the nodulous horn of a male ibex.) The callipygous Venuses reappear after the Ice Age, and are central to the early proto-historic mythologies. Consequently during the Palaeolithic, the female image, always with pronounced primary sexual characteristics, occurs in deep sanctuaries such as Pech-Merle (Lot), where it has been painted with fingers on the ceiling of the great hall, and again at the back of the cave, where the figure's bent posture evokes an invitation to copulation. Leroi-Gourhan has called these last figures 'bison-women'.

In the Magdalenian, the female image disappears from the deep sanctuaries, with the exception of some highly stylized rumps such as those engraved at Les Combarelles or Laroche (Dordogne). On the other hand, female images do occur in the bas-relief sculptures of exterior sanctuaries such as La Madeleine (Tarn) and Angles-sur-Anglin (Vienne), where the sexual characteristics are very marked. The representation of the vulva in more or less schematized form is frequent both in deep sanctuaries and in mobiliary art; the latter is plentiful from the Magdalenian onwards and sometimes combines female representations with reindeer in engravings on bone, plaques of Pyrenean schist or on limestone slabs such as those in the cave of La Marche. These slabs have been studied by Dr Pales and provide many details about clothing, ornaments, hairstyles and posture in the Middle Magdalenian. No women at all are represented at Lascaux.

These vulvas, engraved in relief with a pick, are among the earliest representations in the history of art. They are in Leroi-Gourhan's Style I. La Ferrassie (Dordogne). Aurignacian civilization, 30,000 years old.

Above: two female forms carved on rock. The figure on the left has a fringe and line marking the length of her hair. Terme-Pialat (Dordogne). Gravettian civilization, about 25,000 years old.

Right: on this block of stone fallen from the ceiling of the Castanet shelter an Aurignacian artist has engraved vulvas, female sexual symbols. These are the earliest evidence of human art. Style I (Leroi-Gourhan), about 30,000 years old.

Men, sorcerers or shamans

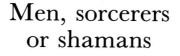

The theme of a man pierced by spears occurs only in the caves at Quercy (Lot). This image is from the cave of Cougnac. Solutrean civilization, about 18,000 years old.

Apart from rare depictions of penises on stone blocks and in mobiliary art, male figures are almost completely absent throughout the early period of the Venuses. They make an unobtrusive appearance in sanctuaries about 20,000 years ago, during the Solutrean, and occur throughout the Magdalenian, in a curious position of inferiority with regard to the animals. The men are shown with deformed faces – sometimes masked – which are stretched out like muzzles; in fact this elongation of the nose seems to be a stylistic trait. It is notable too that the sexual aspect of the figures is emphasized: indeed, the schematized figures of men silhouetted on cave walls and in mobiliary art are often ithyphallic. In the sanctuary of Le Portel (Ariège), the human figures are drawn around rock projections or stalagmites which suggest erections.

Among these male images are some particularly enigmatic ones which suggest the presence among these people of those who have become known as 'sorcerers' or 'horned gods'. From the Magdalenian onwards these strange figures are found in sanctuaries, where they occupy marginal positions. The 'sorcerer' seems to be a bystander in the animal scenes, but sometimes, because of his disguise, he merges with the animals: he is masked, and dressed in an animal skin, wearing deer or bison horns; he may have legs that end in hooves and a tail borrowed from some other species. He seems to be hopping along, half-way between man and animal. The figure in the sanctuary of Le Gabillou wearing a bison mask is contemporary with the man in the Shaft at Lascaux who has a bird mask and is placed next to a staff which also has a bird at its end.

The famous 'sorcerer' of Les Trois Frères, dating from the Middle Magdalenian (14,000 years ago), no doubt represents the most sophisticated image of what might be called a 'shaman': a masked, leaping figure in a strange costume, with antlers on his head – a kind of entranced demiurge in direct contact with the animal world. Until very recently the shamans of the Indian caribou hunters and other Arctic and Subarctic peoples did the same. This particular image makes it seem plausible that 'magic' rites were performed in

the sanctuaries. The Trois Frères sanctuary also contains another figure of a shaman, disguised and masked as a bison and holding a curious instrument shaped like a bow which seems to be coming out of his mouth, possibly representing the emission of a sound. He advances as a suitor, displaying his intentions to a female reindeer, but, as if jokingly, the head she turns towards him is that of a bison. There are several instances from different periods where this curious character, with his Dionysian appearance, seems ready to take part in what we should perhaps hesitate to call a fertility rite, since, as we have said, it is not known whether Palaeolithic people were aware of the biological connection between copulation and reproduction. Is it possible, however, that the shaman, transformed into a spirit, became the fecundating link that assured the continuity and abundance of species and perhaps the reincarnation of the animals killed in the hunt? The only scientific answer to such intriguing questions is provided by ethnographic comparisons – otherwise one is relying on the imagination.

Above: ithyphallic men are fairly frequent in the Magdalenian, appearing both on the walls of sanctuaries, notably in the Shaft at Lascaux, and engraved on bone or stone plaques in mobiliary art. Note the intentional 'bestialization' of the face. Later Magdalenian, about 12,000 years old. (Photo Delluc)

Left and below: disguised figures perhaps evoking shamanistic rites. Cave of Les Trois Frères (Ariège). Middle Magdalenian, about 13,000 years old.

The sacred function of hands

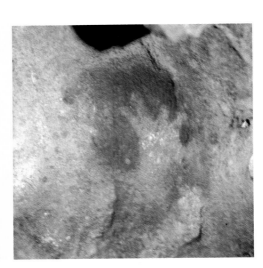

This red 'negative' hand from the cave of Gargas was painted about 25,000 years ago. It probably dates from the final phase of the Gravettian civilization.

Above: little devils engraved on a spear-straightener from Teyjat (Dordogne). Late Magdalenian, about 10,000 years old.

On the walls of a certain number of Palaeolithic caves and shelters in the Franco-Cantabrian region negative and occasionally positive imprints of human hands appear. The negative imprints are produced by stencilling, dabbing colour onto the wall around the hand with a sponge or brush, the positive ones by placing a palm smeared with paint against the wall. There are also engraved imprints, but these are rarer. The hands first appear more than 25,000 years ago in the Gravettian period and occur thereafter all through the Ice Age. They raise an unsolved problem which is probably connected with religion and the rites practised by tribes not only in prehistoric Europe, but also in Africa, Australia and even South America until relatively recent times. In the cave of Gargas more than 150 black, red and blackish-brown ochre hands have been counted, many of which have phalanges or whole fingers missing. A number of theories have been suggested to explain this absence of fingers, including ritual mutilation or frostbite caused by the severity of the climate. The fact that the mutilations are found only at Gargas, and not in the fairly large number of caves where the hands are complete, is an argument against such theories.

Leroi-Gourhan noted that at Gargas some hands were applied to the cave wall with their backs against the rock and that the fingers were deliberately bent in accordance with certain schemas, in which a number of recognizable 'combinations' have been shown statistically to recur. He sees this as a sort of sign language related to hunting and referring to animals. But in most sanctuaries the hands are applied with the palms facing the rock, sometimes singly, or in small groups, and very occasionally accompanied by rows of dots. Their positions make it hard to relate them chronologically to the pictorial compositions, although they may be close in date. Often they are the hands of women or adolescents – and at Gargas there are imprints of the hands of children aged about two or three, who must have been carried into the sanctuary by their parents and hoisted up at arm's length to reach the right height for the stencilling.

The Abbé Breuil counted more left hands than right, and came to the conclusion that Palaeolithic people were right-handed and used one hand to paint the other. But it is obvious that children of three could not have done this by torchlight; consequently it is possible that the hand painting was the work of a single person. Up to now the technical aspect of this operation has not been considered; in fact, it must have required a high degree of professionalism and it is most improbable that a person applying their hand to the wall, in an extremely awkward position, would have had enough control to execute such delicate work as the tracing of the incomplete hands of Gargas, or indeed the other Palaeolithic hands. It may be that during the initiation rites the shaman, as the only person empowered to designate the participants, would give them

the necessary instructions, choose the locations and use his superior technical skill to execute perfect images of hands without mistakes.

What can they mean, these mysterious hands, which look like our own, but which may be more than 20,000 years old? They have a symbolic power and must contain some striking message, but what it is we do not know. Are they signatures? An affirmation of self or of personality? Marks of initiates? Tribal identification? Do they denote ethnic groups?

We have seen in the course of this chapter that prehistoric religion has vanished with the passing of time, with all its rituals and ceremonies, its artists and shamans, and its mythology. All we can do is consider the few known facts and study the incomplete remains, and these will never reveal the essentials of the religion. Palaeolithic myths must have survived after the Ice Age and merged into the religions of the Epipalaeolithic and Neolithic tribes, to re-emerge in the mythologies of the first metal civilizations and continue in a mysterious way down to the religions of our own day.

The study of prehistory is a vocation demanding a sort of second degree initiation and the prehistorian's work is an investigation in which science goes hand in hand with imagination. Using ever more refined techniques the material existence of the Palaeolithic tribes can be examined in the smallest detail, but when it comes to their spiritual and religious life, researches are frustrated and there is uncertainty. Thanks to the work of prehistorians we can say that the Magdalenian hunters were prodigious artists and undertook extraordinary underground expeditions to decorate deep sanctuaries, but we do not know what their motivation was. They did not use the sanctuaries like

Bouriat shaman from Siberia. Hunting peoples whose way of life is still close to that of prehistoric times have retained the extraordinary figure of the shaman, who very probably existed in the Magdalenian. He is in charge of the rites, a diviner and healer, the mediator between the complex world of the animal spirits and the vital activity of the hunter. Perhaps he was also in some cases the artist who had the power to depict the mysterious Palaeolithic compositions on the virgin walls of caves. (Photo Toumanoff – Musée de l'Homme, Paris/Photoeb.)

catacombs: the dead were not placed inside them but were ritually buried, with their weapons, ornaments and garments, outside the caves or in the entrances and sometimes in the rock-shelters.

Nevertheless, on our journey through the Upper Palaeolithic and its sanctuaries in this book we can see how the artists developed within their milieu. Magdalenian animal art approached a naturalistic perfection not found in the many other rock civilizations scattered over several continents. To find a comparable mastery of the forms one must move forward almost 8,000 years to the Greek world. But the Magdalenian hunters concealed one important aspect regarding themselves: they did not leave us images of their faces, bodies and postures showing themselves as they lived and hunted. This is true even of the cave walls at Lascaux, where their beautiful and daring compositions have earned the cave the name 'the prehistoric Sistine Chapel'. There is probably some religious explanation for this strange attitude, which is difficult for us to comprehend, originating as it does in a mentality so distant from our own that it seems to belong to the inhabitants of an unknown planet.

We shall end this chapter with the question posed by André Leroi-Gourhan: 'After we have ruled out the hypotheses of hunters' magic, of literal representations of trapped animals, of weapons and huts for spirits, of the simplistic symbolism of the pregnant animals, what hypothesis is left? Clearly, the core of the system rests upon the alternation, complementarity, or antagonism between male and female values, and one might think of "a fertility cult". If we weigh the matter carefully, this answer is at the same time satisfying and laughable, for there are few religions, primitive or evolved, that do not somewhere involve a confrontation of the same values, whether divine couples such as Jupiter and Juno are concerned, or principles such as *yang* and *yin*. There is little doubt that Palaeolithic people were familiar with the division of the animal and human world into two opposite halves, or that they supposed the union of these halves to govern the economy of living beings. Did they conceive of this union the way we do, or in the fashion of Australian Aborigines and Kanakas? Did they conceive of fertilization as biologists do, or did they suppose that the action of the male merely nourishes the spirit which has entered the body of the female? Theirs was probably some other explanation that we cannot imagine.'

THE SANCTUARY OF LASCAUX

The discovery
of the cave
by the
Magdalenians

The countryside around the cave of Lascaux today in no way resembles the landscape the Magdalenians would have known about 17,000 years ago. Everything about it has changed. The great pine wood that surrounds the site was planted in the last century to replace vines that had been ravaged by phylloxera. At the prehistoric period when the cave was frequented the earth on the hill was at the level of the stairway built for tourists after the Second World War. The entrance to the cave was higher up and further forward. To reach it people followed the fossilized bed of an old stream, partly obstructed by recent rock falls. In much earlier times, the watercourse had been considerably bigger and had worn away a path through the limestone, emerging on the side of the hill. This stream, a tributary of the 'palaeo-Vézère', created the underground network of caves at Lascaux.

Before the arrival of the Magdalenians the roof of the entrance had partly fallen in – no doubt as a result of earth tremors. To penetrate underground it was necessary to climb over a mound of rubble, forcing a way through the brambles and ferns. A widening gallery sloped down for more than 22 yards and opened into the Rotunda, where weak daylight penetrated. By the faltering light of their torches the Palaeolithic explorers moved forward over the damp, muddy, slippery ground, composed of clay and sand. The stratigraphic sections made by the Abbé Glory in 1958 have provided interesting information about those very first incursions. The diagram below (p. 98) shows the positions of the various archaeological sections. Unfortunately the abbé was forced to work in very difficult conditions; the cave was then in the process of being fitted up for tourism, and the archaeologist was surrounded by teams of workmen digging up the ground and destroying irrecoverably all trace of prehistoric life.

A cross-section showing the entrance at the time of the Magdalenian artists, the present-day entrance and the very narrow entrance used by Ravidat, Marsal, Agnel and Coëncas – the four youths who discovered the cave – on 12 September 1940. The roof (marked O) had collapsed after the end of the Ice Age, blocking the Palaeolithic entrance.

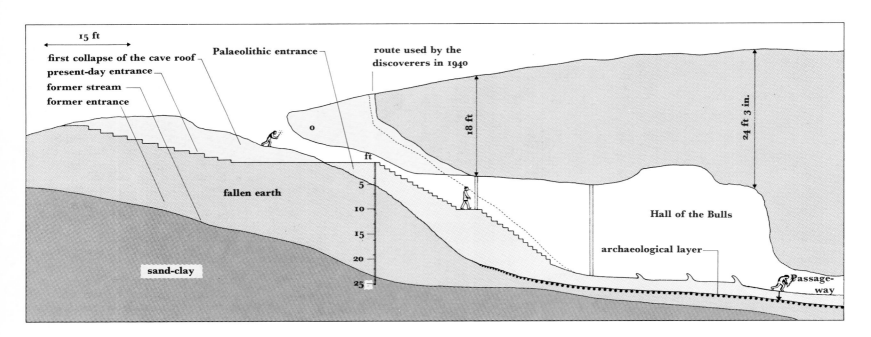

The stratigraphic study, together with the analysis of the charcoal from the torches, provides evidence of the first visit of explorers who descended as far as the bottom of the Shaft, 26 feet vertically down, some time before the period when the cave was frequented by the artists, who for their part left considerable remains. This interval is represented by the accumulation of a layer of barren sandy clay $\frac{1}{32}$ inch thick. The $\frac{5}{32}$ inch layer containing the earliest charcoal lies below this. Unfortunately it is impossible for us to establish any connection between the two visits. We can only suppose that the first visits were brief and furtive since the people left no object on the ground apart from the residue from their burning torches.

Is it conceivable that the first explorers were impressed by the mysterious beauty of the cave and its religious atmosphere, and brought other members of the tribe to it some time later? Or was it just chance and coincidence that, later still, other Magdalenians rediscovered the entrance and converted the cave into a sanctuary? What is certain is that the Magdalenian artists were truly overwhelmed by the sight of the cave walls in the flickering light of the torches: where the calcite had crystallized, the walls were dazzling white, and the natural forms evoked by the relief of the rock surface seemed to be brought to life by the shadows. The original sanctuary was already there, imbued with a holy aura and ready to receive the great mythological images, perhaps representing the first genesis. The artists set to work in successive periods within a fairly short overall time span, leaving some evidence of their endeavours everywhere in the cave, to be rediscovered later by archaeologists.

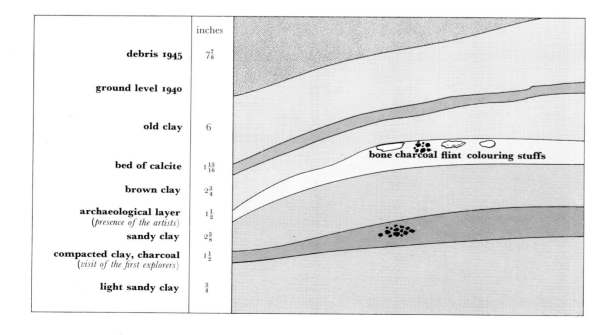

	inches
debris 1945	$7\frac{7}{8}$
ground level 1940	
old clay	6
bed of calcite	$1\frac{13}{16}$
brown clay	$2\frac{3}{4}$
archaeological layer (*presence of the artists*)	$1\frac{1}{2}$
sandy clay	$2\frac{3}{8}$
compacted clay, charcoal (*visit of the first explorers*)	$1\frac{1}{2}$
light sandy clay	$\frac{3}{4}$

bone charcoal flint colouring stuffs

The base of the west wall of the Nave, below the painting of the first stag, at section L. The Abbé Glory gave the following description of what he found in section L (measurements converted from metric):

'$7\frac{7}{8}$ inches (thickness): modern debris up to 1958; 6 inches: light sandy clay the surface of which was the ground level in 1940; $1\frac{13}{16}$ inches: sandy brownish calcite. This layer increases in thickness downstream where the slope is quite steep. On the east wall, at the foot of the cornered bison, it is 9 inches thick, and reaches 12 at the bottom of the gallery towards the narrow passage leading to the passage of the felines; $2\frac{3}{4}$ inches: sandy brownish clay; $1\frac{1}{2}$ inches: archaeological layer with slab of dark red ochre and much flint, bone, charcoal and colouring stuffs; it also contains an antler, a mandible and a jaw bone of a reindeer; $2\frac{3}{8}$ inches: light powdery sandy clay; $\frac{3}{4}$ to $1\frac{1}{2}$ inches: compacted brown clay, with a few pieces of charcoal. This layer never contains any flint or other archaeological object. There is a trace of it at the end of the passage (section I) at this point in the Nave, as well as at the bottom of the Shaft. Hence it seems that people went through the cave, probably with torches, but did not stay there at all (there are no bones, flint or ochre), and this happened shortly before the arrival of the painters of Lascaux. The base of the section is made up of sandy clay and sand.'

The work
of the
first painters

What would the scene have been like in the Rotunda about 17,000 years ago during a period of activity?

The hunters pass to and fro carrying things to the cave entrance. All kinds of materials are brought from the outside and piled up there: trunks of young trees cut down near the cave and branches for the construction of ladders and scaffolding, together with coils of plaited rope for tying them together. There are piles of flint nodules ready to be shaped into blades, burins and various flakes, and heavy slabs of ochre like those found at the bottom of the Shaft. Sacks and pouches are filled with colouring materials extracted from natural quarries sometimes at a considerable distance. Skins still with their hair or fur are spread out at certain places, even on the bare ground, for the purposes of resting and bivouacking. Reserve supplies of flat stones gathered from nearby are to be used for lamps and there are bags filled with fat to provide fuel for them. The artists insist on being made comfortable; the discovery of pollens from grass and flowers led Arlette Leroi-Gourhan to propose an interesting hypothesis: 'These grasses seem to have been placed on the ground at several places, in particular in the Passageway where the Magdalenians had to sit down to paint and engrave the walls.'

These materials were probably first all stored in the entrance to the cave and then brought in as the artists needed them, to be distributed among the workshops in various areas of the cave. It is quite clear that the painter, perched aloft on scaffolding sometimes in unstable and dangerous positions, would have to rely on the help of assistants. This sort of organization implies the existence of a spirit of enterprise imposed by a master in charge of a hierarchically organized group. Referring to the reserve supplies of lamps in the Nave, the Abbé Glory says: 'There were centres of supply and kinds of stockpiles' (Glory 1960).

The archaeological layers
The Abbé Glory gives the following description of sections G and H in the Passageway: 'We took a sample piece of this soil for examination under binocular magnifying glasses; it is composed of ten to twelve superposed thin layers made up of straw-coloured clayey and sandy material, granulations of red ochre and manganese, and a few particles of charcoal, some burned and some turned to peat. Put in simple language, this optical examination shows that within a space of time represented by the accumulation of a centimetre of earth brought in by men, animals and erosion (decalcification of the walls, dust from the air) there were ten to twelve successive ground-levels, which were trodden down by people passing over them. This represents, therefore, ten to twelve periods of occupation followed by ten to twelve periods of absence. Each varve has a sprinkling of coloured powder (the surplus from the painting), with burned wood smuts that had fallen from the lamps and soft wood brought in from the outside, the result of wood working, wood chips 8 to 12 centimetres long and 1 to 5 centimetres wide (from the handles of tools and scaffolding).' (Glory 1965).

Stylistic and
archaeological unity

The Abbé Glory's excavations revealed ten or twelve periods of occupation (his findings are quoted in the margin). It is quite likely that as time passed the tribe of Lascaux would periodically emigrate to other more distant hunting-grounds, returning later to settle again at an encampment nearby and once more frequent the sanctuary, the memory of which had been preserved by the initiates and had been handed down by oral tradition. Consequently new painters and engravers, but steeped in the same religious thought and bound by the same system of signs and symbols inherent in the culture of their ethnic group, would make their own contribution to the decoration of the cave. As André Leroi-Gourhan has rightly remarked, the hundreds of images inscribed on the walls of Lascaux, both paintings and engravings, all display the same stylistic conventions and a great homogeneity in execution. The artists would have been the same people, belonging to a single tribe, or else their children or descendants, the inheritors of an impressive culture and skill together with a mastery of complex technique. The stratigraphic study confirms that in a very short time – perhaps within two or three generations – the sanctuary was decorated, frequented and then abandoned. The art at Lascaux suggests the existence of a real 'school' with its representatives continuing to give instruction over several generations.

The first artists came to the cave after the explorers had visited it. They immediately went over it from top to bottom, right down to the lowest part of the Shaft. They seem to have worked out the spaces for the big pictorial compositions and the positioning of the principal themes in advance, but it is very difficult, in the present state of research techniques, to tell which figures were executed first. To our eyes the many superimposed and overlapping figures gave an impression of confusion. Except in very particular cases, such as the Great Black Cow in the Nave, which is executed on top of the procession of horses, it is difficult to make any suppositions about the figure painted first and another executed later partially or completely covering the earlier one. The very most one can suggest is some sort of chronology based on the stylistic evolution of certain details like the shape of animals' hooves.

In other cases – and this is what is so fascinating – the creation of several figures in different parts of the cave can be attributed to a single artist. The 'tricks' of an individual, choice of colours, line and other details, are like signatures. Thus the famous 'Chinese horses', of the Axial Gallery, with their ball-shaped hooves, are by the same hand as some of the horses in the entourage of the Great Black Cow. The same artist did the manganese drawing of the horse and the four large aurochses that make up the giant frieze of the Rotunda, and also no doubt the solitary head of a black bull in the middle of the Axial Gallery above the five ponies. Was this the first of a series of painters? The question must remain open.

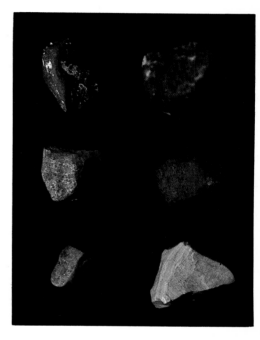

Blocks of pigments found in the Nave at Lascaux. They were the artists' raw materials and have marks of wear and scraping.

The layout of the cave

The cave is part of a karst network hollowed out of the Coniacian and Santonian limestones (Upper Cretaceous). This karst comprises an upper network, which is the decorated part of the cave, as well as a lower level, which has been shown to have a greater capacity although so far it has proved impenetrable. Access is made impossible by barriers of clay and rocks, as well as the presence of carbon dioxide that sometimes rises through the Shaft. The chances of there being a continuation of the decoration of the cave at this lower level are practically nonexistent. The upper part is made up of a wide entrance gallery, the *Rotunda (Hall of the Bulls)*, 22 yards long, which extends into the *Axial Gallery*, a narrower gallery continuing along the same north-west/south-west axis and almost the same length. In the Hall of the Bulls, to the right of the

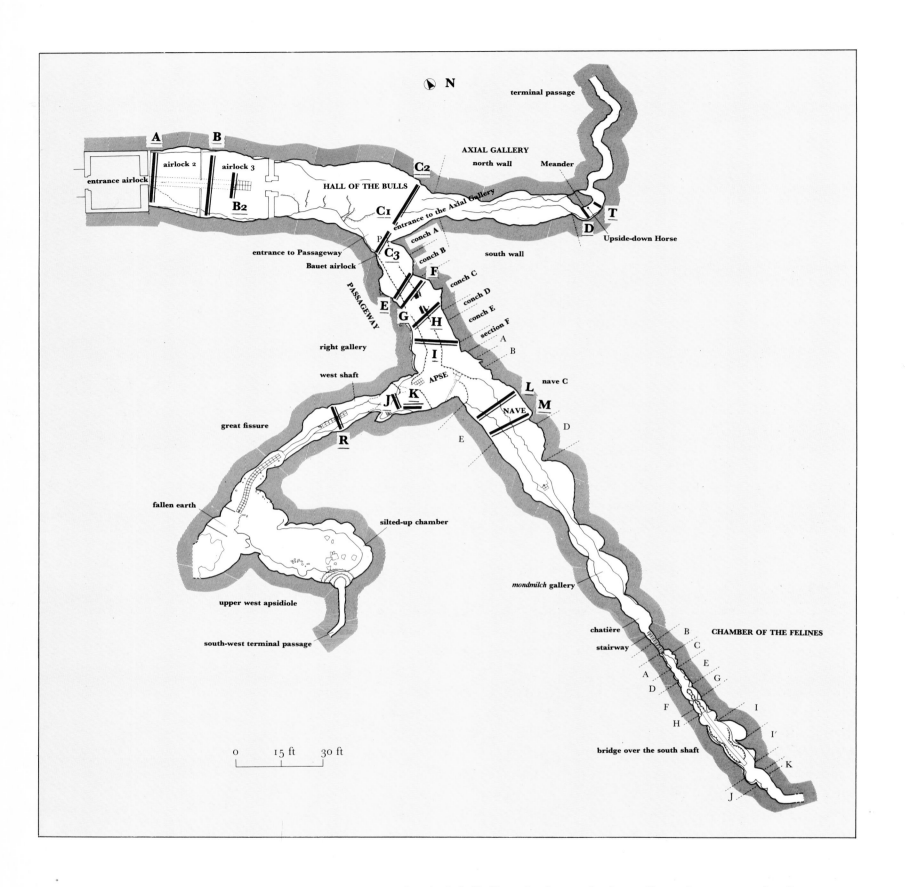

Labels on the plan:

N

terminal passage

A **B**

airlock 2   airlock 3

entrance airlock

B2

HALL OF THE BULLS

C2

AXIAL GALLERY

north wall   Meander

C1

entrance to the Axial Gallery

T

D

Upside-down Horse

entrance to Passageway   conch A

Bauet airlock   **C3**   conch B   south wall

F   conch C

PASSAGEWAY   conch D

E   conch E

right gallery   **G**   **H**   section F

A

I   B

west shaft   APSE   nave C

L

great fissure   **J**   **K**   **M**   NAVE

R   D

E

fallen earth

silted-up chamber   mondmilch gallery

B   CHAMBER OF THE FELINES

chatière   C

upper west apsidiole   stairway   E

G

south-west terminal passage   A

D   I

F   I'

H

bridge over the south shaft   K

J

0   15 ft   30 ft

A general plan of the cave made by Claude Bassier. The positions of the sections made by the Abbé Glory have been indicated with underlined letters, as well as the two small sections *J* and *K* made by the Abbé Breuil and the section *T* drawn by M. Girard.

entrance to the Axial Gallery is the end of a gallery, known as the *Passageway*, which leads to the *Nave* and the *Chamber of the Felines*. The length of the whole of this north/south sequence is about 88 yards.

At the junction of the Passageway and the Nave there is an opening on the west side extending for about 22 yards, known as the *Apse* and the *Shaft*. These complete the area that can be decorated, in all 270 yards long, the only undecorated portions being a few yards of *mondmilch* (a coating of spongy calcite), which is unsuitable for any kind of art. The walls with the most figures, including the ceilings, are those of the Passageway and especially the Apse, which alone contain 450 individually identifiable animals. The size of the panels varies a great deal from one group to another, and is of significance only as far as it affects the length of the figures. It is important to remember that the different parts of this karst form very distinct topographical units: a diversity that strikes even the visitor who has not been told about it in advance.

THE ROTUNDA OR HALL OF THE BULLS

The Rotunda contains the most majestic pictorial composition and the largest figures known from prehistoric times. It is 55 feet long, 22 feet wide and 19 feet high, roughly U-shaped with the back of the hall forming the curve of the U. The walls with the paintings are covered in a white granular calcite and curve inwards towards the roof. The whiteness ends, 5 feet from the ground, at a brown ledge forming a kind of regular shelf round the decorated part, and acting as an 'imaginary ground level' for the pictures. This marvellous setting dazzled the Palaeolithic hunters: they saw before them an enormous virgin canvas provided by the divine powers which rule the primitive imagination, a sort of panoramic screen ready to receive the images of the animal-gods – a potential sanctuary.

Today the ground in the Rotunda slopes slightly and is covered in a series of three petrified pools of white calcite – formerly connected basins filled with clear water. They were created when the stream became active again at some point after the period when the Magdalenians were there. They seal in the archaeological layer; beneath them there must be many remains of human occupation. In 1950 these areas were pierced by the Abbé Breuil, then the leading authority on prehistory, causing them all to empty at once and precipitating a small disaster (see margin overleaf).

To enter the Rotunda, the modern visitor has first to make a preparatory journey – a kind of 'Descent into Hell'. This ritual somehow seems appropriate; it gears the visitor up for the experiences ahead. Watched by the big police dog which guards the cave, the small group of visitors descend the twenty or so steps of the exterior stairway cut into the hillside. Jacques Marsal (one of the four discoverers of Lascaux, now its official guide) half opens a large reinforced door, and closes it behind them. Everybody comes to a sudden halt in a small antichamber in front of the 'Styx', a basin of formalin in which they must wet the soles of their boots to remove any algae and pollens. There is a patter of running water against the ceiling. The electric torches are lit. The first plastic air-lock opens, revealing a dimly lit, concrete stairway with nineteen steps. The smell of damp clay fills the nostrils and the sound of the rainwater dripping through the rock grows louder, discouraging any conversation. Half-way along

Subsidence. The Abbé Breuil describes how the ground gave way: 'In order to photograph the figures on the neighbouring walls without distortion I had to cut into the white calcite crust at the bottom of this basin in several places . . . The water from the stream filled a deep funnel two-thirds of the way along the Hall of the Bulls, half blocked with sand and clay; when I pierced the pools ["gours"], thousands of gallons of water gushed into this funnel, and there were loud noises caused by loose rocks in the chimney collapsing and falling into the lower, inaccessible galleries. The following day we tried to go along the Axial Gallery, a slightly lower extension of the Hall, but the ground gave way beneath our feet, collapsing more than a metre.' Nowadays, when photography is rather simpler, such a procedure seems remarkably inept. Irrecoverable archaeological layers were swept away, and the subsidence in the Axial Gallery has distorted the stratigraphy.

is a small platform in front of the second plastic door, which is sprung so that it shuts automatically. The privileged visitors then have to go down another twenty-four steps before they reach the level of the Rotunda through an opening in a concrete wall. On their right before they enter the Hall are chambers containing the equipment that controls the atmosphere in the cave and the alarm systems that register the slightly atmospheric change.

The visitors' descent will have taken them about three or four minutes and their eyes will have gradually become accustomed to the gloom in the famous sanctuary. It takes another few moments before they can make out the great polychrome compositions by the glimmer of the little nightlights scattered along the walls. The pictures begin on the right (north wall) with the head and neck of a small russet-coloured horse with fuzzy mane facing towards the entrance. The second and strangest figure seems to be entering the cave. This is the so-called Unicorn – a curious name since it has two horns on its fairly small head. Its eyes are round and its body has thick limbs, a swollen belly, and six circular markings which resemble the spots on a jaguar. Close examination reveals also the sketchy profile of a horse, reddish in colour, drawn on the flank of this strange mythical, rather unnerving beast. Many opinions have been expressed about the Unicorn. Is it a feline – a lynx, perhaps, or panther? Or a rhinoceros depicted as it might have been described in oral tradition? Or hunters disguised under an animal skin like a pantomime monster to deceive their prey? Or a shaman merging into the spirit of an animal? No doubt we shall never find out the true explanation of what must have seemed perfectly obvious to a Magdalenian.

Gradually the whole of the decoration becomes visible on several levels, dominated by the 'giant aurochs frieze' which is spread over the whole expanse of the white calcite surface, curving round the end of the Rotunda and returning along the opposite wall. Here and there flakes of calcite have come away from the paintings and caused gaps. Some of these flakes had fallen before the coming of the artists, who then had to paint over the gaps (for example, the head of the first aurochs). Other flakes fell later, damaging figures that had already been painted (such as the fourth aurochs). In some instances important parts have disappeared and this has led to mistakes in interpretation. This was the case

with the first figure in the frieze: only the tip of the muzzle and the top of the head remained of an animal identified and described as an aurochs. The plaque that fitted the gap was never replaced; it was left on the ground for years while the tourists passed through and today it is barely recognizable. Fortunately, Windels, Lascaux's first photographer, photographed it shortly after the discovery of the cave. Brigitte and Gilles Delluc have made an ingenious reconstruction based on photographs and have come up with the revelation that the first aurochs is, in fact, most probably a horse, and that the same plaque also contained a smaller black horse's head which came immediately before the Unicorn.

The frieze in the Hall of the Bulls (Rotunda). In the text, figure 9 is called the first aurochs, 13 the second aurochs, 15 the third aurochs and 18 the fourth aurochs.

The first picture in Lascaux: a horse's head and neck with a fuzzy mane, coming before the Unicorn.

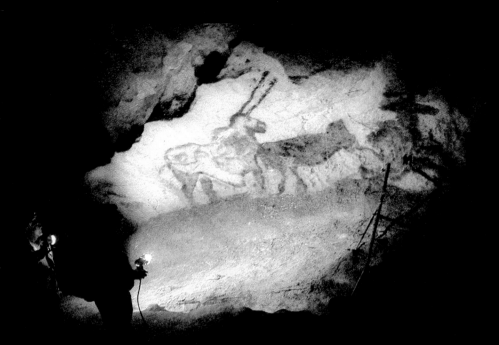

The panel with the Unicorn. This is approximately how the Magdalenian artists saw it by the light of their lamps 17,000 years ago.

The north wall of the Rotunda. At the back is the entrance to the Axial Gallery. On the ground in the middle is the concrete path which was laid for tourist access. To the right are the calcite walls of the pools ('gours') which were full of water at the time of the cave's discovery. The archaeological layer lies below them. Note the 'imaginary ground-level' on which all the animals on the wall are standing. Photo Colorphoto Hinz.

Aurochses 9 and 13, facing each other and separated by the Floating Horse and small red deer stags. Aurochs 9 is escorted by horses, one of which is preceded by a composite sign. Aurochs 13 has a disjointed sign on its breast. It is passing a cow and her calf going in the opposite direction, perhaps part of an earlier pictorial decoration. Note the half-twisted perspective of the horns. Rotunda, north wall.

The great frieze thus begins with a horse's head preceding the head of the first aurochs, followed by its neck and the line of its back. Both of them face towards the back of the Hall and are advancing to meet the other bovines that are moving majestically forward in the opposite direction round the end of the Rotunda. The fourth of these is the largest known prehistoric figure, $18\frac{1}{2}$ feet long. Behind it is the profile of an aurochs head, also drawn in black manganese, situated beyond the entrance to the Passageway. Its neck, which is barely visible, follows the shape of a natural projection in the wall at the height of its shoulders. This figure is often neglected in descriptions; it is not drawn on the white calcite, which ends with the fourth aurochs, but on the natural, yellowish rock, and is perhaps less well preserved than the rest of the great frieze of which it is probably a part.

Is this the earliest composition painted in the Rotunda? Judging by technique and style, it is the work of a single artist: the figures are created by an outline drawn in manganese and filled in with black dots, unlike the other works in the Hall all of which are completely filled in with polychrome paintwork. Moreover, the large-scale painting seems to act as a structure organizing the

whole ensemble. The figures are very large and very high up. 'The highest marks are 3.50 metres or 4 metres [11½ to 13 feet] from the present floor level. It is not possible to climb up to reach these panels' (B. and G. Delluc, *Lascaux inconnu*).

This would be understandable if the ground-level had been higher at the time of the artists, but in fact the archaeological layer is situated at a *lower* level, beneath the calcite pools. It is therefore clear that scaffolding must have been used. 'For example, a tree trunk with the beginning of its branches could be used as a ladder, with one end of the central beam leaning against the ledge and the other on a prop or stilt . . .' (*ibid.*) A person with outstretched arm can reach nearly 7 feet high, but that does not mean they are able to draw accurately in that posture, especially since the higher the figures are, the more they curve inwards on the arching walls; this forces the artist to work in a very uncomfortable position, leaning backwards on the rock for support with one hand, while painting with the other.

To draw the head and line of the back of the fourth aurochs, the artist must have moved sideways. The feet are more than 6½ feet high and the animal is at

Aurochs 15 is preceded by incomplete horses and has a small black stag (16) cutting across it. Hidden in the line of its belly is the small purple bear facing in the other direction, preceded by a cow followed by her calf, and executed by the same artist as aurochs 13. Above, the head of aurochs 18 separated by a disjointed, sword-shaped sign. Rotunda, south wall.

least $19\frac{1}{2}$ feet long, which suggests a large elevated structure, perhaps with movable parts. Also on this scaffolding there would certainly have been assistants to hand the artist coloured paste or manganese crayons, and 'painting rags' made of skin or fur. The wall would have been illuminated by several lamps, which would be placed on the scaffolding or held by the assistants – all of which implies a collective organization in the service of the artist.

An examination of the figures in the Rotunda, beginning with the famous Unicorn at the end of the north wall, continues with the hindquarters of a horse overlapping it, which forms part of a group of five dappled horses. The latter, with their wind-blown manes, gallop towards the back of the Rotunda in a remarkable concerted movement on the 'imaginary ground' formed by the clay ledge. The two chargers in front – particularly the first of them – seem to be leaping over some obstacle. These also suggest the 'manner' or 'style' of a single artist who came after the Unicorn artist and the Aurochs artist.

Other, larger horses facing in the same direction seem to have been added later by another painter. They are pink-ochre in colour, with black heads, necks and outlines. The first of them is depicted inside the first aurochs and it is clear that the artist was careful not to allow the legs to overlap the earlier cavalcade. Its black head follows exactly the shape of the shoulders of the aurochs beneath. A red line – perhaps a small spear – seems to be embedded in its forehead; it is

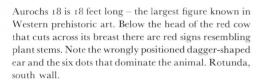

Aurochs 18 is 18 feet long – the largest figure known in Western prehistoric art. Below the head of the red cow that cuts across its breast there are red signs resembling plant stems. Note the wrongly positioned dagger-shaped ear and the six dots that dominate the animal. Rotunda, south wall.

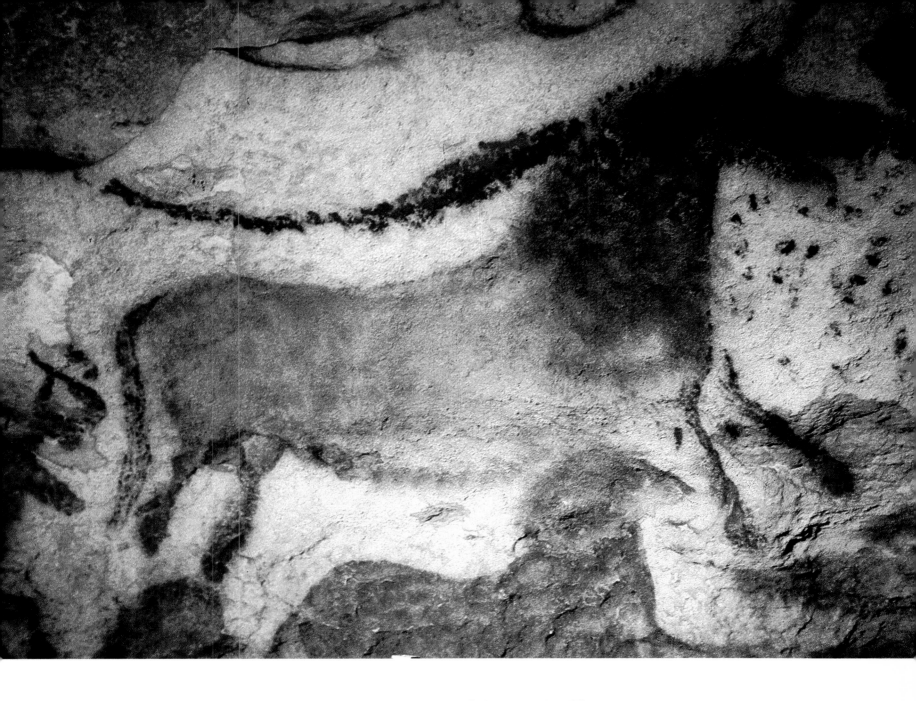

the same red colour as the outline added along the horns of the aurochs. The second, known as the Floating Horse, is in the same colours but incomplete. It shows the care taken not to interfere with the confrontation between the first and second aurochs. The figure is delicately placed very high up in the available space. The muzzle of the Floating Horse, a marvellous piece of draughtsmanship, comes between the converging horns of the second aurochs, which are shown in what has been called 'twisted perspective'.

To conclude this list of horses some small figures must be mentioned: a black head and neck next to the penultimate hoof of the second aurochs; a red neck with no head (the head was on a flake that has fallen off) on the breast of the third aurochs, and a small incomplete horse on its front leg; three sketches of horses facing the Axial Gallery and apparently associated with the Roaring Stag. All the horses in the Rotunda move from left to right, unlike the second, third and fourth aurochs.

Two red cows, similar in technique, move in the same direction as the horses. They are placed on either side of the Axial Gallery. The first of them cuts across the line of the belly of the second aurochs, and the second, followed by its calf, cuts across that of the third aurochs. It is hard to tell whether they were executed before or after the aurochs frieze, because the black colour is denser and shows through the red tints.

The pink-ochre horse painted inside aurochs 9. Behind it is the muzzle of the horse that was reconstructed by Brigitte and Gilles Delluc. Rotunda, north wall.

A reconstruction by Brigitte and Gilles Delluc of the missing part, using the flake that had fallen and was photographed in 1940 by F. Windels. It shows that the first figure (3) in the great aurochs frieze is a horse.

107

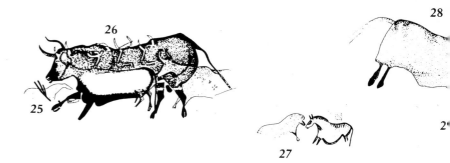

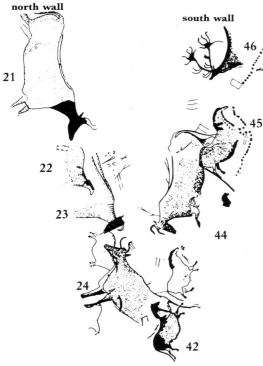

north wall

south wall

21

46

45

22

23

44

24

42

ceiling of the first compartment

Above: the ceiling of the first compartment of the Axial Gallery. The figures climb towards the ceiling and intersect each other there. This is a horse-bovine-cervid group.

Below: the entrance to the Axial Gallery. The pictorial composition was worked out in advance to take account of the shape of the cave. The artist has placed the point of intersection of the second and third aurochs of the Rotunda exactly at the entrance to the Gallery.

26

25

28

27

2

Below the Floating Horse on the north wall the decoration of the Rotunda ends with the addition of four small deer painted in ochre, facing the entrance to the cave. The last of these overlaps the breast of the second aurochs. On the south wall one small deer, black this time, cuts across the breast of the third aurochs. Finally, hidden in the shadow of the thick line marking the belly of the third aurochs is a character who is always enigmatic in prehistoric art – a little bear, tinged slightly purple, with only its head and two clawed back feet showing.

Decorating the Rotunda must have caused great difficulties to the Magdalenian artists because the coarse granular texture of the white calcite makes it hard to apply colours and draw precise lines without smudges. Moreover, they would have had to prepare a great deal of paint to penetrate in between the granules. The figures of the animals seem to have been filled in by means of a series of dabs using animal hair or furs, with movable maskings along the outlines to avoid any smudges which would be very difficult to erase. Some fully painted animals, like the horses in the first aurochs, were then given painted outlines which must have been applied with brushes. However, it is possible that the line was drawn by applying the dry colour unevenly with an ochre or manganese crayon and then evening it out by passing a wet brush over it. This technique would also make it possible to 'gradate' the outlines and give the effect of relief.

A convincing example of this is provided by the second aurochs. The outline of the head, legs and line of the belly varies in thickness to suggest shadows, and shows the gradations achieved by the brush working from a preliminary outer line; but the line of the back and the horns was too high and difficult to work on, and so the initial, coarser line was retained unaltered. The spots may have been made with the fingers, but it is hard to imagine that this rudimentary, imprecise and messy technique could have been used for outlines more than 22 yards from the ground, like that of the second aurochs. Moreover, it would have taken a long time to draw very long lines in paint with a finger and it would have resulted in innumerable spots and smudges which are not found on the wall. The fine lines around the small deer suggest the use of rather fine brushes with stiff, resistant fibres, dipped in a very thick emulsion.

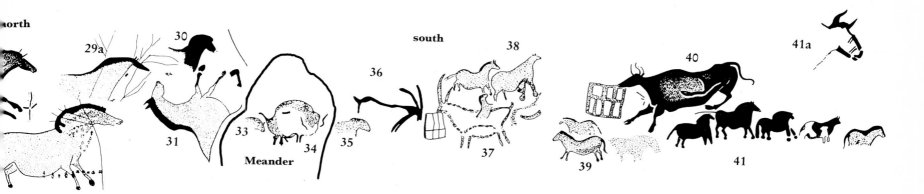

29a

30

31

33

Meander

34

35

36

38

37

39

40

41

41a

THE AXIAL GALLERY

The entrance to the Gallery resembles a key-hole opening from the Rotunda along its central axis between the second and third aurochses at the far end. It is a winding corridor 20 yards long and narrow at the bottom, though there are places where two people can pass. On each side the walls gradually widen towards the top, where they form a fine rounded vault which is covered in white calcite down to the height of a person above a brown ledge forming a shelf running along the wall. The ceiling is $11\frac{1}{2}$ to 13 feet above the ground. The uneven walls have projections, hollows and natural divisions which the artists used to frame some panels (like that of the Great Black Aurochs), or as pre-sculpted shapes (as in the Cow with the Collar or the Upside-down Horse).

At the back the Gallery becomes lower and narrower. It turns left at a right angle around a pier, narrows even more until it is only 1 foot 4 inches wide, and ends up as an impenetrable tunnel. This pier marks the beginning of the section known as the Meander. Although it is extremely narrow, several fairly large figures were painted here, the last of which, at the very end, is impossible to photograph. A sickle-shaped sign and a dot, both red, mark the place where further penetration becomes impossible.

First compartment: The great procession of animals along the north wall (on the left) begins with a real masterpiece: the Cow with the Collar. Its body is painted in a beautiful red ochre and modelled by the rock wall on which it is painted so that the rib-cage and the shoulder project forwards. Its very long, hanging tail marks the division between the Rotunda and the Gallery. The black head and neck plunge towards the back of the cave. It is the first of a group of four and is opposite the large figure of the Roaring Stag on the south (right-hand) wall, which has its head forward as if escaping from the Rotunda. Of this large deer only the enormous antlers, head, neck and line of its back are depicted. It has a strange appearance, made more dramatic by a long line of seventeen dots ending in a quadrangular sign, all executed in black. It is a very suggestive but indecipherable image . . . the key to some enigma. Such roaring is part of the behaviour of the rutting stag at the end of winter, and perhaps this indicates a direct and sonorous link with the other pictures in the Gallery: further along the same wall two ibexes confront each other, displaying behaviour also associated with the rut, as does the male Chinese horse chasing a mare. There is nothing to prevent one imagining such a resonance and the impulse it may have evoked in prehistoric mythology.

Further along the Gallery a second cow appears on the north wall. It too is red, but incomplete; its belly becomes blurred and shelters a yellow horse with a black mane as if it were a calf. Oddly enough, on the wall opposite is another red cow – the third one – and from its belly emerges another yellow dappled horse,

Above: the ensemble of paintings on the walls of the second compartment. The north and south walls are separated by the Meander.

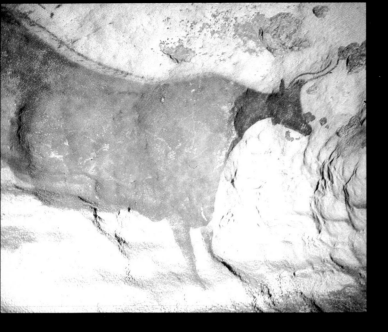
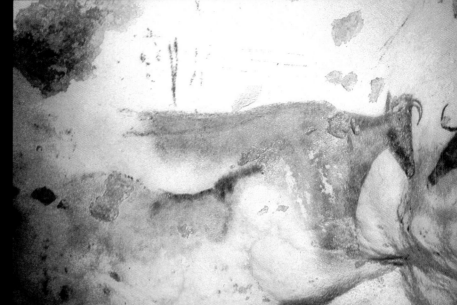

Above: the Cow with the Collar (21), the first figure in the Axial Gallery, faces towards the back of the cave. The artist has made good use of the natural irregularities of the surface to give volume to the animal's rib cage. Axial Gallery, north wall.

Above right: the second cow accompanied by a yellow foal (22 and 23). Axial Gallery, north wall.

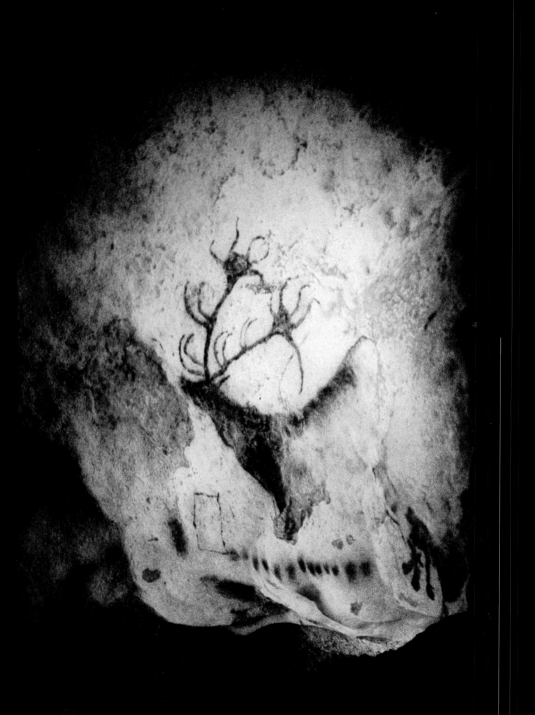

Right: at the entrance to the Gallery and opposite the Cow with the Collar is a stag (46) roaring towards the back of the Gallery. Below it are a rectangular sign and a row of dots. Axial Gallery, south wall.

Opposite, above: in front of the stag, a cow (44) is also accompanied by a foal, this time facing in the opposite direction. The row of dots beginning below the stag seems to mark the ground-level. Note the black belly which indicates both shadow and the animal's winter coat. Axial Gallery, south wall.

Opposite, below: on the ceiling of the Axial Gallery the cow (24) in the middle is only half painted. A line penetrates its breast. The line of its back runs between the Chinese horses on the south wall and the figures are accompanied by numerous abstract signs.

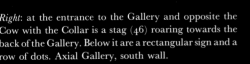

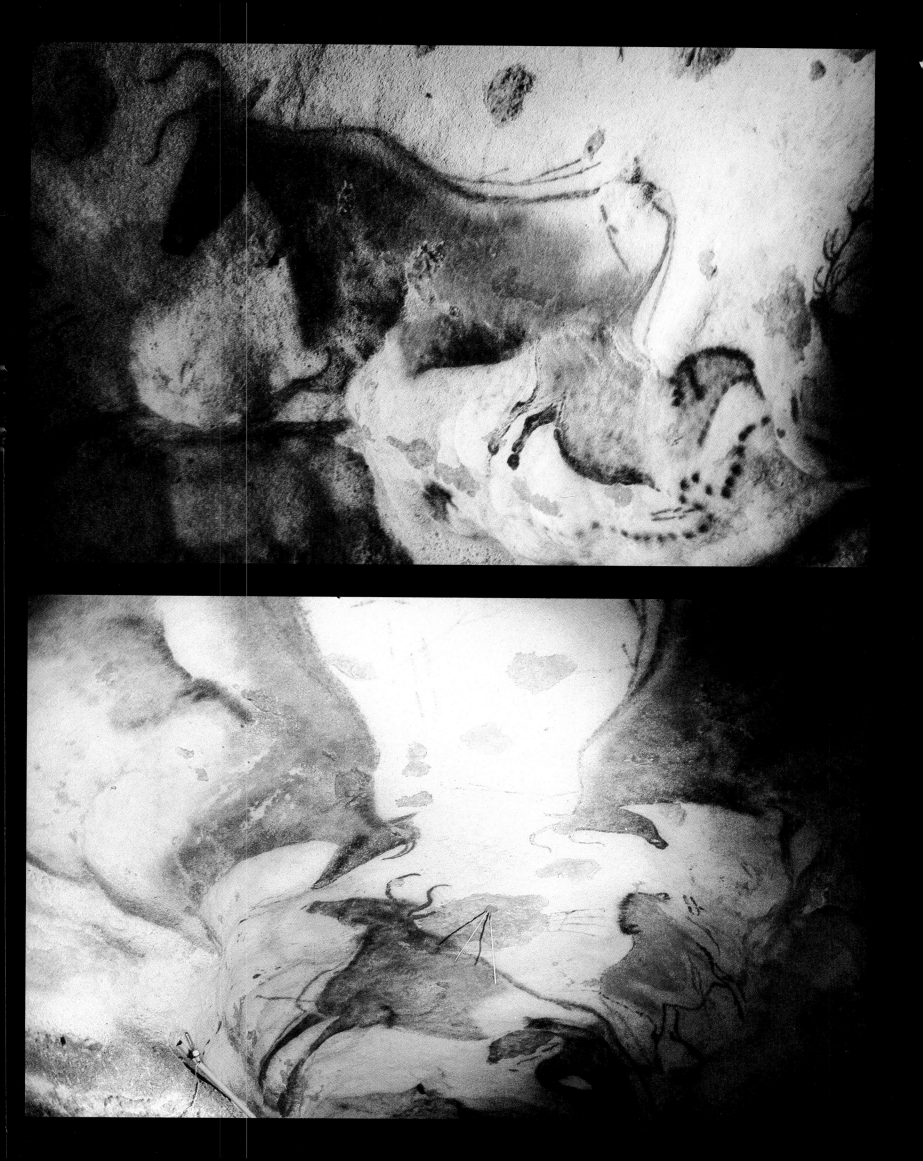

the first of the three Chinese horses. Next comes the fourth cow, which crosses the ceiling to face the second cow on the north wall. It is the largest of the group; only the front half is painted and the line of its back is extended down the south wall, separating the second and third Chinese horses. This grand composition occupies both sides of the Axial Gallery, forming a coherent ensemble which can almost certainly be regarded as the work of a single artist.

To some extent the space is defined as a natural compartment by the narrowing of the Axial Gallery, as the walls come closer together at the point where the Great Black Cow appears on the ceiling. The third Chinese horse, galloping in pursuit of a mare, is situated at the beginning of this bottleneck and its front leg cuts across the line of the back of the Great Black Cow. The animals are accompanied by a host of abstract signs, which will be discussed later.

The ceiling of the first compartment, looking towards the entrance Cow 24 can be seen upside down. The gallery narrows, separating the first compartment from the second. On the left are the Chinese horses. Axial Gallery.

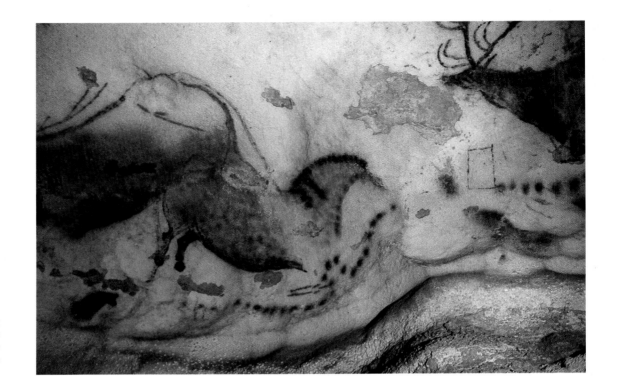

Right: a detail of the south wall between cow 44 and stag 46. Note the disjointed sign on the hindquarters of the cow, the curious arrangement of the row of dots and the sign composed of five elements below the breast of horse 45.

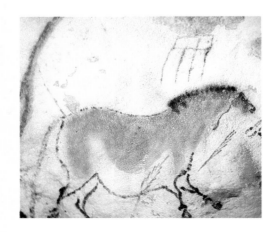

The last figure in the first compartment, a Chinese horse (42) with hatching along its belly (*above*) is chasing a yellow mare (*below*) whose hindquarters are pierced by a line. Note the composite signs resembling arrows.

The attentive visitor will have noticed some of the most unobtrusive of all the depictions of horses. The first of these is straw-coloured. It has its neck buried in the neck of the Cow on the ceiling, whose muzzle cuts across the line of its back. It is placed symmetrically, back to back and head to tail with the second Chinese horse, which is a yellow ochre colour and is galloping in the opposite direction along the facing wall. The two horses also look very alike, although the first is coarser in technique, perhaps because of its position on the ceiling. Just above its hindquarters – and very difficult to make out at first – is a small horse's neck carefully drawn in black, probably at a later date and by a different artist in the space between the heads of the three cows. The second horse, situated behind the hooves of the Cow on the ceiling, is of a darker yellow, with only the front part coloured, facing the end of the Gallery like all the horses on the north wall. As the Gallery narrows, it seems to form the link with the next panel.

Second Compartment: Continuing our examination of the Palaeolithic 'Sistine Chapel' along the north wall we must pass in single file through about 13 feet of narrow, undecorated corridor before the Gallery suddenly widens to the left forming a concave space. This recess is invisible until one reaches it and the sudden revelation of the impressive composition there is an emotional experience. Curving round the niche is the Great Black Aurochs with its slanting eye, preceded by a red monochrome horse with a black trident-shaped sign across it. The bull aurochs, whose forequarters are very finely executed, probably with the help of stencils, is charging towards the entrance of the Gallery – in the opposite direction to all the figures preceding it on the north wall. It gives a formidable impression of power and its sexual characteristics are clearly depicted. The hindquarters are less detailed, and become blurred towards the back. The huge animal seems to have been painted over the top of

already existing figures. It covers two fine reddish dappled cows moving forward in single file in the same direction, which are the work of a single artist.

The head of the first is inscribed inside the head of the male aurochs and her breast follows the curve of his. Only her back legs and long, hanging tail extend beyond his outline. The cow's red ochre colouring was applied in dabs and skilfully outlined in black. A brush was used to spread the manganese in gradations from the very dark strip round the edge towards the interior of the neck, hindquarters and thighs. The Palaeolithic artist succeeds perfectly in modelling in relief, but unfortunately this marvellous figure is difficult to make out and needs special lighting. Indeed, if one compares its present state with the earliest photographs taken more than twenty-five years ago, it seems to have merged increasingly with the bull aurochs. Half of a second cow follows in the footsteps of the first. Its head and neck are inside the hindquarters of the bull and a single line divides the breast of the cow from the hind leg of the male. The hindquarters of the cow are not shown. Two cross-signs are marked in black on its breast. Finally, there are four other heads of cows in the Great Aurochs. They are above the first cow and almost impossible to see, drawn in yellow and facing in the same direction, only their horns projecting beyond the edge of the bull.

The following figures do not seem to be integrated into the panel. Two dark brown equine animals (perhaps hemiones) with long necks, placed head to head, are positioned lower down, within human reach, forming a sort of aside.

The Great Black Aurochs (26) curves round a niche in the rock and is preceded by a sign (with three branches) and a small red horse which does not overlap it. The aurochs covers two superb cows probably painted in an earlier phase. Along the line of its back is a row of sketchily executed yellow bovine heads.

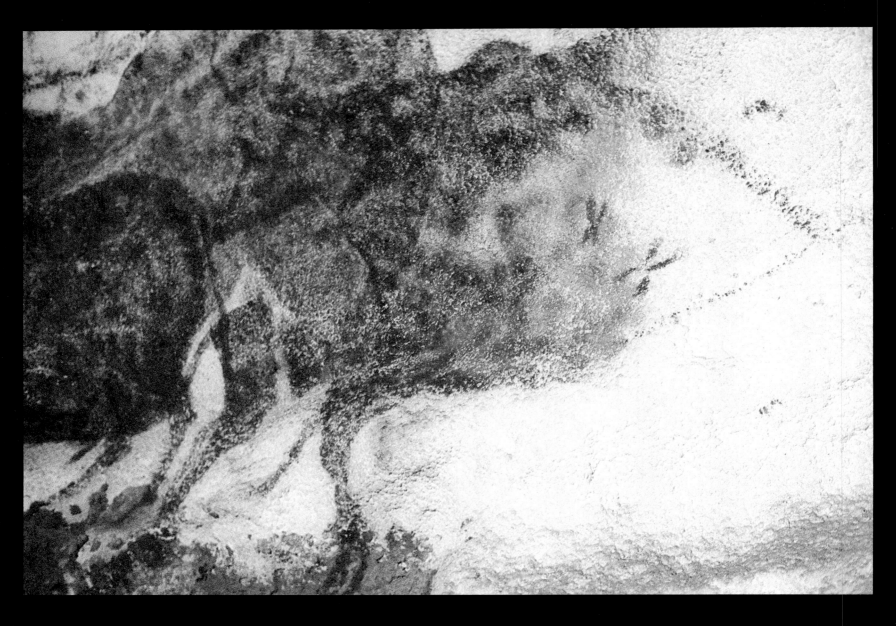

Above: inside the hindquarters of the Great Black Aurochs (26) is the second cow, which is incomplete. Note the cruciform signs. Axial Gallery, second compartment, north wall.

Right: the fleeing horse (28) gallops along the rock ledge which serves as the ground-level. Its neck curves round the end of the Gallery. Everything about this superb figure is expressive of speed: the forward-leaning head and neck, the position of the legs and the tail which is detached from the crupper to create an effect of wind and energy. The figure is more than 8 feet from the ground and was executed from scaffolding. Axial Gallery, north wall.

Facing page: the fleeing horse, detail. The outline of the neck and legs must have been painted with the help of masking and stencils to obtain a clean line on the very granular wall. The ears and nostrils were drawn with manganese crayon. Note the perspective effect created by placing a white space between the further of the legs and the horse's breast. The disjointed cruciform sign is inscribed in a space that had been prepared by scraping. Axial Gallery, north wall.

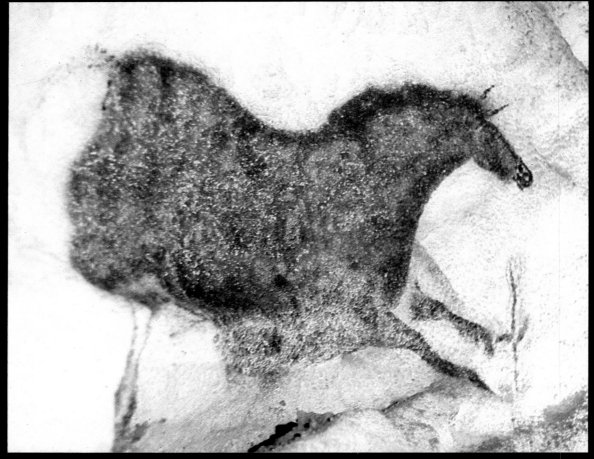

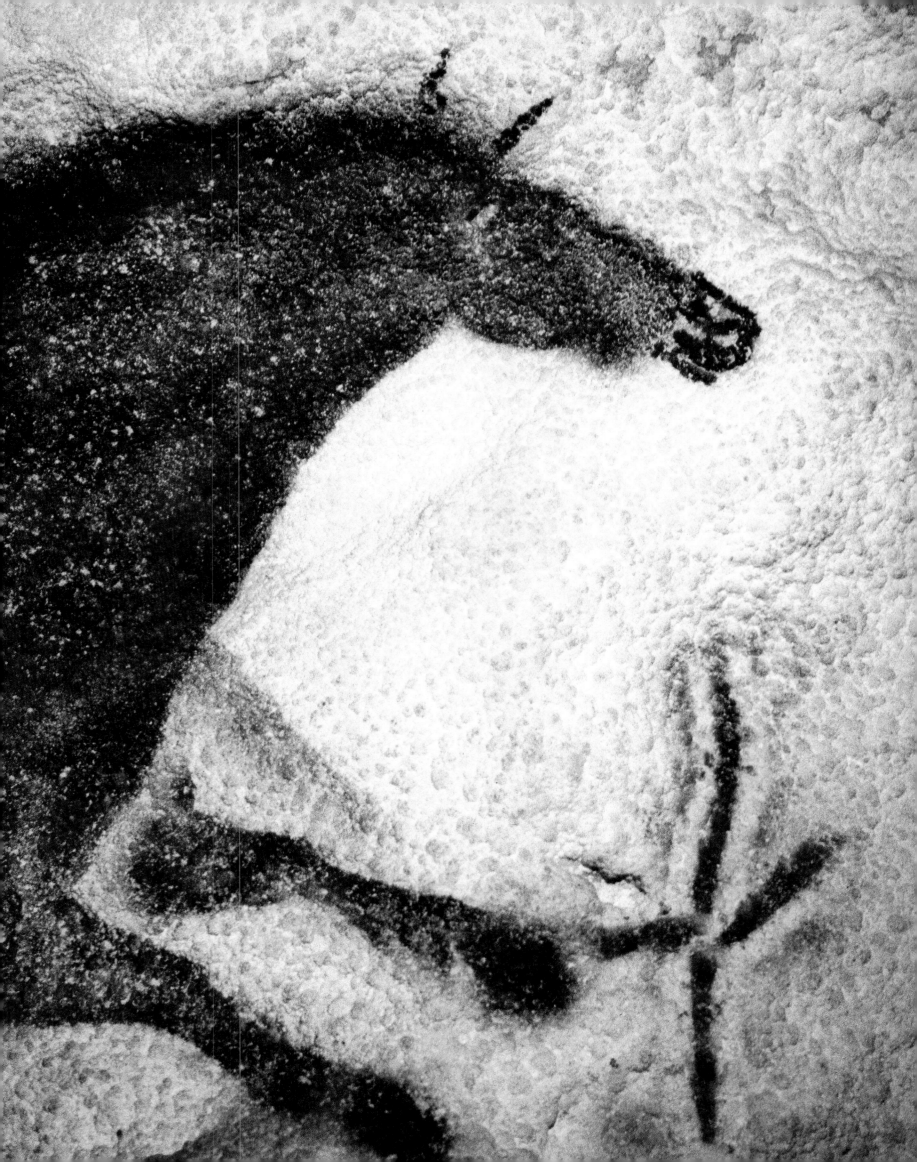

Finally, $16\frac{1}{2}$ feet from the Black Aurochs, a large blackish-brown horse, with a purplish neck and a long delicate head, is galloping towards the end of the Gallery.

The Meander

Above: two very different types of horses (29 and 29a). The upper animal is perhaps a wild ass, while the one below is a stallion with a fuzzy mane, which has probably been outlined with a brush. The animal is surrounded by branching signs and has a row of dots cutting across it. End of the Axial Gallery.

Opposite, top: a detail of the horse with a fuzzy mane. Note the very granular surface, which made the application of paint extremely difficult. The carefully drawn nostrils seem to be by the same artist as the fleeing horse.

Opposite, bottom: the final sign, shaped like a boomerang accompanied by a dot; at this point the Meander becomes impenetrable.

We have reached the end of the Gallery. The ceiling suddenly becomes lower. The walls converge unevenly at right angles and mask a narrow passage turning eastwards, which is known as the Meander. The white calcite covering on the north wall reaches down to the ground and forms a sort of false pier, on which are squeezed several more or less complete horses in various postures facing right. They are painted in red ochre and manganese and surrounded by branching lines reminiscent of primitive vegetation, which André Leroi-Gourhan sees as symbolizing the branches of deers' antlers. There are two of them, one above the other. The higher one has such a long neck and small head that it could be taken for a different species. Towards the middle the animals become shorter and shorter; they are arranged at various levels and their differences in shape suggest several breeds of horse. One of them seems to be emerging upright from the ground waving its hooves in the air. It comes before one of the most extraordinary figures in the cave, the Upside-down Horse, wound round the corner pier in a dramatic posture. Its head is pointing right, its legs are beating the air and its half-open muzzle seems to be whinnying. Several explanations of the picture have been suggested, including the hypothesis that the horse has fallen down a precipice while escaping from its pursuers, or that it is a stallion rolling happily in the grass to scratch itself.

The head and half the body are in the Gallery, but to see the hindquarters we must enter the Meander and turn left. The back legs, the rump and tail of the Upside-down Horse are very carefully executed – an incredible achievement in such a cramped space. One must imagine a horse painted upside-down and curving half-way round a barrel, all in a passage only about $2\frac{1}{2}$ feet wide, so narrow that it has to be entered sideways! It is quite impossible to photograph the Upside-down Horse – there is not room to stand far enough back – but it is one of the many cases where only the movie camera can record the arrangement of the whole composition. In the course of making the film *Corpus Lascaux* my cameraman Michel Bonnat managed to move from the Meander round the corner in a crouching position. Holding a camera, he was able to film the whole of this incredible figure as we shone our quartz lamps onto it. The position of the Upside-down Horse strengthens the impression that prehistoric cave art was made to be seen as one moves forward – just as the Magdalenian initiates would have done – not standing still in front of the images as in a museum.

The Upside-down Horse is the last figure on the left wall, which from now on becomes very bumpy and unsuitable for any art. One would have thought that the extreme narrowness of the Meander in this tortuous and uninviting passage would have put the prehistoric artist off; however, this was not the case. On the opposite wall, barely three feet away, are three figures: a bison and two horses, all of equal size, which are moving forward from the back of the cavity. In the case of the first two, the curvature of the wall creates an astonishing effect of perspective and the artist made good use of this: the bison appears first, set at an angle with its head as it were in full face. The horse behind it is very carefully executed, since the rock on which it is painted is smoother and has a better calcite coating. It turns its neck to follow the shape of the cavity and its head with its parallel ears appears in three-quarter view. The last horse – painted like the others in red ochre – is coarsely executed because the cracked and bumpy surface makes any fine work impossible. Visitors must enter this narrow pocket

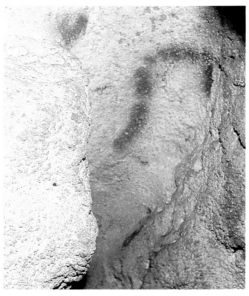

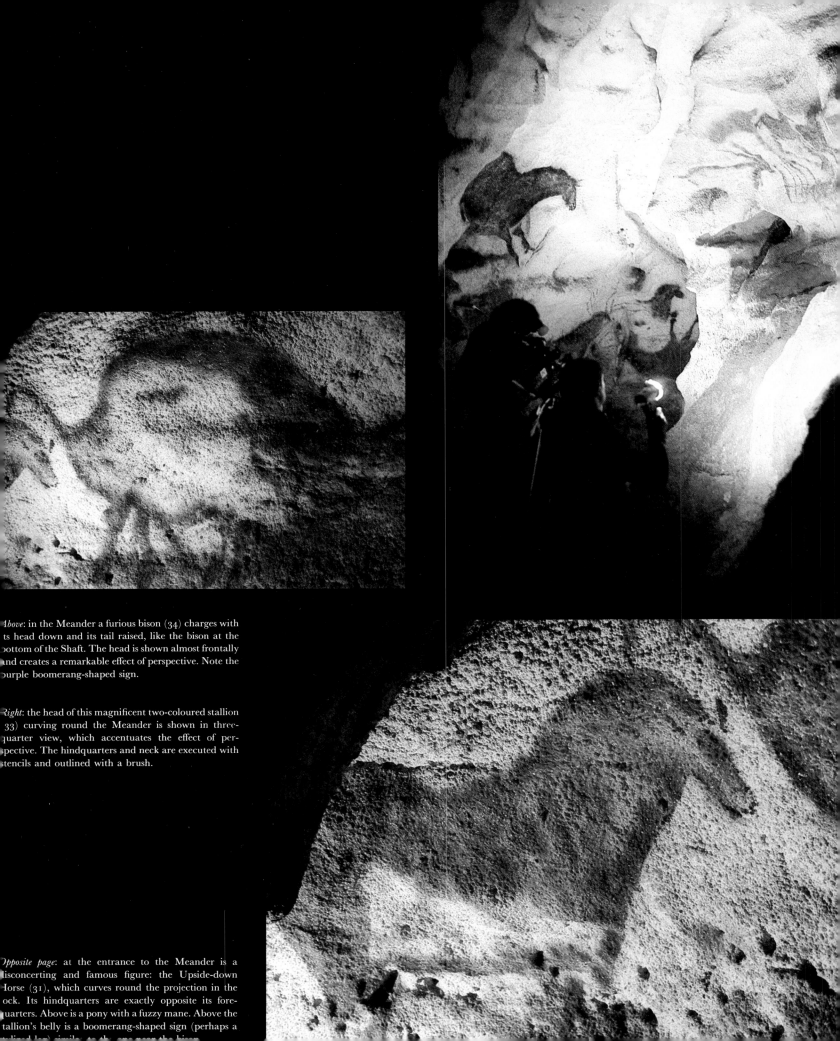

Above: in the Meander a furious bison (34) charges with its head down and its tail raised, like the bison at the bottom of the Shaft. The head is shown almost frontally and creates a remarkable effect of perspective. Note the purple boomerang-shaped sign.

Right: the head of this magnificent two-coloured stallion (33) curving round the Meander is shown in three-quarter view, which accentuates the effect of perspective. The hindquarters and neck are executed with stencils and outlined with a brush.

Opposite page: at the entrance to the Meander is a disconcerting and famous figure: the Upside-down Horse (31), which curves round the projection in the rock. Its hindquarters are exactly opposite its forequarters. Above is a pony with a fuzzy mane. Above the stallion's belly is a boomerang-shaped sign (perhaps a inclined leg) similar to the one near the bison.

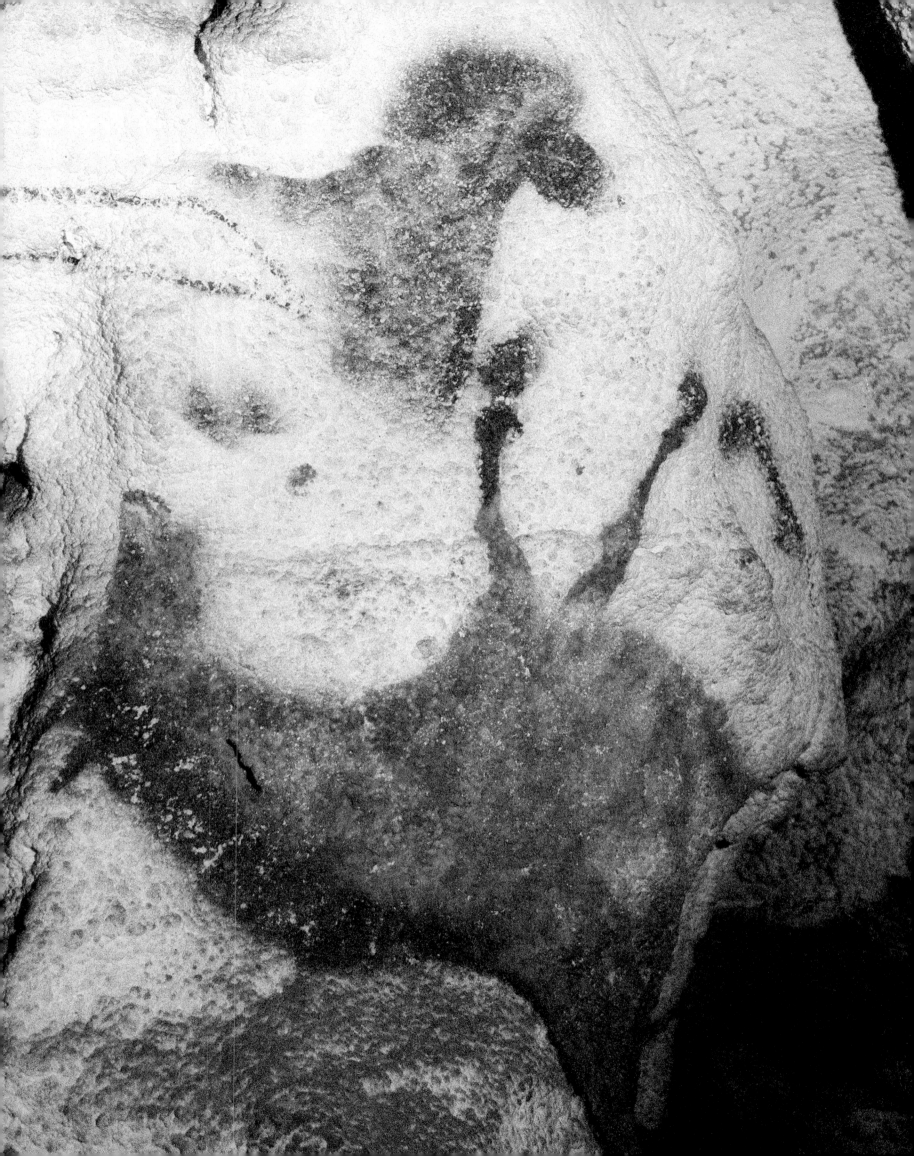

The confronted ibexes (36 and 37) separated by a grid-shaped sign are surrounded by complete or sketched-out horses which face towards the entrance. One of them seems to be emerging from the back of the red ibex, composed of a series of dabs of colour. Axial Gallery, second compartment, south wall.

The confrontation between the horses connected with the ibexes and the horses preceding the Falling Cow. Below is a carefully painted horse with a thick winter coat; its long hair was painted with a brush. Axial Gallery, second compartment, south wall.

Axial Gallery:
south wall

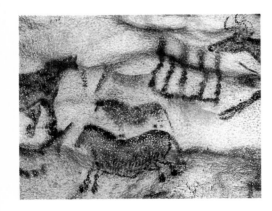

alone, and then retrace their steps. A pause is necessary to recover from the experience, for one has seen the final red sign and been seized by the mystical atmosphere of this strange place. Emerging from the Meander one explores the south wall of the Gallery. This is the beginning of a very different journey: the groups of figures on the south wall are composed almost entirely of horses – from simple sketches to finished pictures – creating a varied and disparate ensemble very unlike the wall opposite.

On re-entering the Gallery the visitor sees a series of horses charging up the uneven, granular, yellow-white rock face. They are arranged in tiers and are all moving in the same direction, apparently as a continuation of the horses on the wall opposite. About ten horses – some carefully painted and others incompletely sketched – are placed around two ibexes, one black and the other red, which face each other. The ibexes were painted quickly in a series of dabs and are separated by one of the numerous 'grid' signs characteristic of Lascaux (the only other place where these grids are found is the small sanctuary of Le Gabillou, which is contemporary with Lascaux). The horses are of various colours, from yellow ochre to dark red-brown; some are more or less outlined in black or brown. Beyond the ibex on the left (the black one), the rock wall becomes very uneven and forms horizontal folds on which the painted figures undulate slightly against a coarse granular background, which discouraged artists from working here.

The positioning of the ibexes and their entourage, composed entirely of horses, deserves some comment. A horse's neck overlaps the first ibex, while a small incomplete figure, also of a horse, leaps across the line of the second ibex's back. Four more horses, brown and ochre in colour, some complete and others merely sketches, surround the red ibex. Finally, another group of four horses, three of which are placed one above the other, bar the way of horses surrounding the red ibex by moving in the opposite direction, thus creating a second confrontation in the composition, besides the ibexes themselves.

Another grid sign heralds the most representative figure of the whole wall, the Falling Cow, painted in a compartment formed by the rock. It faces towards the end of the Gallery. Immediately in front of it is a line (perhaps a spear embedded in the animal's neck) and a horse's neck. The upper part of the Cow's body is painted in a gully-shaped recess in the rock, and the animal slants towards the roof, its front legs hanging over the vertical calcite-covered ledge beneath. The angle between the two legs creates an astonishing effect of perspective. The artist's ingenuity is also shown in the placing of one of the hind legs bent inwards along the flank of the animal, so that the animal appears to be trying to find its balance before touching the ground. In style and technique the Falling Cow differs from all the other figures on the south wall, but echoes the Black Aurochs facing it on the opposite side of the Gallery (north wall) and the Fleeing Horse. They could well be components of one composition with figures executed by a single artist reflecting each other across the space, as Professor Leroi-Gourhan suggested to me when we were editing the *Corpus Lascaux* film.

The Falling Cow (40) is preceded by a grid sign. It has a spear stuck in its breast. The left hind leg follows the line of its body and it is trying to find its balance with its forelegs, which are shown in perspective. Some small ponies (41) are in the lower level.

Below the strange, solitary aurochs head (41a), in the same style as the Rotunda aurochses, the ponies make their way towards the exit of the Gallery.

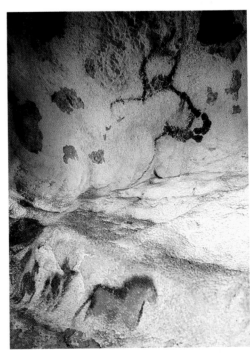

The series of ponies (41) near the Falling Cow. Axial Gallery, south wall.

The ensemble of the panel of the Falling Cow. Note the slanting niche containing the cow, and the scaffolding hole in the centre below the woolly horse. Axial Gallery, second compartment, south wall.

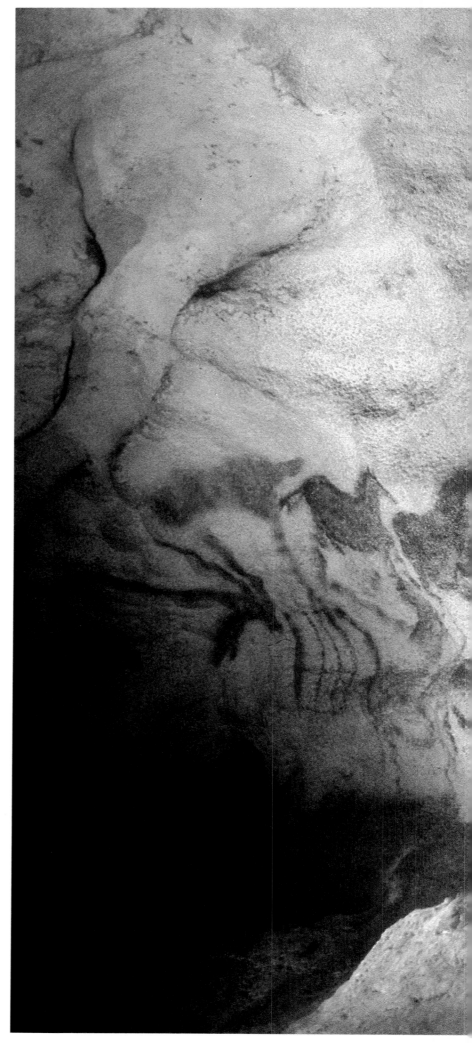

Below the recess of the Falling Cow is a very fine procession of ponies curving round the south wall as the Gallery narrows. Here the artist has made use of the long narrow whitish shelf that rests on the clay ledge. The shelf marks out the pictorial space available and the ledge defines the 'imaginary ground-level' on which the five ponies are walking. In front of them is the brown outline of an unfinished horse, barely sketched in beneath the front hooves of the Cow. The painter's imagination has been given free rein in the distribution of the various shapes and colours in this little procession. The second, 'tachiste' pony is created simply by the contrast between the white calcite background and the black markings on its coat. This procession has an extraordinary feeling of movement: its angle changes with the shape of the wall as the viewer moves forward towards the end of the Gallery.

This would conclude the description of the Axial Gallery were it not for a strange and solitary figure, unrelated to the rest of the ensemble – the head and neck of an aurochs drawn in simple black outline almost on the ceiling and facing in the direction of the Rotunda to which it seems to belong, as far as its technique and expression are concerned. It is certainly reminiscent of the great aurochs frieze.

This completes the tour of the second compartment. Further on, the south wall opens out after the bottleneck, and as one's steps are retraced, the visitor's lamp lights up the galloping silhouette of the third Chinese horse, surrounded by what look like feathered arrows. It belongs with the figures in the first compartment already discussed at the start of this chapter.

The scaffolding in the axial gallery

A scaffolding hole. The paintings of the Axial Gallery were executed from scaffolding. The prehistoric artists used picks to make holes for the beams which ran across the Gallery. They were pointed at the ends and held in place with compressed clay.

For a long time a number of researchers have been interested in the question of prehistoric scaffolding, particularly at Lascaux. The Abbé Glory recorded wood chips buried in the archaeological layer, which had come from the wood used for scaffolding, and *holes* in the walls of the Axial Gallery. Laming-Emperaire suggested that lightweight scaffolding made of branches etc. was used in the Apse and Nave. Jacques Marsal told me he was the first to point out natural or artificial holes in the calcite crust of the Axial Gallery which were full of compressed clay. This surprising activity of the Magdalenians has been studied in detail by the prehistorians B. and G. Delluc (*Lascaux inconnu*). Excavation showed that when the cave was decorated the Palaeolithic ground-level was almost the same as the level at the time of the discovery in 1940. All the figures were beyond arm's length, except for those in the Meander. Raised structures must therefore have been necessary to enable the artists to reach the walls up to the level of the ceiling 13 feet from the ground.

Lascaux 17,000 years ago would have been an extraordinary sight. The Magdalenian hunters would be using sharp flint picks to fell young trees, cut off their branches, square off the trunks and then cut them up so that they could be carried into the cave and across the Rotunda. In the narrow Gallery they would be fitting the wood into the holes in the rock by the light of the lamps, and fixing it there with lumps of firmly compressed clay. They probably arranged branches across them and covered these with skins, to form a temporary platform. Once this was finished, the artist would perch up there, 6 feet from the ground; assistants would pass paint receptacles, brushes, sponges, rags and flint scrapers, and move the lamps. In all, a remarkable undertaking 16,500 years before Michelangelo's work in the Sistine Chapel.

The archaeology of the axial gallery

Interesting remains left by the artists were found by the Abbé Glory during his excavations. Unfortunately the archaeological layer had been largely destroyed by the alterations made for tourism. Arlette Leroi-Gourhan recalls it: 'At the end of the Axial Gallery the rock walls opened out around a false pier, on

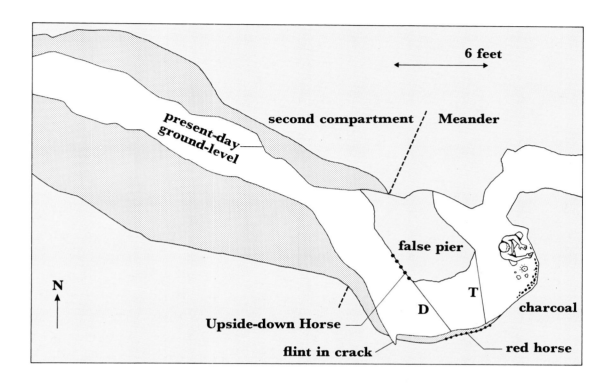

which the Upside-down Horse is painted. The Magdalenian layer was fifty centimetres [20 inches] below the base of the pier, in other words, it was possible to reach the Meander by the passage on the left, but only by bending down, while to the right the height of the ceiling was nearly three metres [10 feet]. In this wide space (which the Abbé Glory called the 'Cabinet du Cheval renversé') the Magdalenian floor surface was horizontal and situated a metre lower down. It was incidentally one of the few comfortable places in the cave: one could sit down at one's ease and put objects below the pier. It is therefore not surprising that many of the Palaeolithic remains should have been found in this area.'

The Abbé Glory noted that 'the compacted earth contained ochre; it was covered with black and yellow *nuclei* and the debris of flint knapping: a few pieces of charcoal often spread out in plaques, flakes, bladelets of flint, fragments of black, red, pink, brown and yellow colouring matter. Three flint blades with edges showing signs of wear and covered in red paint had been hidden together in a hole in the wall, opposite the panel of the Upside-down Horse.' Elsewhere in the Gallery various pieces of reindeer bone, perhaps the remains of a meal, were discovered in the archaeological layer, as well as three flint blades which had probably fallen from the scaffolding, since the narrowness of the place makes it impossible to stand comfortably anywhere.

Arlette Leroi-Gourhan's analysis of the pollens mixed in with the archaeological layer produced some very curious data: it seems that the artists

The Passageway was made larger for tourism; it was barely 3–5 feet high at the period when the Magdalenians visited it. It contains many niches or 'conches' full of engravings made with flint points. These are difficult to see and decipher. The walls used to be painted: there are occasional vestiges of colour, but most of it was eroded during a period when the underground watercourses were active.

made cushions from heaps of grass – no doubt for reasons of comfort. The paintings were certainly executed by the light of fat-burning lamps, which have the advantage over torches that they do not give off smoke. Evidence for their use is the presence in the archaeological layer of juniper wood which was used for the wicks.

Finally, the narrowness and inconvenience of the walk through the Axial Gallery, combined with the windings of the passage, once again raises a basic problem in prehistoric cave art, which has to do with its mysterious religious meaning. Were the artists and their assistants the only people to penetrate this far? Was this place out of bounds for others? Who were those few furtive initiates who left so few traces behind on the ground in an inhabited cave reserved for spiritual activities? For what reason did those adults and adolescents go along this narrow, tortuous passage by the flickering light of their lamps, revealing this sequence of great mythological compositions, the execution of which had required so much effort and talent? Should one think in terms of a revelation expressed by the very people who had participated in its representation on the white walls? At various different periods did a single artist visit the cave, helped by assistants who were being initiated? These unanswerable questions fill our minds as we leave the Gallery and re-enter the Rotunda. Once again we pass beneath the Roaring Stag and along the third and fourth aurochses, descend a few steps, pass through a plastic airlock that closes behind us, and arrive at the entrance to the Passageway.

The Abbé Glory noted that 'near section H a spear, a perforated needle and a burin were found, and in the middle of the Passageway (section G) several flints, a branch of deer antler 25 centimetres [10 inches] long, bones and charcoal'.

THE PASSAGEWAY

The Passageway is a low gallery 55 feet long and 10 to 13 feet wide, linking the Rotunda to the Apse and the Nave. Visitors who pass along it today can walk upright with space above their heads – but this is only after hundreds of barrowfuls of clayey sand were removed from the floor during the alterations made for tourism. In 1940 when the four young discoverers of the cave entered the Passageway – the first people to do so since the last Magdalenians – they went on all fours and had to crawl on their stomachs at some points. The floor was a good 5 feet higher and was covered by a layer of calcite on which petrified

pools had formed. Moreover, this floor sloped to the right, towards the bed of the stream which used to cross the Rotunda. The four boys were the first humans to reconnoitre and cross this calcite floor. It was formed 7,000 years after the coming of the prehistoric artists, during the great climatic upheavals and diluvial rains at the end of the Ice Age.

Palaeolithic people 17,000 years ago also crawled along the Passageway on all fours on a sloping floor of clayey sand which now lies 6 inches below the calcite and the pools, as is revealed by the archaeological layer with its many pieces of charcoal and various remains. The walls of the Passageway are made up of a series of eroded concave areas known as 'conches' and identified by the letters A, B, C, D and E, starting at the plastic airlock which leads to the Rotunda. When the first artists arrived, much of the surface of these walls was covered – as in the Axial Gallery – by a coating of white calcite with a coarsely granular 'cauliflower' texture, on which they painted polychrome figures. These survive only in odd patches; apparently some sort of erosion occurred after their execution and stripped the surfaces not covered with calcite, causing the figures to disappear. This revealed the underlying bare rock on which other artists continued to exercise their talent as engravers.

Many of these engravings – as well as figures which are both painted and engraved – are difficult to read, even when obliquely lit. Although the eye can grasp polychrome paintings or manganese drawings immediately, it finds it

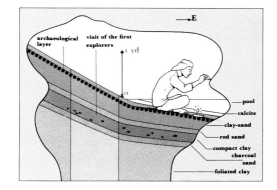

Section H in the Passageway. Note the low roof. All the layers shown have been removed and today's visitor can walk upright.

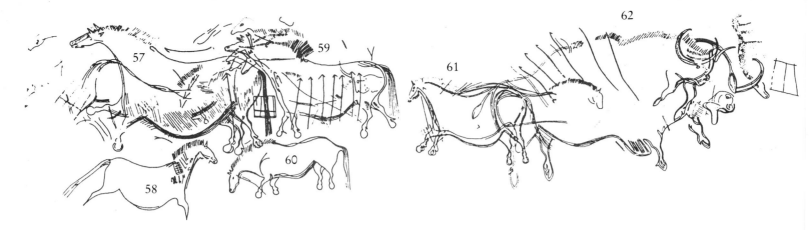

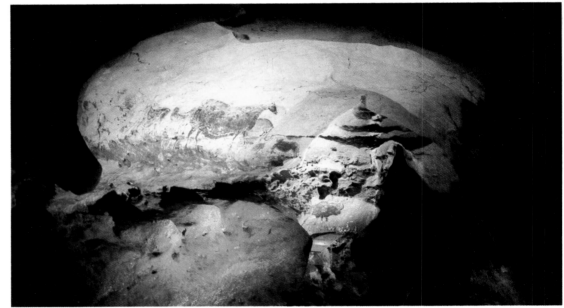

The many engraved paintings were executed from scaffolding that was no doubt built above the rock ledge. In the centre of the niche the Crossed Bison can be seen, with the frieze of stags on the far left. In the darkness at the back is the entrance to the Chamber of the Felines. Nave.

The engravings. During the ten years from 1950 to 1960 that the Abbé Glory worked at Lascaux, he interpreted and recorded on tracings nearly all the 286 engravings in the conches of the Passageway (especially on the west wall). Denis Vialou, in his excellent study of the engravings (in *Lascaux inconnu*), notes that they can be classified as follows:

horses	155	crosses	5
remains of animals	34	signs	5
bovids (aurochses)	18	grids	4
bison	17	*antilopidae*	1
ibexes	17	elk	1
various	11	bear	1
arrows and spears	10	small branches, liana	1
cervids	5	wolf (?)	1

hard to follow the fine sinuous lines inscribed in the conches and sometimes superimposed and intertwined along the rock edges. Moreover, the wearing away of the rock face, particularly in the Passageway, weakens the lines and makes photography practically impossible. In many cases the figures can only be reconstructed from tracings, especially when they are on a large scale. Most of the horses resemble the Chinese horses in the Axial Gallery: they have small heads, swollen bellies (often edged with long hair), round or pear-shaped hooves and short manes. Some have beards. They are in 'Style III' according to André Leroi-Gourhan's classification.

The interest of these engravings is different from that of the pictorial compositions. In the Passageway, where the ceiling was 3 to 5 feet above the ground, the engravers were forced by lack of space to incise small or medium-sized figures. Many of these are incomplete and look like stylistic exercises. They seem to be evocations of associations rather than compositions, and are more like sketches of movements taken from life. The artists were freed from the constraints characteristic of the large paintings with their 'imaginary ground-levels' and could find a more personal means of expression. Using a flint burin or flake they could enjoy a more transient and private expression, depicting the attitudes of the animals they had observed with greater freedom, as in a sketchbook. The pale limestone wall is directly within arm's reach, and the artists, squatting on armfuls of grass brought from the outside, with their feet in the dry bed of the stream and their lamp on the damp clay, would be working in uncomfortable positions, impossible to keep for long.

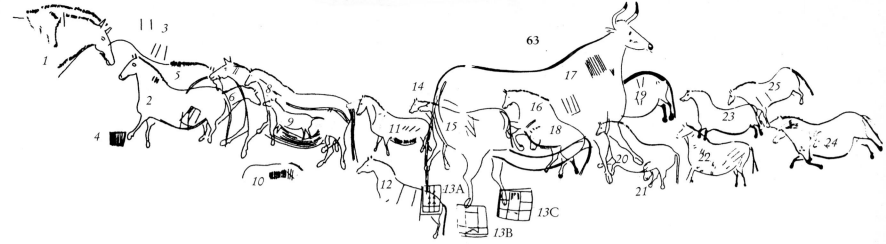

A detailed examination of the engravings would require a book in itself and the visitor to Lascaux would have to spend whole weeks looking for them, identifying them, and illuminating them so that they could be read – but would still be amazed by the perfection of their draughtsmanship, their mastery of form and their remarkable beauty. The stylistic conventions in the Lascaux engravings are closely related to the paintings. One is often tempted to recognize an engraved horse in the Passageway as the work of one of the painters of the Axial Gallery or the Nave. Finally the number and density of works in this part of the cave, and in the Apse, suggest that, unlike the Axial Gallery, they were much frequented.

THE NAVE

Visitors have now come through the Passageway comfortably without even having to lower their heads, and now emerge suddenly into a much vaster intersection at the meeting of the Apse and the Nave. At the time of the cave's discovery, before the conversion work began, visitors would have reached this point on all fours, holding an acetylene lamp before them, and would have been confronted by a great heap of clay which made the Apse on the right 5 feet higher. This was unfortunately destroyed, without any preliminary excavation, in the course of the conversion work. In the gloom on the left a slippery slope could be seen falling sharply away down to the Nave and disappearing into the darkness.

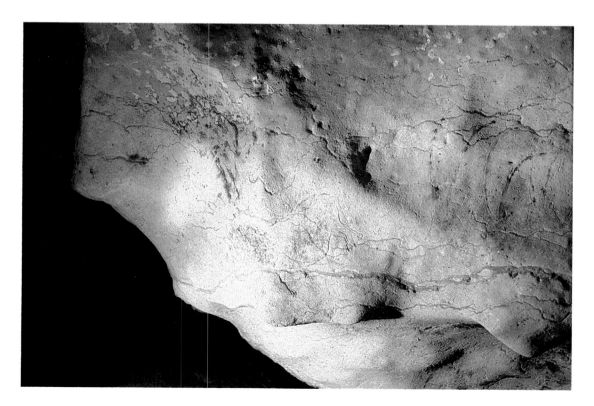

The engraved horse and the first three ibexes have lost almost all their paint. The entrance to the Nave, east wall.

Above, both pages: on the left is the group of figures in the Panel of the Imprint. On the right the group of figures in the Panel of the Black Cow; they are identified by numbers followed by the letter N.

Since then the floor has been hollowed out and levelled by the removal of hundreds of barrowfuls of clay. Nowadays the Apse is reached by a dozen steps and is fenced off by an iron railing. Visitors now follow the left-hand wall, as they did in the Rotunda and Axial Gallery, and arrive at the descent to the Nave where great artistic experiences await them.

The Nave is a tall oblong gallery on a fairly steep slope, and slightly reminiscent of the Axial Gallery in its shape, though much larger. The walls are very close together at ground-level, then form horizontal brown ledges, and widen out considerably to provide large concave recesses covered in a fine yellowish-white calcite. The clay ledges form the 'imaginary ground-level' on which a number of figures rest. The Nave extends along the same axis as the Passageway and the floor served as an overflow for the stream that ran along it. Its length is 22 yards, the width is 21 feet at the level of the concave recesses, 5 feet 3 inches at ground-level, and the height is 18 feet. At the very end the walls come together to form a narrow passage which first leads to the *mondmilch* gallery and then extends for 22 yards to the Chamber of the Felines.

Unlike the Rotunda and Axial Gallery, the wall surfaces in the Nave can be used for fine engravings which the artists executed with flint tools. Almost all the figures are engraved and many are painted as well. The transition between the Passageway and the Nave occurs after conch E (the final conch on the east wall). The west wall opposite turns at a right angle into the Apse and the ridge that divides the two spaces cuts across a delightful engraving of a horse with an expressive bearded head. Its mane and neck are drawn on one wall (in the Passageway) while the belly and back legs are on the other (in the Nave).

This figure immediately precedes the first composition, which shows a row of seven ibexes in profile facing towards the Passageway. They are engraved and were painted, though only occasional traces of paint survive. Only the necks, heads and very long nodular horns are depicted. The last three, separated from the first animals by a rectangular sign, have only their horns and eyes engraved. An earlier engraving of the head of a hind facing right (the only hind in the Nave) cuts across the penultimate ibex. The ibex panel recalls, of course, the 'clubs' of male ibexes who live by themselves and only rejoin the females in the rutting season.

The Panel of the Imprint

Denis Vialou notes that this panel 'measures more than four metres [13 feet] long and is situated in the lower register of the same wall as the ibexes'. It 'seems at first sight to be composed of five horses and a bison. They are painted in dark brown, with their outlines engraved. In fact – if one includes incomplete figures – there are fourteen horses, four ibexes and four rectangular signs'. The

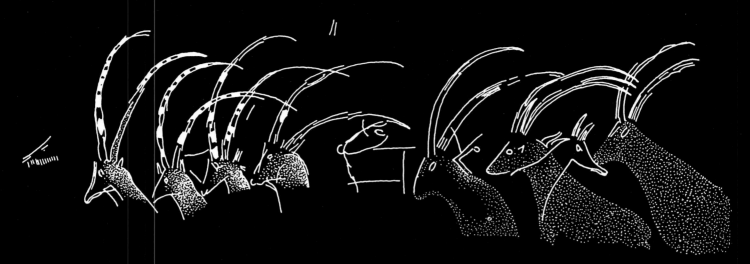

The engravings of the panel of the seven ibexes. Note the hind's head on the neck of the sixth ibex. (Copy by the Abbé Glory)

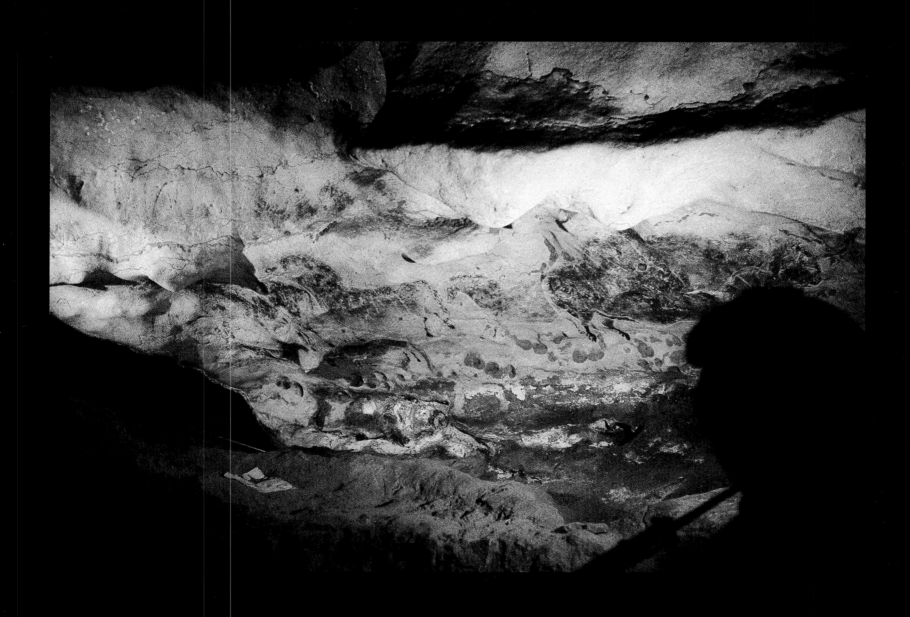

The group of the Panel of the Imprint. (Below the bison is my cameraman Michel Bonnat.)

Opposite page, top: below the ibexes the Panel of the Imprint begins. Horses 57 and 59 followed by 61 are above horses 58 and 60. Horse 59 is marked with seven 'spear-wound' signs. This theme is repeated several times at Lascaux.

Opposite page, bottom: the bison of the Imprint is preceded by a 'grid' sign and like horse 59 is cut across by seven lines (perhaps spears). The animal has two heads, one behind the other.

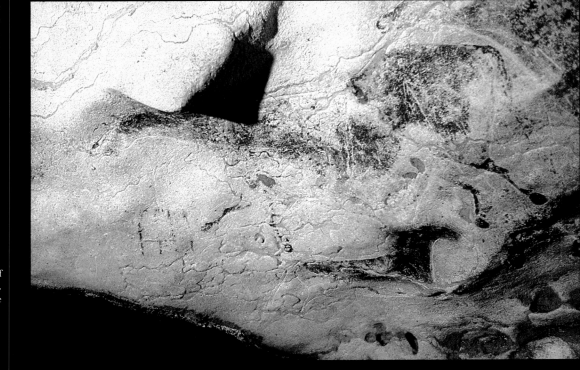

Right: horses 57 and 58 at the beginning of the Panel of the Imprint in the Nave are painted in uniform colour. Note the spear-wound sign and nested chevrons on horse 57. In front of it is a grid sign.

Below: horse 60 advances, sniffing the ground.

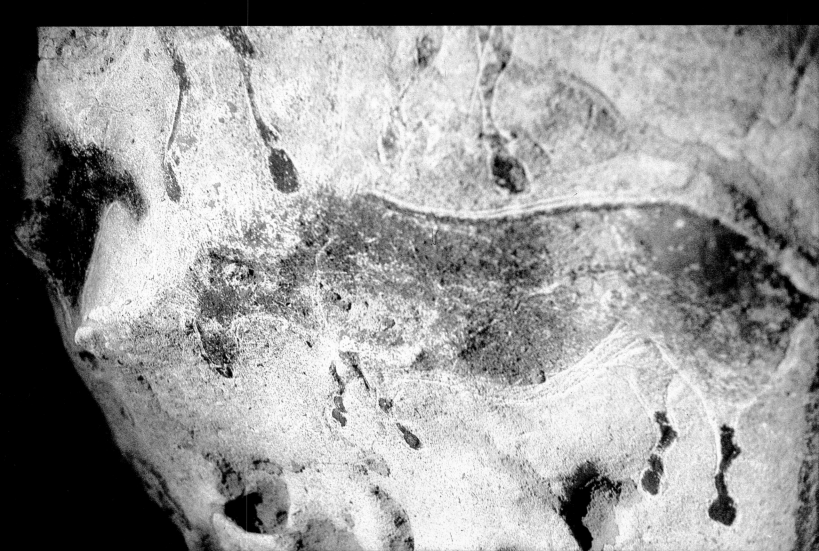

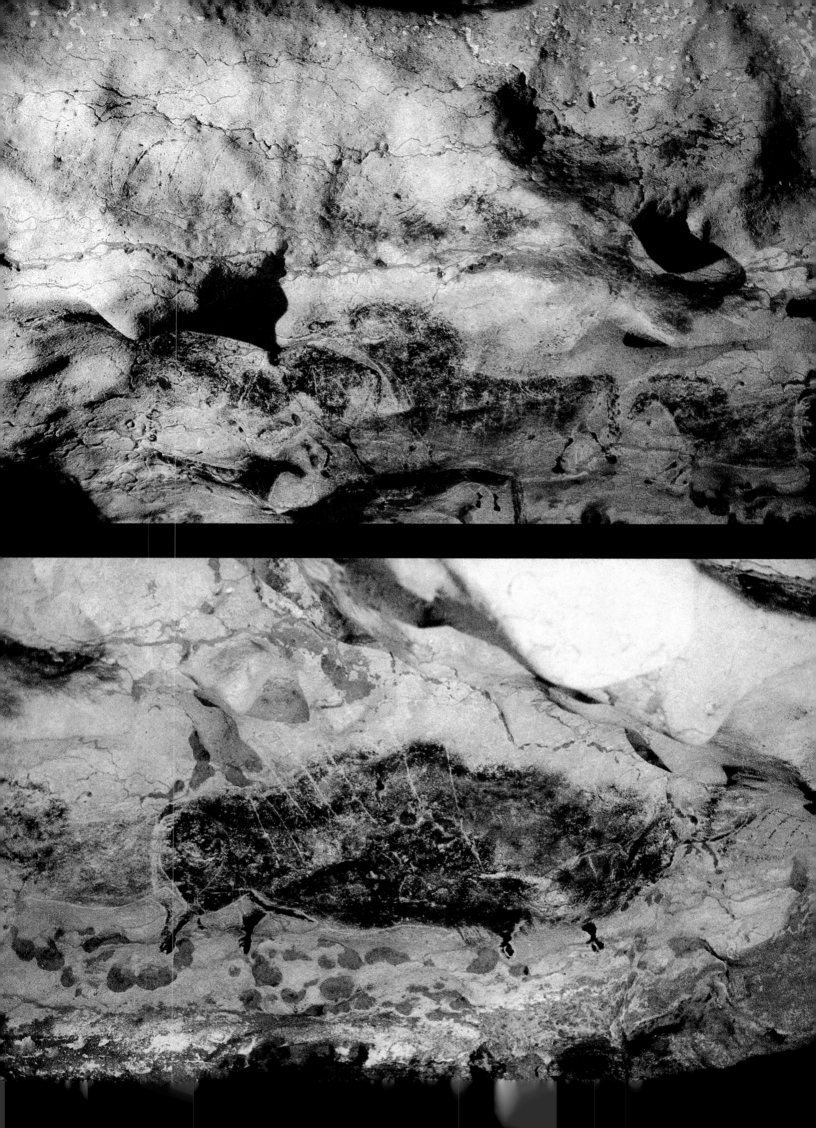

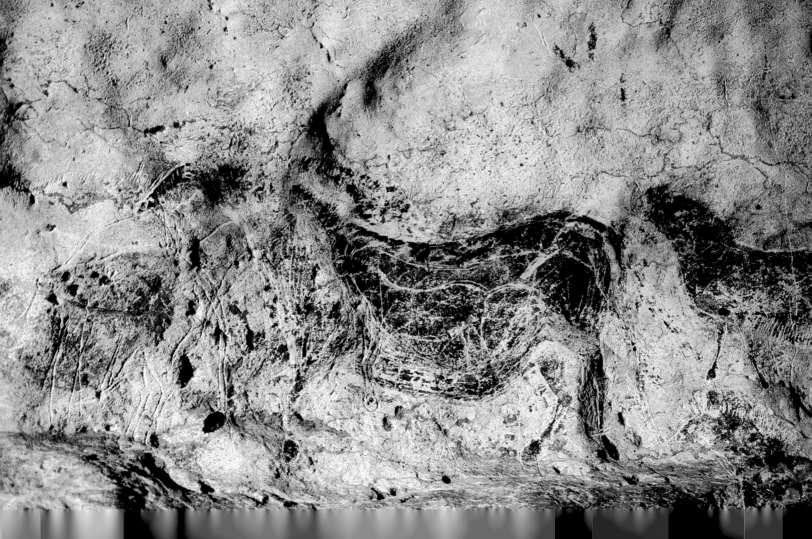

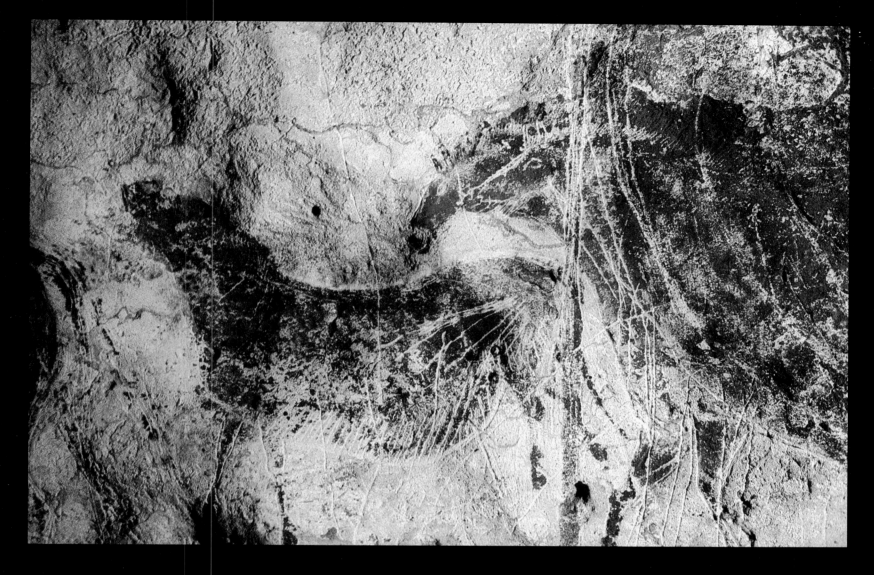

Above: hindquarters of the Great Black Cow. Detail with horses 11, 14 and 15.

Left: escort preceding the Black Cow. A sequence of horses (1, 2, 5, 6, 7, 8, 9, 10, 11 and 12), which are both engraved and painted.

Opposite page, top: beginning of the Panel of the Great Black Cow. Horses 1, 2 and 5 (barely visible) and part of horse 7. Nave.

Opposite page, bottom: horse 6 is engraved. Horse 7 has a black head. 8 contains another smaller horse (9). Parts of horses 11 (left) and 12 (lower left) are also visible.

very uneven wall surface has protuberances, hollows and bumps, but these did not prevent the artists from inscribing figures that follow the irregularities of the rock face. Most are engraved and many have preserved their paint, while others have more or less lost theirs.

Numerous signs accompany the animals or are inscribed above them. They include rectangular signs, 'wounds' (represented by V signs) and hooks. Some signs consist of a series of seven to nine parallel lines. These are characteristic of Lascaux, and evoke arrows – as, for example, along the flank of a horse with several heads or the two-headed bison (see the chapter 'Signs and Prehistoric Language', pp. 154–60). Some figures have been reworked: one horse has several necks, some animals have five legs or three ears; one has five heads and four manes; another has had a second coat of paint covering up some signs.

Like the engravings, the many figures in the Nave are read in a much more private way than the paintings in the Rotunda and the Axial Gallery. Their small scale and their arrangement raise a basic question: whom were they intended for? Apart from the people who had to get into uncomfortable positions to paint and engrave them on the rock, who else, before the modern prehistorians, would really have seen them at close quarters?

To film them and move from one figure to another without omitting the minute details invisible 20 inches away my cameraman had to approach them in very uncomfortable postures, which the average visitor would certainly never adopt. On the other hand – as Leroi-Gourhan observed when he saw our rushes – the lenses we used brought out details that had not been seen before. A very uneven area of the rock face separates the Panel of the Imprint from the Panel of the Black Cow (the only aurochs in the Nave), which is at a high level since the floor has been sloping gradually downwards.

The Great Black Cow

This majestic figure, 13 feet from the floor, is one of the most beautiful to have survived from prehistoric times. It has given its name – a little unfairly – to the whole panel which extends for 23 feet above a large ledge that can be reached by climbing up. The cow partly covers the earlier paintings of the first horses in a sequence of eight heading towards the Passageway. Behind it are another dozen horses which continue this movement – only three of them, more or less complete, are walking in the opposite direction. There are some differences between the two groups: the ones behind the cow have pear-shaped hooves drawn in profile, and this stylistic feature is accepted as being later than the 'ball-shaped' hooves which characterize the group in front. The horses are painted in a pleasing variety of tones; most are brown or reddish brown, but three are yellow, dark orange-red and purplish grey.

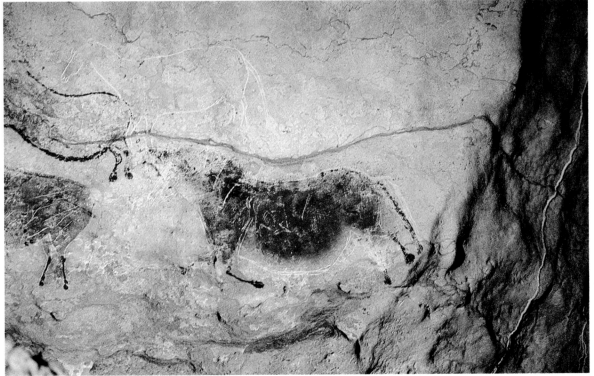

Above: panel of the Great Black Cow (63 N). The animal was painted at a second period and covers part of the frieze of horses. Note the delicate horns, which are reminiscent of the horns of the Cow with the Collar (Axial Gallery) and are placed more than 16½ feet above the archaeological ground-level. On the rock ledge lamps and pigments were found. Polychrome 'blazons' can be seen beneath the hind legs.

Horse 25 is an engraving. Horse 24, in the centre, has two tails and two heads, and inside it are two ibex heads.

The arrangement of this group of horses, and the variety of their attitudes, shapes and colours, make it perhaps the most beautiful work in the cave. Some of the animals in front of the cow could be by 'the same hand' as the Chinese horses in the Axial Gallery. Several have been retouched, perhaps 'improved', and have more than one outline. The last one on the east wall has two tails and more than one mane. In its interior paintwork are the preliminary engravings of two ibex heads. The cow herself, with her beautiful deep matt-black coat, is the highest figure in the Nave and faces the end of the chamber. She is 7 feet $10\frac{1}{2}$ inches long, 5 feet 11 inches wide and the pointed black tips of her horns are shown in 'twisted perspective' 20 feet from the ground. In front of her muzzle is a small detached protuberance which may be her tongue.

The engraving that outlines the Cow and continues the drawing of the front legs into her breast is a true masterpiece, with a modernity which seems to relate it to some of Picasso's works. Beneath the back hooves of the Great Black Cow are the famous 'blazons' made up of grids divided into squares that were painted and then engraved. They are an example of abstract art comparable to tribal signs. These blazons are discussed in the chapter 'Signs and Prehistoric Language (pp. 154–60).

After the last of the horses accompanying the Black Cow there is a fissure in the wall that reaches the ceiling, creating a deep fold which renders the darker upper parts inaccessible. Visitors lower their heads and move forward a few paces. There is a diagonal descent of 10 feet between the last horse in the preceding composition and a separate concave recess situated at a lower level further forward towards the back of the Nave. Here the figures of two large male bison passing each other are almost at the height of a human being; they are painted in black and ochre, without any added engraving.

The Crossed Bison

This scene is one of the most successful Palaeolithic studies in perspective. In the regular concave niche the artist has placed the two bison so that they are shown moving in opposite directions and intimidating each other at the beginning of the rut. Their blackish winter wool is coming away in patches as it does at the end of spring to reveal a lighter coat. Their hindquarters, raised tails and back legs overlap. Several observations can be made about this extraordinarily powerful scene.

It is not one of the panels containing groups of a mythological character, where codified figures are placed together and oppose or echo each other in accordance with a ritual prescribed since the beginning of cave art. The rules of the classic groups, 'horse–bovine–ibex' on the east face, as in the Axial Gallery,

or even 'horse–aurochs–deer' in the Rotunda, are not applicable to the 'crossed bison', which form a unit on their own.

The two bison measure 8 feet across. They are a study of animal behaviour taken from nature, in the context of the season when the animals experience the awakening of the sexual impulse, rivalry between males and struggle for supremacy. It is a symbol of natural selection: an image with a philosophical meaning. From the artistic point of view, the style and the impressive quality of execution – particularly at the level of the legs and hooves – show that the Palaeolithic painter had a mastery of form combined with an interest in depicting perspective – a phenomenon which reappears 16,500 years later in the Italian Renaissance.

Visitors have now reached the end of the Nave rising majestically above them. They turn to look back towards the upper end of the hall along the way they have come. After taking a last look at the Great Cow, which now appears at an angle 16½ feet above them, they turn to the west wall opposite. They are surprised to see, 13 feet up, five stags with large antlers swimming towards the back of the cave. The frieze is 11½ feet long and curves round the rock face; it is the only composition on the west wall.

The Crossed Bison have a niche apart, further down the Nave after the Great Black Cow. The two males (their sex is clearly marked) are intimidating each other. The one on the left is shedding its winter wool. Note the perspective effect in the positioning of the legs.

F or a better view of the stags visitors take a few steps back up the sandy path of the Nave. Now they can see them all; they are shown in single file but in different attitudes. Only the necks, heads and tall charcoal antlers are visible; the rest of the bodies vanish into a mass of dark, misty rock, which forms the

The Swimming Stags

'imaginary ground', or rather the 'imaginary river'. The first four figures were drawn very quickly with manganese crayon and were not coloured in because of the shape of the wall, which made them difficult to reach and necessitated the use of mobile scaffolding. Yet this large-scale sketch thrown, so to speak, on to the rock face, has a remarkable dynamism. The first deer holds its head back and sets foot on the bank, the second is walking on the bottom of the river, the third and fourth are swimming in the water, while the fact that the fifth is drawn in brown clay, perhaps using a finger, suggests that the artist ran out of manganese.

The coarse yet precise quality of the line does not detract from the magnificent drawing. The movement of the swimming herd recalls the fords that were regularly used by deer and this gives the procession of animals the sense of being documentary evidence taken from life. It is an example of yet another 'style' of the Lascaux artists. One needs a practised eye to spot the neck of a little horse painted in red and underlined with a row of dots, very high up in the antlers of the penultimate stag. It was executed with care and even engraved, before the arrival of the 'Master of the Stags'. It should be remembered that, although there are numerous deer in the Apse, these five stags are the only ones in the Nave. There are none on the richly decorated east wall. The Magdalenian hunters would have found a deep significance in this evocation of swimming deer. It is along fords across rivers that the Siberian, Indian and Eskimo hunters lie in wait to sprint out at the last moment and plant their harpoons or spears in the animals when they are off their guard. At Pincevent on the Seine the later Magdalenians studied by Leroi-Gourhan would immobilize and attack reindeer in the shallow waters of the fords.

Scaffolding in the nave

In order to film the Swimming Stags in the *Corpus Lascaux*, we had to use a small step-ladder a little more than 6½ feet high. Two of us went up it, my cameraman Noël Very, with his Aaton camera, and myself, with a battery-powered quartz lamp. An assistant held firmly on to the base of the ladder to stop us falling off. Jacques Marsal – who incidently is a genius at cinematic lighting – held a second lamp at the end of a pole. However, our modern ladder was barely adequate for framing and filming the figures and would have been quite useless for drawing the firm, vigorous lines for the many branches of the antlers 13 feet from the ground.

A more extensive, higher and more solid structure would have been necessary, and we came to realize that the Nave must have seen periods of great activity in the construction and adjusting of various sorts of scaffolding – particularly for executing the Great Black Cow and its entourage – even though

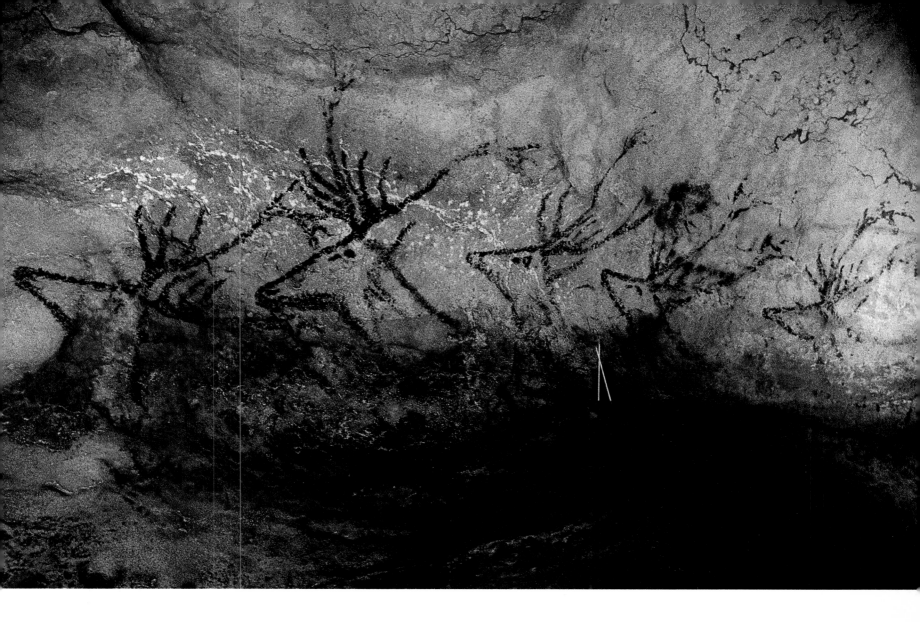

the ground-level at that time was about 20 inches higher. 'It seems simpler to envisage the figures on the east wall (Black Cow, horses) which are approximately on the same horizontal level, being executed by one or more people moving comfortably along the fairly wide shelf-like ledge below' (B. and G. Delluc, *Lascaux inconnu*).

I must admit that this was the only instance where our experience in the making of the film contradicted the otherwise excellent study by Brigitte and Gilles Delluc. Three people were needed to get my cameraman, Michel Bonnat (together with his camera), up to the ledge and keep him balanced there. Besides this difficulty, there was also the problem of stepping back, which is as necessary for the film-maker as it is for the artist at work: the ledge is much too close to the wall, and too uneven and narrow for it alone to have been used as a support for the Magdalenian painters. The Black Cow's horns extend 7 feet above the ledge and their line is so perfect that they must have been drawn with a steady, sure hand. They are engraved and the tips are finely filled with black, which implies that the artist could spend some time with his feet at least 3 feet above the ledge and with sufficient room to step back.

The same goes for the animal's back situated 13 feet above the ledge. Finally, the careful filling in of this 8-foot long figure required a great deal of paint; and many movements were needed to engrave the 15 yards or so of outlines. Again there must have been a construction made of wooden posts placed vertically on the floor of the Nave running the length of the ledge and supporting raised, perhaps mobile, platforms, tied together and wedged above the level of the

The frieze of swimming stags was drawn quickly with a manganese crayon – or in the case of the stag on the left, with a lump of clay. It is almost 10 feet from the ground-level, and mobile scaffolding must have been necessary. The artist seems to have used the dark colouring of the rock to represent the river that the deer are swimming across. In the antlers of the penultimate stag, on the right, is the neck of a horse and a row of seven red dots.

The ledge below the Great Black Cow narrows towards the front, proving that it would have been impossible for the artist to paint in this location without using large-scale scaffolding, which would no doubt have rested on the floor nearly 10 feet below.

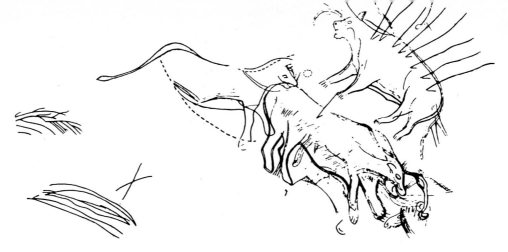

ledge. Only structures of this sort could have saved the artists and their assistants from the danger of slipping and breaking their necks in the Nave. They probably also assured the minimum of comfort necessary for executing figures as large as the Great Black Cow and her entourage, which are painted and engraved with such meticulous care.

The archaeology of the nave

Many objects were left where they were by the artists and have been discovered either in the archaeological layer buried in the ground under the mantle of calcite or on the clay ledges: eleven lamps, two palettes (one of which contains powdered colouring matter), fragments of black, yellow and grey pigments, flints for engraving (with signs of wear), six flint bladelets, a scraper, two burins, a bone object, several tools and pigments below the blazons and on the ledge near the Black Cow.

THE CHAMBER OF THE FELINES

It is very difficult to get into the Chamber of the Felines. During the filming of the *Corpus Lascaux*, I only received permission to send my cameraman there twice, and for no longer than twenty minutes! We would have needed several days' work to film the many engravings and the even more numerous signs; there would also have been enormous difficulties. I myself went there only once, accompanied by Jacques Marsal. We had only one 50-watt battery-powered quartz lamp, protected with a heat shield of thick glass. I must confess that without my companion's deep knowledge of the cave and skilful lighting, I should not have noticed many of the barely perceptible engravings and signs.

A visit to the Chamber of the Felines is a little expedition of its own. Going out of the Nave one seems to leave Lascaux and penetrate a tiny sanctuary. One has to stoop all the time, sometimes crawling on all fours and worming one's way into narrow cracks. The first of these is the 'chatière', after which comes a fairly steep metal ramp with about ten steps. One then passes through what is usually called the '*mondmilch* gallery', coated with a soft chalky substance. In the Chamber of the Felines itself one has to crouch down. The cats are mostly visible on the west wall, entangled with a large number of signs, manes, incomplete figures of aurochses and horses – among them the famous frontal view of a horse. At first sight the felines appear to be executed rather naïvely and with much less care than the horses of the Nave. They are large cave lions with no manes, resembling big domestic cats. A closer examination reveals other features which once again show how the artists captured animal behaviour from life.

At the top of the panel a male lion is about to mount a female, in simulation of mating. This act seems to cause its companion great distress, which she shows by

flattening her ears and opening her mouth in a rictus of anger. Another more peaceful-looking lion walks above them in the opposite direction and has eight long parallel hooked lines on its flank, which suggest spears. We have already noticed these signs on two horses and on the bison in the Panel of the Imprint.

The scene below is also a realistic one. It shows three cats bitterly disputing territorial boundaries. The first lion is moving towards the right and stretching out its paws with their threatening claws. It is face to face with a second cat coming from the opposite direction, whose attitude is, to say the least, hostile. It is standing still and emitting a loud growl, indicated by the sound waves coming from its muzzle. Its tail lashes the air above it and it shoots out a jet of urine, 'marking out' its territory. Behind it a third cat, perhaps a lioness, takes an interest in the scene. This behaviour in the mating season can often be seen in the domestic cat. Beneath the apparent crudity of the engraving there is evidence of excellent observation of animals. From all those thousands of years ago we can learn the interesting information that big lions were living in Ice Age Europe in the vicinity of Lascaux and that Palaeolithic reindeer hunters could observe them from such close quarters that they were able to describe vividly the animals' amatory behaviour.

The Chamber of the Felines also contains many other engravings and signs covering the series of small limestone niches through which privileged visitors now worm their way, lamp in hand. The emotional experience of penetrating the narrow, barely passable tunnels in search of prehistoric works of art is different from that engendered by the vast halls decorated with polychrome compositions. One needs to adjust one's eyes to follow the engraved line, the curve of a small ridge in the rock which serves as the muzzle of a bison with long horns protruding on either side, to run one's finger along the line of a horse's back – in short, the physical process of visual appreciation here brings one very close to the prehistoric engraver.

After the felines, the natural conches form compartments. They contain grid signs, ibexes very like those in the first panel in the Nave, other signs painted in manganese, scrape marks, rectangular blazons, hatched manes, horses (accompanied by more or less complete bison) and horns. Then comes the panel of the engraved horses, surrounded by signs; only their pear-shaped hooves have preserved some of their paint filling, in rather the same way as the antlers of the stags in the Apse. Others are painted and their bodies are superimposed: one raises its head and seems to be whinnying, another lowers its head to the ground. Suddenly the ground gives way: a deep vault, forming a 20-foot vertical shaft, bars the way – but the Magdalenians went down it. The finds beyond the Shaft of pigments, flint for engraving and a hearth right at the end of this narrow passage, make one realize that the Magdalenians must have crossed this chasm – which today's visitor traverses by means of a 40-foot-long metal footbridge.

Six to eight feline engravings can be made out in the Chamber of the Felines. The tracing of the figures is uncertain, on account of the difficulties posed by the narrowness of the Chamber. (Copy by the Abbé Glory)

'Beyond the gap, at the foot of the first bison, the ground contains a hearth 30 centimetres [12 inches] down, composed of charcoal and a long thick bone broken into several pieces (9). At the beginning of the terminal Chamber which we attempted to unblock, we collected an upper milk molar belonging to a large sized *Equus* [horse], and also, buried deep in the clay, a hiding place for colouring matter. This was in the form of a pocket 25 to 30 centimetres [10–12 inches] deep and 15 to 20 centimetres [6–8 inches] wide. It contained manganese in a powdered state, a nugget of mineralized manganese, and a piece of golden yellow ochre the size of an orange' (Glory).

This bison, seen in three-quarter view and pierced by two spear-wound signs, is the last figure in the Chamber of Felines. (Copy by the Abbé Glory)

On the edge of the Shaft the Abbé Glory and Marc Gazay made a false move, as a result of which part of the clay cap was broken off, revealing the imprint of a twisted rope made of vegetable material – the oldest rope in the world. Beyond the footbridge the gallery slopes upwards. It is extraordinary that even here there are engravings, signs and the figure of a bison with long semicircular horns; its head is engraved in three-quarter view and along its flank are two arrow-like lines. Opposite it is the final sign: six dots drawn in dark ochre, in rows of three like the six on a domino placed horizontally. The same sign is found behind the rhinoceros at the bottom of the Shaft in the Apse. This is the end, one cannot go any further. The Chamber narrows and becomes impenetrable; the visitor turns back. It takes ten minutes to worm one's way slowly back to the Nave by the light of one's lamp, taking back many unanswerable questions and the memory of images probably never to be seen again.

THE APSE

The Apse and the Shaft (which is an extension of it) form the strangest and most mysterious part of the cave, and the part which remains most vividly in the imagination. It is the place with the most signs, images and symbols – though these are sometimes very difficult to make out. It is also the most sacred place in the cave: here ritual ceremonies were performed, though all trace of them has vanished with the passing of thousands of years. This part of the cave has been worn down and eaten away by erosion, with the result that the friezes painted in the natural dome have disappeared or been almost completely erased. Now that their bodies have disappeared, all that remains of the sequence of large deer is their hooves and jet black antlers painted in manganese.

The extraordinary result is described by Leroi-Gourhan as follows: '. . . from the time the cave was discovered, people have been struck by the contrast that exists between the greater part of the cave, decorated with majestic paintings of animals and signs, and the Apse above the Shaft where hundreds of small engraved figures are packed next to each other, mixed in with barbed signs, comets, ovals and series of straight lines, apparently in complete confusion. In this quite exceptional case the figures are superimposed on a painted decoration, much of which has deteriorated. This suggests that this incoherent decoration was later, perhaps much later, in date than the large painted figures, when some of the subjects explicitly represented, such as the stags and the horses, do not show the same details in treatment as the large figures. The scrapings must have begun very early and have continued in this area all through the period the sanctuary was used' (*Préhistoire de l'art occidental*).

Curiously enough, the Apse seems to be dedicated to the deer, which is accompanied, on the curving walls, by the classic processions of horses, bovines

and ibexes. The list is impressive and includes more than a thousand engravings: 125 horses, 39 bovines (mostly aurochses with some bison), 70 cervids (including one reindeer), 17 ibexes and 377 signs. With dogged persistence the Abbé Glory spent over a thousand night-time hours identifying each of these figures and then tracing them on 140 square yards of tracing paper! This truly titanic effort, unique in prehistoric studies, provided the data for the detailed study by Denis Vialou, the only work dealing with this extraordinary and unparalleled ensemble.

At the time of the discovery in 1940 the sandy clay floor was higher than it is now and the archaeological layer was very close to the surface. There was no calcite mantle over it because the stream which formed the petrified pools and limestone layers disappeared into the rock in the Nave once it had passed through the Rotunda and the Passageway, thus avoiding the Apse. Arlette Leroi-Gourhan notes: 'The old floor (prior to the Palaeolithic presence) rose from the Passageway and the Nave towards the Apse at an angle of up to 45°. It then became horizontal towards the back, where, at the entrance to the Shaft, the surface was 1.50 metres [5 feet] higher than the present coping. This is where the earliest engravings were, situated a few centimetres above the ground. In the Apse the height of the ceiling varied between 1.60 and 2.70 metres [$5\frac{1}{2}$ and 9 feet].' This implies that here too scaffolding was erected by the Magdalenians, especially since the higher areas are extensively decorated. Furthermore, the width of the Apse suggests that the raised platforms could have reached a height of 8 feet without touching the walls.

Spades and barrows were used to remove 5 feet of sand and clay from the Apse, making access for tourists easier. A great deal of earth was taken and spread outside the cave to facilitate access to the Shaft, which had previously been reached by crawling through a passage opening from the Apsidiole. Today an iron ladder 26 feet long has replaced the plant-fibre rope which the prehistoric people must have used.

One would need several volumes – a veritable corpus, in fact – to reconstruct the obliterated paintings, and to describe, analyse and photograph the almost inextricable tangle of engravings and signs which line the Apse; they are particularly dense in the Apsidiole, a little chapel over the entrance to the Shaft. It is difficult, indeed almost impossible, to deal with the artistic figurations in the Apse: the eye soon tires of following the countless outlines that intertwine on the walls. Only an initiate with a real passion for reading them can move into that inaccessible world which lies beyond our twentieth-century understanding. For whom was this accumulation of graphic art intended? Who drew these thousands of graffiti with their pointed flints?

Here a film-maker finds that neither the eye nor the camera lens can cope with the maze of lines: they cannot select – as with the tracings – and so are

The Major Stag, more than $6\frac{1}{2}$ feet long, is the largest engraving in the cave.

A small deer, marked with two spear signs, differs greatly in style from the Major Stag. (Copies by the Abbé Glory)

confused by the play of light and shade created by the unevenness of the rock surface. There are some very large engraved figures, more than 8 feet long, such as the Major Stag with its quite deeply engraved head and antlers, which makes a cinematic approach feasible for details. But as soon as one moves away to take in the whole ensemble, the finely engraved contour becomes invisible both to the human eye and to the camera.

I was struck by this fact, and wondered if this huge image had ever really been seen as a whole. Perhaps by the light of lamps, in the course of a ceremony 17,000 years ago, a shaman engraved the figure of a deified stag before a group of initiates as he told its story. The movements of his hand holding a flint tool were only meaningful when the act of drawing was combined for a few moments with the evocation of an image that would no longer be perceptible to participants who came later.

This superb yellow stallion has lost almost all its colour, as have all the paintings in the Apse. It was painted and engraved on the ceiling nearly 13 feet from the former ground-level, on a wall covered with graffiti and overlapping figures. Note the way the outline of the neck is emphasized by being scratched with a flint.

This sacred place is the heart of the sanctuary. It is difficult to visit; I went down it three times, together with Jacques Marsal and one of my cameramen, taking only one camera and two lightweight battery-powered lamps. We had to do things quickly; the excessive administrative restrictions had allowed only fifteen minutes for filming and this left little time for contemplation. Marsal would lift a trapdoor in the Apsidiole and through it we would see the first steps of the iron ladder disappearing into the darkness. We would light the lamps on our foreheads and one by one descend vertically into the hole, with our equipment attached to straps. The camera was fitted with a new magazine which had only just been loaded and would assure us of ten minutes' shooting. Once we arrived at the bottom we would light our lamps and gradually illuminate the walls, which are covered with a beautiful layer of white and yellow speckled calcite.

It is impossible for someone who has never descended to this point to imagine the dense, mystic, impressive atmosphere that reigns in a place so charged with

THE SHAFT

The dramatic scene at the bottom of the Shaft. The wounded bison, its entrails hanging out, has two manes, one horizontal and the other vertical, which give the effect of the movement of lowering the head. Below the man is a bird and a disjointed sign. Note the difference in technique between this group of figures and those on the opposite page.

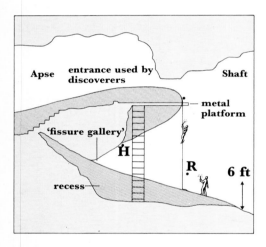

The dark areas on the plan show how much the excavators removed to facilitate access to the Shaft. The Magdalenians must have entered by the route used by the discoverers of the cave, crawling along a narrow tunnel which opened on to a deep drop. The bottom of the Shaft could only be reached by a rope. Nowadays this has been replaced by an iron ladder. H = horse, R = rhinoceros.

occult power. One experiences a sort of metaphysical shock and begins to speak in a hushed voice, almost a whisper, while the light travels along the vertical walls and suddenly reveals the famous scene. There is the bison, its entrails hanging out, its tail lashing the air in rage. A long spear cuts across it. The bison has two manes, a device used by the artist to signify the movement of the animal as it lowers its head to gore its enemy. That enemy is the man, a puppet dressed up in a bird mask, thrashing about with arms that are almost as spindly as his legs, with only four fingers on his hands. He is falling backwards with the stiffness of one consenting to his own murder – and so re-establishing the order of nature. Around the man are the now useless weapons that he has abandoned: the spear and the staff surmounted by a bird's head which some have interpreted as a spear-thrower. In fact, the hooked sign with a cross at its base is much closer in shape to a spear-thrower than the staff is. It has fallen near the point of the spear. The last figure in this dramatic panel is a woolly rhinoceros – the only such animal in the cave – which seems to be innocently going about its own business. It appears to be by the same hand as the man and the bison. The Abbé Breuil interpreted the scene thus: the rhinoceros has disembowelled the bison and the man is attempting to take advantage of this and seize the wounded animal, which still finds enough strength to lift itself up and charge.

But why is the man wearing a bird mask? It is a fact that the few human figures from prehistoric times almost always have faces that are masked or deliberately distorted.

'Like people', writes Evelyne Lot-Falk, 'animals have one or more souls and a language. Furthermore, they often understand the language of humans, while the reverse is not true, except for the shamans.' This emerges from a study of the primitive hunting peoples of Siberia and of Canada. One could spend a long time trying to penetrate the mystery of the 'pictogram', the painted or engraved event which was no doubt created in order that it might gradually become a myth in the collective memory and perhaps be incorporated into an epic.

There are other examples of a man being charged by a bison, notably in the sanctuary of Villars, which is contemporary with Lascaux. The Magdalenians were very religious and nothing in their art is explained merely by chance or materialistic logic. Within the framework of nature, where animals are persons, with the same rights as humans, life obeyed a very detailed code of practices, customs, rites, pacts and prohibitions. Perhaps the dying man has flouted such a prohibition and is suffering the inexorable consequences of his act. This powerful image would thus evoke the law and encourage respect through the very fear it inspires.

A fine, eloquent and simple figure of a horse, reminiscent of much older images, is drawn in manganese to the left of the ladder on the wall opposite the

bison. It is facing towards the bottom and the artist has depicted only the head, neck and the line of the back. It is the very last figure in Lascaux.

The Archaeology of the Shaft

The Shaft has been considerably altered since the discovery of the cave. The top of it is no longer in the same place: a thick tongue of clay, now removed, used to extend horizontally up to the point above the rhinoceros's horns. The young discoverers of the cave had to crawl along to reach the former coping, and one of them, the eighteen-year-old Marcel Ravidat, remembers that they first lowered a lighted lantern at the end of a piece of string to illuminate the bottom. Then they uncoiled their rope, but it proved to be too short. Marcel found himself suspended in mid-air and had to jump the last 5 feet. He became the first person since the Magdalenians to see the paintings. In order that his friends could go down too, he had to climb up more than 20 feet of the same rope, now made slippery by the clay. Marcel has bad memories of his

A detail from the scene in the Shaft. The rock curves in at a right angle just behind the man, and the rhinoceros seems to be depicted on a separate panel. Note the six black dots below its tail; the same sign is found at the end of the Chamber of the Felines.

This rarely photographed horse's neck is at the bottom of the Shaft on the wall opposite the bison. It is identical in technique and style to the bison and rhinoceros.

three companions, who were younger and less strong than he was, being unable to climb up the rope. He had to pull them up one by one with his bare arms.

The Shaft, incidentally, is not a well, as its French name, 'le Puits', suggests; it is a fault in the rock connected by cracks with the network of caves beneath. Some have thought that Palaeolithic people might have entered from below, through another entrance which has now vanished without trace. In archaeological terms, the Shaft is by far the most fruitful place in the cave, having provided the most information and objects. The first excavations, undertaken rather hastily by the Abbé Breuil and S. Blanc in 1947, examined a hypothetical burial place, that of the man charged by the bison. In 1959 further excavations were conducted by the Abbé Glory.

A great profusion of objects left or deliberately deposited by the Magdalenians has been dug up. The lamps are dealt with in the section on 'Prehistoric Lighting' (pp. 28–30); the many pigments are discussed in the appendices. Three carved, pierced or sawn shells found in the Shaft were worn as decoration. They may have fallen from the necklaces worn by the Palaeolithic visitors, during their acrobatic incursions into this awkward part of the cave.

The layers, containing many pieces of charcoal, can be dated relatively precisely. There were two periods of human presence, separated by a fairly short interval, as has already been described at the beginning of the chapter. Only the second of these periods provides evidence of frequent use of the Shaft: the many pieces of reindeer bone found there are likely to be the remains of 'picnics'.

Visitors now climb slowly back up the iron ladder. They have to return through the Apse, the Passageway and the solemn Rotunda, then climb back up the stairs and through the airlock to return to the outside world and the twentieth century. They are no longer quite the same people as before. Their eyesight has been sharpened, they have learned how to decipher images in the gloom, and they take with them abiding memories. In the course of their initiation in the depths of the sanctuary, they have come close to the remains of the first civilization in the West and have witnessed the artistic explosion of the early Magdalenian, one of the most beautiful periods of art in the history of mankind.

As I climbed back up this ladder for the last time at the end of our wonderful cinematographic adventure, I remembered the three reindeer-antler spears found here in the archaeological deposits. They were no doubt offerings. In the tombs, sprinkled with red ochre, spears often accompanied the Magdalenian hunters into the afterlife. The people of Lascaux had placed their precious weapons in the most inaccessible place, in front of the fateful scene in the innermost depths of the sanctuary, reached only after a perilous descent. Was this for conjuration, expiation, exorcism, propitiatory or funeral rites? Perhaps we shall never know – it all happened 17,000 years ago.

THE SIGNS AND PREHISTORIC LANGUAGE

In the course of their underground tour, visitors will have noticed innumerable abstract signs – some of them geometric – painted and engraved on the animals, or placed near them on the cave walls, and extending into the most secret and confined places. There are more than 400 of them in the cave and 228 in the Apse alone. They are not found in these quantities elsewhere: other sanctuaries have no more than a few dozen.

What do these signs mean? This is the most difficult question of all, and it is impossible with the knowledge at present available to give any direct answers or precise explanations. Instead we must rely on intuition, probability and comparison.

Small numbers of signs first appeared on the walls of shelters and caves at the time of the earliest art, during the Aurignacian period 30,000 years ago. They are found throughout the Upper Palaeolithic and increase in number during the Solutrean and Magdalenian. This tendency to have two modes of expression – one abstract and the other figurative – reveals the complex thought processes of *Homo Sapiens fossilis*. The discovery of the great symbolic power of signs was of fundamental importance: after the Ice Age they continued to develop among all prehistoric peoples, through the Mesolithic and Neolithic, and contributed to the formation of scripts in the civilizations of the metal periods. It would be correct to say that the initial phase of writing based on signs and symbols was one of the first intellectual manifestations of *Homo sapiens fossilis* spreading over the earth.

The early prehistorians found the problem of the signs very difficult and it is sometimes surprising to see the meanings that were attributed to the more complex ones. Piette said that a sign accompanying a bison was 'the signature of the artist'. Others saw the 'tectiform' shapes as 'spirit huts', and the 'grids' as animal traps. The first person to make a statistical survey of the Palaeolithic signs was André Leroi-Gourhan, and it is to him that we owe the first coherent

Above: rectilinear signs, a series of parallel double lines. Passageway. (Copy by the Abbé Glory)

Right: on this engraved panel in the Chamber of the Felines the figures of horses and a stag are accompanied by numerous signs. From right to left: above, many parallel lines and short strokes extending as far as the horse, which is marked with V-signs (= wounds). Below: many dots and short strokes. On the big horse is a large disjointed sign and crosses, and below it a 'hut-shaped' sign with many parallel lines.

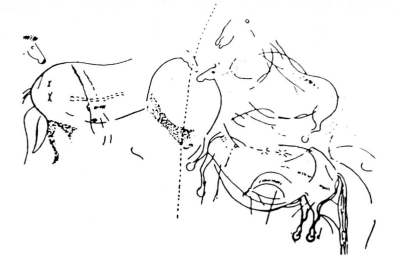

hypotheses about the variety of signs and their distribution both in caves and in mobiliary art. This chapter is inspired by the invaluable study in which he emphasizes the regionalization of certain signs and their attribution to 'ethnic identities'.

Straight lines, which are found in large numbers, painted and engraved, may in some cases be incomplete signs. We noticed several in the Rotunda, Axial Gallery and Nave apparently planted in the animals and perhaps indicating projectile weapons. It is also possible that some long, single lines, drawn in an apparently inexplicable manner across the animal figurations, indicate the imaginary trajectory of projectile weapons.

Parallel lines: double parallel lines are the most frequent all over the cave and are also a feature of mobiliary art.

Multiple lines are series of parallel lines, sometimes numbering several dozen. There are also short lines grouped in long, curvilinear series to represent the manes of horses and bison.

Disjunction: The presence at Lascaux of a central 'star-shaped' sign, both on a spear and on the back of a horse in the Passageway has led to many comments and comparisons. It is one of the proofs that the art on the cave walls is contemporary with that on the mobiliary art. A whole system of signs characterized 'by the suppression of part of their elements', and a 'gap in the joining of the lines' is derived from this star-shaped sign (André Leroi-Gourhan, *Lascaux inconnu*). The interpretation of these is not at all certain. Leroi-Gourhan suggests that perhaps they should be seen as 'the evocation of the badges of distinct social groups, the indications of various functions or individuals, votive signs or hunters' marks'. Such a system raises interesting questions about the complexity of Magdalenian thought.

Branching shapes form a group of signs found only at Lascaux. They are subdivided into 'lianas' or 'plumes', 'fans', 'ribbons' and 'antlers'. (The last of these occur only in the Axial Gallery; they are inspired by the antlers of deer and form a category of their own.)

Nested convergent lines are very common in the cave. They tend to be strung together in a way which seems to support the hypothesis that they represent the tracks of animals. Brigitte and Gilles Delluc (*Histoire et Archéologie*, no. 90) have followed up this idea and in their study of Palaeolithic signs derived from animal tracks in the snow or mud they suggest that the rows of convergent lines at Lascaux may represent the tracks of reindeer, while those on the 'burner' in the Shaft may represent the tracks of ungulates like the wild boar.

On the left of this group of figures are two diagonal crosses and a series of 'bracket' signs which suggest a track (convergent nested lines). Above right: lines and branching signs. Below: two 'asterisk' signs (see the diagram below showing disjunction). Passageway.

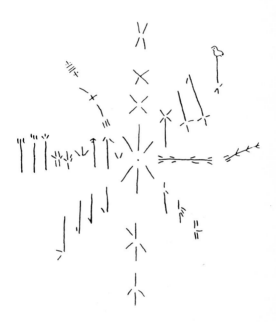

Disjunction. A general diagram of the 'disjointed' signs typical of Lascaux.

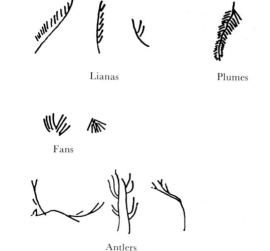

Lianas

Plumes

Fans

Antlers

Convergent nested lines

A horse and a stag superimposed 6½ feet above the Palaeolithic ground-level. Note the rows of nested lines. At the axis of the Passageway and Nave. (Copy by the Abbé Glory)

Huts

Nested signs on the lamp found in the Shaft.

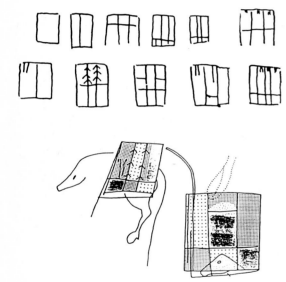

Quadrilaterals, grids and blazons

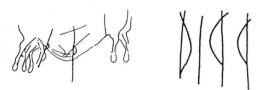

Claviform signs. Nearly 3,000 years separate the claviform signs of Lascaux (on the belly of the horse above) from those at Les Trois Frères (across the whole of the horse below).

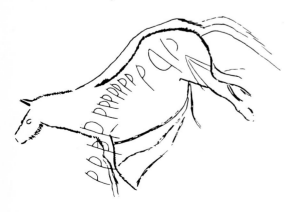

The Huts. This is the name given to some 'enclosed' signs 'of female connotation' (Leroi-Gourhan) engraved in the Apse and the Chamber of the Felines.

Quadrangular signs: 'Each area in the Franco-Spanish decorated cave region has its own "enclosed" signs (Cantabria has horizontal quadrilaterals, Quercy bird-shaped signs, Ariège signs shaped like a female silhouette). The "enclosed" signs at Lascaux belong to the group of vertical rectangles, known as "blazons", which are divided by a line running through the centre. There are many variations on this theme which is also found at Gabillou, near Mussidan (Dordogne). The rectangular signs are found in a variety of situations. Although they are absent from the Rotunda, they are found at four points in the Axial Gallery: the Great Black Stag, the second Chinese Horse, the Falling Cow and the Confronted Ibexes. All these quadrilaterals are on the right-hand (south) wall; the north wall, which includes the Great Black Bull, has no rectangular signs but does have many branching signs which come into the category of signs with male connotation (thin signs).

'Of the rectangular signs at Lascaux more than forty are in the Apse, with sixteen in the rest of the cave: five in the Axial Gallery, four in the Panel of the Imprint (Nave), five are the "blazons" in the panel of the Great Black Cow (Nave), two in the Chamber of the Felines. It is curious that very few of the "enclosed" signs are found on the decorated artifacts. Furthermore, the "enclosed" signs have numerous individual variations and are found only in the underground sanctuaries. The meaning of these partitioned rectangles probably required that they be executed only in the secrecy of the caves. It seems probable that, since they have the same origins in space, they were bound up with restrictions of a religious or magical nature. The fact that they are divided into well-defined geographical regions suggests they are signs of ethnic identity.' (A. Leroi-Gourhan, *L'Art des Cavernes*).

Claviform signs are present in small numbers in the cave, notably over the Shaft. They are also found in the Pyrenees and the Asturias, which suggests that there may have been links between Lascaux and the southern regions of Palaeolithic art.

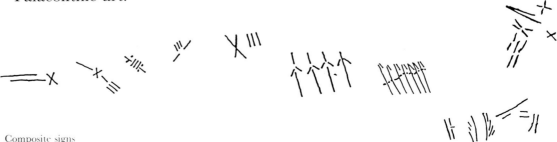

Composite signs

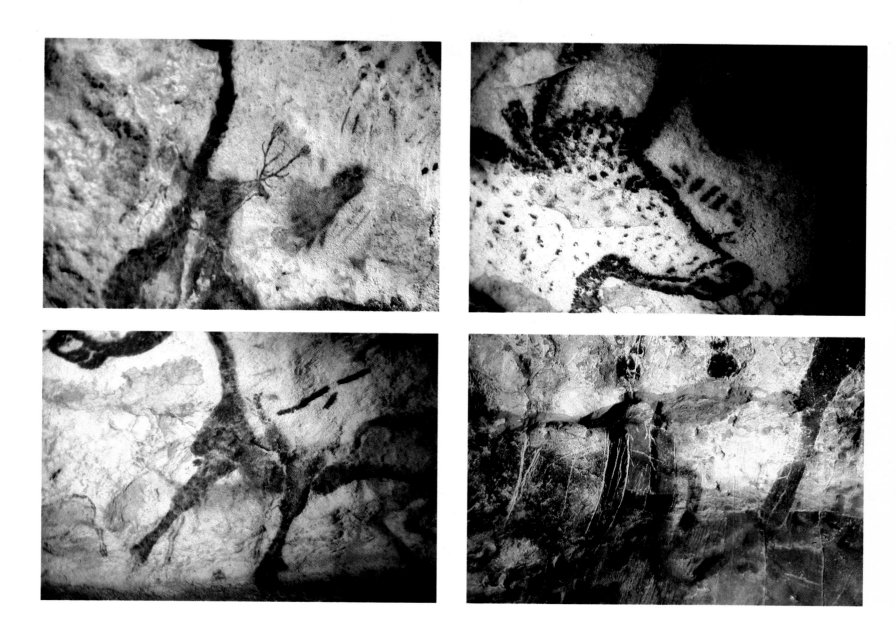

Composite signs (see opposite) are different in nature. They consist of hooked, parallel lines which cut across figures of animals, either singly or in groups of seven or eight, and may evoke the relation between spear and wound. This observation by Leroi-Gourhan is based on the position of V-shaped signs, which are so common in the Magdalenian, on the bodies and necks of animals where the spear could reach the vital organs. From the centre of these V-shaped signs, suggestive of wounds, a line often emerges cutting across the animal, thus signifying 'spear-causes-wound'. A more personal hypothesis was suggested to him by the relation spear (male), wound (female), symbolizing both the complementary nature and the joining of the male sign and female sign.

Lastly, the *Paired signs* are associations between the 'thin' signs and the 'enclosed' signs. Leroi-Gourhan sees them as symbols which are 'explicitly genital, male and female, the latter being represented at Lascaux only by the "rectangles" and the "huts"'.

From left to right and top to bottom: in front of the small stag, two parallel red lines, a theme that is repeated in front of the horse and above the line of dots. Rotunda, south wall.

Aurochs with a red composite sign. Rotunda, north wall.

On the breast of the aurochs, a disjointed sign surmounted by two signs composed of V = wound. In front of the dewlap is a single black dot. Rotunda, north wall.

Polychrome blazons below the Black Cow. Nave, east wall.

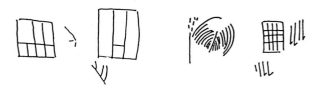

Paired signs.

Dots

Groups of dots, arranged in rows or over surfaces, as well as short strokes, are found in several caves, where they 'mark the beginning and end of the whole decoration or of different parts of it. In the deeper sections they are generally well preserved (Castillo, Font-de-Gaume, Le Portel), but examples at the entrances are rarer (Bernifal, Niaux). At Lascaux it is not known whether dots marked the beginning of the decoration, but eight localized groups of them in various parts of the cave make it possible to list their positions and topography.' (André Leroi-Gourhan, *Lascaux inconnu*).

In the Rotunda: six dots on the shoulder of the fourth aurochs and four dots on the breast of the third aurochs.

In the Axial Gallery: a row of thirteen dots under the Roaring Stag on the right at the entrance to the Gallery. The dot in the middle is set back and the ensemble may be read as two groups of seven. Twenty-six dots under the third Chinese horse (emerging from the cow) on the right-hand wall. Seven dots on the front legs of the horse at the back of the Gallery. Five dots in the Meander. Seven dots in groups of three and four in the antlers of the fourth stag in the Nave seem to be emerging from the breast of a small horse. There are also two groups, each of six dots in lines of three, in the most inaccessible parts of the cave: at the bottom of the Shaft and at the end of the Chamber of the Felines. All the evidence suggests that they mark the extreme limits of the cave decoration.

'The repetition of the number seven in almost all the rows of dots may be a matter of chance, but it is not impossible that, as B. A. Forlov believes, this number played an important role in Upper Palaeolithic thought' (Leroi-Gourhan). The 'hooked signs' on the bison and on one of the horses in the panel of the Imprint in the Nave are also seven in number.

Lastly, a few other dots, not so far mentioned, are visible in the cave: a red dot at the level of the clay ledge (in front of the first aurochs); five red dots under the feet of the bear (south wall, third aurochs); one dot at the back of the Meander next to the 'sickle-shaped' sign, which may be composed of a series of juxtaposed dots drawn unsurely because of the narrowness of the place; two dark dots under the belly of the Unicorn, on either side of what looks like a pair of bent legs emerging from its paunch, and another in front of it, at the level of the back leg of the horse that overlaps the Unicorn's breast; six ochre dots (divided into three pairs) under the belly and tail of the eighth horse in the group around the Black Cow in the Nave; two ochre dots below the six black dots at the back of the Chamber of the Felines; and finally three purplish signs shaped like a boomerang or the arc of a circle situated in the Axial Gallery and the Meander, the first on the breast of the Great Cow on the ceiling, above the Upside-down Horse, and the second on the horse that comes behind the bison in the Meander. These last seem to have been dabbed on as a sign marking the end of the Meander.

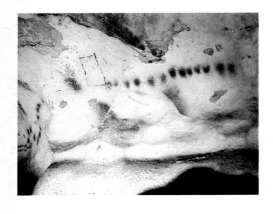

Above: below the stag in the Axial Gallery. From right to left: a row of dots and a quadrilateral sign. Note the four red parallel lines in the centre. Above the little black horse on the left is the sketch of a horse's neck. Several red and black short strokes are scattered around the rectangle.

Opposite: polychrome blazon below the Black Cow in the Nave. This photograph was taken more than thirty years ago. Since then, because of the conversion work, a layer of soot and dust has considerably obscured the blazons. (Photo Colorphoto Hinz)

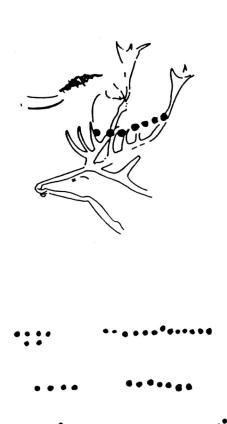

Lascaux has the most important collection of prehistoric signs known, and a further study of them would probably come up with new discoveries.

The prehistoric signs inscribed on the walls of caves, or on decorated artifacts, probably correspond to words, actions and situations which were expressed by articulate sounds in the archaic languages spoken by the Palaeolithic tribes. Although to us the signs are unfathomably mysterious, they must have seemed quite the contrary to the Magdalenians. When the light from their lamps fell on a 'line of dots', a 'quadrilateral' or a 'branched shape', situated in a precise relationship with the figures of animals, at the beginning or end of the sequence, at the intersection of chambers or galleries, or accompanying decorated ensembles, the signs would have been translated using the spoken language.

There are even some Palaeolithic caves, notably in Spain, which contain nothing but signs – with no figures of animals at all. These examples might tempt one to jump to the perhaps rather hasty conclusion that the Palaeolithic people who read them and drew them had already gone some way in the invention of writing. No doubt future research techniques will enrich our understanding in this frustrating area. I remember an afternoon spent with Professor Leroi-Gourhan during the editing of the *Corpus Lascaux*. When I mentioned the problem of the signs he said: 'Ah, if only we could put spoken words to those signs!'

Top: a row of seven dots cutting across the antlers of the fourth stag in the Nave. They accompany the small horses going in the opposite direction.

Above: rows of dots. Note the recurrence of the numbers seven and six, as in the spear-wound signs on the bison and horse in the Nave. Below are the 'terminal' signs: left, behind the rhinoceros; right, at the back of the Chamber of the Felines.

Right: below the pony is a curious arrangement of a row of dots. Note the red disjointed signs, one on the neck and the other below the breast.

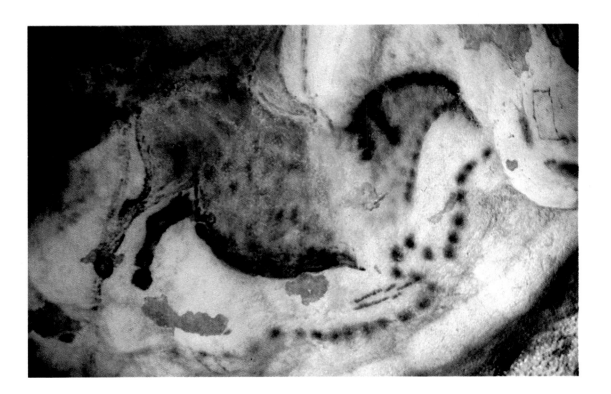

THE EYE OF THE HUNTER AND
THE GENIUS OF THE ARTIST

Only the representations of animals will be dealt with in the following survey. The signs are discussed in another chapter in this book. We have often relied on the work of our teacher André Leroi-Gourhan (notably his unpublished lectures at the Collège de France, 1970–1982), as well as the veterinarian Dr Michel Rousseau and our friend Denis Vialou (particularly their contributions to the 1979 colloquium *La contribution de l'éthologie à l'interprétation de l'art des peuples chasseurs préhistoriques*, Fribourg, 1984).

The paintings and painted engravings of animals in the cave are referred to by the numbers given to them by Fernand Windels and Annette Laming (in *The Lascaux Cave Paintings*, London, 1949); for the remaining engravings we have retained the numbering of the Abbé André Glory, whose detailed records of them were later studied by A. Leroi-Gourhan and D. Vialou (see *Lascaux inconnu*, Paris, 1979). We have indicated their position by one of the following abbreviations: HB = Hall of the Bulls (Rotunda); AG = Axial Gallery; P = Passageway; A = Apse; S = Shaft; N = Nave; CF = Chamber of the Felines. For the painted engravings in the Nave (the group around the Black Cow and the horses) Windels' number (63) is followed by the number given by Glory to each of the animals (63 N 1 to 63 N 24).

The development of Palaeolithic cave art may be summed up as 15,000 years of apprenticeship followed by 8,000 years of academicism. At the turning-point in this evolution stands Lascaux. The artists of the paintings and engravings in this cave created a harmonious style of their own and used it for religious purposes in the service of the community – their art is thus original and 'committed'. As they transcribed it on to the rock wall, they deliberately deformed nature, extracting it from its material surroundings and subjecting it to the rules that they had created, though they did not follow them slavishly. So 17,000 years ago the art 'against fate' – which André Malraux was to speak of in *Les voix du silence* – was already expressing the 'victory of each artist over his servitude'. Our aesthetic reaction to it depends on this originality and commitment.

However, while the artists of Lascaux were certainly professionals within their community, they were still hunters. They copied as much as they created and the works at Lascaux are a unique mixture of truth and convention, of authentic details and workshop mannerisms. In this chapter we shall try to demonstrate the 'tricks' used by the artists and their close observation of the familiar animals in nature.

Anything but an art gallery

The Lascaux style has been well known since the publications of André Leroi-Gourhan: the main features of its animals are swollen bodies, small heads, short lively legs, and the coats often indicated. It would be impossible to superimpose the proportions of an animal from Lascaux on to the silhouette of its living model. Moreover, the dimensions of the various species were not used consistently: they differ from one figure to the next.

There are further confusing features. Since the artists were aiming not at truth but at the most explicit anatomical drawing and convincing rendering of volumes, they invented an original kind of artificial but convincing perspective. The position on the wall of each of these animals – in relation to the topography of the cave, to the edges and irregularities of the panels, to the natural or imaginary ground-level and to the neighbouring animals – is not a matter of chance, but the result of a deliberate choice, corresponding to a sort of syntax which we still do not understand.

The beginning: the bare rock. The cave at Lascaux is not an exhibition of paintings or an art gallery with animal pictures hanging on rails; it is arranged as a sanctuary in which the paintings and engravings are perfectly integrated with the rock on which they are executed. Even before it was painted, the cave chosen was one of the most beautiful – if not the most beautiful – of the many

caves in the Vézère valley. This is because it is below a layer of impermeable marl which prevented the formation of stalactites and stalagmites. Most of the paintings are in immaculate panels covered with coarse calcite crystals (HB, AG and formerly P [see note in the margin for a key to these abbreviations]), which have not spread much since Magdalenian times (bottom of AG); the engravings and engraved paintings are on other surfaces where the ochre-coloured, granular limestone is bare. These walls are almost intact. Flakes of rock have come away in places, both before the arrival of the painters (2, 9, 11, 12, 23, 24, 42, 46 [see margin]), and, more rarely, after their departure (3, 4, 11, 15, 18). The walls of the Passageway have been worn away by slow air currents; only engravings set back in small conches and the faint vestiges of large painted animals have survived there.

There are of course limits to the dimensions of the panels, and their shape and surface determine how the decoration is arranged: friezes run along the passages (AG, P, N, S, CF), or curve round the semi-circle of the Rotunda and the dome of the Apse. Irregularities in the rock form natural frames for some groups: the small conches containing the engravings in the Passageway, wider cavities for the Panels of the Imprint (57–62) or of the two Crossed Bison (65), as well as the dihedral round which the Upside-down Horse is wound (31). Sometimes the lack of space within the panel forced the artists to pile one animal on another: the back of a bison (65 left) or the back of a horse (33). Other reliefs in the rock were sometimes used and became part of the silhouette of an animal: a flake forms the back of one horse (12) and the neck of another (43); a small hole has become the eye of a third (33). Rounded projections emphasize part of the

The statistics of the species in the paintings and engravings in Lascaux is very unusual. Compared with other decorated caves, Lascaux is a sanctuary with very many horses, a good many aurochses and deer, but few bison. The representation of the other animals is average. This is how the 597 identifiable animals are divided up: 355 horses, or 59.46% of the figures (compared with the average of 24.4% in other caves; 87 aurochses, or 14.57% (6%); 85 stags, or 14.24% (4.5%); only 3 hinds, or 0.5% (5.5%); 20 bison, or 3.35% (20.5%); 35 ibexes, or 5.86% (7.1%); 7 felines, or 1.17% (1.1%); 1 reindeer, or 0.17% (3.6%); 2 bears, or 0.33% (1.5%); 1 rhinoceros, or 0.17% (0.7%); 1 human, or 0.17% (very rare). But these overall statistics hide some surprising topographical peculiarities. The horses and aurochses (bulls and cows) are in the most visible position, and are particularly numerous in the Passageway and the Apse (which have a total of 230 horses and 61 aurochses). A few bison are found everywhere, but frequently where the galleries bend and branch. Most of the stags are on the walls of the Apse (68 figures). The felines and the rhinoceros, ferocious animals, are hidden away at the end of galleries.

outline of one of the deer (11), the head and hindquarters of the small bear (17) – and perhaps the hindquarters of a bison (14). A clay plaque, darker than the rock, provides the colour for another bison (52a).

Moreover, not all these panels were easily accessible to the artists, and this difficulty no doubt explains the rather rudimentary and rapid character of some of the lines: at the bottom of the Shaft (52a), places where the artist had to climb up (64), and the small-scale engravings in the narrow Chamber of the Felines.

There is also the limitation imposed by the size of the human body: the hand of an artist standing still more or less describes a circle with a diameter of about 3 feet. The engravings at Lascaux conform to this scale, as do some of the paintings (11, 16, 30, 33, 36, 37–9, 41, 52a, 56a, 57–61, the horses of 63 and 64). But some of the animals are much more imposing (up to 18 feet long in the case of bull aurochs 18) and to paint these the artist had to move along the wall, which was not always easy.

The imaginary ground-level. The ground on which the animals of Lascaux move is never indicated explicitly by a painted or engraved line, yet it is almost always present in the form of a natural ledge (which also contains some secondary reliefs: 28, 40, 42–5). It runs along the walls, separating the decorated, regular, paler panels above from the irregular and darker surfaces below, which contain only occasional paintings (27, 33, 34, 52a, 65, walls of the Apse) or engravings with lighter, incised lines standing out against the dark background (many of the figures in the Apse). The animals stand or move on the ground-level formed by this ledge, though they are occasionally on a completely imaginary ground. They are upright, with bodies horizontal or sometimes at a slight angle (26, 28, 42, 45, 46, 63 right, 64 N1). The Upside-down Horse (31) at the end of the Axial Gallery, and the man stretched out (52a) at the bottom of the Shaft are the only – almost certainly deliberate – exceptions. Some figures painted (22–4) and engraved (P, A, CF) on the ceiling or the upper parts of the walls have no ground-level and so appear to be floating as it were randomly in space.

A whole bestiary

The animals within each decorated panel are not arranged in a disorderly way, or juxtaposed or superimposed according to the inspiration of the individual artist. There is a clear pattern behind their arrangement. A recurring theme is the association of a large bovine (bull or cow, aurochs or bison) and a troop of small horses strung out in a line, most of which are walking in the opposite direction (1–13, 35–41, 42–5, 57–62, 63). Other groupings represent the natural behaviour of the various species: ibexes confronting each other (36 and 37), herds of male ibexes (56a) or stags (64), bison back-to-back (65), a group of felines (56–8 and 61–3). We shall return to these later. However, the

symmetrical arrangement of other figures does not seem to us to derive from natural models: for instance the two large groups of aurochses and horses facing each other in the Rotunda of the Hall of the Bulls, the rosette in the ceiling formed by the heads of cows (23, 24 and 44), a bull (26) and a horse (28), which are moving away from each other (each one towards a branching sign), a hemione (27) and facing it a horse (61) and a bison (62) with their hindquarters superimposed.

The orientation of the figures is not dictated by narrative criteria but seems to correspond to certain conventions. Only one animal (a horse, CF 50) is depicted frontally; the bodies of all the other animals are seen in profile. The horses in the Hall of the Bulls (except the first of them) face towards the right, as do almost all the horses in the Axial Gallery (except 39 and 47). Those in the Nave, on the other hand, are walking or trotting towards the left (except for 58 and 63 N1). The ibexes are usually looking towards the left, as are the painted deer (except for 16). The preferred orientation for the other animals seems to us impossible to work out for the time being, so there is no evidence for supposing that there were more right-handed than left-handed artists at Lascaux.

The third dimension

Painting or engraving consists in the transcription on to a single two-dimensional plane of what is seen in nature in three-dimensional relief. It is a very old invention, dating back to the Aurignacians of the Vézère valley and the earliest Cro-Magnons. To the Magdalenians of Lascaux it was already ancient history – prehistory almost – since it had happened 15,000 years earlier, and they now had other requirements: the details in the schema of the animal's body had to be made clear to enable the species to be immediately recognizable; the volumes had to be treated in a way that made them intelligible – even tangible – in order to represent accurately the anatomy of the animals. For these reasons they developed very mannered conventions of perspective.

Trick perspective. The head and body of the animals are seen in profile, but the other features of the silhouette are drawn in a three-quarters front view (or back view), which makes them very clear and avoids overlaps. The Abbé Breuil

Trick perspective. The treatment of the forequarters and hindquarters of the animals follows similar rules. They are usually seen in three-quarter view from the front, which can be schematized thus (f = front; b = back; r = right; l = left; the head faces in the direction of the arrow):

fr	br		bl	fl
←		or		
fl	bl		br	fr

It is much rarer for them to be seen in three-quarter view from behind, like for example the bison and rhinoceros (52a):

fr	br
→	
fl	bl

or the Upside-down Horse (31):

bl	fl
	→
br	fr

The other formulas appear by chance, especially among the engraved deer and horses.

The forequarters are sometimes seen in three-quarter view from the front, and the hindquarters in three-quarter view from behind:

fr br
←   (stag A 522 and horse P 133)
fl bl

and

bl fl   (horses A 412,
→   A 462 and
br fr   bison A 128).

Sometimes the forequarters are seen in three-quarter view from behind and the hindquarters in three-quarter view from the front:

fr br
←   (horse P 189)
fl bl

and

bl fl
→   (stag A 513)
br fr

Cows 23 and 24 in the Axial Gallery. Note the horns shown in semi-twisted perspective (on the right) and turning downwards (on the left). The 'dagger-like' ear is conventionally placed too far back. Note the *pentimento* where the artist has corrected the drawing of the breast which has a spear sign stuck in it.

called this 45° turn 'semi-twisted perspective', and reserved the term 'twisted perspective' for when there was a 90° turn (for example when the two horns of a bison are shown frontally as a U-shape, while the head and body of the animal remain in profile).

However, at Lascaux the bulls and cows generally have one S-shaped horn (the one nearer the viewer) and one C-shaped (the one further away) (9, 13, 15, 18, 26, 41a etc); much more rarely – though this looks a little more normal – both horns are S-shaped, with curves running parallel (21, 40). The horns of the bison (and sometimes those of engraved aurochses such as A 94) tend to be shown in frontal view, like two brackets, with their concave sides facing each other (14, 34, P 19, A 128, A 161, CF 1, but not 52a) or else this is simplified to a single C-shape (65, A323) rather like the bison in the cave at Pech-Merle (Lot).

Stags' antlers are represented by a very similar schema: one antler is vertical with the spikes pointing forwards, the other is placed obliquely behind it with the spikes pointing forwards and upwards (11, 16, 46, 64 and engravings). They are very occasionally seen frontally in a V-shape, with the spikes pointing symmetrically downwards (A 522). The horns of ibexes are drawn one beneath the other, almost parallel (36, 37, 56a and CF); they are never seen in V-shaped frontal view (except for A 398, which is one of the very few representations of this type in the whole of Palaeolithic cave art).

The pointed ears of horses and hinds, and the rounded ears of bears and felines are shown in frontal view as two identical appendages juxtaposed on the top of the head. The rectangular or triangular ear of the aurochses, and the pointed ear of the cervids and ibexes is strangely positioned on the back of the neck, driven in like a dagger behind the horns or antlers, while the other ear (the one closer to the viewer) is sometimes stuck very oddly on the side of the neck and points towards the ground (stag 64, a few stags in the Apse, and horse P 189). The ears of bison, when they are visible, seem to be in their natural position a little behind and below where the horns begin (A 128, CF 1).

The hooves of the ungulates are usually drawn frontally. Those of horses are shown as if seen by a viewer who is standing upright, in the form of circles or ovals below a projection indicating the fetlock on the back of each leg, and often streaked to indicate the hair on the fetlock. Both round and oval hooves are sometimes found on the same animal (42 and 43). It is odd that the hooves of horses 63 N 2–63 N 11 are oval while those of horses 63 N 12–63 N 24 (following them) are round. The hooves of bovines and cervids, which also have fetlocks, are oval with more or less pointed tips; the bovines' hooves are solid, but those of the cervids (and of cow 63 N 17) tend to be split in two parts by a thin line separating the two ungulae, as if they were being seen from below. Occasionally, indeed, the tip actually takes the form of pincers (26, 40) or of a fork (bison 52a), or is omitted (9, 13, 15, 21). The legs of the ibexes, when they appear, are not

The round hooves of horses 16, 19, 20 and 22. The Black Cow has pincer-shaped hooves. The joining of the legs to the body, engraved with a flint point, shows remarkable skill; it is almost unparalleled in Palaeolithic art. Nave, east wall.

shown in detail. The felines have their claws extended like short-toothed combs. The non-retractile, sickle-shaped claws of the bears (17 and P 14) are also very visible. The man holds his arms away from his body to make them more apparent, and extends his fingers (four on each hand); his legs are seen in three-quarter view as if from a slightly higher position in front. The erect appearance of the phallus is perhaps only a way of clearly displaying it and may have no other connotation.

The animals' eyes are in the normal position, though they are often missing in the animals painted in flat colour. The nostrils are stereotyped: a dot, a short stroke or a loop in the middle of a C representing the muzzle. The muzzle itself overhangs the short stroke that indicates the lower lip.

One animal may conceal another. A three-dimensional effect, as a series of planes, is also created by the superimposition of figures – at least in the case of the paintings and painted engravings. Some animals overlap the silhouettes of their neighbours and are therefore in a plane nearer to the viewer: horse 4 overlaps the 'Unicorn' 2; horse 8 overlaps bull 9; bull 18 overlaps bull 15; cow 63 N 17 overlaps 63 N 14–63 N 16 and 63 N 18–63 N 20; the hindquarters of the bison on the left overlap the hindquarters of its fellow (65). These superimpositions are very interesting from the point of view of chronology when one can distinguish the various layers of paint – but were these layers separated by an interval of a hour or a century? Elsewhere the figures are superimposed with no indication of the depth of field (cow 44 and horse 45, horse 61 and bison 62, not to mention of course the jumble of engravings). The same goes, at least nowadays, for the red bovines (14, 19 and 19a) which overlap, or are overlapped by, aurochses 13, 15 and 18; for the two red cows and the four horned heads which seem to be concealed under bull 26; and for stag 16 and bear 17 painted over or beneath aurochs 15.

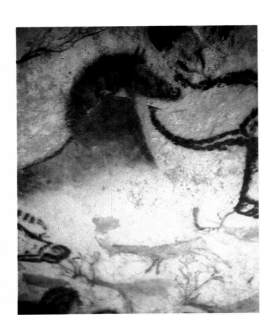

The Floating Horse (12) is incomplete. The artist has here avoided any superimposition over the pre-existing figures; thus the horse's muzzle is delicately inserted between the horns of aurochs 13.

Elsewhere, the superimposition of animals has been carefully avoided, sometimes at the cost of interrupting one of the figures or creating an anomaly in the drawing. An incomplete horse (12) creeps in between bulls 9 and 13; the tail of horse 41 is raised in a curious manner and slips in between the head of another 'pony' and the hind legs of the rolling cow (40); 25 fits in between the head and legs of bull 26; 29a lifts its front legs right up to avoid 29; 30 was left incomplete so as not to obliterate 31; and the same goes for some of the unfinished horses of 38 and 39. Cows 24 and 44, which would have overlapped the horses next to them, were left unfinished. The back of cow 19a does not become confused with the nearby line of the belly of bull 18, and the antlers of the first stag 64 frame the head of the second member of the herd.

Other tricks. There are other methods for creating the impression of three dimensions: by the gradation of colours (as in the cheek of bull 18 and the rump of horse 42 and cow 44), by the markings on the animal's coat (for example, horse 43) – which will be considered later – and the painting of the legs, belly, breast and muzzle black (the large bulls in the Hall of the Bulls).

A very elegant method is to break up the outline and interior painting of the animal to indicate where a front or back leg furthest away from the viewer is attached. A white line of the underlying calcite is revealed and serves to indicate the difference between the breast in the foreground and the front leg set further back in space, or the distance between the points where the two back legs join the body (2, 8, 21, 24, 26, 28, 40, 42, 43, and 65). There is a similar white line around the massive dewlaps of bulls 13, 15 and 18 and one of their shoulders. In a few cases where the animals appear with their hindquarters in three-quarter view from behind, the inside of the upper leg furthest from the viewer is left uncoloured (rhinoceros and bison 52a). The overlapping of the left-hand bison on the right-hand bison (65) is also indicated by leaving an unpainted white strip. There are areas left unpainted in the flat painting on some surfaces; these sometimes represent an eye (46), a nostril (26) or the wide distance between the ungulae (65).

The distortion of certain animals may have been intentional if the artist was anxious to preserve a realistic silhouette despite the viewer's distorting angle of vision. This would explain why the bulls in the right-hand part of the Hall of the Bulls are larger than those in the left-hand part (they are further away from the viewer), why the right front leg of bull 15 is longer than the left leg (it is receding diagonally into the Axial Gallery), why the legs and tail of cow 21 are so long (they are painted on a concave surface normally seen from below). It has even been suggested that as a rule the abdomens of the animals were systematically shown as bloated for the same reasons, but it is very difficult to differentiate such possible anamorphoses – which would have fascinated the perspectivists of the seventeenth century – from purely stylistic distortions.

Lascaux is like a theatre where the lights have suddenly gone out: some of the actors are frozen in natural attitudes of rest, their legs vertical and extended, but more often the artist has caught them in action, animating the whole of their silhouette – or just a leg, tail or head. In many cases the animals are firmly planted on the ground, their front legs rigid and pointing obliquely forwards, their back legs – though not as noticeably – pointing backwards (bovines 13, 18, 19a, 21, 62, 63, 65 and engravings). Often the pace is indicated: horses are shown trotting or galloping, sniffing the ground or grazing, or preparing to mate; a cat is springing, a bison charging, and some of the stags are collapsing.

Oddly enough, however, this animation may be very localized, only affecting a very limited portion of the animal. Some of the animals are raising their tails in a lively way (cow 40, bison and rhinoceros 52a, bison 65). One of the painted bulls (26) and many of the engraved horses, although apparently quite immobile, are in fact moving a leg, sometimes in an unnatural way (P 110, P 133, A 422, A 577, 63 N 24). Cow 40 and horse P 65 are rolling on the ground, throwing out their back legs in a strange manner. Ibex 36 is lowering its head and preparing to fight. The bison in the Shaft (52a) is charging at the outstretched man, and in order to express this aggression the artist has simply turned the otherwise peaceful-looking bison's massive head approximately 90° in an anticlockwise direction, so that the animal is showing its face and pointing its horns forward; the mane is thus made up of two discontinuous segments and the beard is in an isolated position at the top of the dewlap.

Sometimes the movement is broken down into several successive images. Many of the horses have multiple heads (8, 59, A 429, P 23, P 30), extra manes (P 31, P 33, P 38, A 576, 63 N 1) or additional legs (47, P 23, P 30, A 429). These repeated strokes do not seem to represent various versions tried out in a sketch but a graphic reconstruction of movement which is curiously modern in effect.

The animals are very much alive. Even the breath from their muzzles is occasionally marked by a dot or a short stroke (cows 24 and 63 N 17, aurochses 18 and perhaps 13). Stag 46 is belling or roaring, its head haloed by a faint red cloud which may indicate its breath. The feline CF 57 has been pierced by a spear and may be growling or spitting blood from its mouth, while at the time urinating to mark out its territory.

In fact there are a number of wounded animals, their wounds taking the form of a diagonal stroke or a V joining the long straight line of small or large spear (so that the images occasionally seem to have schematized arrows like those used in diagrams). Examples of this are the felines CF 56, CF 57 and CF 62, bison CF 1, horses 57 and 59, and bison 62. Bison 52a has been disembowelled by a long barbed spear. Other animals seem to have been hit by several simple lines without any apparent injury (aurochses 9 and 18, cows 21, 24, 44, horse 43,

Animals full of life

Chinese horse 42 pursuing a mare preliminary to mating. Note the hatching on the animal's belly, the detachment of the further front leg (to indicate perspective) and the 'ball-shaped' hooves like those of horses 16, 19, 20 and 22 in the Nave. This is in the Axial Gallery.

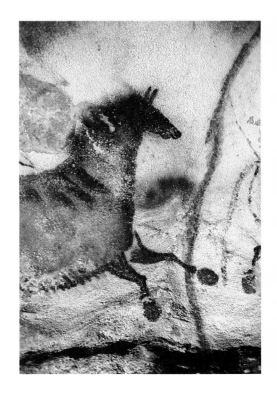

bison 56 (left). But in fact none of the animals at Lascaux (except for the bison 52a and the feline CF 57) seems to be affected by its wound.

The gestures of the artists

To some extent the works of art at Lascaux can help us to enter into human thought at the beginning of the Magdalenian – a mixture of a profound religious sense, a feeling for beauty and, no doubt, magical beliefs. The art also enables us to reconstruct the gestures of the artists – rather as in a police investigation. And as in every investigation the search for the truth relies on material clues and the reconstruction of events.

The clues here are the objects discovered in the archaeological layer (crayons made of pigments, coloured powders, palettes, pestles and mortars, engraving tools) and theories can be derived from close examination of the painted and engraved figures. When the facsimile Lascaux II was created it was possible to reconstruct the actions of the painters: the fresco-painter Monique Peytral often worked using the Magdalenian methods, with the same materials (ochres and manganese), seeking out good binding agents (the hard water from the limestone is perfectly suitable) and the best ways of applying the pigments. In her experience it would have taken half a day to execute one of the large aurochses in the Rotunda, two or three days for the bull (26) in the Axial Gallery, and only one or two hours for the scene in the Shaft (52a).

Twelve examples of the powdered colours used by the artists of Lascaux. Most of the iron oxides come from the cave itself and the surrounding area. Some of the tints were obtained by heating the ochres. See appendix: *The pigments and the art of painting*, page 193. (Photo J. Oster – Musée de l'Homme, Paris)

Ochre and Manganese. Her prehistoric predecessors would also have prepared 'crayons' of colour from small blocks of natural pigments, and coloured powders and pastes by crushing or scraping them. They would have applied the pigment in powder or paste form on to the damp, rough wall surface using a finger, spatula or stick, while some lines would have been drawn with 'pastel' crayons. No doubt they would also have used flexible instruments for the powders: brushes made of hair or vegetable fibres, 'sponges' of fur or tufts of horse-hair. It has been suggested that the dappled appearance of some animals was created by their being painted with a 'spray gun', the powdered or liquid pigment being blown with the mouth or even with the help of a pipe or a small bone tube. This is an attractive idea, but the method must have been very seldom used: it would have been impossible for painting the body (and tail) of cow 21, the coat of horse 8 or of horse 45, each of which is composed of several hundred dots, without smudging and going beyond the outlines. A simpler theory is that the pigment was applied in small 'brush' strokes, using a piece of fur. The hazy manes and beards of the horses were probably created by light 'sponging' of this sort. The very sharp outline of some of the horses' necks (28 and 45 in particular) suggests the use of a movable masking instrument (made of skin, for instance).

However, not all the animals are executed in the same manner: seven basic methods can be distinguished:

1 Silhouettes with a black outline, possibly filled with black markings, with a partial filling in of the legs, belly and breast, creating a three-dimensional effect ('Unicorn' 2, large bulls 9, 13, 15, 18, 20 and 41a, bison scene 52a, herd of stags 64, the last of which is, however, executed in ochre clay).

2 Animals with or without a black outline, filled in with flat red or bistre colour which may be diffuse or dappled (very many of the figures).

3 Animals filled with black or reddish black (horses 3–7, 10, 28, 41 and 47, bear 17, bull 26, cow 40, and right-hand bison 65). The pigment is sometimes applied in small parallel dabs (coat of stag 46 is reminiscent of that of horse 12).

4 Animals filled with two colours (horses 8, 12, cow 21, left-hand bison 65).

5 Animals with a sooty black outline, as if drawn with the smoke from a lamp or torch (36), or composed of dots joined together (37).

6 Superengraved paintings, on the left-hand side of the Nave (56a to 63).

7 Engravings (sometimes with traces of pigment).

No 'sketchbooks' (for example, on small slabs or rock) have been discovered; the artists worked directly on the walls without reference to preparatory models. However, the line of a preliminary sketch is occasionally still visible in the painting (a red line for horse 43, black for stag 46), and sometimes a *pentimento* can be seen where the painter had a change of mind and chose a different line (back of 21, breast of 24, horns of 9 and 19a). The long hair and front legs of the rhinoceros (52a) have been left in their rough state.

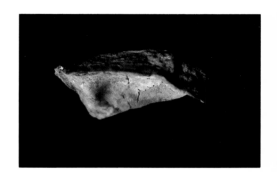

This oyster shell found at Lascaux was used as a cup for painting.

Twenty-five different tints were identified by the Abbé Glory and Claude Couraud: ten reds of varying brightness, six yellows with various degrees of brown and red, six blacks and one white. Analysis revealed the black pigments to be manganese oxides (MnO_2) or mineral carbon, the ochres to be mixtures of clay Al_2O_3, sand SiO_2 and iron oxides which are yellow if more hydrated and red if less so, often with the addition of a quantity of quartz or calcite. Any mixing of these colours is carried out on the wall itself (28, 41) and not on a palette (A. Glory). It is very likely that the red ochres were obtained by means of calcination.

Hand-held flints

The engravers worked with flint tools – simple flakes (more or less modified), blades and, in a single instance, a burin – which have been found with their edges blunted and worn away by rubbing against the rock. Using these very modest pointed or cutting tools, they incised into the limestone lines with a triangular cross-section only a fraction of an inch wide and deep. Some of the lines stand out as ochre against a darker background (the handrail in the Apse); very often they can only be seen today in oblique light, and this was no doubt more or less true in the past.

The painted engravings (left-hand wall of the Nave: 56a to 63) seem to have been executed in several stages:

1 A rough image was engraved (horse 63 N 25 was left in this state).

2 The interior of the rough image was filled in with the chosen pigment.

3 The contours of the silhouette were re-engraved by scraping and incisions.

4 Any wounds and signs were added.

However, since prehistoric cave art does not permit erasure or obliteration, it is not surprising to find a fair number of *pentimenti*, revisions and reworkings. The coats of the Unicorn (2) and cow 40 seem to be spotted with red patches. Bull 26 obscures other figures that have been abandoned unfinished. The line of the sketch can still clearly be seen on some unfinished figures (19a, 24). The lines of the back and belly of 63 N 17 have been redrawn, enlarging the silhouette, and this repainting has led to debate about whether it represents the transformation of a large elegant stag into a cow, which nevertheless retains the pointed hooves of the cervid. We can only cite the fact that the engraved animals frequently have multiple lines and silhouettes abbreviated in a way that suggests they were left unfinished or have been worn away – or perhaps were simply votive graffiti.

Here and there an attentive observer can spot marks of wear: the coping of the Shaft is blackened and shiny, and there are countless incisions and slight scratches on the engraved panels in the Nave and especially in the Apse. These are on top of the animal engravings and usually consist of series of short parallel strokes, in more or less undulating bands, looking like fencing or huts.

Lastly, people also left traces that are perhaps even more personal and moving: the objects they used preserved in the archaeological layer, the imprints of a hand and a foot on a bank of clay (Hall of the Bulls) and, on the wall itself, the coloured finger marks (near the horns of 24, below 17, and, according to Annette Laming-Emperaire, below the rhinoceros 52a).

The animals as they really were

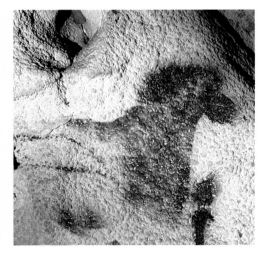

A small grey horse (30) with an upright fuzzy mane. Axial Gallery.

In spite of all this the animals of Lascaux are real animals, and the details of their morphology and natural behaviour are often accurately observed.

Horses of all colours. The coats of the horses have been studied by Michel Rousseau. They are either plain (with the hair of the coat and that of the mane and tail the same colour) or composite (the hair of the mane and tail is black). The first of these are chestnut horses (light brown, with a more or less coppery tinge) or black (sometimes shown here with red highlights). The second are bays (the basic colour of the coat is brown or red, or cerise like 63 N 24) or greyish yellow (63 N 19). This coat is sometimes dappled (8 and 45). No white marks can be seen on the head, nor are there 'white stockings' or stripes on the legs. The mule stripe along the back is not visible on the animals seen in profile (except perhaps on 39 and 41 no. 1). On the other hand, the line on the shoulder (the cross band or cross of Jerusalem) is very frequently indicated: there may be one or more of these – up to five or six, which is unusual nowadays – (28, 33, 42, 43, 47), but they are not found on the engraved horses. The summer coat with a lighter M-shaped mark on the abdomen (as found on the Przevalski horse and even on modern breeds of horses) appears especially on the large horses (43, 57–61, 63 N 7, 63 N 11, 63 N 24, A 10). The winter coat is found mostly on the smaller horses (41). This darker phase is accompanied sometimes by more or less

A horse with a 'flying gallop' (10) hovering above the imaginary ground-level. Rotunda, north wall.

vertical strokes on the line of the belly, probably indicating the long winter hair (8, 39, 42, P 120, P 133, P 135). Only one stallion has its sexual parts indicated (A 10). The upright manes of these primitive horses are hazy in the paintings and composed of parallel hatching in the engravings; the same goes for the beards (paintings and engravings such as P 188 and P 189). The ears may be laid back (Upside-down Horse 31) or pointing forwards (galloping horse 28), clearly displaying behaviour associated with fear and alertness.

The postures are often accurately observed and well rendered. Horse 63 N 16 is rearing up as in a fight between stallions before mating; 60 is sniffing the ground or grazing; P 65 is probably rolling in the dust. One of the stallions is preparing to mate with a mare (42–3).

Herds of mares with their rumps in the air are watched by a stallion facing in the opposite direction (1–10, 35–41, 57–61, 63 N 1–63 N 24). It is known that there were usually six to eight females for each male. Horse 43 seems to be ambling (M. Rousseau); the back legs of some others are both bent, as if jumping or galloping (5, 29a); many seem to be trotting (59, 63 N 24, A 577 etc.). Some of them may be foals, such as the black 'ponies' with red highlights (41), and 63 N 9, which is superimposed on the belly of its 'mother' (not shown inside a transparent womb, as has sometimes been claimed).

Some aspects, however, are very unusual. Quite a number of horses are represented in a 'flying gallop' (extending all four legs like a cat jumping), which results in an exaggerated lengthening of the body (4, 7, 8, 28, 58, P 832, P 188). This is an error that persisted (in English engravings, for example) until the American Eadweard Muybridge's investigation of animal locomotion in the 1880s. There are several horses with 'rat tails' (4, 28, 31, 42–5) or tails like enormous brushes (P 107, P 118, P 120). The bellies (i.e. the thoracic-abdominal regions) are swollen, sometimes so much so that they touch the ground – though this does not indicate pregnancy, as was once thought. The belly of the hemione (27) reaches down to its hooves.

Impressive aurochses. Although the last aurochs vanished from the face of the earth in 1627, the anatomy of the animal is well known through old drawings and the *in vivo* reconstructions by L. and H. Heck in Germany. The aurochses at

Lascaux show the obvious sexual dimorphism typical of the species. The male is recognizable by his massive head, his white muzzle, his neck and breast, his shoulders and the length of his light-coloured horns with their black points. The external genitalia are represented by a very low-hanging scrotum (13, 15, 18, 26), but the sheath is not depicted. The cows are a reddish colour (with, perhaps, a lighter band on the back, 21, 63). The udders are not shown – they retract quickly when lactation ceases. One of the cows appears to be followed by her calf (19a and 19). It is amusing to note that the ears of the bulls are rectangular, while those of the cows are triangular. On top of the heads of most of the bovines is a projection formed by a tuft of sometimes streaked hair between the horns (9, 13, 15, 18, 19a, 21, 23, 24, 44, P 121, A 49, A 98 and near A 69). Some of these figures are animated: two of them have curving tails (21, 40); one is rolling on the ground (40); bull 26 seems to be scratching the ground with his right foreleg. The others, however, are usually shown standing firmly on the ground and tend to have apparently elongated bodies (15, 18, 26).

A few of the beasts are unusual in that their hindquarters (26, 63 N 17) or their legs (21) are not properly finished. The tails of some are too long (21, 63 N 17 and perhaps 9, whose tail some people believe is in fact the 'horns' of the 'Unicorn' 2). Sometimes the forequarters are made up of 'fins' (19, like those of bison 14), or the horns may be pointing downwards (23, 44) – though present-day bovines occasionally have the same features. One cow is two-coloured with a black head (21), and the coat of the bulls does not seem to be black (like 26 or the aurochses reconstructed in recent times), but white with black patches.

Certain signs composed of short paired lines, either straight or bracket-shaped and sometimes fitted into each other like telescope lenses, may represent the tracks of cloven-footed ungulates (bovines or cervids): the artist-hunters must have been very familiar with the tracks of the animals they hunted.

Aggressive bison. The silhouette of the bison is usually accurately depicted with its three characteristic humps (the top of its head, the hair at the back of its neck and its back) (A 128), its upright mane and dewlap (52a, 62, 65, A 161 and A 128, CF 1) and the beard on its chin (52a, CF 1) – which sometimes looks rather pharaonic (62). The end of the tail widens into a tuft (52a, 62, A 128, CF 71). The scrotum is missing (except in CF 1), but the sheath is often depicted (34, 65, A 128, A 161, CF 1), and the bison have other clearly male features: massive forequarters, lop-sided appearance and convex noses.

Unlike present-day bison, all the bison at Lascaux have enormous horns, which are seen frontally and seem (because of the thickness of their hair on the head) to be placed very low. One animal (A 419), with wide horns apparently stuck to its head and curving back at the ends to form thin hooks, is more reminiscent of the ovibos or musk-ox from the Far North. Nearly all the bison

An engraving of a bison in the Apse. (Copy by the Abbé Glory)

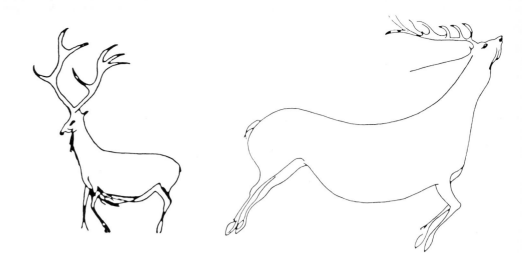

are animated and are depicted somewhere between a standing posture and a flying gallop (65, A 128, A 161). Some of the details are well observed: the coils of the herbivore's long intestine in the scene with the disembowelled bison (52a), the trotting hind legs of CF 71, the spring-time moulting of 65 (left), the back-to-back posture of the bison (65), which Leroi-Gourhan believes represents a classic attitude of intimidation adopted by males in the rutting season.

Elegant deer. The cervids deserve to be discussed at length. They are red deer stags for the most part (there are only three hinds) and very probably a reindeer. The latter (A 141) is recognizable by the unusual tine of its antlers, the way it carries its head low, showing a prominent shoulder hump and the forward curve of its antlers (though these last two characteristics may also be seen on older stags, and the other on stags such as A 25).

Three red deer stags. Above right is the famous 'Fend la bise' stag, copied by the Abbé Glory.

The silhouettes of the stags are very elegant. Their necks are narrow (too narrow in fact), the throat and dewlap are only occasionally given the prominence they should have (A 44, A 195, A 522), especially in autumn and winter, and the shoulder ridge is missing. The white belly is indicated by a double line (A 195, A 499, A 513) and sometimes has curiously long hair (A 300). One stag seems to be two-coloured (110), while other engraved stags have long strips of pigment along their backs, bellies and necks (frieze of A 308, A 310, A 313, A 317). None of them has its genitalia indicated. The ear is generally stuck on to the back of the neck, and sometimes the ear nearer the viewer is stuck to the side of the neck (two stags in the frieze 64). The ears of the hinds and of a stag (A 313) are seen frontally. The eye is oval or round, and tends to have the lachrymal gland marked.

Some stags are motionless, others are galloping or leaping (such as the Abbé A. Glory's 'Fend la bise' A 74) or are collapsing (A 44, A 513). Some of them seem to be roaring or belling during the mating season, which occurs between mid-September and mid-October (46). The old males in the frieze (64) form a single-sex group, as is often the case in the winter. (They appear to some to be swimming across a river.)

A few herds of ibexes. The ibexes depicted are not Pyrenean but Alpine ibexes (*Capra ibex*): their horns have a simple curve and are not twisted into an S-shape (36, 37, 56a, P 86, A 398, A 399, CF 44). In spite of their long, heavy horns, the males often have thin necks (56a). The growth knots on the horns are not represented, nor is the beard (except on 36 and perhaps 37), and the tail, when it is shown, does not turn back on itself. The abdomen and legs are often sketchily drawn or omitted. The belly of ibex 37, however, is distinguished by a curved line marking the border between the dark coat on the belly and the coat on the flank, which is lighter in colour on the Alpine ibex. A very few of the ibexes have short, upright manes (P 86, A 398) or two pointed ears seen from the

The study of the antlers is fascinating. Their presence is evidence that the animals were 'sketched' by the artist between the end of June and March. The main horns, seen frontally, have the classic shapes well known in venery: heart-shaped (the stags are thought to be prudent), V-shaped (reckless) and U-shaped (friendly). Often the two antlers are artificially made to grow from a single point or share the same trunk (two stags in the frieze 64); sometimes one seems to branch from the first segment of the other (Apse). The points – the first ('brow') tines, second tines ('bays'), third tines ('trays') and fourth tines – are drawn in profile, pointing forward and upward, and rarely symmetrically downward (A 522). The antlers end with a wider fork or 'palm'.

Some features are unexpected. A few of the stags are not well armed, having thin antlers, but most are very well armed – usually quite old (ten points or old ten points). Some antlers are very exuberant, particularly their 'palms', which are shaped very like hands (11, 16, 46, P 177, A 44, A 469) and are vaguely reminiscent of the antlers of a fallow deer or a megaceros deer. There are others that have two twin brow antlers or even bays on a single horn, so that these pairs are curiously spaced along the antler (11, 46, A 217, A 513, A 527).

front on either side of the beginning of the horns (56a, the second ibex).

As in the wild, in summer and autumn the old males in the frieze 56a (black ones on the left and red ones on the right) are grouped in a sort of single-sex club. Ibexes 36 and 37 are preparing to clash heads: one of them has already lowered his head, but they have not yet found a firm footing.

Other animals. The rhinoceros in the Shaft (52a) is unquestionably a woolly rhinoceros (*R. tichorhinus*), which had a thick fleece as well as long stiff hairs. It resembles the examples of the species that have been found frozen in Siberia. It is not clear whether it is a participant in the scene with the man and the bison, but the presence of this disturbing animal is not surprising here at the end of a gallery.

The same applies to the felines at the end of the Chamber to which they have given their name (CF 56–8, CF 61–3). The gregarious nature of cats is well known: here there are six of them – half of which have spear wounds. Their round eyes and square muzzles, strong legs with pointed claws and long tails (with a tuft at the end in the case of CF 62) are typical of the species. One of them appears to be leaping, with its legs extended (CF 57); another is perhaps getting ready to spring (CF 61). CF 57 is wounded and seems to be growling, or spitting or vomiting blood; in all Palaeolithic cave art only the two wounded bears in the cave of Les Trois Frères (Ariège) can be compared to it in this respect. Finally, the same feline, clearly a male, is urinating backwards to mark out its territory. These felines had no manes or bibs, nor were they spotted, but they were probably very similar to the present-day lion. Similarly, the heads of bears (17 and P 14) with their straight, not convex, foreheads, are those of brown bears, like our Pyrenean bears, and not cave bears.

The 'Unicorn' (2) remains an enigma. The zoological mystery surrounding it has provided much scope for scholarly and imaginative suggestions. It has been thought to be a representation of a Tibetan antelope, a Russian rhinoceros (both with unpronounceable Latin names), a lynx (with truly enormous ears), the skin of an animal patterned with eyes concealing two hunters, and even a bearded man with a profile reminiscent of the late President Paul Doumer. Two hypotheses seem a little more reasonable: that it is a composite animal (a very surrealist 'exquisite corpse', with the body of a rhinoceros, the shoulder ridge of a bear or bison, the head and markings of a feline and the tail of a deer), or – and this is even more likely – that it is a feline drawn not from the living model but from a 'verbal portrait' handed down by oral tradition.

It is the first important figure the visitor encounters on entering the cave and it begins the frieze in the Hall of the Bulls. It also closes this chapter which Mario Ruspoli kindly asked us to contribute. It is the symbol of all that we still do not know about the cave of Lascaux, a trial attempt and at the same time a masterstroke by the earliest Magdalenians.

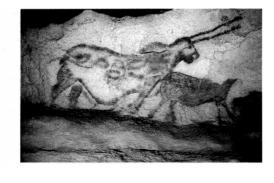

The enigmatic Unicorn. This is an old photograph taken by the Abbé Glory and his team in the 1950s. The profile of a horse can be seen inscribed in the figure. Is the Unicorn an imaginary animal? A lynx? A shaman in disguise? (Note the two red legs hanging below the belly.) The question remains open.

BRIGITTE AND GILLES DELLUC

A CINEMATIC APPROACH TO LASCAUX

For three consecutive years, at the request of the Ministry of Cultural Affairs, I directed the filming of the *Corpus Lascaux*, which was intended to be as complete as possible a cinematic record of the cave. This treasure-store of images on 16-millimetre film is divided into four parts, each lasting about two hours. It is the first attempt to apply this kind of scientific approach to almost the whole of a Palaeolithic sanctuary. The film was put together and edited in collaboration with Professor Leroi-Gourhan, who showed a friendly interest in this new sort of venture and was closely involved in the project from the time we left for the Dordogne until the final screening.

I had been chosen to make this film record because of my long experience of filming underground – sometimes in difficult conditions – and because I had an interest in research into cave art as well as a concern for its preservation. I had the opportunity to make two preliminary visits to Lascaux, on the second of which I was accompanied by Denis Vialou, a prehistorian and friend, who knew the cave very well. I must acknowledge the debt we owe him for his contribution to the success of our mission.

The filming was entrusted to a small team that I had formed, using portable equipment which is described in the marginal note on page 179. All the cinematic 'baggage', particularly the lighting equipment, was first examined by the CNRS (National Centre of Scientific Research) to check whether it conformed to the severe ecological restrictions which regulate and protect the 17,000-year-old artistic masterpiece.

In order to film underground in accordance with these strict ecological rules, the film team had to undergo an initiation. Before we left, I had taken care to inspire my technicians with a lively interest in prehistory, and I had chosen two cameramen who had accompanied me on previous filming expeditions to caves: Noël Véry and I had had the valuable experience of visiting more than fifteen sanctuaries with camera in hand and Michel Bonnat had filmed the Etruscan tombs of Tarquinia with me.

Heat and light

Filming in the fragile underground world, even with our techniques, presented the double problem of heat and light. Caves have a climate of their own and their natural, biological balance in the slow rhythm of the seasons and variations in global climatic conditions; the internal temperature oscillates with the seasons, but within the very narrow margin of a few degrees. Moreover, there are variations in humidity due to the changes in the circulation of water by capillary action and percolation, both in the cave walls and in the surrounding air. Each cave has its own climate, and how it 'breathes' is determined by the volume and interior shape, the number of exterior openings, the circulation of air and the percolation of water.

It goes without saying that any disturbance in this natural balance, such as the arrival of crowds of people or building works, will be detrimental. That is what happened at Lascaux: the art there had been preserved over so many thousands of years because the temperature never rose beyond 15°C. (59°F.) and the level of humidity was maintained naturally, but the coming of more than a thousand people a year, after the alterations made for tourism, disturbed this balance by raising the temperature above 30°C. (86°F.) As a consequence of this, the rapid deterioration of the works of art became so apparent that cures had to be found for the 'green disease' that was eating the paintings, and the 'white disease' caused by a build-up of crystals; the cave was closed to tourism in 1963. Scientific studies have since been undertaken over the last twenty years or so into the most appropriate means of preserving these underground works of prehistoric art in the future. But while this conservationist thinking is admirable in itself, it has led to the cave being controlled according to an ultra-protectionist régime which sometimes verges on the absurd.

Lascaux was opened to us for about twenty days a year in March to April; that is, when the cave had stored the maximum cold winter temperature. Filming was accomplished in record time, since our hours underground were restricted by a draconian timetable and reduced to shooting sessions varying from three hours for the Rotunda to twenty minutes for the Passageway, Axial Gallery and Chamber of the Felines. All this could be done only at intervals of two or three days, so that the cave could dissipate our body heat.

The problem of the heat that emanated from our bodies, as well as the heat from our lamps, had been carefully considered. If quartz lamps fitted with heat shields tested by the CNRS were directed for fifteen minutes at an absorbent brown surface 3 feet away, they raised the temperature of the surface by 1°C. (2°F.) In practice, for rapid shots lasting no more than a few dozen seconds, the heat rise was negligible. Human bodies, on the other hand, give off much more heat than quartz lamps, especially in the narrower parts of the cave where the air does not circulate, so that this heat builds up and is only evacuated slowly. There is even a noticeable difference between the heat radiated by someone who has not eaten and that radiated by the same person after a good meal, when they give off the most calories, especially if they are being physically active.

A team of six people working in a narrow and winding gallery for a quarter of an hour raises the temperature of the surrounding air by a few degrees. It also increases the level of carbon dioxide and water vapour, which condenses on the walls. For this reason I had to reduce the team to two or three persons when working in narrow places such as the Chamber of the Felines or the Shaft.

There was also the question of whether the beams from our lamps would damage the pigments of the paintings. This possible long-term problem was impossible to measure and was therefore dismissed.

Filming the *Corpus* in the Axial Gallery. From left to right: Jacques Marsal and Mario Ruspoli holding the Minette lamps, Michel Bonnat and Noël Véry filming simultaneously. (Photo G. Galmiche – TF1)

Cinematic equipment used in the filming of the *Corpus Lascaux*:
2 Aaton 16 mm cameras, 4 120 mm magazines
Lenses
2 Angénieux zooms 12–120 mm
1 Angénieux zoom 16–44 mm, f 1.1
1 Zeiss 9.5 mm, f 1.2
1 Zeiss 12 mm, f 1.2
1 Angénieux 28 mm, f 1.2
1 Kinopfik 5.7 mm, f 2.2
Stands
2 large stands, with a Ronford F.4 head
2 small tripods, with a Ronford F.4 head
Lighting (all battery powered)
4 Minettes with 30-watt batteries: 150-watt quartz: L.T.M.
4 spotlights (12 volts): 100-watt and 50-watt quartz: L.T.M.
2 reflector bowls: 150 watts: L.T.M.
Heat shields

The lamps

The lighting for almost all the shots in the *Corpus Lascaux* was provided by two small hand-held 100-watt quartz lamps powered by portable batteries weighing about 11 pounds, which were supported by a shoulder strap. Generally, prehistorians who have studied and listed the paintings and engravings on the walls of caves have used makeshift lighting: candles, acetylene lamps, torches and weak electric lamps. It was therefore very hard work for them to make out any faint traces or signs barely sketched inside the figures or around them. Our precision lenses sometimes surpassed the powers of perception of the naked eye, bringing out details which were only just discernible, particularly in the painted surfaces and around the figures.

At first it seemed that it would be impossible to film with so little light, especially since the film we were using, Fuji negative 100 ASA, was not particularly sensitive – but in actual fact the opposite proved to be true. The lamps which gave us such excellent results were of two types: the smaller ones, 'Minettes', contained a $\frac{3}{4}$ inch quartz tube fixed to the back of the reflector; three catches made it possible to adjust a special thick glass screen which considerably reduced the heat radiation directed at the wall; the larger ones, 'Manderines', could take either 200- or 300-watt tubes, but we only had recourse to these for particular shots of larger areas. For a tracking shot in the Rotunda one morning, when we were using a platform running on closely laid rails, we had to have all the pictures in the chamber appearing in a single plane – which was not possible with our small lamps. So in this single instance we resorted to an HMI iodine and cold light reflector for illumination.

The filming methods

We followed the guidelines that I had proposed to my team before filming began. These were dictated by the ecological restrictions and aimed at making the most of the limited time available.

Each take was filmed by two cameras simultaneously with the centrings and various movements worked out in advance. The preparation took place in darkness lit only by pocket lamps. Then, when the cameras were already rolling, the hand-held quartz lamps were switched on at floor-level. In accordance with verbal instructions given by the director the light was then raised up the cave wall to bring out the variations in the relief of the surface. The lights were never held on a particular spot for longer than twenty seconds, and at the end of each take they were turned up to the ceiling or down to the floor, causing the image to fade into darkness. The lamps were always held at least $6\frac{1}{2}$ feet away from the surfaces being filmed. For details and the small engraved figures filmed in close-up, weaker 50-watt quartz lamps giving off much less heat were used. The cameras were usually held on the shoulder for moving shots or screwed onto a tripod for fixed or small-scale shots.

Left: before the descent, the ritual foot-bath in a trough of formalin to kill algae and pollen. From left to right: Jacques Marsal, Norbert Aujoulat (from the Centre de Préhistoire), Michel Bonnat, Mario Ruspoli and Noël Véry. (Photo G. Galmiche – TF1)

Above: the blazons in the Nave were difficult to film. Michel Bonnat with the camera is being held by Maurice Bunio, while Jacques Marsal lights up the Black Cow.

Many of the 'tracking' shots were done on foot and required considerable physical fitness on the part of the cameraman. Usually for the twenty seconds needed for a difficult piece of filming it was necessary for him to stop breathing in order to avoid shaking the camera. A human scale was provided in some of the more general shots by including a person moving about holding a lamp. As the camera was moving, the focusing was adjusted by the cameraman's assistant or the lighting assistant, or sometimes by the director himself, to rectify any variations in distance. After shooting it was advisable not to light the lamps for a little while in order to allow the slight rise in temperature caused by the bodies and the quartz lamps – however minute this might be – to disperse. To avoid any build-up of heat in moderately confined areas we would interrupt the filming after remaining in one place for a few minutes and move to another part of the cave, returning to our earlier position again later once the heat had dissipated.

The magazines were loaded on to the cameras in the Rotunda, since it is better ventilated and therefore less subject to build-ups of heat, and the cameras were left in the cold of the cave so as to avoid the condensation that could result from the changes in temperature if they were brought in from the outside. We took care not to position our cameras in front of beautiful aesthetic images, but to film the cave in its totality with all the details of the prehistoric wall surface and especially its relief.

The exposed films were sent every evening to Paris by fast train from the station of Brive-La Gaillarde. A courier collected them on their arrival and took them early in the morning to the laboratory for immediate development. The rushes would be sent back straightaway to the Dordogne, to be collected by our assistant at Brive station in the evening, when the day's films were dispatched. The rushes were then taken by car to the Hôtel du Soleil d'Or at Montignac, where the team were staying, and screened, after dinner, using a 16 millimetre projector. In this way we could see our film as it was in the process of being made, with a delay of only two days at the most, and also invite prehistorians and friends to the screenings.

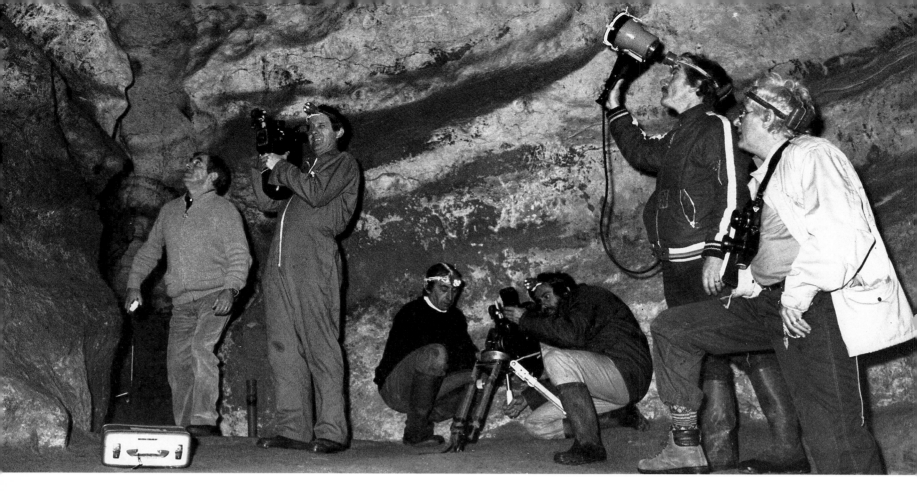

The experience of filming

The ecological constraints under which we were working (especially as regards lighting) and the brevity of our stays in the cave should, at first sight, have detracted from an undertaking like ours. But, on the contrary, our modest resources and the extremely restricted lighting that was permitted made us take a new cinematic approach to the art on the cave walls. 'This economy in manpower and material', remarked Noël Véry, 'meant that we had to use swift, precise and spontaneous takes, the camera moving forward through the dark cave and disclosing the space as it emerged, without ever losing its sense of magic. The movements of the camera and light, as well as the filmed movements of a person, made it possible to show the shapes of the cave and the relief of the surfaces, while the size of the figures was indicated by a human scale and their relationship to each other.'

This slow unfolding of the images in the silence of the cave took us to the edge of another world. I remember Leroi-Gourhan's remark that modern people confronted with the prehistoric world were 'like Martians visiting the cathedrals of a vanished civilization'. We became aware of the great fascination that the prehistoric images held for us and we ourselves gradually began to feel like initiates. Each 'plunge' into the depths of the earth came as a sort of metaphysical jolt followed by the impression of travelling in space-time. Our quartz lamps were lighting exactly what people 17,000 years ago had seen and our cameras recording images of prehistoric life as if we had landed on an unknown planet.

We decided to have a slight movement of the camera almost continuously while we were filming, so that the figures would be related to each other, with the least possible discontinuity between takes – even if this meant concentrating on the details of each figure afterwards.

The positioning of the often oblique lighting that accompanied the movements of the camera brought out all the relief of the cave wall surface and made us realize how much the prehistoric artists had been inspired by the

Filming the *Corpus* in the Apse. From left to right: Jacques Marsal, Michel Bonnat, Philippe Grolleau, Noël Véry, Michel Boyreau, Mario Ruspoli. Two cameras are being used at once. (Photo G. Galmiche – TF1)

natural sculpture of the rock itself right down to the smallest details. This use of the rock structures is particularly evident in the Axial Gallery. The Cow with a Collar is placed over natural protuberances which emphasize the muscles of the shoulder and the thoracic cage. Its neck cuts across a ridge in the rock and this slight change in orientation creates the impression that the animal is turning its head. The Upside-down Horse curves round a pier and the Great Black Aurochs makes use of the curious relief of its concave niche: when it is seen at an angle from the end of the Gallery, only its head is visible; the body is concealed behind a projection in the rock and is only revealed when one moves towards it.

We noticed all this as we advanced, lamps in hand, along the wall towards the back of the cave. The painted figures emerged gradually from their hiding-places in the rock and this movement made them seem to come alive. The Magdalenian artists used all the ingenuity of Style III to create these movements, which are removed from the rigid constraints of Style II (see the definition of styles on page 197), particularly the articulation of the legs, feet and hooves, which evoke walking, trotting, galloping, kicking, treading the air and jumping. An example of this can be seen in the horses of the north wall of the Rotunda in front of the Unicorn: one of them is jumping, depicted in mid-air, its mane flying in the wind, as if clearing some obstacle. This interest in movement is connected with an interest in perspective, and both these features of Magdalenian art are found only in the Franco-Cantabrian region; they do not occur in the rock art of other prehistoric peoples. To appreciate the use of perspective (which has been discussed in the earlier chapters) one has only to look at the curve of the Meander where the bison is advancing at an angle and showing a front view of its head, while the horse behind it is turning its head so that it appears in three-quarter view.

It became clear to us that the cave art at Lascaux was not made to be viewed like a series of fixed paintings, but as images in movement glimpsed by the Palaeolithic initiates as they walked through the dark. The power of the images as they loom out of the blackness as if in a dream, taking one by surprise, would have shown them – as they did us – the revelatory power of the religious and magical forces which fuelled the Palaeolithic imagination. To the members of my team and myself Lascaux became a sort of second homeland – a world outside the real world – where we communicated through the medium of art with the mysterious impulses of prehistoric mankind. We shall never forget it.

The experience of walking through the cave, following the walls by the light of two little 'Minettes', with a camera on one's shoulder, must have been very similar to the way the Magdalenians experienced the cave, as they advanced with their lamps in their hands. The prehistoric images, full of mystery and revelatory power, emerged from the darkness and vanished again as soon as we had passed, to be replaced by other images.

The *Corpus Lascaux*

The cinematic *Corpus* of Lascaux was filmed in 1981–2 and 1983. It is divided into four parts and it took almost two years to put together, in collaboration with André Leroi-Gourhan, to whom this book is dedicated. Each part consists of a silent 16 millimetre film lasting two hours. The contents are as follows:

Rotunda

Pictures of the discovery of Lascaux, exteriors, landscapes, helicopter views, a complete and detailed examination of the Rotunda, the Dellucs' reconstruction of the first figure in the Aurochs Frieze, examination of the human imprints.

Axial Gallery

Structure and complete examination of the figures in the Gallery first along the north wall then the south wall. The revealing of the Upside-down Horse, the figures in the Meander. Complete examination of the south wall from the Meander to the entrance. The scaffolding holes. Demonstration of Leroi-Gourhan's theory that the panels 'echo each other' across the Gallery.

Passageway, Apse and Shaft

Structure of the Passageway. Position of the 'conches' with engravings. Filming of the essentials of the engraved figures, many of which are not 'visible' to the camera. Structure of the Apse and examination of the paintings and engravings (mostly in a very poor state of preservation). Descent down the Shaft, the complete imagery of the scene of the bison and the other figures (horse and rhinoceros).

Nave and Chamber of the Felines

Complete imagery of the Nave, east and west walls. Details of all the paintings and engravings as well as the frieze of stags on the west. The essential imagery of the Chamber of the Felines as far as the back. Return, moving back to the entrance to the cave.

Each section of the *Corpus* was preceded by a filmed journey from the cave entrance to the area being examined. After each panel a recapitulation of the decoration of the whole wall to enable viewers to orientate themselves again. Explanatory boards were shown giving the standard names of the panels and figures. Each section also included an animated map of the area studied.

Besides the *Corpus*, the Ministry of Cultural Affairs also has available a large set of plans, as well as classified and numbered cuttings, and lists of these.

The television films

Parallel with the *Corpus*, and using the same team, I also made a series of television programmes for TF1 in 16 millimetres, which were broadcast on three occasions in 1983 and 1984. They were called *L'Art au Monde des Ténèbres* (a co-production of the Ministry of Cultural Affairs and TF1) and were intended as an introduction to and popularization of prehistory. Prominence was given to the images filmed at Lascaux and the following caves, shelters and sites were also featured:

Filming in a narrow passage. Noël Véry is holding his Aaton camera while Jacques Marsal lights the wall with a 25-watt Minette lamp. (Photo G. Galmiche – TF1)

Dordogne: Font-de-Gaume, La Grèze, Rouffignac, Combarelles, Villars, Teyjat, Abri du Cap Blanc, Abri du Poisson, Laugerie Haute, the museums at Les Eyzies and Périgueux.

Lot: Pech-Merle and Cougnac.

Aquitaine: Pair-non-Pair.

Pyrenees: Niaux, Enlène, Le Portel, Le Mas d'Azil, Gargas, the museum at Foix, the Bégouën collection.

The series comprised four parts, each lasting fifty-two minutes:

1 *The Origins* – man and the first manifestations of art – flint working – engraving, sculpture, beginnings of painting.

2 *The Reindeer Age* – introduction to prehistoric painting – the Rotunda at Lascaux – other sanctuaries.

3 *The Great Inventions of Lascaux* – technical, artistic and archaeological

approach to Lascaux. Painting methods and pigments, scaffolding – Axial Gallery, Passageway, Apse, Shaft, Nave, Chamber of the Felines.

4   *Magdalenian Civilization* – the Palaeolithic and its art after Lascaux – life in the Magdalenian period – mobiliary art and body ornaments. The sanctuaries of Font-de-Gaume, Rouffignac, Niaux, Teyjat – the cave of Enlène, the Bégouën collection.

This series of films has also been given regular public showings as part of the educational programme at the Musée de l'Homme in Paris, as well as being frequently screened in schools.

Audio-visual archive material and television

Subterranean prehistoric images are fragile and subject to natural erosion and those that have come down to us over thousands of years must be jealously protected and preserved. Unfortunately, this conservation is incompatible with mass tourism, with the result that increasingly severe ecological regulations have restricted access to the most famous sanctuaries. This trend can only increase: it has already affected Lascaux, Niaux in Ariège and Altamira in Cantabrian Spain.

The future will see the construction of more facsimiles open to the public and accompanied by an educational programme. The only example of this so far is Lascaux II, a faithful reproduction of the Rotunda and the Axial Gallery, situated near the cave.

However, cinematic records of the underground decorated sanctuaries represent a new approach which opens up many audio-visual perspectives. It is suited to scientific means of communication and popularization. Archive material in the form of a *corpus*, with images from each decorated cave, is not merely a means of protecting the art and a store of information for research, it is also a way of bringing the oldest artistic heritage of mankind to a worldwide public.

This cultural and educational perspective should be entrusted to film-makers and popularizers who specialize in filming subterranean prehistoric remains. Various countries could take it upon themselves to use the media of cinema and television to spread awareness of those parts of their artistic and archaeological heritage which are otherwise closed to the general public.

The *Corpus Lascaux* is the first such cinematic monograph of a Palaeolithic sanctuary, a unique document for the understanding of prehistoric civilizations.

APPENDICES

THE DISCOVERY OF LASCAUX

In the nineteenth century the hill of the small estate where the manor house of Lascaux stood was planted with vines. When these fell victim to the ravages of phylloxera they were grubbed up and replaced by pines, one of which fell down more than twenty years before the discovery of the cave, lifting up with its roots a large mass of earth and uncovering a narrow crack at the bottom of which was an opening like a fox-hole. Soon brambles had formed impenetrable undergrowth, but people remembered having seen the 'hole' before the 1914 war, and it was known to huntsmen and farmers who kept it blocked to prevent cattle falling down it.

The remarkable discovery of the most beautiful decorated prehistoric sanctuary was due to an adventurous group of youngsters. In fact, the explorers were looking for a hypothetical underground passage to the old manor house. On 8 September 1940, Marcel Ravidat, a strong young apprentice garage hand from Montignac, accompanied by three friends, went to look at a hole, to which he had been drawn by the barking of his dog, Robot, who had disappeared into it. To rescue his dog Ravidat cut a path with his knife through the brambles, helped by his friends Jean Clausel, Louis Périer and Maurice Queyroy. They found a dead donkey, and at the bottom of the hole was a narrow vertical shaft which they widened using the knife. They dropped stones and heard them fall far below underground. This was what they had been looking for and the youngsters decided to come back better equipped.

Four days later, on 12, then 13 September, the great expedition took place. This time there was a different team composed of Ravidat, who was seventeen, and his friend Jacques Marsal (fifteen), both from Montignac, and two young refugees (this was during the German occupation and Montignac was in the Free Zone), Jojo Agnel, from Nogent-sur-Seine, and Simon Coencas, aged sixteen and fifteen respectively. These four were about to make an amazing discovery.

The following is the full text of the report written by Ravidat, together with other extracts from documents of the time published by Brigitte and Gilles Delluc in the invaluable *Lascaux inconnu*.

M. Ravidat: '*Having no work for three or four days and tired of wandering the streets I took a walk in the woods. That was how I was reminded of a fairly deep hole that I had discovered with some friends and I decided to go and explore it. I made myself a very rustic but quite adequate lamp from an old oil pump and a few metres of string: this was not marvellous but I had to content myself with it. As I was going to the spot I ran into several school friends and invited them to come along for the adventure, since, like me, they were fascinated by it (as indeed were most of the young people of Montignac). When we arrived at the hole I rolled some large stones into it and was surprised at the time they took to reach the bottom and the loud noise produced by their fall. I set to work with my big knife (I had made this myself and it had a blade that had been tested) to widen the hole so that we could get into it. After an hour's difficult work I tried to penetrate into the interior, but without success because my shoulders were too broad. I began to work away again with a will and then tried another tactic: entering head first with my legs in the air, I managed to get 5 or 6 metres down. You cannot imagine the difficulty I had covering this short distance. At this point I lit my lamp and took a look round, but I had hardly gone a step when I lost my balance on a heap of clay debris and tumbled down to the bottom.*

'*I was bent double when I got up and relit my lamp, which I had had the presence of mind to hold on to. I made sure that the descent was not too dangerous and called my three companions, who had stayed up above, warning them to take great care. They came to where I was (Marsal, Agnel and Coencas) and once reunited we began to explore the cave; looking to the right and left we made slow progress because the lamp*

was not working properly. It was thus that we crossed a large hall 30 metres long, 12 metres wide and 10 metres high [98 × 39 × 32 ft]. There was nothing in our way and we entered a narrow, but fairly high, passage. It was there that we raised the lamp to the height of the walls and saw in its flickering light several lines in various colours. Intrigued by these coloured lines, we set about meticulously exploring the walls and, to our great surprise, discovered several fair-sized animal figures there. It was at this point that it occurred to us that we had discovered a cave with paintings. Encouraged by this success we began to go through the cave, moving from one discovery to the next. Our joy was indescribable. A band of savages doing a war dance could not have done better. There and then we made a promise to say nothing to anyone about our discovery for the time being and to come back the next day with stronger lamps.

'*The next day, armed with our essential equipment, we set off at ten-minute intervals, taking different routes, like a band of Indians covering their tracks. When we arrived at our "treasure" (that was the name we had given to our discovery) we set about improving the entrance and then headed once more into the unknown. As we moved from one wonderful find to the next we came to a vertical hole which we could not see to the bottom of. There we paused. Who would go down first?*'

[On this occasion, on 13 September, the four had been joined by Maurice Coencas, the brother of Simon.]

'*At the entrance to the shaft the ground-level was 1.50 metres [5 feet] higher than the present-day edge and was made up of a large tongue of earth which sloped steeply down to the nave (at about 45 degrees) . . . At the foot of the shaft the ground-level was 1.50 metres higher and there another tongue of earth sloped down steeply under fallen debris leading to chambers that were blocked with sand*' (Marsal 1965).

'*My friends were all afraid that they would not be able to get back up, because they had to climb up a smooth rope. That was not the reason why I hesitated: I had confidence in the strength of my own arms – but not in the strength of my companions, who would have to hold my weight of 70 kilograms [154 pounds] at arm's length, without any support. When I had made sure that the three would hold me, I began the descent, my heart beating, and soon arrived at the bottom. There I raised my head and saw that I had come down about ten metres [32 feet]. I quickly reassured my companions and set off on my adventure. I had only gone about 20 or 30 metres when I came up against a mass of fallen earth. So I turned back and inspected the walls. I was very surprised to see there was a human figure with the head of a bird and only four fingers, knocked down by a bison, forming a picture about 2 metres long (Laval archives). After having explored the smallest corners I climbed back up – not without difficulty – to the place where my friends were. When I told them about my strange discovery they all wanted to go down. I could not argue with them, but pointed out the difficulties in getting back up.*

'*I was confident I was strong enough and they went down one by one into this shaft – but getting back up again was another story: I had to haul them up one after another at arm's length and without being sure of my balance. When I had finally managed to get them all up, it was with rather pale faces that they told me of the effect the unexpected painting had had on them.*

'*We were agreed about what had to be done about our discovery, and put all our trust in our old schoolmaster, Monsieur Laval*' (Laval 1954).

The following extracts describe what happened on the days that followed:

14 September. J. Marsal: '[*Visit to the cave by*] *the first five plus another four boys from Montignac*' (Marsal 1965).

16 September. J. Marsal: '*Since our discovery was attracting most of the children in the region, we decided to inform M. Laval (our old schoolmaster who was interested in archaeology); he was away that day, so he was only informed on the*

following day. Like a trail of gunpowder the rumour of our discovery had spread through the region' (Marsal 1965).

L. Laval: '*Young Marsal came to tell me about it . . . I did not immediately believe the importance of this find and wondered whether it might not be a series of natural marks in the rock such as occur frequently in the region. To make sure I asked one of my former pupils, Georges Estréguil, to do me some basic drawings of what could be seen in the cave. These simple sketches brought home to me the fact that these figurations really were prehistoric*' (Laval 1954).

J. Bouyssonie: '*The Abbé Breuil, in danger of being arrested by the occupying forces in Paris, had sought refuge at Brive at the house of his friends the Abbés Bouyssonie, at the Ecole Bossuet*' (Roussot 1966).

17 September. J. Marsal: '*Georges Estréguil, aged nineteen, made several sketches of paintings which he showed to M. Laval, who had not really believed in the importance of our discovery*' (Marsal 1965).

Abbé H. Breuil: '*Thaon telephones me at Brive from Montignac to tell me of the discovery of the painted cave at Lascaux*' (Breuil 1960).

J. Marsal: '*After a day's work we had widened the hole enough to allow a man to pass. But our teacher was no longer very young and did not go down. After a few days, however, everyone all over the town was talking of nothing but the cave, so the entrance was widened so that anybody could enter*' (Laval archives).

J. Marsal: '*After clearing the entrance and cutting a few rough steps in the earth, M. Laval went down for the first time, accompanied by most of the youngsters of the area and a few curiosity-seekers*' (Marsal 1965).

L. Laval '*In my turn I leaned over the brambly opening, which was about a metre wide, and began the descent. My face, scratched by the brambles, was bleeding. I noticed this when I passed my hand over the face and moved back. A peasant woman from the region was there near the hole and said: "Well now, I'll go down and have a look!" In order not to seem more cowardly than a woman (so much for man's courage!) I slid along as best I could behind her. After the vertical descent I had to crawl between the clay earth and stalactites which gave me an unpleasant tickling sensation. Once I arrived in the great hall accompanied by my young heroes, I uttered cries of admiration at the magnificent sight that met my eyes . . . Thus I visited all the galleries, and remained just as enthusiastic when confronted with the unexpected revelations, which increased as I advanced. I had literally gone mad*' (Laval 1954).

Abbé A. Glory: '*The Syndicat d'Initiative is active. The cave had only been known for three days before its president had a sign put up pointing to the way out of the town, which read: Grotte de Lascaux, 2 kilometres*' (Glory 1944, p. 94).

After the discovery of the cave there was a period of naïvety. Everyone came as individual tourists to marvel, sometimes bringing their own candles, but the visits were difficult and muddy. Acetylene lamps were not very effective for lighting the large ensembles of paintings on the cave walls and calcium carbide was hard to find, even on the black market. This was the time of the German occupation: there were few cars because

petrol was scarce, and vehicles were run on gas. Furthermore, there was no road suitable for vehicles leading to the cave, so one had to climb up on foot. But the stir caused by the discovery and the public's fascination with the art of the early Magdalenians – miraculously preserved and looking as fresh as if it had been executed yesterday – were such that people went there in spite of the difficulties, and went back again. Marsal and Ravidat acted as guides and spent most of their time underground orchestrating the unending passage of visitors.

It did not occur to anyone that in the long run the cave would have to be closed. Quite the reverse – more and more alterations were made to facilitate visits. After the war, things were to get worse with the beginnings of international tourism.

In conjunction with the alteration works for tourists in the decade after the war, archaeological excavations were conducted at various times by, among others, the Abbé Breuil and later the Abbé Glory, who took on an enormous task. He made archaeological sections and also, working by night with the help of assistants, he filled 141 square yards of paper with tracings which form an invaluable corpus of the prehistoric engravings in the cave.

The abbé was surrounded with young people, friends, amateur and unpaid excavators. I am delighted to include here an unpublished text by one of these. Marc Gazay, the head of the animation service of the Red Cross after the war, was a friend and companion of the Abbé Glory who assisted the abbé during those long nights working underground, and I asked him if he would recount some of his memories of those times. He was witness to one of the most famous discoveries at Lascaux: that of the oldest known rope in the world.

The Abbé Glory in the Apse. The Magdalenian scaffolding would have been at about the same height. (Photo J. Lagrange)

The Tracings and the Rope

In those days, when I was young, I was fascinated with prehistory. Because I happened to be geographically nearby, I had come into contact with the Abbé Glory, who was then teaching at the Collège Saint-Etienne at Strasbourg. I had even had the opportunity to get him, on two occasions, I believe, to give a lecture on speleology, prehistory, of course, and in particular the decorated caves in the Ardèche valley, Chabot and Figuier, in which he was working at that time.

One day in July 1949 or 1950 he told me he was going to go to the Dordogne for a few days, where he had been asked, under the exalted direction of the Abbé Breuil, to make a record on tracing paper of the countless engravings that the Magdalenians had made on the walls and ceilings of the galleries in the cave at Lascaux. While the worldwide fame of the paintings of Lascaux was firmly established, the engravings were still practically unknown. He asked me if I would accompany him.

The task that was assigned to me and to another chance companion (a Parisian who was to become a dental surgeon) might seem rather tedious. We were in the middle of the tourist season when hundreds upon hundreds of people poured in through the heavy bronze door. For this reason it was decided that our work should be done by night, usually between 9 p.m. and 2 a.m., so that we should not be disturbed and could erect our scaffolding and set up our ladders wherever necessary.

I shall always remember those extraordinary nights of work and I can still see myself entering the sanctuary for the first time, moving slowly forward, filled with emotion and wonder by the paintings of animals on the walls. Fortunately, the heavy atmosphere left behind by the many daytime visitors was occasionally stirred by a faint draught of fresh air.

We were soon initiated by the abbé into our new role and I very quickly realized what we were to expect. It would be our job to hold the large sheets of tracing paper on which he traced in charcoal, evening after evening, the lines which could be seen on the walls by the oblique beams of our lamps. For my part, at the beginning at least, I could distinguish nothing more than an unimaginable tangle of lines intersecting each other in all directions. One night the Abbé Breuil himself gave us a magisterial lesson in reading, or rather deciphering, these in the horizontal light from our lamps, following with his finger the outline of wonderful little horses which we would have been incapable of detecting by ourselves. The walls and ceilings of the galleries were populated with hundreds of horses, finely engraved in the rock with flint.

As the work progressed we would move the scaffolding with its raised platforms of planks, which allowed us to work on our backs with our arms in the air holding the tracing paper, while the abbé went on with the copying of all the existing lines. It was only afterwards that he proceeded to read them systematically.

It will be appreciated that in such a position we needed frequent breaks, as the arms of all three or four of us were liable to ache. However, my memory of this is very far from all bad – thanks to the abbé's radio receiver, our efforts were sustained by divine music: what a delight it was to listen to Mozart at Lascaux in the peace of the night!

Around midnight we could allow ourselves a good few minutes' rest. Depending on the day, our little group would go to enjoy their cigarettes or pipes at the entrance to the cave in the fresh air beneath the starry sky, or else I would make use of a remarkable privilege, which I was probably the only person to take advantage of. I would go down the rope ladder, my lamp in my hand, and into the famous Shaft of Lascaux. When I got to the bottom and had sat down on the clay floor, letting my light rest gently on the rhinoceros, the 'sorcerer' and his dart, I would light there the most delicious of pipes and, as one can easily imagine, my thoughts would go back over thousands of years. What extraordinary times I passed in front of that scene, now so famous in the world of prehistory!

It was when we were moving the scaffolding on one occasion that I, together with my companions, witnessed and was responsible for an important discovery: the finding of a fragment of Magdalenian rope made of vegetable fibre – the oldest in the world – miraculously preserved in its coating of clay. Because of a false move one of the feet of

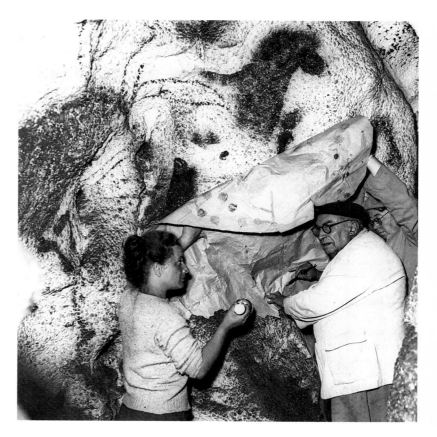

Above: the imprint of the oldest rope in the world, found in the Chamber of the Felines. (Photo A. Glory – Coll. Archives IPH) *Right*: the Abbé Breuil making a tracing at the end of the Axial Gallery, the Falling Horse. (Photo Windels – Musée de l'Homme, Paris/Photoeb.)

the scaffolding knocked against the little bank of clay which ran along the gallery leading to the Shaft from the Chamber of the Felines. The pieces of clay contained the rope. I can still see the Abbé Glory's delight. The rest of us were sceptical; we found it hard to believe!

Marc Gazay

Brigitte and Gilles Delluc recall that at the time of the archaeological excavations 'up to two thousand tourists were counted every day . . .' This sort of tourism was fatal since the enormous accumulation of carbon dioxide emitted by the visitors filled the cave and the temperature more than doubled because of the heat of their bodies. Water vapour condensed and ran down the walls, and the air was evacuated only very slowly: sometimes tourists fainted because they were unable to stand the tainted atmosphere.

In 1958 a complex machine was installed to change the air in the cave and allow the visitors to breathe. The air was taken from the outside, dehydrated and forced into the cave through channels buried in the floor, which was thus dug up, making any further careful archaeological excavation impossible. 'At the very most the Abbé Glory was permitted to be present at the building work to glean any objects thrown up by the shovels or the pneumatic drills, without delaying the men at work. The only place where he conducted a normal excavation was at the bottom of the Shaft.'

It had not been realized that the visitors' feet were bringing in pollen and algae which were then spread everywhere; the new machine gave them air and scattered them into the furthest corners of the cave. This was the so-called 'green leprosy': whole colonies of algae, nourished by diatoms, proliferated on the walls and spread from the entrance of the Rotunda. Ravidat first noticed them on the little red horse which precedes the Unicorn to the right as one enters. He went away on holiday and when he returned the famous Falling Horse at the back of the Axial Gallery was disappearing 'in a prairie' of greenish algae. The micro-organisms were proliferating and ravaging the paintings.

The Green Disease and the White Disease

Marcel Ravidat had thus indicated 'the first attacks of the green disease'. This proliferation of vegetable and animal micro-organisms was to lead to the closure of the cave in April 1963. Antibiotics and diluted formalin soon put a stop to the problem. However, an examination of the decorated surfaces revealed a more insidious 'white disease' threatening the long-term future of the art on the cave walls. This was the development of opaque crystals of calcite encouraged by the increase in the levels of carbon dioxide, humidity and temperature caused by the

presence of visitors. It was therefore advisable to maintain these at a safe level and, after long and costly years of research, it was decided to return the cave to its previous condition: it was closed to the public, slow air currents were reintroduced, a low temperature was maintained to avoid condensation, carbon dioxide was pumped out of the Shaft and it was protected against seepage of water. Although it is perhaps too soon to judge, these measures seem to be effective.

THE REPLICA OF LASCAUX

At the same time the creation of a replica of this remarkable decorated cave was envisaged. In the early 1960s the animal paintings on the famous ceiling of the cave of Altamira in Spain had been reproduced full size on a modelled background copied from the contours measured *in situ* by means of stereophotogrammetry (the Archaeological Museum in Madrid and the Deutsches Museum in Munich). At Lascaux the Institut National Géographique (IGN) had used the same method to take measurements of the whole cave down to the nearest millimetre. A reconstruction of the Hall of the Bulls based partly on these measurements was exhibited at the Grand-Palais in Paris in 1980, but its decoration was created by transposing photographs from film (rather in the manner of transfers) on to the polyester resin support made according to the records of the IGN. This facsimile is on exhibition at the Musée des Antiquités Nationales at Saint-Germain-en-Laye. Lascaux II is a much more ambitious project. Work on it began in 1972–5 but was interrupted for several years until it was taken up again in March 1980 by the authorities of the department of the Dordogne (the owners of the facsimile since 1978). It was to be completed (under the direction of Daniel Debaye) by the departmental office of tourism. The new cave is situated in an enormous concrete blockhouse which is now buried in a disused open quarry on the hill at Lascaux about 200 yards from the original cave. The two parts of the cave reproduced are the Hall of the Bulls and the Axial Gallery. They represent more than a third (35 metres) of the total extent of the cave, and include the greater part of the paintings at Lascaux.

The walls of this tunnel are constructed of a metal framework composed of profiles that reproduce, on a slightly larger scale, the cross-sections of the cave as calculated by the IGN. On the inner face of this skeleton a coating is applied consisting of three layers of galvanized fine wire mesh. This framework is sandwiched between two layers of projecting concrete, forming a structure resting on breezeblock supports. For even greater security, in the Hall of the Bulls it is suspended from a structure of steel girders.

The outer layer of the walls of the gallery thus constructed has been modelled by the addition of a special mortar. In the Axial Gallery the accuracy of the reproduction has been achieved by measurements taken directly in the original cave and transferred manually to the facsimile. In the Hall of the Bulls, which is much larger, it was achieved by using a machine invented by Renaud Sanson. This made it possible to locate in space some 2,500 important points chosen by the sculptors (about ten artists working in teams of three or four) and calculated by the IGN, using stereoscopic photographs as memory aids. Thus, even before the paintings were added to this structure, Lascaux II was already a remarkable work of modelled concrete (about 500 tons of it), reproducing the smallest details in the relief of the original to within a few inches.

The work of the painter, Monique Peytral, was based on constant reference to the original. The many drawings in relief of the walls and frescoes were compared with projections of slides and with relief photographs. To begin with she was concerned with the reproduction of the various tints of the rock surfaces and – working in conjunction with the modellers – with recreating the grain of the rock (microreliefs and areas covered with calcite or clay). Then, of course, she had to reproduce as faithfully as possible the figures of animals and the signs. The colours used were natural pigments: iron oxides (yellow and red ochres) and manganese oxides (especially the dioxide MnO_2, which is very black). Some of the unpurified mineral pigments came from the cave itself, while a large number of the purified ones came from nearby sites. The dark reds, for example, were obtained from a fine burnt clay from Thiviers. The pigments were applied in various ways: by throwing clay mixed with water in increasing intensity for the coloured areas, by applying pigments by finger for lines, in a spray of resinated water, and by pulverization of coloured powder. The ledges and the ceiling of the Hall of the Bulls were treated in a different manner (the concrete itself was coloured and a 'patina of age' was added). With the exception of the Frieze of the Stags, the painted figures in the Nave and Shaft, and a few fragmentary figures in the other galleries, all the paintings of Lascaux are reproduced. It is not feasible – in the short term, at least – to attempt to reproduce the five hundred or so engravings in the cave. They are so finely incised and so entangled that they are often barely visible even to an experienced and patient viewer. Besides the frescoes of the galleries so far copied (the Hall of the Bulls and the Axial Gallery), Lascaux II – Le Thot also includes the paintings of the Shaft and the Crossed Bison. No doubt within quite a short time these will be joined by a reproduction of the Frieze of the Stags and the Nave to complete the group. All the paintings of Lascaux will then be visible in facsimile. Today's visitor to Lascaux II is thus presented with practically everything that used to be admired at Lascaux itself. Three hundred thousand people each year have visited the facsimile since it opened in 1984. Better still, there is an information display in the entrance lobby to the new concrete cave preparing the visitors for viewing the frescoes and explaining to them about how the creation of a facsimile was justified by the deterioration of the cave. They are also given information about the circumstances of the discovery, the various features that have made it possible to reconstruct the life and actions of the artists, and the archaeological material used to understand and date Lascaux. As some enthusiasts have said, it is 'as if Lascaux had just reopened'.

Brigitte and Gilles Delluc

THE PIGMENTS AND THE ART OF PAINTING

In order to draw and colour in the many polychrome figures at Lascaux, and later at Font-de-Gaume and Altamira, Palaeolithic artists had to research and experiment with all sorts of raw materials, make implements and even, in some cases, use a kind of chemistry. The art of getting together the necessary equipment to 'create art' was not acquired in a single day, and there must have been very many pictorial images handed down from generation to generation and from tribe to tribe using media other than the cave walls of the sanctuaries.

All we know is that hunting peoples, such as the Australian Aborigines – who are the inheritors of techniques several thousand years old and who have maintained an impressive continuity in images on rock from prehistoric times until our own day – also paint on other objects and on eucalyptus bark, and in a ritual context reproduce themes from their mythology on their own bodies. Unfortunately, nothing at all survives from prehistoric times of such works of art executed on wood bark or skins.

Most of the Palaeolithic images that have come down to us on cave walls or mobiliary art – a tiny proportion of what must have existed in daily life – reveal not only a great 'sureness in execution', which is the result of an apprenticeship, but also the use of precise techniques relying on more or less elaborate implements which were then in general use but which have almost all disappeared. The practice of body-painting among the Magdalenians is only an assumption, although it is almost certain if one considers the amount of pigments found in the habitation levels and the encampments. Did they also paint on the skins or coverings of the tents? Or on cliffs exposed to the weather where the figures have not been preserved? We can easily imagine that in their time there would have been whole open-air cliffs in Western Europe, decorated with thousands of figures which have not survived the rain and the glacial winds, unlike the paintings that have been preserved in the dry climate of the Australian deserts.

Where did the Magdalenian artists learn to paint with such a disconcerting sureness of line? There is no answer to such puzzling questions.

Large quantities of paint, prepared in advance, were used to decorate among others the sanctuary of Lascaux, without taking into account the wastage inevitable in any pictorial work. To gather the pigments in their natural state in sufficient quantities, the Palaeolithic hunters had to seek out deposits containing colouring matter in natural quarries and outcrops situated sometimes nearly 25 miles from the cave. It is also possible that some pigments were to be found in deposits nearer the sanctuary which have now been buried without trace. The pigments were collected in their natural state and so to obtain pure colours they had to be washed, concentrated and have impurities removed. The reserves of colouring matter brought back from collecting excursions in skin pouches holding about 20 pounds were taken to the cave, to be stored and then prepared. This probably took place outside, to avoid unnecessary wastage of lamps.

The pigments found at Lascaux are the subject of a remarkable study by Claude Couraud and A. Laming-Emperaire, published in *Lascaux inconnu*. They consisted principally of a wide range of iron oxides: ochres, haematite, oligist, iron peroxide (blood-red), black and grey magnetite. As well as these there were also the silicates associated with iron silicate: limonite, iron hydroxide (yellow), xanthosiderite (yellow or red), turgite (brown), goethite (dark brown, orange or red), lepidocrocite (red), aetite, stilpnosiderite (brown yellow and dark brown). The list also includes ochre, glauconite (yellow), laterite (bright red or red-brown), raw sienna and raw umber. This collection of 'ochres' is resistant to heat and light, and covers well.

An historic visit in 1940 by the light of acetylene lamps. In the middle, with arms outstretched, are the old Count Bégouën and the Abbé Breuil; seated, Jacques Marsal and Marcel Ravidat. (Photo M. Larivière – Laval archives)

Another group of colours (manganese) provides the blacks (hausmanite, manganite, braunite, polianite). Lastly comes black ochre or 'black earth', which is rich in manganese dioxide and graphite.

Prehistoric Chemistry. By heating iron oxides it is possible to change their original colour. It seems that prehistoric people used this method from the Châtelperronian onwards (36,000 to 32,000 years ago). When André Leroi-Gourhan was digging in the Cave of the Reindeer at Arcy-sur-Cure (Yonne), he found in the hearths small plaques of ochre at various stages of oxidization (delicate red and yellow). It is possible that, as Claude Couraud notes, this method of changing the colours was used at Lascaux. As the temperature is raised by hundreds of degrees to 1,000°C. (1,832°F.) the ochre gradually darkens and changes from yellow to yellow-brown, then to red, to red-purple and finally, at about 1,000°C., from red to black (experiment by Bauchonnet, 1911). When raw sienna is heated it becomes burnt sienna and raw umber burnt umber.

Hypotheses. We do not have nearly enough archaeological evidence to be able to explain the technique of painting: how the artists and their assistants organized their work as they stood on scaffolding in the light of their lamps before the virgin whiteness of the calcite wall surface at Lascaux. They would have shaped and made every piece of their artistic

equipment in advance, as they had seen the artists before them doing, and the creation of beautiful wall compositions depended on the care taken over their implements. Of this equipment only the objects made of hard materials have survived: grinders, palettes and mortars or natural stones used to prepare the powdered colours, and an oyster shell covered with paint. The rest has vanished.

There is no doubt that the coloured emulsions were prepared in receptacles made of wood, bark or thick leather, with the help of spatulas and wooden sticks, after the pigments had been ground down and washed. The artist must have tried out all sorts of mixtures before obtaining the desired tints, which were achieved in some instances by heating ochres.

Experiments. The researchers in *Lascaux inconnu* carried out a range of experiments in an attempt to obtain results close to those of the Palaeolithic artists. These led to a number of observations.

The first is important: the quality of the whitish calcite that covers the rock is remarkable, although in some places in the cave it has a lumpy 'cauliflower' texture. The absorbency of the calcite allowed the surface to be well impregnated and thus fixed the colour perfectly. Also the constant humidity of the atmosphere, the darkness and the regularity of the oscillations in temperature meant that this cave was by nature exceptionally well regulated for the preservation of an almost miraculous freshness in the ancient paintings.

Binding Agents. All sorts of binding agents were tried out: blood, glue, fat, bone marrow and water mixed with natural pigments. They all presented problems and could not have lasted for long. The researchers concluded that the only perfect binding agent was quite simply the water in the cave, which is rich in salts of dissolved calcium that 'fix the pigments in the crystalline mass and form a very hard coloured calcite'. Urine and saliva, effective binding agents frequently used by rock artists, notably in Australia, do not seem to have been tried in the experiments, but this does not exclude the probability that Palaeolithic artists used them.

Prehistorians used to believe that paint was applied by blowing through tubes or hollow bones, but this method has been shown to be inaccurate and messy. It leaves dribbles of paint on the wall that are difficult to remove.

The painting methods of the Magdalenians can be described thus. First, they made use of large and small brushes of various shapes and thicknesses, made of animal hair, vegetable stems (tied together or chewed), badger, sable, fox or human hair (as is the case among some hunting peoples), feathers, and other materials found in nature. They used glues and mastics that were strong enough to fix flint to handles, so it is unlikely that the sticking of tufts of hair to the end of a wooden stick would have presented them with any difficulty.

Many 'crayons' of dense or compressed colouring matter have been found at Lascaux and in other caves, and bear traces of wear. They were probably used for drawing the outlines, which the artist would then go over with a wet brush.

The many spongings or dabbings used to fill in the figures form dots and even complete outlines, as with the ibexes in the Axial Gallery. But what exactly was the technique used? Experiments have been done with balls of fur impregnated with colour but these soon become soft.

My own theory, based on personal experience, seems to me the most convincing: these 'sponging' effects can easily be obtained by using a relatively fine skin, from a fallow deer or a chamois, for instance. A 'sponge' is then made by forming a ball of thick fairly short animal hair mixed with vegetable fibre and combined with coloured paste the consistency of toothpaste. This ball, which has a certain elasticity, is wrapped in the piece of skin which is held together at the back and can be twisted in the hand. The front part of the ball is pierced with small holes like those in the rose of a watering-can so that if the skin is squeezed by twisting, the semi-liquid coloured paste oozes through the little holes, facilitating the series of 'spongings'. When the paint inside is used up, the skin is unfolded and the 'sponge' of hair and fibres is soaked once more in the paint receptacle. It is also easy to moisten the outside of the ball once it has been filled, as one would a brush, so obtaining a more or less liquid emulsion.

André Leroi-Gourhan has brilliantly demonstrated that the Magdalenians used 'marks' or 'stencils' cut from skin or bark, without which it would be impossible to trace such precise lines on the lumpy rock as are found in the necks of some animals in the Axial Gallery (the Cow with the Collar, the Great Black Aurochs, the Flying Horse, etc.).

The Magdalenians thus used tempera techniques, with brushes and water-based paints, similar to those practised today. The absence or rarity of dribbles, spots or smudges around the figures shows a care for neatness and suggests that 'rags' were used to wipe away imperfections.

Who drew the figures? Who was the master in charge of the work? These questions can only be answered hypothetically. At the very most

one would imagine that a person who could commune with impunity with the spirits of the deified animals and make them emerge out of the rock was not simply an initiate or an adolescent in the process of becoming one. He was certainly a man invested with a great deal of religious authority, who knew perfectly the myths and the bonds linking the living and spiritual forces that governed life. Perhaps there were steps that the initiates had to pass through. Could the people who went to paint and engrave in the narrow galleries and inaccessible parts of the cave have been going through such a phase in their initiation? Were they being subjected to an ordeal?

Karel Kupka, in his study of the Australian Aborigines, noted that the right to 'the possession of colours' is not given to everybody, and that the precious material, which can be converted into cash and does not lose its value, is placed under the surveillance of the 'ancients'. He also observed that as they created their art the people sang and recited passages from their oral literature about the story of the characters and animals that were being depicted, rather as if these were being called as witnesses.

Many thousands of years separate us from the artistic flowering of the Early Magdalenian, but there is nothing to prevent us imagining that during the initiation rites and the creation of the art the cave would have echoed to laughter and stories that are now lost for ever.

The Archaeology of the Pigments

(by Annette Laming-Emperaire and Claude Couraud, from *Lascaux inconnu*.)

The mineral pigments collected by the Abbé Glory in the various excavations at Lascaux comprise 158 fragments and about 20 tubes containing coloured powder. Some of the locations of the pigments show a correspondence between the colour of the paintings and the raw material found. Thus Glory notes an 'abundance of haematite and an absence of manganese dioxide at the back of the Axial Gallery, which is covered with red figures, but a profusion of manganese in the Nave and the beginning of the Passageway below the black paintings . . .'. The many pigments found include: at the entrance 'a small plaque of iron peroxide'; at the bottom of the Shaft the 'crayon' of figure 118 found in 1959; and 'thick streaks of manganese powder localized at the foot of the rock painting with two minerals of manganese dioxide the size of a hazelnut . . .'. In the last yard of the excavations in 1961 in the Shaft, Glory again collected manganese powder, 'two nuggets of red ochre' and a small plaque containing this same material in its cup (Glory, unpublished manuscript report).

The end of the Axial Gallery produced black, red, pink, brown and yellow material; the Chamber of the Felines contained red, white and pink pigments and, at the far end of the gallery, 'manganese in a powdered state, a nugget of mineralized manganese and a piece of yellow ochre the size of an orange' (these last were found in a 'hiding place 25 to 30 centimetres [10–12 inches] deep and 15 to 20 centimetres [6–8 inches] wide . . .' (Glory, unpublished report, 1953, and Laming 1964, pp. 110–13). Below the panel with the horses in the chamber of the same name, Glory collected some powdered red ochre, besides palettes coloured with red or black paint (Glory, unpublished report, 1953, and Laming 1964, pp. 110–13). Lastly, in the 'chasm' separating the two chambers, charcoal, red ochre and a palette with traces of that colour were discovered (Glory, unpublished manuscript report).

Many of these minerals were near 'palettes', lamps and flint blades, on which there was much paint. Unfortunately only seven of the collection of 158 fragments, and two of the tubes of powder, have their precise locations recorded. They are: one block of black (no. 15), six blocks of red (nos 3, 8, 9, 10, 20, 22), one tube of yellow and one of black powder.

We have divided the pigments into four large colour categories, with their various nuances classified from the darkest to the lightest, using Cailleux and Taylor's code.

Blacks	Number
black	7
J 10, very dark grey	3
J 90, very dark grey	8
H 90, very dark grey	25
H 10, dark grey	61
F 81, dark grey (clay mixed with black)	1
H 82, olive grey	powder
	105 blocks

Reds	
H 21, dark red-brown	1
F 18, red	1
F 22, faint red	5
F 12, faint red	7
E 12, faint red	4
E 14, faint red	1
D 12, pale red	2
D 16, pale red	1
D 46, yellow-red	1
C 48, yellow-red	1
	24 blocks

Yellows	
E 68, bright brown	1
D 63, brown-yellow + 1 tube of powder	3
D 56, yellow-red	8
D 66, yellow-brown	4
D 68, yellow-brown	2
C 66, yellow	1
B 82, pale yellow	4
A 82, pale yellow	3
	26 blocks

White	
A 90, white	3 blocks

CHRONOLOGY AND THE ANALYSIS OF STYLES

(The problem of the chronology of the works, their relationship to the various civilizations which overlapped or succeeded one another, as revealed by archaeological evidence and stylistic evolution, has been the subject of a magisterial survey by André Leroi-Gourhan, which was mentioned briefly in the chapter on Magdalenian Civilization (see p. 16). I have asked Brigitte and Gilles Delluc, who worked with Leroi-Gourhan for many years and who have much experience in the field, to describe this analysis in greater detail.)

In some instances the works on the cave walls have been covered by well-dated archaeological layers: they are therefore earlier than these layers or approximately the same age as them. Hence the engravings in the cave at Pair-non-Pair (Gironde) are attributed to people at the beginning of the Upper Palaeolithic (Gravettians or Aurignacians), while the bas-reliefs at Isturitz (Pyrénées-Atlantiques) seem to date from after the Solutrean and those of Le Roc aux Sorciers at Angles-sur-l'Anglin are clearly dated to the Magdalenian.

Sometimes the chronological connection between the works of art and the archaeological remains is less clear. Archaic-looking art sometimes co-exists in a cave with objects which date back to the beginning of the Upper Palaeolithic, proving that the site was occupied at that time – and it is probably the same age as them. Thus the caves of Bernous and La Croze at Gontran (Dordogne) were perhaps decorated in the Aurignacian, Gargas (Hautes-Pyrénées) in the Gravettian, Chabot and Figuier (Ardèche) in the Lower Solutrean. Similarly, the Magdalenian hunters who occupied the shelter of Cap-Blanc or the cave entrance of Comarque (Dordogne) were very probably the creators of the bas-reliefs in the one and the engravings in the other.

In some very exceptional cases the art on the cave walls and the archaeology of the cave floor can be linked more closely. At the cave of La Tête du Lion (Ardèche) traces of pigment, similar to that used in the wall paintings, were discovered in a layer precisely dated by carbon 14: like this layer, the paintings must date back to the Lower Solutrean.

At Lascaux the works on the cave walls have great stylistic unity, and the archaeological layer is unique in that it has no different superimposed layers. But were the people who owned the objects found in the ground the artists and engravers who decorated the walls? There are two reasons why we can be sure of this: the layer which contains the many elements that make it possible to date the human presence to the Early Magdalenian (particular shapes of flints and spears, pollen, wood and wood charcoal) also contains many pigments (powders and crayons) and objects (lamp and spears) which have the same, highly original, signs that are painted or engraved on the walls of the cave. It follows that the works on the walls and the archaeological remains are indeed contemporary; they are both 17,000 years old. Such precision in the dating of a decorated cave – and the most beautiful and complete of all such caves – is almost miraculous.

Apart from a few cases, usually related to habitation sites or small decorated caves from the beginning of the Upper Palaeolithic, the great majority of the works of cave art, particularly in the deep sanctuaries, are 'orphans': they have no archaeological context and are therefore impossible to date in any definitive way. Since at the present time there is no physical method of determining, for example, the date when the pigments were prepared or the age of the calcite that sometimes covers the works of art, the dating of these difficult examples – *and they form the majority* – is based only on stylistic arguments, that is, on the comparison of these works with other works (on walls or mobiliary art) which can be archaeologically dated. So it is with some regret that one abandons the rigorous discipline of archaeology for the more nebulous field of art history.

What style?

Some twenty-five years ago André Leroi-Gourhan proposed the 'elements of a chronology of style' in Palaeolithic cave art. His classification rapidly rendered obsolete the Abbé Breuil's chronology (in two successive cycles: Aurignaco-Gravettian and Solutreo-Magdalenian) and moved the dates of most of the decorated caves forward. Moreover, the decoration of each of them appeared more homogeneous, composed (with some exceptions) of figures and signs in the same style, not a sort of chronological patchwork.

Leroi-Gourhan's analysis, like the Abbé Breuil's, took into account the perspective of the legs, horns and antlers, as well as the animal silhouette itself (the cervico-dorsal line, endographic or peripheral details, animation or immobility). Geometric signs, classified into three categories (linear, enclosed and rows of dots), were referred to for corroboration, some of these enigmatic patterns being 'ethnic markers' found only in a particular region and/or period (tectiform, claviform, rectangular signs, etc.).

Style I (Aurignacian, about 30,000 years ago) corresponds with the awkward, abbreviated representations of animals in the deposits close to Les Eyzies, often with images of genitals, especially female, and signs (series of cup-shapes or short strokes).

Style II (Gravettian and Early Solutrean, 25,000–20,000 years ago) is the style of the shelters and small caves decorated with animal figures with a very sinuous cervico-dorsal line; the extremities are not depicted and the execution is very summary though the species are still recognizable. There is no animation, the drawing is rigid and the perspective very artificial (shelter of Labattut in the Dordogne, caves of Pair-non-Pair and Gargas).

Style III (Later Solutrean and Early Magdalenian, 20,000–15,000 years ago) shows complete artistic mastery. The animals often still have sinuous dorsal lines, enormous, pseudo-pregnant bodies, small heads, and short, lively legs (caves of Lascaux, Villars and Gabillou, deposits at Le Fourneau du Diable and Roc de Sers). There is often animation, of the whole body or part of it, but the perspective is still very artificial. There are numerous, very polymorphous signs.

Style IV (Middle and Upper Magdalenian, 15,000–10,000 years ago) evolves towards an increasingly elaborate realism, which is almost photographic, with a great richness of detail, animation and very natural perspective. The animals' coats and the modelling of their forms, in particular, are handled with much care. Most of the decorated caves in France and Spain were decorated at this period (Altamira in Spain, Font-de-Gaume, Les Combarelles, Rouffignac and Teyjat in the Dordogne, Niaux and Les Trois Frères in Ariège). In Western Europe, at least, cave art ceased at the end of this very figurative phase.

This classification was fairly soon adopted by everyone. Our recent work on the Aurignacian and Gravettian work in Aquitaine, J. Combier's on the caves of the Lower Solutrean in Ardèche, D. Vialou's on the Magdalenian sanctuaries of Ariège, the current researches of M. Lorblanchet in Lot and those of Spanish prehistorians have added refinements to the chronology. There is little distinction between Styles I and II. The transition from Style II to Style III was probably very gradual and difficult to place in time.

It is not always easy to compare one decorated cave with another. No doubt in the two hundred centuries which saw the beginnings, development and disappearance of cave art, there were important changes in the motivations of those who – for want of a better term – we call the 'artists', as well as in the meaning of the art which in some places decorates a habitation site open to all, and in others a sanctuary hidden

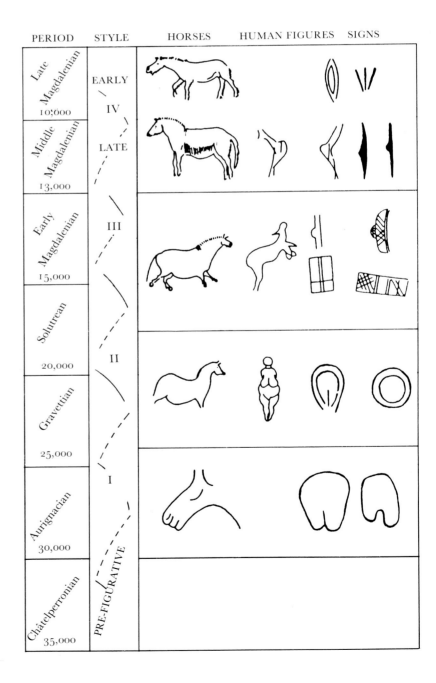

Chronological table of the periods and styles of the Upper Palaeolithic (after André Leroi-Gourhan). The figures in grey indicate the place of Lascaux in this chronology.

deep under ground. Perhaps it is appropriate in a book about Lascaux to propose a division of the art in shelters and caves into three stages: before Lascaux (apprenticeship); at the time of Lascaux (period of originality); and after Lascaux (academicism). It has probably tended to be forgotten that André Leroi-Gourhan's classification is stylistic rather than chronological. The correspondence between styles and chronology cannot be rigorously laid down – does a Tudor-style piece of furniture always date from the Tudor period?

A few examples will confirm this. The animal figures roughly engraved on the granular rock in the first chamber of the cave of La Mouthe and in the cave of La Sudrie (Dordogne) are fairly late (if one looks at the perspective) – perhaps Magdalenian – despite their archaic technical features, because the nature of the rock is not at all favourable, and besides, not all prehistoric artists were geniuses. The animals rather awkwardly incised on the chalky limestone bristling with flints in the cave of Bara Bahau (Dordogne) were for long believed to be Aurignacian or Gravettian, but a closer study of the details and the signs associated with them shows that they are probably much later and date from the Magdalenian. A small, finely grained limestone pebble found at the shelter at Labattut, delicately incised with the figure of a finely detailed horse, and a large block of rough local limestone bearing the vigorously engraved figure of another horse in a very archaic style, both come from the same Gravettian level.

This brings us back to the fact that archaeological methods can in some instances provide us with a very firm basis for dating, whereas stylistic analysis (usually the only possible) is much more approximate. A reasonably reliable approach to chronology requires not just a few features or the statement of an 'expert', but the combination of a number of consistent arguments.

BRIGITTE AND GILLES DELLUC

CHRONOLOGY OF THE PALAEOLITHIC

Around 34,000 BC Neanderthal man gave way to the first modern human, as represented by Cro-Magnon man, a sturdy hunter of proud appearance with a high forehead. The 25,000 years of Cro-Magnon man's existence saw the development of the great civilizations of the Upper Palaeolithic from the Atlantic to the Urals and from the Baltic to the Mediterranean: the Aurignacian, Gravettian, Solutrean, Magdalenian, Epigravettian, Azilian, etc. New discoveries and inventions enriched mankind's cultural inheritance: the speed of laminar stone-working (which reached its apogee with the magnificent foliate points of the Solutrean, c. 18,000 BC), the first appearance of tools made of bone (awls, spears, spear-throwers, harpoons), the earliest use of elements of body ornament (perforated teeth and shells), the intensive use of red ochre in habitation sites and in burials, developments in the treatment of animal skin and the invention of the needle. The people of those times knew how to make proper garments (as in the burials at Sungir). At the same time there were developments in the field of fishing, and daring navigators ventured forth in their flimsy vessels to conquer distant islands or new continents.

But the principal cultural invention of modern man was art: engravings, paintings and even sculptures, which bear witness to the development of symbolic thought.

The Châtelperronian civilization: a civilization in transition

The Châtelperronian, a transitional industry between the Mousterian and the Upper Palaeolithic, developed between 34,000 and 30,000 BC, during a temperate period (the Les Cottés interstadial) followed by a more severe climatic period. Having for long been presented as an industry at the origins of the Gravettian (Lower Perigordian), the Châtelperronian is today regarded as a late example of the Mousterian civilizations.

The people still belonged to the Neanderthal group, as can be seen from the 'burial' at Saint-Césaire (Charente-Maritime) and the human teeth found in the Cave of the Reindeer at Arcy-sur-Cure (Yonne). The tools still consisted mainly of Mousterian types: scrapers, denticulated flints, etc. Nevertheless some new cultural inventions heralded the earliest civilizations of the Upper Palaeolithic: the Châtelperron knife (a blade with a curved back, with abrupt retouches), bone industry (bone awls), elements of ornament (perforated teeth), the use of red ochre and the earliest manifestations of symbolism, apparent in incisions on bone and in geometric signs on small plaques. In the Cave of the Reindeer at Arcy-sur-Cure, people constructed a circular hut out of mammoth tusks.

The Châtelperronian was a Western European manifestation of Mousterian culture, in particular in south-western France (Charente, Périgord), the Pyrenees, Saône-et-Loire, Côte-d'Or and Asturias.

The Aurignacian civilizations: the first manifestations of art

The Aurignacian, the first of the great civilizations of the Upper Palaeolithic, developed between 33,000 and 26,000 BC, during the first two periods of the later Würm glaciation and the temperate interstadials of Arcy (29,000 BC) and Kesselt (26,000 BC). The Aurignacian appears also to derive from certain features of the Mousterian. In the Near and Middle East it seems to have appeared earlier, and some layers similar to the Aurignacian are found between Mousterian layers.

The modern human type is represented by Cro-Magnon man, who is associated with Aurignacian civilizations everywhere. He was tall, reaching nearly 5 feet 11 inches (the old man of Cro-Magnon) and his skull, with its flat forehead, had a large capacity (1,600 cc or 98 cubic inches). He had a strong jaw with a chin. Some examples of Cro-Magnon man have some archaic features still reminiscent of Neanderthal man: strong orbital arches and slightly projecting facial bone structure.

The tools of the Aurignacian civilizations, usually made from blades and more rarely from flakes, as in the preceding civilizations, comprise the stereotyped forms characteristic of the Upper Palaeolithic: scrapers, burins, retouched blades. These tools are often trimmed with characteristic continuous, thick, scaly retouches, known as 'Aurignacian retouches'. The Aurignacian saw the development, for the first time in the history of civilizations, of varied and very elaborate tools made of bone: points with a split base, lozenge-shaped points, biconic points, awls, perforated staffs. There are also abundant body ornaments: perforated teeth and shells in burials, where their arrangement gives an indication of how they were used on garments and head-dresses: the net of the man in the cave of Cavillon at Grimaldi. It was at this time that prehistoric art first appeared, giving evidence of the spread of symbolic thought among the first modern humans: the development of art on blocks of stone showing male, and above all female, sexual images and some schematized animals (Leroi-Gourhan's Style I).

Habitation structures are relatively numerous: circular tents in the Cave of the Reindeer at Arcy-sur-Cure, the back of a rectangular cabin in the cave of Cueva Morin in Spain, an oval cabin at Tibava in Slovakia and encampments with pits at Barca in Moravia.

The Aurignacian civilizations developed over more than 7,000 years and occupied the greater part of Europe, from the Near East to the Atlantic, extending through Anatolia and the Balkans.

The Gravettian civilizations: the development of prehistoric art

The Gravettian civilizations developed between 27,000 and 19,000 BC, during the Kesselt interstadial (26,000–25,000 BC), a cold period (24,000–22,000 BC), the Tursac interstadial and the period of maximum cold in the later Würm (20,000–19,000 BC). For two thousand years (27,000–25,000 BC) these civilizations were contemporary with the last of the Aurignacian civilizations.

LOWER PALAEOLITHIC	MIDDLE PALAEOLITHIC
Acheulian civilizations hand-axes Levallois flint technique	**Mousterian civilizations** hand-axes diversified Levallois technique
beginning of the Acheulian *c.* **450,000 BC** ←	*La Chapelle-aux-Saints* *Neanderthal Cave*
Homo erectus	*Homo sapiens neanderthaliensis* (Neanderthal man)

100,000 years

Note: Although it is very difficult to schematize the various overlapping civilizations of the Palaeolithic, this table

The people of this civilization were still of the Cro-Magnon type: tall and thin (Pataud shelter in the Dordogne, Paglicci in Italy, Pavlov, Dolni Vestonice and Predmost in Czechoslovakia. Their anatomy still has some archaic features reminiscent of Neanderthal man, for instance the prominent arches below the orbits.

The most characteristic tool of the Gravettian civilizations is the La Gravette point (a blade pointed with a cut-away rectangular back), and associated with it are a large number of burins with retouched truncations of the stems. Several successive or regional cultures can be distinguished in the Gravettian civilizations. The bone industry, less varied than in the Aurignacian civilizations, consisted basically of long bevelled or biconic spears. The Gravettian deposits in Central Europe contain many tools made of mammoth ivory. The elements of body ornament are extremely varied and particularly abundant in the burials where they were used as decoration of the clothes. In the burials of Sungir near Vladimir in the Soviet Union a large number of perforated roundels of mammoth ivory were found arranged in rows along the arms and legs: they had been sewn on to the sleeves and trouser legs. Over the 8,000 years of the Gravettian civilizations, prehistoric art developed in the form of engravings, paintings and sculptures. Most numerous were the still schematized images of animals. The artists emphasized the cervico-dorsal line and part of the animal was shown in twisted perspective (Leroi-Gourhan's Style II). Mobiliary art was augmented by many objects made of engraved bone, antler, ivory or small plaques. At Dolni Vestonice many figurines of animals were sculpted in the round or modelled in clay and fired: mammoths, rhinoceros, bears, horses and lions. The remarkable female statues of the Gravettian – in ivory, bone or stone – bear witness to the relative cultural unity of these civilizations which were found right across Europe, in south-western France (Lespugue, Brassempouy), Italy (Savignano), Austria (Willendorf), the Soviet Union (Avdeevo) and later as far as Siberia (Malta).

There is a remarkable similarity in the habitation structures. All over Europe, particularly in the Ukraine and the great Russian plain, the hunters of the Reindeer Age were very well adapted for the severe climate and inhospitable environment. They constructed large round cabins, using stones for centring (Villerest in the Massif Central), or the bones of mammoths (Mezhirich in the Ukraine). At Pavlov (Moravia) a single habitation structure consisted of several individual dwellings. For 7,000 years the Gravettian civilizations occupied the whole of Europe (France, Spain, Italy, Belgium, Central Europe, the Ukraine and the great Russian plain).

The Solutrean civilizations: the apogee of flint-working

The relatively homogeneous Solutrean civilizations developed between 20,000 and 16,000 BC, during the coldest part of the Würm glaciation (20,000–18,000 BC) and the warmer climate of the Laugerie interstadial (17,000 BC).

The people of the Solutrean (e.g. in the burials of Roc-de-Sers) were smaller and less sturdy than their predecessors. Their tools mark the apogee of flint-working and are characterized by the flat-faced points of the Early Solutrean, the laurel-leaf points of the Middle Solutrean and the notched points of the Late Solutrean. The magnificent large foliate points of the Middle Solutrean, found at the site of Volgu (Saône-et-Loire), are evidence of the remarkable skill of the Solutrean craftsmen in working with hard stone. There is little variety in bone industry: small hooks, spears, perforated staffs. It was during the Upper Solutrean that the first perforated needles appeared. Monumental sculpture and the earliest bas-reliefs are also found in this period (Leroi-Gourhan's Style III). The cave of La Tête-du-Lion in the Ardèche gorges was visited 18,000 years ago by a group of Solutrean hunters who painted a cow, a stag and two ibex heads in a niche. The artists left behind on the cave floor a few flakes, some paint marks and wood charcoal (the remains of the torches that had lit their way through the darkness). Several habitation structures from the Solutrean have been discovered: a rectangular hut at Le Fourneau du Diable, a semicircular encampment at Chufin in Cantabrian Spain.

The Solutrean civilizations extended over 4,000 years and were basically restricted to central France, around the Massif Central and the Rhône valley, south-western France, the central, western and Cantabrian Pyrenees, and Asturias.

The Magdalenian civilizations: the apogee of Palaeolithic art

The great Magdalenian civilizations were established between 16,000 and 10,000 BC, during the Lascaux interstadial (15,000 BC), the Lower Dryas I phase, the Pre-Bölling interstadial (12,000 BC), Upper Dryas I, the Bölling interstadial (11,000 BC), and Dryas II.

The people were Cro-Magnoid, but frailer and smaller in size (5 feet 1 inch) than their predecessors. The dimensions of the cranium diminished lengthwise (Chancelade, Les Hoteaux, Saint-Germain-La-Rivière). There is evidence of several successive cultures in south-eastern France, distinguished by their lithic industry and bone tools.

ARCHAEOLOGICAL PLANS OF LASCAUX AND MAP OF FRANCO-CANTABRIAN SANCTUARIES

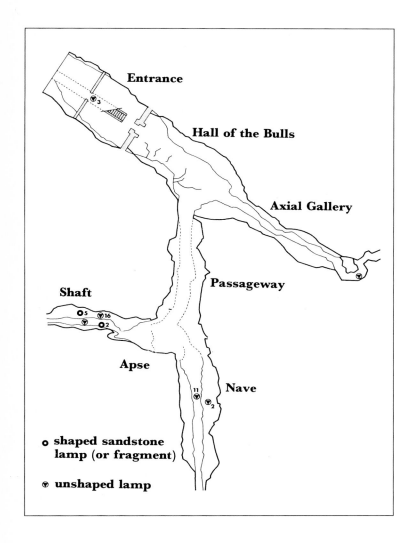

Above: positions of the over one hundred lamps found in the cave. In the Nave the Abbé Glory discovered whole stacks of limestone plaques placed one on top of another, some of which had not yet been used as lamps. In the Shaft the Abbé Breuil discovered inverted lamps arranged as a sort of paving. The famous 'incense burner' was found at point 5.

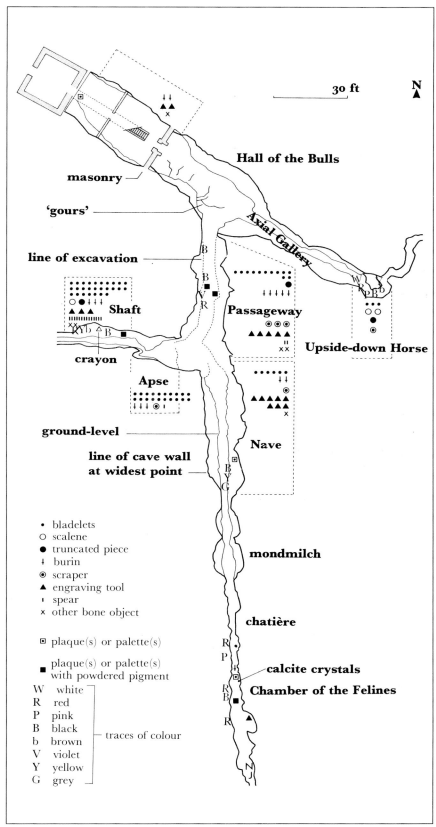

Right: positions of the archaeological finds in the cave – flint tools, hunting weapons (spears) and other bone objects. Artists' materials, pigments (in powder or solid form), crayons, palettes and receptacles. As recorded by Arlette Leroi-Gourhan.

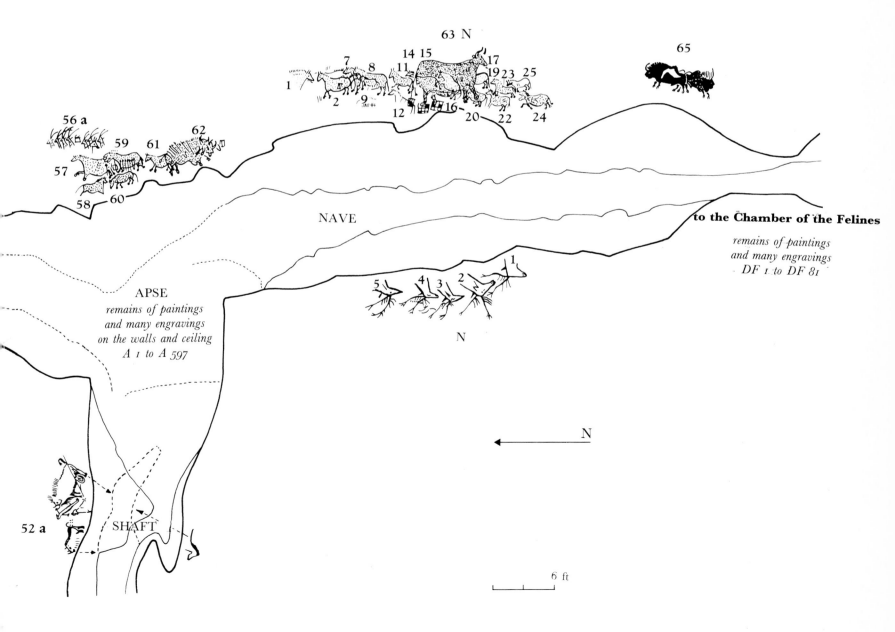

63 N

65

7
14 15
17
8
19 23 25
1
11
56 a
2
9
16
20 22 24
59
61
62
12
57
58 60

NAVE

to the **Chamber of the Felines**

*remains of paintings
and many engravings
DF 1 to DF 81*

1

APSE

*remains of paintings
and many engravings
on the walls and ceiling
A 1 to A 597*

5
4 3
2

N

N

52 a

SHAFT

6 ft

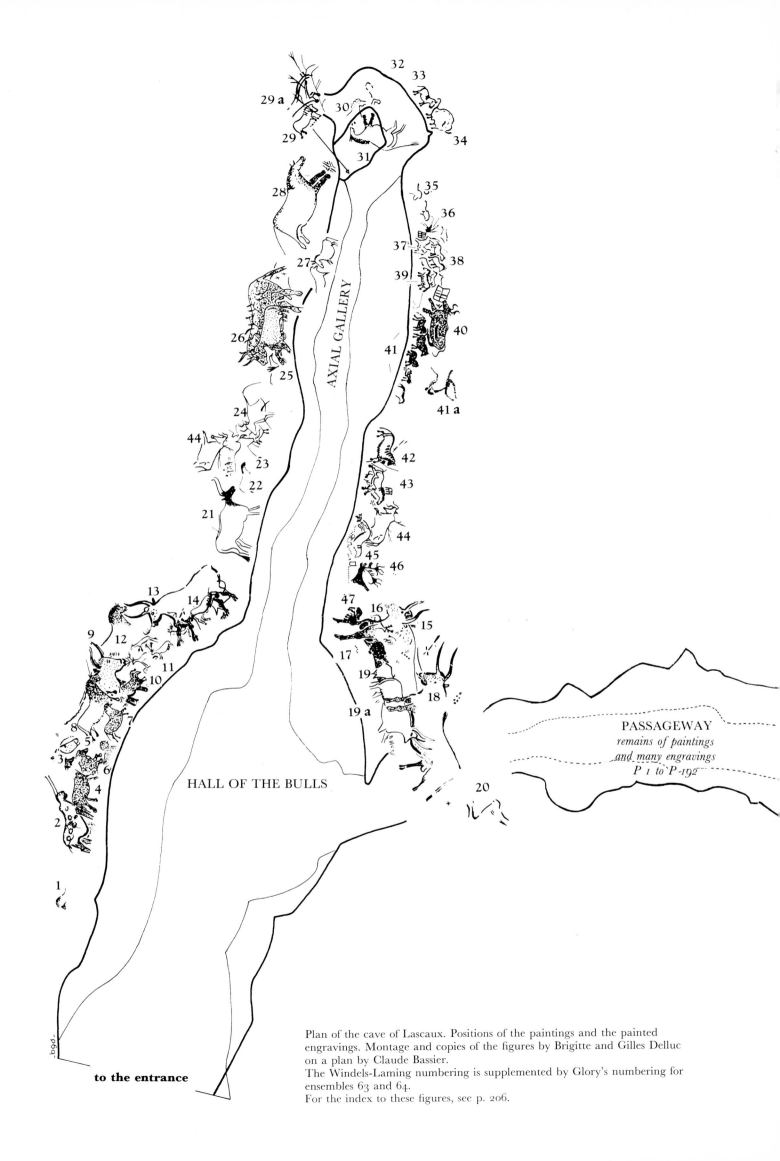

AXIAL GALLERY

HALL OF THE BULLS

PASSAGEWAY
*remains of paintings
and many engravings
P 1 to P-192*

Plan of the cave of Lascaux. Positions of the paintings and the painted engravings. Montage and copies of the figures by Brigitte and Gilles Delluc on a plan by Claude Bassier.
The Windels-Laming numbering is supplemented by Glory's numbering for ensembles 63 and 64.
For the index to these figures, see p. 206.

to the entrance

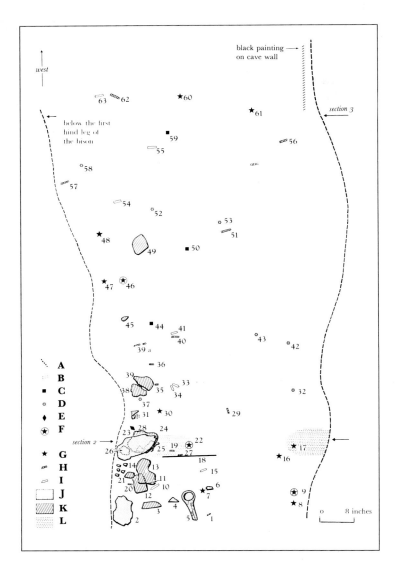

The Abbé Glory's plan of the excavations in the Shaft, redrawn by Michel Orliac. *Key*: A: approximate contour of the wall at the archaeological ground-level; B: remains found in earth debris; C: large fragment of charcoal; D: colouring matter; E: engraving tool; F: backed blade with traces of mastic; G: backed bladelet; H: lithic remains; I: bone remains; J: lamp or fragment of lamp; K: plaque, palette; L: layer of red ochre and manganese. *Inventory of the objects from the Shaft, by the Abbé Glory – 1960*: **1**: black flint bladelet. **2**: limestone lamp against the rock. **3**: silica palette. **4**: debris of triangular limestone lamp. **5**: pink sandstone lamp. **6**: debris of rectangular limestone lamp. **7**: light-coloured flint. **8**: backed flint. **9**: flint bladelet. **10**: grooved bone. **11**: light-coloured flint. **12** and **13**: limestone plaques with ochre colour. **14**: five fragments of a limestone lamp. **15**: bone debris. **16**: light-coloured flint bladelet. **17**: backed black flint (with a grain of red). **18**: celluloid cup. **19**: black flint bladelet; many charcoal fragments. **20**: light-coloured flint. **21**: limestone plaque. **22**: flint bladelet. **23–26**: five horizontal plaques laid against the wall, forming a makeshift lamp (according to the Abbé Glory). Below is a bed of manganese and then charcoal. Large pieces of branch, $1\frac{1}{2} \times \frac{3}{4}$ inch in diameter. Pile of clay blocks. **27**: flint from the section. Acetocelluloid. **28**: black flint. **29**: atypical black flint bladelet. **30**: atypical black flint bladelet. **31**: along the wall, limestone and charcoal debris. Debris from limestone lamp-making. Fragment of sandstone. **32**: small piece of manganese ore. Charcoal. **33**: grooved bone filled with charcoal. **34**: bone diaphysis. **35**: charcoal, flint debris. **36**: black flint debris. **37**: small piece of manganese. **38**: two plaques against the wall. Charcoal. **39**: two plaques against the wall. Charcoal – *1961*: **39a**: black flint bladelet with flake. **40**: brown flint flake. **41**: small bone. **42**: manganese. **43**: small piece of red ochre. **44**: large piece of charcoal. **45**: limestone debris in the shape of a pot against the wall, held by three balls of compressed clay. Red ochre in the cup-shaped part. **46**: black flint bladelet at the base of earth debris. **47**: black flint bladelet at the base of earth debris. **48**: black flint bladelet in earth debris. **49**: cup-shaped limestone plaque, inverted. **50**: large pieces of charcoal. **51**: atypical light-coloured flint at a depth of $4\frac{4}{4}$ inches with charcoal debris. **52**: nodule of manganese. **53**: triangular piece of mineralized manganese. **54**: small bone. **54a**: backed flint. **55**: rodent's tooth. **56**: sausage-shaped lump of flint. **57**: debris of black flint bladelet, not retouched. **58**: ball of manganese. **59**: large piece of charcoal. **60**: fragment of charcoal at the base of the archaeological layer, on the barren clays. **61**: backed bladelet, flaked by pressure, black flint. Length: $1\frac{3}{4}$ inches. **62**: fragment of brown flint. **63**: fragment of spear. Debris.

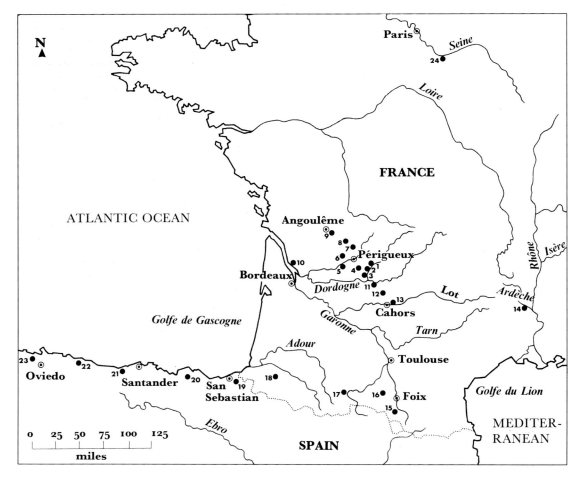

Principal sanctuaries decorated by Cro-Magnon Man in Western Europe.

1. Lascaux
2. Sergeac: shelters of Castanet, Labattut, Blanchard, Belcayre, Cellier
3. Les Eyzies: shelters of La Ferrassie, Pataud, La Madeleine, Laugerie-Haute, Laugerie-Basse, Cro-Magnon; caves of Font-de-Gaume, Les Combarelles 1 and 2, La Mouthe
4. Rouffignac
5. Le Gabillou
6. Le Fourneau du Diable
7. Villars
8. Teyjat
9. Roc-de-Sers
10. Pair-non-Pair
11. Saint-Front-de-Domme
12. Cougnac
13. Pech-Merle
14. Caves of Ardèche: Tête-du-Lion and Chabot (Solutrean), Le Figuier and Ebbou (Magdalenian)
15. Niaux, Fontanet
16. Le Mas-d'Azil, Le Portel, Les Trois Frères, Le Tuc-d'Audoubert, Enlène
17. Gargas
18. Etcheberriko-Karbia
19. Ekaïn, Altxerri
20. Santimamine
21. Altamira, El Castillo, La Pasiega, Las Chimeneas, Hornos de la Peña
22. Tito Bustillo
23. Peña de Candamo
24. Pincevent (undecorated open-air camp)

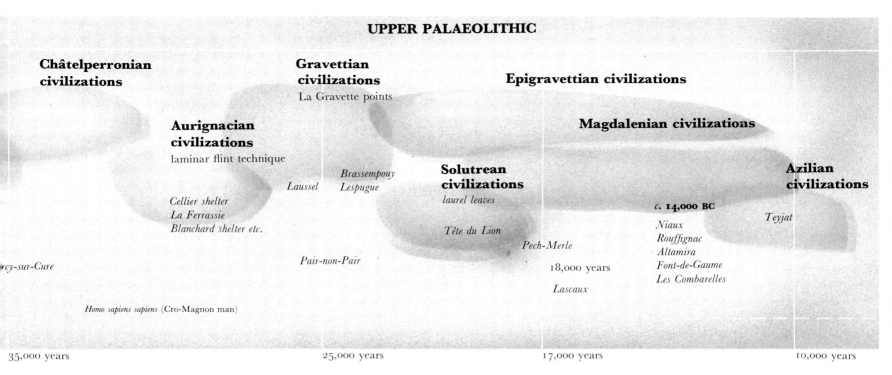

Châtelperronian civilizations

Gravettian civilizations
La Gravette points

Epigravettian civilizations

Aurignacian civilizations
laminar flint technique

Brassempouy
Lespugue

Magdalenian civilizations

Laussel

Solutrean civilizations
laurel leaves

Azilian civilizations

Cellier shelter
La Ferrassie
Blanchard shelter etc.

Tête du Lion

c. **14,000 BC**

Teyjat

Niaux
Rouffignac
Altamira
Font-de-Gaume
Les Combarelles

cy-sur-Cure

Pair-non-Pair

Pech-Merle

18,000 years

Lascaux

Homo sapiens sapiens (Cro-Magnon man)

35,000 years   25,000 years   17,000 years   10,000 years

he reader some idea of the chronology of the evolution of flint-working techniques.

The lithic industry is characterized by an abundance of burins (often dihedral), end-blade scrapers, borers and backed blades. It was during the Middle and Upper Magdalenian that small backed bladelets, with trimmed edges, became particularly numerous. One of the original features of the Magdalenian is the remarkable development of bone industry: cylindrical spears with broad bevels in Magdalenian I, biconic spears in Magdalenian II, grooved spears and semi-rounded rods in Magdalenian III, spear-throwers and proto-harpoons in Magdalenian IV, harpoons with one row of barbs in Magdalenian V and harpoons with two rows of barbs in Magdalenian VI. The Magdalenian represents the apogee of Palaeolithic art. At present we know of more than 150 decorated caves which can be considered as Palaeolithic sanctuaries, dating from this period. The art of the Early Magdalenian (Leroi-Gourhan's Style III) is demonstrated by a number of particularly remarkable sanctuaries: the caves of Lascaux and Le Gabillou. The scene in the Shaft at Lascaux is especially interesting as it seems to be one of a very few narrative compositions, if not the only one in Quaternary art. A dead, ithyphallic man with the head of a straight-beaked bird, his arms half extended and his fingers spread, seems to have been knocked down by a wounded bison with its entrails hanging out, which is pierced by a long spear with a single row of barbs. Below the fallen man is a vertical barbed sign with a bird at its end, which has sometimes been interpreted as a hooked spear-thrower; to the right is another, diagonal, barbed sign. To the left, a rhinoceros, with six dots arranged in two rows below its tail, seems to be moving away from the scene. The art of the Middle and Later Magdalenian (Leroi-Gourhan's Style IV), characterized by engravings and polychrome paintings, is widespread in south-western France (Font-de-Gaume, Les Combarelles, Rouffignac), in the Pyrenees (Niaux) and in Cantabrian Spain (Altamira). The famous clay bison modelled by the Magdalenians at Le Tuc d'Audoubert (Montesquieu-Avantès in Ariège) remain exceptional in Palaeolithic art. Mobiliary art objects, made of bone, reindeer antler and ivory, are particularly impressive: the silhouettes of animals cut out of flat bones are very characteristic. The habitation structures remain in the tradition of the Gravettian civilizations. Notable encampments have been revealed in the Dordogne (Le Cerisier and Le Breuil) and in the Paris basin (Pincevent, Etiolles, Marsangy).

The Magdalenian civilizations occupied a large part of Western Europe. Whereas the Early Magdalenian was confined mainly to south-western France and Spain, the Upper Magdalenian was spread over a much wider area, extending to southern France, Switzerland, Jura, Germany, Belgium and even Poland.

The Epigravettian

In areas beyond the classical Magdalenian region – south-eastern Europe (Italy), as well as Central and Eastern Europe (Austria, the Soviet Union) – cultures derived from the Gravettian developed. These Epigravettian civilizations are not as rich in cave art and mobiliary art as the Magdalenian civilizations. However, various works of mobiliary art on blocks of stone, pebbles and bone have been discovered at several sites.

The Azilian

The Azilian civilization developed out of the final stage of the Late Magdalenian between 10,000 and 8,000 BC, during the climatic oscillation of the Alleröd phase and during Dryas III. The milder climate which followed the end of the glacial period brought with it alterations in the landscape as forests spread across the open spaces. This was when deer gradually replaced reindeer.

Azilian tool-making is characterized by small circular and thumb-nail scrapers, and small bladelets with curved backs (Azilian points). The bone tools consist of flat harpoons made of deer antler with a hole in the base. There was a decline in prehistoric art. The great animal paintings on cave walls practically ceased, and mobiliary art is characterized by engraved or painted pebbles, and bones decorated with various, often geometric, signs.

The Azilian civilizations covered almost the same geographical area as the civilizations of the Late Magdalenian.

Sauveterrian and Tardenoisian

The Mesolithic civilizations, with their geometric microliths, developed after 8,000 BC: the Sauveterrian (8,000–7,000 BC) basically identified by triangles and the Sauveterre point, and the Tardenoisian (7,000–5,500 BC) characterized by trapeze-shapes and the Tardenois point. The Sauveterrian occupied the early part of the Preboreal, and the Tardenoisian the late Preboreal and the Boreal. The geometric microliths were intended to be inserted into wooden or bone handles to form harpoons, which replaced those made of deer antler in the Azilian and reindeer antler in the Magdalenian. The habitation sites of this period are characterized by large heaps of snail shells or, near the coasts, the shells of marine molluscs – evidence of an intensive gathering of shellfish in this period.   HENRY DE LUMLEY

BIBLIOGRAPHIC NOTES

Countless books, monographs and articles have been devoted to Lascaux: there are certainly several hundred of them. Nevertheless, there is more to be said about the cave; for example, we do not yet have a good study of the paintings using traced drawings.

Some items now have only historic interest: examples are Léon Laval's booklet, and the chapter in Henri Breuil's *Four Hundred Centuries of Cave Art* which is devoted to Lascaux:

> LAVAL, L. (1954), *La caverne peinte de Lascaux*. Éditions du Périgord Noir, Montignac, 36 pp., 10 pl. (photos by Windels), followed by the *Rapport de M. l'abbé Breuil sur la grotte de Lascaux*, presented to the Académie des Inscriptions et Belles Lettres at its meeting on 11 October 1940.
>
> BREUIL, H. (1952), *Four Hundred Centuries of Cave Art*. Centre d'études et de documentation préhistoriques, Montignac, 417 pp., 531 figs, 1 pl.

These can be consulted in libraries (the Breuil book, featuring the decorated caves which he studied, was reissued in its French edition, *Quatre Cents Siècles d'Art Pariétal*, in 1974 by éds. Max Fourny, Paris). They provide an account of the discovery and a list of the figures known at the time. Lascaux was then thought to be the work of Gravettians. These books are now very out of date.

Two other works are almost as old, but remain of great interest:

> WINDELS, F. & LAMING, A. (1949), *The Lascaux Cave Paintings*, Faber, London. 138 pp., illustrated.
>
> LAMING, A. (1959), *Lascaux: Paintings & Engravings*, Pelican, Harmondsworth, 208 pp., 29 figs, 48 pl.

These two texts are the work of Annette Laming-Emperaire, an eminent specialist in cave art who died tragically and prematurely in 1976. They are rich in details, gathered together with precision and intelligence. They have never been reprinted. Abbé André Glory, who also died prematurely, did not leave an overall view of his research at Lascaux. However, one should mention a small booklet (now out of print) which gave a very succinct account of his main results:

> GLORY, A. (1971), *Lascaux, Versailles de la Préhistoire*, Imp. Jaclemous, Périgueux, 38 pp., illustrated (reissued in 1978, Imp. Leymarie, Périgueux).

Professor André Leroi-Gourhan deals with Lascaux in many articles and books. The following are particularly important:

> LEROI-GOURHAN, A. (1968). *The Art of Prehistoric Man in Western Europe*, Thames and Hudson, London, 543 pp., 702 ills, 242 figs. (One chapter of this fat volume gives the latest position on the paintings, the style and the organization of Lascaux).
>
> LEROI-GOURHAN, A. (1982). *The Dawn of European Art. An Introduction to Palaeolithic Cave Painting*, Cambridge University Press, 77 pp., 132 figs. (This book is the summary of the masterly courses given by the author at the Collège de France from 1970 to 1982. Lascaux is often mentioned.)
>
> LEROI-GOURHAN, A. (1984). 'Grotte de Lascaux', in: *L'Art des Cavernes* (Atlas Archéologique de la France), Ministère de la Culture, Paris, pp. 180–200, 30 figs. (A. Leroi-Gourhan wrote an article of a few pages for this large book.)

Arlette Leroi-Gourhan, his wife, directed an exceptional, multi-disciplinary study of the cave of Lascaux which comprises the work of 18 authors. It is the principal scientific work on the archaeology and the engravings of Lascaux. The paintings of the Nave and the Shaft are also covered in it. Abbé A. Glory's research (and especially his tracings of the engravings) are set out and commented upon in the work. The reference is as follows:

> LEROI-GOURHAN, Arl. & ALLAIN, J. (eds), (1979). *Lascaux inconnu* (12th Supplement to *Gallia Préhistoire*, Éd. du C.N.R.S., Paris, 381 pp., 387 figs.

The principal chapters of this important study (all in French) are:
Lascaux, the first ten years from written accounts by the witnesses, by B. and G. DELLUC.
Geological study and hydrokarstic origin, by J. VOUVÉ.
Representation of the cave of Lascaux in plan and volume, by C. BASSIER.
Stratigraphy and excavations in the cave of Lascaux according to the texts and notes of H. Breuil, A. Glory, S. Blanc, by Arl. LEROI-GOURHAN.
Pollen analyses of the cave of Lascaux, by Arl. LEROI-GOURHAN and M. GIRARD.
The dating of Lascaux, by Arl. LEROI-GOURHAN and J. ÉVIN:
I – History.
II – Summary of the radiocarbon dates.
The stone and bone industry of Lascaux, by J. ALLAIN.
Lighting, by B. and G. DELLUC.
The shells of Lascaux, by Y. TABORIN.
The fauna of the cave of Lascaux, by J. BOUCHUD.
Colouring materials, by C. COURAUD and A. LAMING-EMPERAIRE.
Technical study of coloured powders, by O. BALLET, A. BOCQUET, R. BOUCHEZ, J-M. COEY and A. CORNU.
Access to the walls, by B. and G. DELLUC.
The wood, by Arl. LEROI-GOURHAN, F. SCHWEINGRUBER, M. GIRARD.
The engravings of the Passage and the Apse, by D. VIALOU.
The engravings of the Nave and the Chamber of the Felines, by A. LEROI-GOURHAN.
Animals and Signs, by A. LEROI-GOURHAN.

Two articles put together by Arl. LEROI-GOURHAN constitute a summary of the book:

> LEROI-GOURHAN, Arl. (1982). 'The archaeology of Lascaux cave', *Scientific American*, vol. 246, no. 6, pp. 80–88, illustrated.
>
> LEROI-GOURHAN, Arl. (1980). 'Lascaux', *La Recherche*, vol. 11, no. 110, pp. 412–420, 6 figs.

Two further syntheses by Brigitte and Gilles Delluc present the results of this study and also provide a description of the cave. They can be bought at the site:

> DELLUC, B. and G. (1984). *Lascaux. Art et Archéologie*, les éditions du Périgord Noir, Emmanuel Leymarie, Périgueux, 93 pp., 18 figs, 4 pl., 4 plans.
>
> DELLUC, B. and G. (1985). *Tout Lascaux*, small newspaper format, single issue, Office du Tourisme de la Dordogne and Éditions du Périgord Noir, Périgueux, 4 pp., illustrated.

Some publications concern a part of Lascaux's riches:

> APELLÁNIZ, J-M. (1984). 'L'auteur des grands taureaux de Lascaux et ses successeurs', *L'Anthropologie*, vol. 88, no. 4, pp. 539–61, 22 figs.
>
> BATAILLE, G. (1955). *Prehistoric Painting: Lascaux; or, the Birth of Art*. Macmillan, London. 149 pp., 68 ills, 6 pl. (This book is abundantly illustrated with colour photographs of the paintings and the paintings/engravings. The text is of debatable interest in the eyes of the prehistorian.)
>
> DELLUC, B. and G. (1981). 'Le bloc peint de la Salle des Taureaux', *Bull. Soc. historique et archéologique du Périgord*, 108, 1, pp. 34–47, 5 pl. (A photographic reconstruction of a decorated area which flaked away

from a panel in the Hall of the Bulls, and which is now very weathered.)

VIALOU, D. (1984). 'Les cervidés de Lascaux', in: *La contribution de la zoologie et de l'éthologie à l'interprétation de l'art des peuples chasseurs préhistoriques* (3rd colloque de la Société suisse des sciences humaines, Berne, 1979), pp. 199–216, 12 figs (a study of the 91 cervid figures in Lascaux).

Lascaux's place in the development of Palaeolithic cave art can be studied in André Leroi-Gourhan's *The Art of Prehistoric Man in Western Europe*, and also in the following recent publications:

DELLUC, B. and G. (1984). 'L'art pariétal avant Lascaux', *Dossiers Histoire et Archéologie*, no. 87, pp. 52–60, 15 figs.

DELLUC, B. and G. (1985). 'De l'empreinte au signe', *Dossiers Histoire et Archéologie*, no. 90, pp. 56–62, 10 figs.

VIALOU, D. (1976). *Guide des grottes ornées paléolithiques ouvertes au public.* Masson, Paris, 128 pp., illustrated.

VIALOU, D. (1984). 'Lascaux et l'art magdalénien', *Dossiers Histoire et Archéologie*, no. 87, pp. 61–9, 17 figs.

LUMLEY, H. de, COURAUD, C., DELLUC, B. and G., DELPORTE, H., LEROY-PROST, C., LUMLEY, M-A. de, PERPÈRE, M., VIALOU, D. (1984). *Art et civilisations des chasseurs de la Préhistoire (34,000–8,000 av. J.-C.),* Édit. du Laboratoire de Préhistoire du Musée de l'Homme-Muséum national d'Histoire naturelle, Paris, 415 pp., 199 figs.

The 'illnesses' which afflicted Lascaux and the remedies taken against them can be studied by reading a few works published by the specialists in this removal of pollution:

LAPORTE, G-S., (1971). 'Au chevet de Lascaux . . . (les travaux de la Commission Scientifique pour la sauvegarde des peintures rupestres de la grotte préhistorique)', *Bulletin de l'Ordre des Pharmaciens* no. 143, 39 pp., 2 photos.

LEFEVRE, M. (1974). 'La maladie verte de Lascaux', *Studies in Conservation,* 19, pp. 126–56.

BRUNET, J., MARSAL, J. and VIDAL, P. (1980). 'Lascaux. Où en sont les travaux de conservation?', *Archéologia* no. 149 (December 1980), pp. 35–50, illustrated.

VOUVÉ, J., BRUNET, J., VIDAL, P. and MARSAL, J. (1982). *Lascaux en Périgord Noir.* Fanlac, Périgueux, 87 pp., illustrated.

BRUNET, J., VIDAL, P., VOUVÉ, J. (1985). *Conservation de l'art rupestre (deux études, glossaire illustré),* Études et documents sur le patrimoine culturel, Unesco, 107 pp., illustrated (an interesting synthesis of the work, presented in about 50 pages).

Finally, the fabrication of the facsimile of Lascaux is explained in:

DELLUC, B. and G. (1984). 'Lascaux II, a faithful copy', *Antiquity,* vol. 58, pp. 194–6, 2 pl.

DEBAYE, D. (1986). *Catalogue de Lascaux II* (forthcoming).

Numerous publications were consulted during the writing of this book. The following are a few of the references used:

BÉGOUËN, H. and BREUIL, H. (1958). *Les cavernes du Volp,* Arts et Métiers graphiques, Paris, 124 pp., 115 figs, 32 pl.

BULLETIN DE LA SOCIÉTÉ PRÉHISTORIQUE FRANÇAISE.

GESSAIN, R. (1981). *Ovibos, la grande aventure des hommes et des boeufs musqués,* éd. Robert Laffont, Paris, 303 pp., figs.

HAINARD, R. (1972). *Mammifères sauvages d'Europe,* éd. Delachaux et Niestlé, Paris, 352 pp., 72 drawings, 40 pl.

KUPKA, K. (1965). *Dawn of Art: painting and sculpture of Australian Aborigines,* Angus and Robertson, Sydney.

LAMING-EMPERAIRE, A. (1962). *La signification de l'art rupestre paléolithique,* éd. Picard, Paris. 424 pp., 50 figs.

LEROI-GOURHAN, A. (1964, 1st ed.). *Les religions de la préhistoire (Paléolithique).* P.U.F. (coll. *Mythes et religions*), Paris, 154 pp., 16 ills.

LEROI-GOURHAN, A. (1982). *Les Racines du Monde* (interviews with Cl.-H. Rocquet), Belfond, Paris, 279 pp., full bibliography.

LEROI-GOURHAN, A. (1983). *Le fil du temps – Ethnologie et Préhistoire 1935–1970,* Fayard (coll. *Le temps des Sciences*), Paris, 384 pp., illustrated.

The following books are the major recent (and not-so-recent) English-language introductions to the subject of Palaeolithic art; they all refer to Lascaux:

BANDI, H-G. *et al.* (1961) *The Art of the Stone Age. Forty thousand years of rock art.* Methuen, London (2nd edition 1970).

GIEDION, S. (1962) *The Eternal Present. The Beginnings of Art.* New York, Bellingen Foundation (Bellingen Series, xxxv, 6, 1).

GRAND, P. M. (1967) *Prehistoric Art. Paleolithic Painting and Sculpture.* New York Graphic Society, Greenwich, Connecticut (Pallas Library of Art, vol. III).

GRAZIOSI, P. (1960) *Palaeolithic Art.* Faber & Faber, London.

GRIGSON, G. (1957) *The Painted Caves.* Phoenix House, London.

MARINGER, J. & BANDI, H-G. (1953) *Art in the Ice Age, Spanish Levant Art, Arctic Art,* Allen & Unwin, London.

MARSHACK, A. (1972) *The Roots of Civilisation.* Weidenfeld & Nicolson, London.

PFEIFFER, J. E. (1982) *The Creative Explosion. An inquiry into the origins of art and religion.* Harper & Row, New York.

SANDARS, N. K. (1968) *Prehistoric Art in Europe,* Penguin, Harmondsworth.

SIEVEKING, A. (1979) *The Cave Artists.* Thames and Hudson, London.

STERN, P. van D. (1973) *The Beginnings of Art,* Four Winds Press, New York.

UCKO, P. J. & ROSENFELD, A. (1967) *Palaeolithic Cave Art.* World University Library, Weidenfeld & Nicolson, London.

Some recent popular articles also are of interest:

CONKEY, M. W. (1981) 'A century of palaeolithic cave art', *Archaeology,* vol. 34, no. 4, pp. 20–28.

MARSHACK, A. (1975) 'Exploring the mind of Ice Age Man', *National Geographic,* vol. 147, no. 1, pp. 62–89.

PFEIFFER, J. E. (1980) Icons in the shadows, *Science 80,* vol. 1, no. 4, pp. 72–7.

BRIGITTE AND GILLES DELLUC, PAUL G. BAHN.

INDEX

This index includes the names of the civilizations (except for the Magdalenian which recurs frequently throughout), Palaeolithic sites and caves, animals and objects mentioned in the book, as well as the names of people who have contributed to our knowledge of the decorated caves.

The page numbers printed in *italic* refer to the captions of illustrations, the page numbers in **bold** type indicate where a subject is discussed in some detail (this may also include picture captions).

Leroi-Gourhan, Arlette 21, 26, 27, 56, 96, 126, 127, 147
Levallois (flint-working) 12, 13, *14*, *15*
lion, cave 26, 32, 35, **54–5**, 66, 82, 84, 85, 198
Lorblanchet, Michel 196
Lot-Falk, Evelyne 62, 63, 150
Lumley, Henri de *15*, 199
Lyell, Charles *64*
lynx 32, 34, 44, 50, 85, 100, 176

Madeleine, La [Dordogne] *13*, 78, 81, 87
magic 49, 62, 63, 64, *66*, 79, 82
mammoth 15, *17*, 18, 24–5, 26, *48*, 53, **58–60**, 63, 68, 73, 84, 85, 198
manganese 16, *38*, *53*, 96, 104, 106, 108, 115, *116*, 118, 129, 142, 145, 146, 150, 170, 171, 192, 193, 194
Marche, La (cave) 87
Marsal, Jacques *94*, 99, 126, 142, 144, 149, 178, *179*, *181*, *182*, *185*, 188, 189, 190, 193
Marsoulas 79
Mas-d'Azil (cave) [Ariège] 61, *70*, 79, 185
Massat (cave) [Ariège] 55
Meander 27, 42, 109, **118–22**, 126, 127, 158, 183, 184
Megaceros giganteus 26, **60**, *61*, 84, 85
Melanesian 70
Mesolithic *21*, 27, 68, 154
microfauna and small mammals 58
Mindel (glaciation) 12
mobiliary art **20**, 21, 22, *76*, 87, 155, 192, 196, 198, 199
Montagnais (Indians) 49, 52
Montespan 83
Montignac [Dordogne] 36, 181, 188, **189**
Mourer-Chauviré, Cécile 72
Mousterian **13**, *14*, 197
Mouthe, La (cave) 197
musk-ox (ovibos) **39**, 73, 175

Nave 28, 29, *33*, 37, 38, 42, 44, 45, 49, *63*, 86, *95*, 96, 97, 98, 126, 128, **131–44**, 145, 147, 155, *156*, *157*, *158*, *159*, 162, 163, 165, *167*, *169*, 171, 172, 179, *181*, 184, 186, 192, 194
Neanderthal **13**, 14, 15, 23, 51, 55, 74, 84, 197
needle, perforated *17*, 51, 69, *70*, 72, *128*, 198
Neolithic 73, 76, 91, 154, 199
Niaux (cave) [Ariège] 35, *36*, 45, *46*, 74, *75*, 79, 82, **83**, 86, 158, 185, 186, 196, 199
nomads 61
nucleus 27, 127

Oberthur 43
ochre 13, 16, 23, 30, 73, *90*, *95*, 96, 106, 108, 109, 114, 115, 118, 119, 122, 127, 140, 145, 146, 152, 158, 170, 171, 192, 193, 194, 197
offering 15, 24, 28, 64, 152
Olduvai 67
ornament *14*, 16, 23, *24*, 42, 44, 52, 56, 61, 71, 87, 92, 152, 197, 198
Ostrorog 38
otter 61
owl, snowy 73
ovibos, see musk-ox

pachyderm 58, *59*, 85
Pair-non-Pair (cave) [Gironde] 26, *40*, **45**, 84, 185, 195, 196
Palaeolithic, Lower 12, 39
Palaeolithic, Middle 13
Palaeolithic, Upper 12, 15, 16, 24, 28, 37, 39, 48, 49, 55, 67, 72, 74, 84, 87, 92, 154, 158, 195, 197
Pales, Dr 87
palette 19, 29, 144, 170, 193, 194, 195
panther 32, 35, 82, 100
Passageway 27, 42, 49, 96, 98, 99, 104, **128–31**, 132, 138, 147, 152, 155, *156*, 162, 163, 164, 166, 179, 186, 194

Pataud (shelter) [Dordogne] *86*, 198
Pech-Merle (cave) [Lot] 17, 74, 82, 83, 87, 166, 185
pendant 23, 44, 73
penis 88
perforator 69, 73
percussor 51, 52
Pessac-sur-Dordogne 73
Peyrony, Denis *13*, 80
Peytral, Monique 170, 192
pictogram 150
Piette, Ed. 78, 154
pigments 15, 16, 17, 26, 29, 30, 82, *95*, 96, 97, 106, 127, 139, 144, 145, 152, 170, 179, 185, 192, **194**, 195
Pincevent [Seine-et-Marne] 21, 22, 23, *24*, 51, 76, 142, 199
pit 35, 54, 59, 66
plaque, engraved 20, 21, *25*, 87, *89*, 197, 198
point (of antler) 175
points, notched 71, 198
Poisson (Abri du) [Dordogne] 75
pollen 15, 21, **26**, 27, 96, 127, 195
pony 16, 40, 42, 168
Portel, Le (cave) [Ariège] 17, 42, 82, 88, 157, 185
pots 19, 29, 52
Przevalski horse 39, 40, **42**, 172
Pszczyna [Silesia] 34

quadrilateral (sign) 110, 132, 156, 157, *158*, 160

rabbit 25, 26, 57, 61, 76, 85
Ravidat, Marcel *94*, 151, 188, *189*, 190, 191, 193
reindeer 15, *16*, 18, 19, 21, *23*, *24*, 25, 26, 32, 44, 45, 46, **49–52**, 55, 57, 58, 61, *64*, 67, 68, 69, 74, 75, *76*, 84, 85, 87, 89, *95*, 127, 142, 152, 155, 164, 175, 199
religion 16, **23**, 62, 64, 78, 80, **84**, 90, 91
rhinoceros, woolly 25, 26, **53–4**, 67, 84, 85, 100, 164, 168, 169, 172, 176, 198
Riss (glaciation) 12, *48*
rites 22, **23**, 28, 56, 63, 64, 84, 88, 90, 91, 92, 146, 150, 152, 194
Roc-aux-Sorciers (Angles-sur-l'Anglin) 195
Roc-de-Sers 196, 198
rod, semi-rounded 20, 21, 199
rodents 21, 57, 58, 61
Roesslin, Dr Amédée 40
rope, plant fibre 30, 96, 146, 147, 190, *191*
Rotunda (or Hall of the Bulls) 16, 27, 37, *38*, 42, *43*, 45, 53, **56**, 86, 94, 96, 97, 99–108, 109, *123*, 124, 126, 128, 129, 132, 138, 141, 147, 152, 155, 156, *157*, 158, 162, 163, 165, 168, 170, 172, *173*, 176, 179, 180, 181, 183, 184, 185, 186, 191, 192
Rouffignac (cave) [Dordogne] 45, *48*, *54*, 55, *59*, *84*, 85, 185, 186, 196, 199
Rousseau, Michel 162, 173

Saint-Front-de-Domme (cave) [Dordogne] *60*
Saint-Germain-La-Rivière 26, 198
Saint-Girons [Ariège] 20
salmon 19, 21, 26, 55, 61, 74, 75, *76*
scaffolding *38*, *60*, 96, 105, 106, *124*, **126**, 130, 142, *143*, 147, 185, 193
Scandinavia 49, 50, 56
scapulomancy 52
sculpture 80, 87, 185, 197, 198
scraper 27, 51, 67, 68, 126, 144, 197, 199
seal 61, 73
Shaft 27, 28, 29, 33, 38, 42, 53, 57, 67, 68, 88, 89, **95**, 96, 97, 145–6, 146, 147, **149–52**, 155, *156*, 158, 162, 163, 164, 169, 170, 172, 176, 179, 184, 186, 188, 190, 192, 199
shaman 22, 52, 84, 88, 89, 90, 91, *92*, 100, 148, 150
shells *14*, 23, 152, 197
Siberia 30, 50, 51, *52*, 53, 56, 59, 63, 74, 76, *92*, 142, 150, 176

sickle (sign) 109
sign 28, 29, 44, *62*, *66*, 67, 68, *69*, 80, 84, 86, 96, *104*, *106*, 109, *110*, 112, *114*, 130, 132, *134*, 138, 144, 145, 146, 147, **154–60**, 195, 196
skin 16, 18, 19, 20, 26, 27, 35, 36, 40, 44, 51, 52, 53, 59, 69, 96, 100, 126, 170, 192, 194, 197
sorcerer 88
spear *18*, *19*, *24*, 28, 29, 40, 44, 51, *62*, *63*, *66*, **67–70**, 72, 75, 106, *123*, *128*, 142, 150, 152, 155, 157, 195, 197, 198, 199
spear-straightener, see staff
spear-thrower 19, 20 **69–70**, *90*, 150, 197
'sponging' 16, 90, 170, 194
staff, perforated or pierced (or spear-straightener) 20, 21, 61, **68–9**, *90*, 150, 197, 198
stag [see also deer, red] 43, *44*, *45*, *69*, 84, *104*, *156*, 164, 166, 167, 168, 169, 171, 175, 198
stencil 16, 90, 194
steppe 33, *38*, 39, 40, 44, 58, 59, 60, 85
stoats 61
stratigraphic section *94*, *95*, *96*, 97
styles 16, 88, **196**, 197
Style I *87*, *88*, 196, 197
Style II *40*, *45*, 183, 196, 198
Style III *37*, *63*, 130, 183, 196, 198, 199
Style IV *35*, *46*, *76*, 196, 199
Sudrie, La [Dordogne] 197
Sungir [USSR] 68

tarpan 40
Tautavel *15*, 39
teeth, deer canine 44
tendon 36, 52, 69, 74, 75
tent 18, 19, 20, 21, 22, *23*, 28, 30, 35, 36, 51, 52, 58, 61, 72, 76, 80, 197
Terme-Pialat 88
Tête-du-Lion [Ardèche] 195, 198
Teyjat (cave) [Dordogne] *16*, *45*, 79, *90*, 185, 186, 196
thongs 30, 40, 45, 52, 69
Thot, Le [Dordogne] 36
thur 38
torch 28, **30**, 82, *95*, 128, 198
Torralba [Spain] 67
traps 35, 52, 63, 64, 66, 73
trimmer 36, 52
Trois-Frères, Les (cave) [Ariège] *18*, 20, 29, 42, 49, *55*, *59*, *62*, *63*, *66*, 88, 89, *156*, 176, 196
trout 26, 55, 61, 74, *75*
Tuc-d'Audoubert (cave) [Ariège] 20, 56, 82, 83, 199
tundra 39, 49, 50, 58, 59
Tursac [Dordogne] *13*
typology **27**

urus, see aurochs

Venus *87*, 88
vertebra 61, *64*, 74
Véry, Noël 142, 178, *179*, *181*, 182, *185*
Vézère, (river) 74, 94, 163, 165
Vialou, Denis 130, 132, 147, 162, 178, 196
Villars (cave) 150, 185
Volp (river) 20
vulva *76*, **87**, *88*

wallow 55
weasels 61
whale, sperm 61, 69
willow-leaf *71*
Windels, F. 101, *107*, 162
wolf 19, 32, 34, *38*, 39, 40, 44, 50, 55, 66, 85, 130
wolverine 32, 46, 50, 85
Würm (glaciation) 12, 13, 18, 25, 27, 32, 39, 46, 50, 54, 59, 197